To Frances
with love from
Barbara
x

Under The July Sun

Barbara Jones

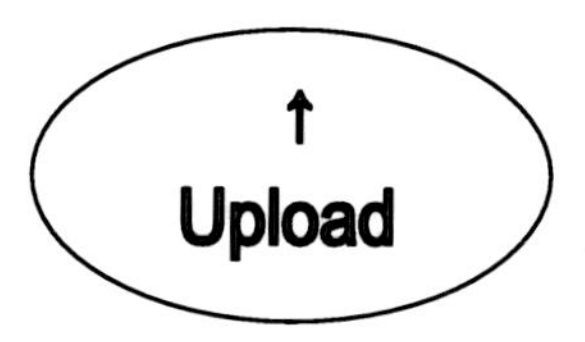

First published in Great Britain January 2011 by Upload Publishers 6 Bay Vue Road, Newhaven, East Sussex BN9 9LH

Printed in the United Kingdom
Parchment Press, Oxford

Second Edition printed in the United Kingdom
Tansley Press, Seaford

This book is fictional and any resemblance to actual people, past or present, is purely coincidental.

A CIP Catalogue record for this book is available from the British Library

ISBN:

978-0-9567821-1-3

Under The July Sun

My thanks to so many people who have supported me in writing this novel, without whom I would probably have consigned it to the waste paper bin.

Enormous gratitude goes to my husband, Chris who has read and re-read the work relentlessly; provided endless cups of tea and meals while I typed and re-typed the manuscript.

Thanks also to members of Writers Reunited: Joan El Faghloumi, Caroline Harris, Maggie Edwards, Kathryn Greig as well as Todd Kingsley-Jones who helped with many editing suggestions.

Gratitude also goes to Steve Myers of Brighton Community of Writers for his input in editing and to Charlotte Cross for her technical help in solving formatting problems with the manuscript.

Finally I must thank Father Brennan of The Sacred Heart Church, Newhaven for his invaluable help with Latin.

This book is dedicated to my family: past, present and future.

Foreword

Shakespeare reflected on the *troubles in Ireland* in his play Richard II, and throughout history the country has been occupied by the English, whose monarchs complained about 'this thorn in England's flesh.' However, it was not a thorn they wished to pluck out and discard entirely. The desire was to remove the pain and enjoy the fruits of their labour.

So it has been for hundreds of years and at the turn of the twentieth century Ireland was still undergoing unrest; so once more England sent in their troops - ostensibly to keep the peace until Home Rule was achieved. But Home Rule was not to be. At the outbreak of World War One the English soldiers moved out to join the war in Europe, so Ireland was left to wait, and struggle on.

As with all occupied countries, breakaway groups of people can take the law into their own hands trying to manipulate situations and gain what they believe to be justice in the move towards peace. Inevitably violence breaks out between those who are for this method of achieving peace and those who are not.

This is the human condition and it will probably ever be so. It is this difference in thinking that sets us apart from other animals; but it also binds us together as a human race. No other species sets about its own kind in the way humans do.

The backcloth to violence is always a territorial imperative: a struggle for wealth, minerals or suchlike. Whatever banner it flies under there can be no excuse for murder, and certainly no justification – whatever our beliefs.

The struggles of Ireland continue and, like all other occupied countries, the original reason for unrest often becomes blurred with the passage of time.

This book tells the story of a family who experience struggles of their own, initiated by the ricochet effect of one such group of people, who believed murder and violence was the way to achieve their goal.

Sometimes it takes a lifetime to realise that this isn't the only way to achieve peace, but by then a lot of heartache has usually taken place in arriving at this understanding.

Barbara Jones

Part One

1
Fethard Town, Tipperary
July 25th 1914

Had it not been for the recent murder, her decision would have been easier. But sympathy, Cat knew, could sway minds, and she could not afford to be labelled as callous; the town was too small for that sort of gossip. Torn with conflict about her situation, Cat steered Bessie along Cashel Road that sizzling hot Saturday afternoon, thoughts spinning in her head; one minute she felt she had reached a resolution, then would waver and wasn't so sure. The timing was all wrong.

Stopping the cart, she gazed across the river and watched people gradually making their way up Main Street towards the football field at the top of the town.

She slackened the reins allowing Bessie to pull the loaded cart at her own pace, and leaning back against the wooden seat, turned her face up to the sky. Not a hint of any rain clouds, just blue and white stretching forever.

It felt good being out in the fresh air driving the cart; it helped her put anxiety aside and she began to feel more relaxed.

As they crossed the bridge spanning the Clashawly River the sound of Bessie's hooves and grinding cartwheels echoed across the emptying town. It seemed to Cat that everyone was going to the football match.

All the houses had their windows open though the stillness in the air made little difference whether folk were inside or not. It was stifling. Cat listened to snatches of conversation as she passed by and aromas of newly baked soda bread drifted on the air, tantalising her hunger.

She waved at the O'Hara sisters, two aged spinsters dressed in black, creeping on spider-thin legs down the steps of The Holy Trinity Church, where Jesus in his stone garb waited in perpetual patience with outstretched arms. Cat shuddered at the thought of ending up like those old women and decided that sort of existence was definitely not for her. No family, no children waiting for them at home, just relying on each other for company - it was not what she would want.

But when she weighed up the alternative and thought about her fiancé Paddy Hogan, her mind returned to the same anguished problem. Why, although being engaged to a handsome man who was financially secure, did she feel she no longer wanted to marry him? Nothing made sense to her except she knew she could no longer pretend she loved him.

Despite his brother being murdered recently, each time she saw Paddy she felt that having to be endlessly compassionate toward him was making her feel even worse and just prolonging things.

A dream she had the previous night, though she knew it was only a dream, had disturbed her and it was as though her deepest worries had presented themselves to her in the form of a nightmare.

As they drew level with her sisters' shop, a normal stopping place, Bessie slowed. Cat knew she should carry on and deliver the potatoes but decided to call in on the girls, so pulled the donkey to a halt and jumped down from the cart.

The shop managed by three of Cat's four sisters, nestled between an abattoir and saddle shop on the hillside half way up Main Street.

When the sisters had taken over the lease it had been an ordinary house, but, with a speed that had surprised the residents of Fethard, they had converted the lower half into shops, stocked up and moved in.

Upstairs there were two bedrooms where the girls now slept; glorying in the freedom of living away from home.

Peggy and Mary had one side of the building as a sweet shop and tobacconist. Breda ran her tailoring service in the other half. Both shop fronts overlooked Main Street and the three sisters had spent a considerable time dressing the windows to attract customers.

Cat was impressed with the sweet shop display. There were jars placed along the windowsill showing a mouth-watering array of honey-coloured barley-sugar twists, blood-red aniseed balls, black and white striped humbug chunks, black liquorice sticks and russet-coloured toffees. She could smell toffee apples and knew Mary must have been busy making her specialty.

She approached the shop and cupped her hands around her eyes to peer through the glass. Seeing Peggy standing on a stepladder handing down a jar of bulls-eyes to Mary, she tapped on the windowpane. Both young women looked towards her and beckoned, but Cat indicated that she was going next door and moved away to look through the other window at Breda. She knocked on the glass but her sister's head was bent down concentrating on her machining, so Cat strolled inside.

'Have ye finished me skirt yet, Breda? I need it for the dance tonight.'

Breda looked up, her mouth full of pins and pointed at a skirt hanging on a hook. She took the pins from her mouth and asked Cat if Paddy was taking her to the dance.

'No. Not now. We *were* goin' together...but with his brother bein' killed an' all, God rest his soul.' She crossed herself, and then moved to stare out across Main Street. 'Anyway, 'twould have been the last time,' she said and waited nervously for Breda's response.

'And *why's* that?'

Cat did not want to tell her the reason, as she knew Breda would be furious. She was jealous that Paddy had chosen her to court. As a result, Breda never missed an opportunity to scorn her for being too casual about her feelings towards Paddy.

So Cat hesitated to answer Breda, but then her conscience pricked her and she knew she should tell the truth, so decided it was best to get it over with and explain how she felt.

Taking a deep breath she said quickly, 'I'm kinda fed up with him.' She waited for Breda's reaction.

'Ye're a *fool,*' Breda snapped, 'ye know he's got plenty of cash.' Her face reddened and she turned the cloth over that she was machining. She did not look up at Cat. Lifting the lever on the sewing machine to raise the needle foot, Breda placed the material beneath it and lowered it before continuing. 'But 'tis up to ye, I *s'pose*!'

Cat winced and felt her face flush before turning round to face her. She hoped her sister would at least listen to her point of view, but Breda began machining again without even casting a glance in her direction, so she stood watching her for a while, feeling like a schoolgirl admonished by a teacher.

Minutes passed in silence except for the sound of the sewing machine. Eventually Cat decided there was no point waiting for Breda to resume the conversation so she slipped quietly through the doorway and crossed the hallway into the sweet shop.

When she entered, Cat raised her eyebrows at Peggy and Mary and inclined her head in Breda's direction, but though Peggy and Mary exchanged glances, they did not comment.

Cat settled down on a chair by the counter, unscrewed the lid to the bull's-eyes and helped herself to one, then shifted the sweet to the side of her mouth where it bulged through her cheek. She crossed her eyes and pulled a face in Breda's direction.

Peggy tutted. 'Stop that, Cat. Ye look like ye've a carbuncle in yer mouth, and yer eyes'll stay like that one day.'

Cat laughed, spattering saliva and bull's-eye juice down her chin, which she wiped away with her hand. 'Listen girls I'd a weird dream last night. 'T'as left me feelin' peculiar. 'Twas about Paddy.'

Mary put up a hand to stop her. 'Wait, don't start yet, we'll get Breda then ye won't have to go repeatin' it for her.' Mary called out, 'Breda, c'mon in here - Cat's had one of her dreams.'

They heard the sewing machine stop and Breda appeared in the doorway, so Cat related her nightmare in shocking detail, telling how a grizzly bear had chased her. When she reached the part where the beast bit off her breast, the sisters shrieked, covering their ears, yelling for her to stop.

'But I haven't finished.'

'Ah well,' Breda said, 'just leave out the gory bits. Sure we'll all be havin' nightmares at this rate.'

'That's about it really, except Paddy Hogan just stood there watchin' and didn't lift a finger to help me.'

Breda drew in her breath. 'Ye let Paddy Hogan see yer bare breast?'

'Don't be stupid. 'Twas a dream and I can't control me dreams.'

Mary looked solemn. 'Ye'll have to go to confession on that score, Cat. They're impure thoughts and ye'll go to Hell if ye don't clear yer conscience.'

Breda glanced at Cat then turned to Peggy and Mary. 'Has she told ye she's fed up with Paddy?'

Cat looked down, sighed and began picking mud from beneath her fingernails while crunching on the bull's-eye. Peggy and Mary looked at her in surprise, waiting for an explanation.

Her shoulders slumped and she realised she would have to give a reason for her decision. 'Sure, I cannot imagine meself bein' married to him.'

The sisters looked at each other, then back at Cat, waiting for her to continue.

'I liked his company once, but that's all gone now. I feel as though I'm missin' somethin' and I cannot go on pretendin'. I'm *not* in love with him!'

Breda was first to speak. 'Ye don't know a good thing when it's lookin' ye in the face!' She blurted out. 'If ye're not serious about him, then tell the man and let one of us have him!'

Yes, Cat thought, *that's what she'd like isn't it*? But she just laughed. 'He's all yers. Take yer pick ladies, which of ye will take him off me hands?'

Peggy spoke up suddenly, surprising them all. 'Quit jokin' about it, Cat. Be serious! Ye'd be an absolute fool to pass Paddy up, especially now his brother's dead. That makes him the sole heir to, let me see now, the stud farm, gun shop and all the other businesses. Ye know the Hogans have their fingers in every pie. Anyway, neither Breda nor I would get a look in if ye were to pass him up;

Bernadette Cullen is waitin' in the wings, so to speak.' She folded her arms and looked at Mary and Breda who nodded in agreement.

Cat listened, but knew in her heart that she would make her own decisions without her sisters' opinions. If Bernadette was to hook Paddy - then so be it!

* * *

Much later than intended, Cat left the shop and Bessie moved off at a steady pace. She toyed with the engagement ring hanging on a cord around her neck, thinking how much she wanted something special to occur. *To experience some excitement. I love living here, but nothing happens*, she thought to herself. One day she decided, she might spread her wings and go to live in London, like some of the other girls had. The thought cheered her and she poked Bessie with a twig to make her trot.

Delivering potatoes to the barracks for her father had meant she missed lunch, but she planned to join him later. They would eat their sandwiches and cheer her brother Tom on as he played football for Tipperary. *Well, I'd better get a move on*, she thought, and shook Bessie's reins to make her gallop up to the top of Main Street where the barracks stood at the end of the shops.

She stopped daydreaming about escaping from Fethard and scrutinised the town walls, remnants of the oldest walled town in Ireland, still with a semblance of its medieval past. Standing at the top of the town, the barracks looked both impressive and menacing with huge wooden gates that remained closed at all times.

Cat had learnt at the convent school that throughout history the town had been occupied. From its foundation in the thirteenth century it had been invaded, most devastatingly by Cromwell's army.

And how the nuns had driven that lesson home to her class, she reflected. Now the English army was again in occupation in the run up to Home Rule. Supposedly, they were there to keep the peace between opposing parties, though recent events had increased tensions. It seemed to her that many people were on edge. Cat sighed, wondering why the English government didn't just give them back the whole country and finish with the matter, but she knew this had gone on for centuries unresolved. Now Irish Nationalists were causing major problems around the country trying to force the issue with violence, a peaceful solution looked a long way off. She wondered how much longer the army would be there and whether Ireland would ever really be free.

Seeing her approach two guards jumped to attention, pointing their rifles at her.

'Put down yer toys, boys,' Cat laughed and, after climbing down from the cart, pulled the reins over Bessie's head to lead her forward.

One of the soldiers demanded to know who she was and would not let her pass. She smiled at them and began to move ahead but suddenly the soldiers slammed their rifles across her chest, their faces only inches from hers. One of them bawled into her face.

'Who are you?'

Annoyed, she yelled back. 'Get outta me way.'

But undeterred, the soldier demanded her name and what reason brought her to the barracks.

'D'ye want to eat tonight, or not?' she asked, irritated by this ridiculous behaviour. She knew her father never had to put up with this nonsense when he delivered produce to the barracks, so why do it to her? She wanted to get the delivery over and be away as quickly as possible, but these two idiots were delaying her.

From behind them a smaller door beside the gates opened and an officer approached and spoke to the soldiers.

'Private White. Private Smith,' he said, 'it's alright, I'm expecting the lady.'

The soldiers stepped back looking straight ahead, as though oblivious to Cat's presence.

The officer turned to her and she simply stared at him, captivated. There was something about him that took her breath away. He was, she estimated, over six feet tall with a tanned complexion and dark brooding eyes beneath finely shaped black eyebrows. She thought he was a good-looking man and liked the sound of his voice.

'Open the gates,' he commanded.

Cat noticed that though his voice was quiet, it was authoritative, and the soldiers lowered their guns.

'Sir. Permission to go off duty?' One of them asked.

'Yes, Private Smith you may.'

They saluted each other and Private Smith disappeared through the gates while Private White opened them fully, then stepped back to allow the donkey cart entry. Bemused, Cat stood waiting to see what she should do. Then the officer smiled and stepped towards her. She felt her heart pounding in her chest as he spoke.

'Miss Delaney? Captain Ross at your service.' He tipped the edge of his hat with his hand, and then looked at the cartload of potatoes. 'I take it these are ours?'

'Sure. Indeed they are.'

'Your father told me last week you would be delivering our order so I've been expecting you, though I thought you'd be earlier. I had hoped to go to the football match. I hear your brother's playing.'

Surprised he not only knew she would be delivering the potatoes, but also about Tom's important match, Cat began explaining that she was late because she had a devil of a job digging them up. 'Sure the ground's like concrete,' she said, avoiding telling him she had been malingering in her sisters' shop blathering on about her nightmare and Paddy Hogan. Her father must have had it planned all week she realised, though he'd only asked her today to do his delivery!

She looked at Captain Ross and he smiled at her as he began leading Bessie through the gates. Cat fell into step alongside him.

The barracks had always intrigued her from the outside; it was a place of fear yet curiosity to all the girls in town. Now she could tell her friends she'd been inside, which was something none of them had done! Then she wondered why they should all be so scared of the English soldiers. They seemed all right and never caused any trouble, and everyone knew they were only there to keep the peace until Home Rule was achieved.

Captain Ross turned to her, interrupting her thoughts and said he'd find someone to unload the cart.

'I'll do it meself.'

'You'll do no such thing. It's a man's job.'

'I can work as well as any man I'll have ye know!'

'Maybe,' he smiled, 'but who earth would keep a dog and bark himself?'

Something in his eyes exhilarated her and she grinned back at him, while an embarrassing blush mushroomed across her neck and face, swathing her skin in a poppy-red glow.

'Would you like tea while the cart is being unloaded, Miss Delaney?'

'Cat,' she said nodding.

'Pardon?'

''Tis Cat.'

'Where?' he asked, looking round for the animal.

''Tis me name. Cat. And thanks, I would.'

'I'm sorry. I've never heard anyone with that name!'

''Tis a nickname for Catherine.'

'Oh! I thought Kate was.'

'Yes, 'tis, but Kate's fine with me too. Whichever ye like.'

'Good, then Cat it is! By the way, call me Louis,' he said, 'I'll just go and arrange for someone to come and unload the cart. Don't go away,' he laughed.

'Sure I won't,' she said amused, 'after all ye have me donkey and cart.'

He turned and smiled at her again, before disappearing through a door.

Suddenly she felt alone and vulnerable as she stood watching two soldiers rubbing down horses. They spotted her looking at them and began to grin and push each other, murmuring comments she couldn't quite hear. She looked away, thinking they were probably being lewd. Perhaps, she decided, she shouldn't have agreed to the tea.

Cat saw one of the men sauntering towards her. She noticed that his shirt was undone and his chest hair glistened with sweat, so she averted her eyes, mortified at the sight of his bare flesh.

''Ow do Miss. Doin' anythin' special tonight?'

Cat looked at his fat blubbery lips. She could smell his sweat and felt disgusted.

'Yes, I'm goin' out with me fiancé,' she lied turning her head away.

'Ah, wha' a pity. 'Ow about disappointin' 'im and makin' my life werf livin' tonight?'

She closed her eyes, repulsed by him, but he was undeterred.

'Come on luv, don't be stuck up.'

Cat had never spoken to a soldier before today and this one wouldn't take no for an answer. *'Póg mo thóin!'*[1] she murmured.

The soldier looked confused, and glanced at his friend before continuing.

'What's that you said luv?'

She turned on him, feeling furious. *'Póg mo thóin*!' she shouted, but as the words left her lips, she realised that the Captain had re-appeared and had heard her, but the relief of seeing him quickly overcame her embarrassment.

The soldier continued to press her for an answer. 'Is that a yes or a no?' He looked puzzled and was about to continue pestering her when the Captain told him to button his shirt up and help unload the cart. He then led Cat away from the yard into a small room where she saw a tray of tea on the table.

They sat down and she sipped the tea, glad to be away from the yard and that nuisance of a man who was now busy helping unload the cart. She could see him through the window, sweating and muttering with every bucket he filled.

After a while she began to find the air in the little room stuffy and longed to roll up her sleeves,

---

[1] 'Póg mo thóin – kiss my arse (pronounced – pug ma hone)

but knew decency wouldn't allow it. She looked through the glass once more to see how much of the pile of potatoes had been unloaded and saw with satisfaction the disgruntled expression on the soldier's face. *Good. That will teach him a lesson,* she thought.

Louis talked, and Cat swallowed her tea trying not to make gulping noises. His voice had a mesmerising effect on her, but then she became aware of her soil-filled fingernails and the fact she hadn't even washed the sweat off her face before setting off today.

Being alone with this man was affecting her. His presence was stirring an emotion she had never experienced with Paddy Hogan, and she began to wonder what it would be like to be kissed by him.

She could not control her thoughts. *God forgive me*, she prayed, and looked down at the floor where her shabby boots peeped from beneath the hemline of her mud-caked skirt.

The clock ticked toward three and she knew she would not see the football match, or witness her brother Tom hopefully make his name for Tipperary. For a moment she felt dispirited but on balance she considered maybe it had been worth it, if it meant being there with Louis.

Eventually there was a soft tapping on the door, and a soldier entered saying the unloading was finished. Louis rose but made no move to leave the room until Cat finished her tea and stood up. Then realising her engagement ring, hanging on a cord around her neck, was visible, she quickly popped it back inside her blouse.

'Thanks for the tea.'

'Will we see you next week?'

'Maybe. Maybe not. I only did this delivery so that me father could go to the match.'

He nodded and opened the door standing back waiting for her to pass through.

'That's a pity.'

'Why? He's waited a long while to see me brother play for the County.'

'No. I meant it'll be a pity if you don't do the deliveries in future.'

'Oh.' she said, and then there followed an awkward silence, which Cat finally broke. 'Well, I'll be off then,' she said. As she walked ahead of him into the yard Cat felt his eyes must have been focussing on her muddy clothes and she cursed her appearance.

She went across to Bessie and stroked her nose murmuring softly to her, and the animal nuzzled her hand. Cat picked up the reins, leading the donkey forward, and Louis walked beside her as they approached the gateway.

At the exit to the barracks she turned and said goodbye, then began leading Bessie away. When she was a little way off she looked back and saw that Louis was still standing by the gates watching her.

'Wait a minute!' he called, 'I want to ask you something.' She stopped walking, let go of the reins and Bessie ambled to the other side of the road to graze on the grass.

He rushed up, caught hold of her arm, and guided her down the road and round a corner out of earshot of Private White on sentry duty outside the gates.

'Well, what is it ye want to ask me?'

'What does *pug ma hone mean*?'

Cat giggled, 'Ye wouldn't want to know.'

'I do! Please tell me. I'd like to learn a little Irish while I'm here. It sounded so charming.'

She grinned up at him impishly. 'It means, kiss me arse!'

Cat could see he was lost for words. She threw her head back laughing, and her headscarf slipped down revealing a mass of tiny black curls, which bounced like miniature springs as she moved.

Suddenly, Cat felt herself thrown off her feet. She flew backwards, the air knocked out of her lungs, and landed heavily on the ground. She felt her arm grazed and an intense pain in her back. She tried to rise, but Louis pushed her back on the ground, covering her body with his own to protect her, as debris hit the ground all around them, some clipping Louis' back. Everything happened so quickly but seemed to be taking place in slow motion. The noise of the explosion had been immense – Cat's ears were still ringing from the sound of the blast.

Over Louis' shoulder, Cat could see smoke and flames roaring swiftly around the barracks, licking hungrily at the sides of the dry timber buildings, as stones and wood showered the area with the wreckage of the once proud structure. Shop fronts shattered showering pavements with glass.

Through the dust Cat saw Bessie galloping at speed down Main Street, the cart left behind like a pile of firewood.

As the smoke cleared she heard people running towards her; men shouting, women screaming and crying. The smell of the explosion hung in the air and her lungs filled with cloying smoke.

They lay there for a few moments and Cat's brain tried to work out what had happened, but numbed with shock she could not comprehend a thing.

Louis rolled off her onto the ground and began to move away but she reached out and grabbed his sleeve. 'Don't leave me. I'm comin' with ye.'

He shook his head, standing up cautiously to peer around the corner. Drawing his gun from its holster he stepped warily onto the roadway and picked his way across the rubble while Cat sat amidst debris, her teeth chattering violently. Someone arrived beside her and placed a shawl around her shoulders, but as she opened her mouth to say something, she found herself unable to utter a word. Warily, she looked around her.

Nothing remained of the barrack gates except a yawning gap and a deep hole gouged into the ground. The walls on either side of the gates had been destroyed for a distance of several yards and part of the barracks inside had collapsed, trapping the men. She could hear them crying out for help.

Private White lay in the road motionless, his uniform blackened and torn, his damaged bloodied limbs and torso exposed. Cat watched Louis dash over to him, and kneel to cradle the dying man in his arms.

She heard soldiers running. They emerged from the barracks, some covered in dust with trails of blood trickling down their whitened bodies. Rifles raised ready to fire, they stood in an orderly row forming a ghostly troop amidst the chaos.

Then another movement caught Cat's attention. There was someone slipping down the alleyway opposite.

It looked like Paddy Hogan.

2
Monroe, Fethard
July 31st 1914

Ned watched his wife Maeve kneading dough, pounding it into a rounded mound; then with a knife she made the sign of a cross on its flaccid surface.

'What time's Paddy bringin' out the new cart Ned?'

He took his pocket watch out, flicked open the case and read the time. 'Should be along soon, 'tis nearly eleven.' Seeing the dough was ready for baking, Ned began turning the bellows wheel, fanning air into the sleeping fire. Gradually the embers sprang to life, gusting hot ash, into the fire basket.

He rose from his stool and ambled across to peer through a little window overlooking the yard while Maeve dusted the loaf with flour, wiped her hands, lifted the bread shovel from its hook, and deftly manoeuvred the dough onto it.

'Ned, will ye open the oven now?'

He moved back to the fire and, with a poker, flipped open the cast iron door. Carefully, as though lifting a baby into its cradle, Maeve moved across the room holding the bread shovel; then with a quick jolt she shoved the dough in and slammed the door shut.

Rubbing his chin, Ned returned to stare out of the window. 'How much longer is Cat goin' to hide away in that barn?'

'Ah! Leave her be, Ned. Sure she's in shock.'

'She's been doin' it for days now!'

'It'll take as long as it takes.'

'Murderin' swines! Sure, I'd like to get me hands on them. Will ye call her out, Maeve, I'm bustin' for a pee?'

'G'w'on round the back.'

'I can't keep dodgin' round the back.'

'Ah! Ye've no patience at all. Praise be to God, she'll come out of it soon enough.'

He sighed and lumbered out of the cottage to the back garden where he relieved himself against a tree. Buttoning his flies he returned to the kitchen and sat on a stool beside the fire watching twists of sweet peat-smelling smoke drift up the chimney.

'Any news of the weddin' yet?'

She pursed her lips, irritated with the question. 'No! And don't ye go askin' her.'

Ned began to whistle.

'Will ye stop that row, Ned? Ye know I can't stand it when ye do that.'

'Ah! Woman there's no pleasin' ye. Will I go and lay on the railway line so ye've got rid of me whistlin' once and for all?'

'Don't be childish Ned, it doesn't become ye.'

'Ha! I'll keep meself quiet then shall I?'

'Well, say somethin' sensible if ye must speak. So long as 'tis not that whistlin'.'

'Well how's this then for conversation? I hear the English Captain is up and about again.'

Maeve raised her eyebrows. 'Is that so? And how's he doin'?'

'Considering everything, I heard he's not so bad. He's mainly cut about the face and hands.'

She picked up a broom and as she swept the floor, Ned began whistling again. Annoyed, Maeve battled with the broom sweeping flour dust across the flagstones toward the door. 'Now,' she said, 'I'll just get cleared up, then see to dinner.'

Ned waited for her to complain about the floor. It was uneven and flour had settled between the cracks in the flagstones, refusing to be swept away. She cursed and asked God's forgiveness alternately, trying to wheedle the brush between the gaps.

He scratched his head and sighed.

Maeve looked at him. 'What are ye sighin' about now?'

'The bombin'. That English Captain is luckier than that poor lad sent back home in a box.'

She nodded. 'Poor boy. And his poor parents too. Lord save us, what's this world comin' to?'

'Thanks be to God for his mercy with Cat,' he said crossing himself.

'Thanks be to God,' she echoed as Ned turned away from the window and went to the milk churn. He ladled out some of the oyster-white frothy liquid into a mug, walked across to the barn, opened the door and shuffled inside. It took a second or two for his eyes to adjust to the gloom before he saw Cat curled up in the corner.

'Cat, 'tis time to come out now,' he coaxed.

'I'm thinkin'.'

'Well, ye can't stay in here forever. Can't ye do yer thinkin' somewhere else?'

'I need to be alone.'

'Here, I've brought ye some milk. Drink it up now, ye'll feel better.'

She didn't answer so he placed the mug on the straw next to her.

'They killed that poor soldier. What harm had he done to anyone?' There was anger in her voice.

'I know, Pet.' His voice was tender as he watched his daughter sit with her knees drawn up under her chin. 'If ever I get my hands on the murderers I swear I'll—'

'Ye'll *what*?' She asked looking up at him. 'What'll ye do?' She stared ahead. 'If ye do anythin' ye'll be just as bad as them.'

'Turn the other cheek eh?'

'I s'pose so.'

'Listen, Pet. I thank the Lord ye weren't hurt. I know Bessie went chargin' off and the cart got broken up, but that's nothin' at all considerin' what could have happened, is it?' He was relieved to see her pick up the mug and drink some milk. 'Paddy's about to arrive. He's bringin' a new cart for me.'

She put the mug down, and Ned saw that the colour had drained from her face. 'I don't want to see him, Dada.'

He raised his eyebrows in surprise. 'C'mon now, Pet, why not?'

'Did ye not hear me? I said I don't want to see him, Dada.'

'But ye have to see him sometime.'

'No I do not. I don't want to see him ever again!'

'Why, Cat?'

'I just want it that way.'

'Cat what're ye sayin'?'

'Get rid of him when he comes, Dada. Just get rid of him, *please*!'

'How? What'll I say?'

'Tell him whatever ye like, but I won't see him.'

Ned sighed. 'Have it yer own way, Cat. 'Tis your life.'

'Dada I *mean* it! I never want anythin' to do with him again!' She began to shake, and Ned could see she was afraid.

He watched her tremble as she sat there in the straw like a little child; then, overcome with tenderness, he put his arm around her shoulders and drew her closer.

'C'mon now, Pet, 'tis alright. Ye don't have to do anythin' ye don't want to do, or see any man ye don't want to see. If Cupid hasn't fired his arrow at ye by now with this man, then maybe ye'd better let him go.' He rubbed her back, kissing the top of her head.

'Ye're not cross then, Dada?'

'No, Pet. Of course not. What's troublin' ye? Can ye tell me?'

'I'm not sure. 'Tis all confused.'

'When ye're ready. When ye're ready then. Take yer time. Here,' he said taking off his jacket, 'put this on, ye're cold,' he said drawing the rough material across her shoulders. 'One thing's botherin' me though, Cat.' He rubbed his ear, feeling awkward. 'I know 'tis a delicate matter to ask, but, well have ye…has Paddy—?'

'Absolutely *not* Dada!'

'Good! Only he'd have to marry ye if that was the case.'

He saw her face lose its pallor and a deep blush sweep up her neck and cheeks. He realised he had embarrassed her. But it had to be asked he felt.

'He won't listen to me, Dada. But if *ye* tell him, he'll have to!'

Ned interrupted her. 'Eist![2] I think I hear Paddy arrivin' with the cart. Stay here and I'll talk to him.' Rolling up his shirtsleeves Ned walked out of the barn, closing the door behind him as he saw Paddy approaching.

'Mornin' Paddy.'

Paddy smiled revealing a row of even white teeth. 'Mornin' Ned. 'Tis a fine day is it not?'

''Tis indeed. 'Tis.' Ned agreed and stood watching Paddy unhook the new cart from his pony before turning to face him.

'Well, here's the cart then, Ned. 'Tis a fine replacement, sure it is.'

'Aye, a fine cart Paddy, I'll say that.' Ned said running his hand over the woodwork. 'Though there's no replacement for that young soldier murdered in cold blood before me own gel's eyes is there?'

---

[2] Eist – listen (pronounced wist)

Paddy did not look up and appeared to be sorting out the reins, but Ned sensed he was avoiding eye contact; so asked him if anything was wrong.

'Wrong? *No*! Not at all. Sure I'd like to speak to Cat if she's about though.'

Ned rubbed the stubble on his chin. 'Ye seem kinda jumpy Paddy.'

Paddy laughed. 'Oh. Just lots to do and not much time to do it in ye know.' He pushed the new cart round to the side of the barn then strolled back towards Ned wiping his brow on the sleeve of his shirt.

'Well, is Cat about then, Ned?'

Ned knew he couldn't avoid the subject any longer, so pulled himself up to his full six foot five, thrust his thumbs inside his belt, and began the speech that would sever his daughter from a life of assured luxury.

'No. Cat's not about, Paddy. Nor will she be for ye again.'

Paddy looked stunned. 'What d'ye mean, Ned?'

'Exactly what I say. She does not want to see ye again.'

Paddy's smile vanished as he realised Ned wasn't joking. His jaws clenched together angrily, his hands balled suddenly into fists as he realised Ned was serious.

Wondering if Paddy was preparing to hit him, Ned took his thumbs out of his belt in readiness. He felt sorry having to be the bearer of the news, but his loyalty was to his daughter even though he didn't understand the reason for her decision.

Trying to conceal his anger Paddy looked down, rolling a stone around on the ground with his boot as he spoke.

'Why?' He sounded curt, and his friendliness had disappeared.

'She doesn't need a reason, Paddy. If my gel says she doesn't want to see a particular fella, then she doesn't see a particular fella, 'tis that simple.'

Hardly able to contain his fury Paddy felt in his pocket and pulled out the bill for the cart. He folded it in two and held it out.

Ned took it and stuffed the paper in his shirt pocket without reading it. 'I'll settle up with ye later.' Then without saying another word, he turned and walked off in the direction of the cottage, leaving Paddy in no doubt that the interview was over.

Hearing Paddy leave, Ned turned and ambled back to lean against the side of the barn. He stood listening to the river running through the brittle dryness of osier beds, thinking about his conversation with Cat. *What was it she wasn't telling him?* He drew a packet of Sweet Afton from his pocket, lit one, and blew smoke rings into the air, watching them float upward, distort, then dissipate.

He scrutinized the cottage roof and thought the thatch would need mending that summer. With its low roof and white walls, it was more than just home to Ned. It was the very centre of his universe and he could never imagine living anywhere else.

One day, he thought, maybe he'd enlarge the window to the main room. It was far too dark inside. Firstly, though, he would fix that floor for Maeve, if only to stop her blathering on about it.

Ned threw his cigarette butt down grinding it underfoot, and pushed the barn door open. 'C'mon, Cat. Ye can come out now, he's gone. We'll go and cut the sallies[3]; I've a few baskets to make.'

Wandering along the riverbank together, Ned scythed the young willows while Cat followed, laying them in lines to dry. They worked in harmony beneath the sun and not a word passed between them about Paddy Hogan. Ned decided he could wait to hear whatever was worrying her. He did wonder, though, if there was a connection between the bombing and Paddy's brother, Tommy. Everyone now knew that the soldier who shot Tommy Hogan was the one killed outside the barrack gates. Was it an act of reprisal, Ned wondered? If that was the case then Cat was better off keeping her distance.

He didn't want to think about it and pushed the worries away replacing them with other thoughts of more immediate concern. Should he begin planting lettuces now or should they use the space for something more profitable?

An hour later Ned called to Cat and she looked up, her hand shielding her eyes from the sun. He saw in the shimmering air, a vision of Maeve as she had been thirty years ago: young,

---

[3] sallies –willow, the leaves of which are used for basket making

pretty - and full of fire. Not young and pretty any more, he thought, but still full of fire!

Cat began walking towards him, smiling. Then, as though sharing a single thought, they both tore off their boots and rushed laughing to the river's edge where they sat down and thrust their bone-white feet into the rippling river while the summer sun scorched their backs.

'Ye know, when I was a boy I used to sit in this very spot with me feet in the water. There's nuttin' like the feel of it is there?'

'Mmm.'

'Yer mother an' me used to walk along this bank when we were courtin'. Did I ever tell ye that?'

'Maybe, but I don't remember. G'w'on tell me about it.'

'We had to be chaperoned in those days and I remember once, yer mother showed her ankle in my presence as she twisted her foot on a stone. Ye should have seen the chaperone's face, old Nell Callaghan 'twas. Like she'd swallowed a cup of vinegar!'

He became silent thinking that here he was now with Cat, sharing the joy of working in this blissful place where he felt they had been hewn from the very rocks of the overlooking mountain - Slievenamon. Then after a while he picked up the story again.

''Twas an arranged marriage, so to speak. Me da asked for a marriage dowry of fifty pounds, but yer granddad couldn't meet the figure, so she was turned down.' He stopped talking and Cat looked at him.

'So what happened then?'

'Well, one day yer grandad met yer mother in town. He saw her comin' toward him in Main Street, but she was so humiliated 'cos she'd been turned down, she couldn't look at him.'

'Poor Mummy.'

'Yer granddad felt sorry for her then, so as she passed by he mentioned that he'd lower the price and take twenty pounds. Then, just like a little child, she looked at him and he could see she was delighted, and she just ran all the way down Main Street as though the Banshee was after her.'

Ned became quiet for a while before continuing. 'How times have changed. I'm glad ye will never have to offer up a dowry, 'Tis all so old-fashioned now. I couldn't bear the thought of any of me daughters bein' bought and sold like cows at market. I'd rather ye all remained spinsters. And if ye don't want Paddy Hogan, for whatever reason, then I'll back ye all the way.'

He lay back watching the blueness above as swallows swooped and soared in concert directed by an invisible conductor. They flew in unison, their little bodies silhouetted black against blue.

Ned thought he would go and see the English Captain. He'd offer the hand of friendship to him just to show that there were decent Irish people who did not resent the presence of English soldiers or condone violence.

Suddenly he felt hungry, pulled his watch from his pocket, flipped open the small silver door.

'Dinner time,' he said, and helped Cat to her feet.

Stepping carefully over the discarded sallies, which lay in the bleaching sun, they picked their way across the crackling osier beds[4]. Then Ned stopped, took out his handkerchief and, wiping sweat from his forehead, turned to Cat. 'After dinner, we'll go on into town; I want to visit the English Captain.'

'His name's Louis,' she said and looked away.

'Is it indeed?' Ned said looking at her. 'G'w'on now, I'll just have a smoke and follow ye in a while.'

He lit the cigarette and watched her walk the well-worn pathway that led to Monroe. She looked back briefly at him and then disappeared from view leaving him staring into the void her departures always left.

---

[4] Osier beds – place where willows grow

3
O'Connell's Hotel, Fethard
July 31st 1914

The hotel bar was full. Ned suggested to Cat they should go in through a side door to Reception. When they entered, his sister Nellie O'Connell was sorting out bills; she smiled and moved out from behind the counter to place an arm around Cat's shoulder.

'How're ye now pet?'

'I'm fine Auntie thanks, just gettin' over the wobbly feelin', and me ears have stopped ringin' now, thanks be to God.'

'Thanks be to God,' Nellie said and turned to Ned. 'And what brings ye here this time of day? Is it thirst?'

'No, not entirely. Though I could be persuaded in a minute if that husband of yers can find time to serve us. Jesus, 'tis busy!' He walked a few paces to the entrance of the public bar, craned his neck above the crowd, and saw Mick O'Connell was busy serving. Mick looked up and nodded to Ned, who then ambled back to Nellie and Cat.

'We've come to see the English soldier, Captain Ross if he's about, Nellie.'

'He's in his room. Will I call him down?'

'Yes, do that will ye? We'll wait in the snug at the end; there's no space in the bar.'

They forced their way through the crowded bar to the far end, opened the door and squeezed inside.

Ned took off his cap and dropped it on a chair. ‘Phew, ’tis worse than bein’ at a match. Sit yerself down now Cat. Take the little leather armchair, ’tis more comfortable than the others. I’ll stand here by the hatch so’s I can see the Captain comin’.’

He opened the window that overlooked the bar and leaned on the sill until he spotted Nellie pointing the Captain in their direction. Ned watched him battle his way through the crowd and, satisfied he knew where to find them, closed the window.

‘I see him comin’ Cat, he’s not lookin’ so good. Still, maybe he’ll look better after a couple of pints.’

Her stomach did a funny little somersault as Louis came through the door and smiled at them.

'Hello, this is a nice surprise,' he said shaking Ned’s hand, 'and Miss Delaney. I'm so glad to see you again under better circumstances. Can I buy you both a drink?’

‘The drinks are on me Captain, and Ned’s the name. What’ll it be – porter?’[5]

'Well, thank you very much. I’ll get the next round, Ned. By the way,’ he said smiling, ‘call me Louis.’

Ned turned to his daughter, ‘Cat, what’ll ye have?’

---

[5] Porter – dark sweet beer

'Just a fruit cordial please, Dada.' The timbre of her voice sounded constrained and high pitched, and she immediately felt annoyed with herself for sounding nervous when she would like to have appeared nonchalant. She took deep breaths to calm herself while Ned bent down to look through the hatch trying to attract Mick's attention, but he was still busy serving down the far end of the bar.

'Ach! We'll wait all day 'til he sees me,' he said and straightened up too soon so bumped his head on the window-frame. 'Oh *feck* it! I'll go out into the bar. I won't be long now,' he said rubbing his head and lumbering towards the snug door.

Cat wished her dad had not uttered such profanity in front of Louis, though if he was shocked, she thought, he covered it up well because she had seen no sign of him flinching at her father's language.

'Shall I come with you, Ned?' the Captain called after him.

'No, 'twon't be necessary, I'll not be long. Make yerself comfortable and have a chat to me daughter.'

Louis sat down as Cat tried pulling her lace gloves off, but she was having difficulty as they were sticking to her fingers in the heat. Aware he was looking at her, she looked up and felt the same frisson inside her as when they had met last week. Out of modesty, she dropped her eyes and continued struggling with the gloves.

'Here, let me help you,' he said kneeling before her; and he began gently pulling on the tips of each lacy finger. She found his nearness uncomfortable, yet exciting! He was so close - she could even smell coal-tar soap on his skin.

While he was busy with her gloves, Cat studied the top of his head. His hair was the colour of deep mahogany under the shaft of light from the window and when he looked up at her, having released the gloves from her fingers, she saw that his eyes were not just dark brown as she had first thought but had little flecks of green in the irises.

Excitement rippled through her but was quickly followed by shame at the sight of her bare hands. She plunged her fists, rough from working on the land, quickly into her jacket pockets and sat further back in the armchair.

He rose and returned to his chair and chatted in a very relaxed manner waiting for Ned.

Mick O'Connell was serving, so Ned waited. Looking round the crowded bar he saw his cousin Brendan, a Royal Irish Constabulary[6] officer in Fethard, standing just inside the door. When Brendan saw him, he gestured for Ned to buy him a drink, raising an imaginary glass to his lips. Ned grinned and pressed through the crowd to speak to him.

'Ye already owe me one from last night, remember? I won the arm wrestle.'

---

[6] The Royal Irish Constabulary (RIC) was one of Ireland's two police forces in the early twentieth century; the other was the Dublin Metropolitan Police.

Brendan pulled a few coins from his pocket indicating he had no money, so Ned grinned and battled through the men again to the bar. Mick took his order and began drawing a pint of porter.

As Mick pulled the pump, he raised an eyebrow and indicated with a sideways jerk of his head that Ned should listen to the conversation taking place to his right. Ned's eyes settled on Paddy Hogan's back.

Paddy shouted in a voice loud enough for Ned to hear above the crowd. 'I just off-loaded that Delaney piece. She was turned in the head, so I'm glad to be rid of her.'

Ned tapped Paddy on the shoulder. Paddy turned and saw Ned, but was unprepared for the fist that smashed into the bridge of his nose with a loud crunch.

He staggered, sprawling into the crowd, knocking some of them off balance causing them to spill their drinks. His arms flailed wildly as he lost his footing and the men roared at him to be careful; but covered in porter with his nose oozing blood, he hit the floor and stared blankly up at Ned who leaned calmly on the bar staring down at him.

'Right now Paddy, maybe we'll tell all these people what really happened, and how 'tis the other way round!'

Paddy remained on the floor saying nothing. Ned was aware of a hush and addressed the onlookers. 'Why so silent? Cat got your tongue, so to speak?'

The men shuffled in anticipation, eager to see what Ned would do next. 'Well then, maybe I'll provide the information! 'Twas me daughter gave this heap of worthless pig-skin here the elbow. *She* doesn't want *him.* So Paddy, perhaps ye'll do the honour of confirmin' this so's we can get back to our porter.'

Paddy took out a hankie and wiped his nose. He didn't answer but just nodded agreement. Then Ned kicked his boot against Paddy's.

'Now then, what is it ye have to say to these people about me daughter?'

Paddy mumbled, 'Cat Delaney and I are finished.'

He kicked Paddy's boot again. 'Still not good enough, Paddy. Try a little harder so's everyone can hear ye.'

'Cat Delaney threw me over.'

'There, that's better isn't it? And now ye'll go to Heaven with all God's other children who learn to tell the truth. 'Tis not so hard now is it?'

Mick O'Connell learned over the bar. 'Paddy, I see ye've settled yer differences with Ned now. Shall I pour him a drink and put it on yer bill?' He grinned and put another glass of porter on the bar for Ned.

Disappointed the excitement was over, the onlookers began mumbling to each other and this soon turned into chatter until soon the familiar buzz of conversation was back.

As Paddy staggered to his feet, Mick held his hand out for money. Paddy paid him. But Mick hadn't finished with him. He began polishing a glass and as he did so, spoke to Paddy.

'Oh and by the way, didn't yer daddy ever tell ye that Ned here was our bare-fist champion before ye were born? *No*, I'm sure he didn't! Well, I thought I'd just tell ye like.' He giggled then put the glass down. 'Now get outta here, I won't have ye blackenin' me niece's name, sure I won't!'

The men parted to allow Paddy through as Ned collected his drinks tray.

As he entered the snug, Ned noticed a shy smile on Cat's face and as he placed the tray on a table, he wondered whether she was throwing her hat at this man. It crossed his mind that maybe this was the reason she'd given Paddy the elbow. He passed the drinks to Louis and Cat.

'Sláinte,'[7] Ned said raising his glass to Louis.

Louis raised his glass. 'Cheers and good health.'

Cat settled back in the armchair sipping cordial, watching Louis. She noticed everything about him: his black eyelashes closing on his olive skin; the rich dark hair falling across his brow; the movement of his Adam's apple as he swallowed; his hands quivering slightly as he placed his glass on the table. She saw small cuts across his face, neck and hands where splinters of wood had caught him in the blast, and the brown healing scabs growing over them, which were slightly reddening in places.

The men chatted easily, and Cat studied Louis intently, until she became aware Ned was

---

[7] Sláinte –health or cheers (pronounced slawn-cha)

watching her. She gulped down her drink and jumped up. 'I have to be off now.'

'Why, where are ye off to?'

'Confession, Dada, are ye coming?'

'But we've only just got here!'

'I must be goin',' she gave a pleading look at Ned, 'are are ye comin' Dada?'

'Ye go on and I'll catch up with ye after. I want to speak to Louis here a little longer; we've hardly said a word.'

Cat turned to Louis. 'Goodbye then, Louis. Nice seein' ye again. I'm glad ye're feelin' better now.'

He looked surprised, and shook her hand. 'Goodbye, Cat. And thank you for coming.'

She felt extremely stupid trying to pull on her lace gloves which refused to slip over her clammy swollen fingers, so, unable to stand Louis watching her ridiculous attempts at looking refined any longer, she rushed out of the door and disappeared into the crowded bar.

Once outside the hotel, Cat crossed Main Street and walked briskly up the pathway to the church. She opened the huge wooden door and slipped into the cool gloom of The Holy Trinity. After the bright sunlight outside, the church appeared dimmer than ever and she paused, allowing her eyes to adjust.

Suddenly someone grabbed her hair from behind and an arm came round her throat as she was dragged away from the entrance, further into the church. She knew instantly that it was Paddy

Hogan. Her fear lifted to be replaced by a rich and powerful anger.

'Let go of me!'

'C'mon ye soldier's whore.' He shoved her against a wall. 'So ye don't want to see me anymore eh?'

She smelt his hot beery breath. 'Get off ye animal,' she shouted and brought her knee up, catching him in the crotch. She heard his sharp intake of breath, but he just tightened his hold. His face was only inches from hers and she could see wildness in his eyes; his top lip curled up in a snarl revealing his teeth and gums. There was spittle at the edges of his mouth and his nose was bleeding.

'Get yer hands off now or—'

'Or what? Tell yer dada? So, if 'tis not me yer seein', then is it that feckin' soldier?'

'No!'

'I *don't* believe ye.'

'Ye can believe what ye like.'

'Ye go out with me and we'll say no more about it.'

'Go to Hell!'

'I'm warnin' ye. Think it over.'

'I've no need to think it over. I've made up me mind. I don't go out with murderers!'

She knew instantly she had made a mistake saying that. His expression changed and he pushed his arm against her throat even harder. Then with his free hand he took out a knife and held it up against her check.

Her head swam. ‘Oh no, Paddy. For the love of God. Let me go and I’ll–’

Paddy cut across her conversation. ‘If ye want yer family to remain safe, then don’t go repeatin’ what ye just said. This is the only warning. Open yer mouth and ye’ll be sorry. D’ya hear?’

She nodded, prepared to concede to anything and felt the pressure of his arm ease from her throat. She bent over gasping for air. Then as quickly as it had all happened, he was gone, leaving her alone in the corner of the church.

She heard a rustling sound coming from the confessional box and realised Father Ryan must be inside and that he would have heard it all. He would help her. She stumbled across the church, wrenched open the door to the confessional box and slumped onto the chair inside. He would console her, make it all better.

It seemed ages before Father Ryan slid the partition aside, and she heard the priest’s familiar voice.

‘Bless me, Father, for I have sinned.’

'How long is it since your last confession my child?'

Already, she felt the awful trembling inside begin to subside. ‘Two weeks, Father. I wasn’t very well last week.’

'And are ye recovered now my child?'

He was concerned about her she felt and soon he would tell her that everything would be all right. Composed she answered him. 'Yes, Father, I am.'

'What is your confession?'

'Father, I have to confess I have had bad thoughts about a man.'

'Ye have my child?'

'Yes, Father'

'What kind of thoughts were they?'

Forbidden thoughts, Father.' There, she had said it!

'And was that what the commotion was all about just now?'

'Yes, Father. Ye see it's all about me not wantin' to marry the man I was engaged to.'

'So are these thoughts about some other man?'

'Yes, Father. 'Tis an English soldier.'

There was a long pause and Cat waited for the penance to be announced. It felt so good to have got it off her chest. Now she would hear the gentle voice of Father Ryan, who had know her all her life, giving her a little penance and telling her to go on her way and sin no more. Relieved of her burden, she waited for the words he would say to soothe away all her troubles.

When Father Ryan spoke, his tone was harsh as he spat out her penance, stinging her with every word. 'As an act of contrition say fifty Our Fathers and fifty Hail Marys each day for two weeks; and pray to God for your soul to be redeemed for such *wickedness!*'

Cat was stunned. She didn't understand. Surely he had heard every word that had passed between her and Paddy? He had witnessed Paddy attacking her. Maybe, she decided there would be words of consolation to follow.

'Yes, but, Father–' The little sliding door slammed shut!

Bewildered, she staggered from the confessional box, made her way across to the other side of the church and sank down onto a pew. Confused and humiliated, she lowered her head to pray. She sat in the darkness waiting, feeling as though time no longer moved nor mattered, until she heard the church door open.

Ned stood as she had done inside the doorway, his eyes adjusting to the gloom; then seeing her waiting he nodded to her.

Her immediate reaction would have been to run to him, seek his protection, cry on his shoulder about Paddy's attack and the unfairness of Father Ryan; but she vowed never to speak of it to anyone.

The peace and security she thought she knew were gone. Her life had changed and whatever happened from now would be steered by her own actions. She could not bear to have her family hurt on her account.

The memory of Private White lying in the road and of Louis kneeling to cradle him in his arms came to her. She knew that a threat she barely understood had moved into her life.

Ned turned towards the confessional box, went inside, and Cat tiptoed over to wait nearby.

She heard Father Ryan slip the wooden slider back, and as she had done, her father began his confession.

'Bless me, Father for I have sinned.'

'How long is it since your last confession my son?'

'A week, Father.'

'What sins do ye want to confess my son?'

'Well, Father, I hit a fella on the nose today.'

'Did ye indeed, and what compelled ye to such action my son?'

'Well ye see, Father, he was tellin' lies.'

'And ye took the redemption of his soul into consideration?'

'I did, Father.'

'Say two Our Fathers and two Hail Marys and ask God to forgive a soldier of His great army when he's fightin' for the truth.'

Ned left the confessional and Cat hurried to his side, linking her arm in his and squeezing it in comfort as they walked out into the summer sun. It felt so good to hold on to him. She now understood why Paddy had been so mad; Ned had punched him on the nose! Well serve him right, she thought and felt the scales had somehow tipped back into balance after the priest's admonishment.

Usually, holding on to her father's arm filled her with security, as he felt substantial and strong, but today she didn't know what had upset her most: Paddy's threats or Father Ryan's attitude. She found herself brooding over both problems.

Ned interrupted her thoughts.

'I thought we'd cut the hay in the high meadow tomorrow, and get yer mother to roast a pig. We'll have a bit of a craic[8] after.'

She didn't answer immediately, even though haymaking was her favourite time. Cat loved it at the end of the day when everyone who had helped stayed on eating, drinking and dancing well into the night.

She was still trying to unscramble her feelings about the encounter with Paddy and Father Ryan's reaction to her confession when Ned, without looking at her, added that Louis had told him he had to attend an inquiry about the bombing in the morning.

'But I asked him to join us afterwards. I thought ye'd like that.'

---

[8] Craic – entertainment (pronounced crack)

4
The Inquiry
Fethard
August 1st 1914

Louis found the room set aside for the inquiry into Tommy Hogan's shooting. Hopefully, he thought, it would be an open and shut case.

He put his papers on a desk and quickly began to flick through his evidence. The report had been drastically reduced each time he read it, and this morning he had cut it even more, hoping to shorten the hearing.

Louis knew that Tommy Hogan was Paddy's brother, and that Cat had been engaged to him until recently. He had already formed conclusions about Paddy Hogan and Private White's murder but this inquiry was not about that, though he would like to have voiced his opinion about the connection in his evidence. He just hoped things went his way during the questioning and that enough was said to tie Paddy Hogan up with both events.

The seats began to fill around nine thirty and Major McIntosh, presiding, arrived at nine fifty, arranged his papers on the desk, and laid out three sharply pointed pencils and a note-pad. At ten o'clock he told the guards to close the doors and after introducing the matter, he nodded to Louis, who stood to make his address.

'This is my account of the incidents leading up to and including the death of Tommy Hogan,' he began to speak looking directly at Major McIntosh, then read from his report.

'Nationalist Tommy Hogan was involved with a company of Irish National Volunteers[9] who had rioted at the Waterford by-elections in May and was consequently jailed for three months. Upon his release, he allegedly planned with Michael Ryan to hold up some R.I.C men in Fethard and take their car and weapons.'

Major McIntosh looked up. 'Allegedly?'

'We have information, Sir, that Tommy Hogan and Michael Ryan planned this together.' He waited, expecting Major McIntosh to intervene once more, but in the silence that followed he decided to continue. Just as he was about to speak, Major McIntosh interrupted again.

'I suppose this comes from a reliable source, this information?'

'Yes sir.'

McIntosh scribbled something down on his pad and nodded at Louis who moved across to a board and easel where a local map was pinned showing where the hold-up took place.

Returning to his desk, he eased a finger between his neck and shirt collar. God it's hot, he thought, and if he keeps interrupting me, this could go on all morning! He waited for permission to

---

[9] The **Irish National Volunteers** were a paramilitary organization established by Irish Nationalists in 1913 aiming 'To Secure and Maintain the Rights and Liberties common to the whole people of Ireland', and to help enforce the imminent Home Rule Act

continue until Major McIntosh finished writing and looked up. 'Go on,' he said.

Louis explained at length the sequence of events and how the police had just surrendered when confronted by Hogan and Ryan until Major McIntosh interrupted him again.

'Wasn't there any resistance from the police?'

'No sir, they just held up their hands and were led away.'

Major McIntosh raised his eyebrows and sighed as Louis continued.

'Michael Ryan took four small calibre revolvers from the R.I.C. Officers and forced them across some fields to a cow shed where he locked them in.' He waited until Major McIntosh finished writing, then continued. 'Tommy Hogan stayed on guard for some time, but later on, he unbolted the door and left. When the policemen discovered the door unbolted, they went into town and alerted the military who turned out to search for the car and weapons.'

'Who led the search?'

'I did, Sir.'

'Right, go on.'

'The following morning we received intelligence that Ryan and Hogan had gone to a nearby farmhouse and had breakfast. The farmhouse was surrounded and shots were fired from a window, then Ryan and Hogan were seen running from the back of the farmhouse across a field.'

McIntosh interrupted him again. 'Was any fire returned by either the military or R.I.C.?'

'Yes Sir, Private White of the 110th Battalion Royal Artillery fired on them, and shot Tommy Hogan in the hip. But he continued to run, so he received another two shots in the back from R.I.C. officers McClure and Quigley, after which he collapsed.' Louis paused. 'Any questions Sir?'

'No. Continue please.'

'Tommy Hogan was taken to Fethard Military Barracks, and then transferred to Tipperary Town Military Hospital. Father Donovan was in attendance and stayed with him until he died at 2.30 pm that afternoon.'

Major McIntosh decided not to call any further witnesses and adjourned the court.

Louis marched quickly down Main Street to O'Connell's Hotel and changed out of his uniform. For once he didn't hang his clothes up, but threw them impatiently on the bed.

His mind shed the depressing courtroom events of the morning, the revulsion falling from him like autumn leaves fluttering in his wake as he left the hotel and headed out of town.

Approaching the fields of Monroe he stood at a distance on the roadside where he could see people cutting hay and smiled, wondering how long it would be before he spotted her.

5
Monroe – Fethard
August 1st 1914

At the meadow, where Ned had said he would find them, Louis leaned on a gate and watched men scything the sweet smelling grass. He felt the tension of the morning melt away as he watched cow parsley blooms swaying crazily back and forth, bowing in unison under the weight of butterflies that landed and took off from their floral platforms.

He felt at peace for the first time since the bombing and knew that getting away from the arena of army life would put him back on an even keel. But more importantly, accepting Ned's invitation gave him the chance to see Cat again.

As he stood watching he realised he was in a world that had evolved at a much slower pace. It was full of sweet smelling country odours and insects that appeared and then disappeared without warning.

The children here could run and play on soft green grass, not the harsh sounding cobbled streets of home in Plumstead. He was breathing air that was heavily scented by the smell of nearby milking cows, and the unmistakable aroma of burning peat wafting from the chimney at Monroe.

There was a quality of stillness in everyone's activity and the only distraction to his sense of calm was the droning buzz of bees.

Afraid of dispelling the dream-like scene he silently opened the gate and stepped forward into long grass unwillingly trampling the emerald cover. He spotted Ned in the distance rhythmically moving from the waist, guillotining the crop with his scythe.

Then as though some intuition had told him of Louis' presence, Ned looked up and waved.

Several people stopped and stared at Louis as he approached. Their faces were bronzed and weathered and the men greeted him by tipping their caps. As they did so, they showed their blue/black hair which glistened like magpie plumes under the white-hot sun, reminding him of peasants he had seen in Italy one summer. He thought how remarkably Mediterranean some of them looked. The women just stared and the youngest children clung to their mothers' skirts, wary of the stranger.

Ned approached. 'Glad to see ye, Louis. C'mon over here and I'll introduce ye to me son.' Ned let his scythe fall and went over to a tall, muscular, fair-headed man.

'Tom this is Louis, the English fella I was tellin' ye about.'

Tom smiled, his eyes crinkling at the corners.

'Hello, how are ye? So ye've come to find out how to cut hay have ye?'

'Yes, your father said he could use an extra pair of hands.'

'We've to get this lot in quickly before the weather changes. ''Twill spoil if we don't cut it today and it rains tomorrow.' He bent to tie up one of the hay-cocks.

Louis watched Tom's huge hands deftly manoeuvre each bundle, and then he remembered the football match the previous week.

'By the way, congratulations on winning the cup last Saturday, I was sorry to have missed it.'

Tom straightened up and smiled, 'Sure 'twas a grand match.'

Ned then asked Louis to follow him and they wandered down the rows of cut crops to where some of the others were tying and stacking haycocks.

Louis' eyes scanned the faces looking for the one he wanted to see most, but she wasn't there. As Ned introduced them all, he felt he would never remember their names; it seemed to him that they were *all* called Tom, Neddy, or Mary!

Ned showed him what to do, then gave him his long-handled scythe and left him to it. Louis took off his jacket and tried to do as Ned had shown him, but however he angled the scythe, nothing was achieved. He just could not get the knack of positioning the blade at the right angle.

Feeling foolish, he called to Tom. 'This sickle won't cut the grass.'

Tom grinned and ambled over to him. 'Stand upright, Louis, then pull the handle in toward yer chest as ye swirl the blade.' Tom took the scythe and demonstrated the action once more.

Then, taking the scythe into his own hands exactly as Tom had, Louis began cutting.

He went slowly at first and then as he perfected the action he was afraid to stop unless he lost the knack, so he went down the field, relentlessly swinging the scythe back and forth beheading the crop. Pleased with himself, he worked his way to the end of the field and when he turned around sweating and laughing - he saw her!

She was walking toward him, the hem of her skirt kicking up in front of her boots. In one arm she cradled a stone jug and hanging on the other arm was a basket swinging to the beat of her body.

The Italians had told him that when *the thunderbolt* hit you, the woman would be the love of your life. He knew he had been hit by *the thunderbolt!*

Louis' tension mounted as she drew nearer; then she stopped to chat to someone. He watched her laughing, throwing back her head, curls bobbing on the shoulders of her white blouse. *Lucky curls,* he thought. He absorbed the sight of her, distracted from his cutting and seduced by her presence. Now she was looking at him, shielding her eyes from the blazing sun, saying something he couldn't hear.

He flushed and called back. 'Sorry, I didn't hear you.'

Smiling, she repeated what she'd said; but when he couldn't hear for the second time, she laughed and walked toward him. His heart pounded and he began practising his battle calming routine, remembering to wait until he saw the whites of her eyes before he moved. He had never felt such emotion, but then *the thunderbolt* had never struck him before.

As she approached he thought for a moment that he was going to rush forward, lose control, and take her in his arms. Instead he raised the scythe and picked off the grass sticking to the blade.

'How about stoppin' for a bite to eat and drink?' She smiled at him, one hand moving self-consciously to her throat where the blouse button was undone.

Suddenly his life as a soldier, the prospect of a war, his home in England, the family, no longer mattered to him. He desired only to watch the flame of beauty burning brightly on her face.

Their eyes met.

She looked away blushing, and then walked quickly back to Tom and with trembling hands, unstopped the stone flask. After a while Louis followed her and flopped down beside Tom who offered him the drink.

'Here, Louis, this'll put hairs on yer chest.'

Louis took the flask and laid it down on the grass beside him as he watched Cat pulling off hunks of bread from a loaf. She passed the bread to Tom, avoiding Louis' eyes.

'Give, Louis some of this bread, Tom and I'll go see where Ellie's got to.'

She strode off across the field and disappeared through the gate while Louis absent-mindedly broke off a piece of bread and pushed it into his mouth to stifle his disappointment. He picked up the flask and took a gulp, then gasped.

'God in heaven, Tom, what the hell's this?'

Tom grinned. 'Tis Mummy's poitín[10]. Careful now ye don't want to drink too much on an empty stomach. Take some more bread with it.'

Louis sucked air into his mouth wiping away tears with the back of his hand while Tom shot him a sideways glance. 'Drink some more, ye'll be fine now ye've some bread inside ye.' Tom reached for the flask and wiped the top with his shirt before taking a swig of the poitín.

Louis lay back on one elbow and tried to sound casual. 'Who's Cat engaged to?'

'Nobody, why?'

'Oh, I just wondered.'

'Well,' Tom said, 'she *was* engaged to Paddy Hogan, but somethin's gone wrong and she won't see him.'

Louis felt a thrill of satisfaction. 'That wouldn't be any relation to Tommy Hogan who was killed recently was it?'

' Yes. 'Twas his brother. A terrible affair. But we don't get involved in that kind of stuff. We mind our own business.'

Louis fell silent, then after a pause, changed the subject. 'Who's Ellie?'

'Oh, she's one of me sisters. She's home for the weekend. She works out at The Grange cookin' and waitin' on the lady of the house.'

'So how many sisters do you have, apart from Cat and Ellie?'

---

[10] Poitín - an Irish, highly alcoholic distilled beverage traditionally distilled in a small pot (pronounced potcheen)

‘Three. They run a little shop in Main Street, Peggy, Mary and Breda. They'll be along tonight after closin’ the shop. We're roastin’ a pig. Mummy’s roast pig is the best to be had hereabouts. D'ya like pig?'

'Yes, I do.'

‘Good, then ye’ll enjoy it after a hard day’s work.’ Tom stood up and continued cutting the hay.

Louis could hardly wait. In a few hours he told himself he would be able to see her for the whole evening; spend time with her; savour the vision of her. Such a small price to pay, he thought, for doing a little hard work.

Eventually the long day slipped its way into early evening as the final yield was bundled onto a donkey cart then pulled downhill to the barn. Swaying from side to side the cart wobbled like tea-party jelly, topped with children hitching a lift as it crossed the field and rumbled its way down the dusty boreen[11].

* * *

As dusk stole unnoticed by the little gathering in the farmyard, the women carved up roast pig and delivered fat juicy slices to everyones’ plates. Chairs appeared in the yard as bats flew overhead and Ned settled down to play his flute to them. Cat began running through preliminary notes on a melodeon and Breda took her violin from its case.

[11] Boreen - a narrow country lane (pronounced bore-een)

Louis looked on fascinated by the trio, wishing he'd brought his own violin with him.

The trio played, filling the honey-suckled night air with a sweet sound that wrapped itself around the breeze, and was carried away across the valley.

Later in the evening, encouraged by drinking a large glass of poitín, Louis borrowed Breda's violin and played to the fascinated audience. They saw the arm that had held a rifle and shot men, rise to command the innocent bow; slowly and sweetly drawing it across the strings to produce the poignant notes of an intermezzo.

When he finished playing, he saw Cat was watching him. Their eyes met briefly before she suddenly looked away, but he had seen something in that look.

The moon coasted high in the night sky, radiating its silver sheen earthward, before it slipped slowly away behind Sleivenamon mountain.The fire beneath the remnants of the pig dimmed and people began to drift away home.

Everyone was thanked for helping and all agreed it had been a grand day. Sleeping children were lifted onto shoulders to be carried by parents who wouldn't bother to go to bed because it was too hot.

Ned insisted Louis stayed on to share a nightcap and they sat talking about the state of affairs in Europe.

Louis sensed Ned was leading up ask him the question he did not want to answer, and eventually he did.

'Will ye stay here long now or will ye be called back to England?'

Louis shrugged. 'Anything's possible,' he replied, but did not add that in a few days they would be gone.

The men were silent when Cat and Ellie hurried past them giggling, and Louis watched them running down the pathway towards the river. He could hear them shrieking and frolicking in the water and it made him feel an agonising mixture of happiness - tinged with sadness.

Louis did not want this night to end or to leave this place and enter the theatre of war which now seemed inevitable. He sat deep in thought listening to their laughter as dawn broke, watching all the stars in the crimson and sapphire sky disappear, one by one.

6
Plumstead, England
August 13, 1914

Louis opened the door to 29 Benares Road, Plumstead and called out, 'I'm home.'

Iris was in the hallway and seeing her uncle, yelled excitedly to her mother. 'Mummy, Uncle Louis' home!'

He scooped the child up into his arms rubbing his bristly chin into her neck, making her squeal. Lize appeared, from the kitchen, wiping her hands on her apron and rushed forward to kiss her brother.

'Why didn't you let us know you were coming home?'

'Oh well, you know how it is. The best laid plans of mice and men and all that,' he began, 'but I only have a twenty-four hour pass, Lize, then we're off.'

She gasped. 'Oh Louise!' But he held his hand up to stop her coming closer.

'Not now, Lize,' he said heaving his kit bag into the hallway, 'let me just enjoy coming home.' He closed the door. Home! At least that was how he'd come to think of it.

Louis followed Lize into the kitchen where his nephew Reggie was sitting at the table munching bread and jam.

'Well that looks good enough to feed a king, Reggie,' Louis said ruffling his hair. Iris slid onto a chair next to Reggie.

'Sit down, Louis and I'll make you some tea,' Lize said offering him the plate of bread and jam. 'Here, take a slice,' she said and added hot water to the teapot. She sat down at the table opposite Louis and began pouring the tea. 'So what's new?'

'Nothing much, really,' he said biting into the bread. He saw Lize looking at his hands.

'Louis, what happened?'

'Oh.' He lowered his hand. 'Just a little accident, nothing to worry about.'

'Come on! You'll have to try harder than that! It doesn't look like *just a little accident*. Were you in a fight?'

'No. There was a bomb outside the barracks and I got hit by some of the flying debris, Lize, that's all.' He swallowed another piece of bread before telling her about Private White's death.

He could see she was upset and it had probably struck a raw nerve as her husband Charlie had already gone to war. She stood up and fetched a handkerchief from her handbag and blew her nose.

'Rotten Irish. Uncivilised, murdering pigs.'

'They're not *all* like that.'

She studied the back of his head before moving round the table to sit opposite him. 'What's her name?'

'Pardon?'

'I said, what's her name?'

'What are you talking about?'

'Come on, Louis, I know you inside out. What's the name of the woman who's stolen your wits?'

He ignored her question and continued drinking tea before checking his pocket watch. 'I have to visit Private White's mother.'

'What now?'

'Yes, she only lives across the common. They were very close, Lize, and she's a widow. She'll be finding it pretty hard.'

Lize didn't answer, but silently cleared away the tea things and told the children to go upstairs and get ready for bed.

In the silence that followed, Lize settled down with her knitting. She poured over the pattern, counting; her lips working silently as her finger pulled each stitch along the needle. Suddenly she stopped, as Louis stood up.

'I'm going to see Mrs. White now. Need to get it over with.'

'Oh, I see.' She sniffed. The needles clicked in the silence as she wound the grey wool round the needle increasing the snake coiling into her lap.

Louis left the house, pulling the front door closed with a soft click, walked to the end of the road, turned the corner and headed towards Roydene Road. He walked quickly, wondering what on earth he was going to say to Mrs. White when he arrived.

Checking the numbers, he stopped outside number seventeen; went through the front gate and knocked on the door. As he waited he noticed that though it was still light, the parlour curtains were drawn across. Mrs. White, in the time-honoured way, was mourning her loss and Louis suddenly felt he was intruding.

He heard footsteps from inside and knew someone was approaching the door. There was a click as the latch was opened, and an eye peered through the crack.

'Yes?'

'Mrs. White?'

'Yes, who wants to know?'

'Captain Ross, Royal Artillery.'

The door opened wider and Mrs. White began to apologise and asked him to step inside. She showed him into the kitchen and after Louis had offered his condolences she relaxed and began to reminisce about her son. She related how he had won a certificate at school for history, how clever he was with his hands and recounted to Louis at length about the letters he had written to her. She told him she had nothing to live for now, and he didn't know how to disagree with her so he just listened.

'He spoke kindly of you, Captain. He wrote often singing your praises. He said you were a good man and looked after the men well. You know, he loved being in the army. Now it's killed him.' She began to cry.

'He died a courageous death, Mrs. White. It was quick... and he didn't suffer at all. I was there. I can assure you of that.'

'Thank you. It helps to know that.'

This was proving harder than he had imagined and he decided he should leave. He stood up to go and Mrs. White looked up at him surprised.

'Going already?'

'Yes. I'm afraid I have to. My sister will be expecting me back.'

'Where does she live?'

'Benares Road'

'Oh what number?'

'Number twenty nine. Look, why don't you call in on her one day? Her name's, Lize and her husband is away at war. It can't be easy for either of you. maybe it would give you both some company. I'm sure Lize would love to meet you.'

'Oh.,. I...err,' her voice trailed off.

Louis could tell she didn't know what to say and decided he would ask Lize to call on her instead.

'Well, goodbye, Mrs. White,' he said. 'I'll look in again next time I'm on leave.'

'Yes, you do that. Thank you.' She walked in front of him to open the door.

Louis stepped into the garden, turned and shook her hand, then went through the gate and walked briskly away. He waved to her as he crossed the road to the common and she nodded to him, before closing the door.

He couldn't erase the image of her lonely little figure and wondered how many times she had waved her son off in just the same way.

* * *

Louis was dreaming. He could hear a tapping noise. But as he awoke, he gradually realised it was the post dropping through the letterbox onto the hall floor. Slowly he eased himself out of bed, pulled his trousers on, and feeling utterly worn out, stumbled downstairs. He had been disturbed by the visit to Mrs. White and when he had returned, he and Lize had spent a difficult evening together. He had suggested she call on Mrs. White but the idea had been rejected when Lize said she didn't even know the woman let alone go calling on her.

'For the love of God, Lize, can't you just visit her? She's lonely and her son has just died,' he had pleaded, but she had stung him with her reply reminding him Mrs. White wasn't the only one to suffer loneliness. Her words were in the forefront of his mind as he went downstairs.

He recognised the familiar brown envelope instantly. The letter was addressed to Lize and the marking across the envelope read, WAR OFFICE. He felt his stomach contract and stuffed the letter into his pocket before going into the kitchen where his hands shook as he filled the kettle and placed it on the range. He needed time to think, but then was aware that Lize was behind him.

'What was the letter, Louis?

He turned to face her, drew the letter from his pocket and handed it to her. She ripped the envelope open and he saw the colour drain from her face. He knew without asking that Charlie had been killed, just one week after the war started.

* * *

'Now before I go Lize, I just want to go over things once more.' She didn't respond but remained sitting in Charlie's chair, staring into space, cradling her cup of tea.

Louis pressed on regardless. He didn't have much time. 'I've made out my Will and everything goes to you and the children if anything happens to me. I'll make arrangements to have my pay cheque forwarded to you while I'm away. I've also got an insurance policy which matures later on and I can't see myself needing it, so you'll be looked after…if…well, you know what I mean.'

He got up and pressed her shoulder. 'Lize, are you listening? It's important that you know you'll be looked after. You won't go short.'

'Thanks, Louis,' she said unenthusiastically.

He checked the time, then emptied his pockets onto the table. 'Here, Lize take this, it's not much but all I've got. I won't need it. Not where I'm going.'

Lize stood up and looked at him then slowly put her arms around him burying her head into his chest.

'Take care of yourself, Louis.'

He hugged her briefly then walked quickly along the hallway, opened the door and left without looking back.

Crossing the common he wondered who was worse off, Charlie or himself. At least Charlie was out of this damned war now. He decided that if he survived he would never deliberately hurt another human being. It wasn't in his nature to be violent. He and others like him, peace-loving, family men were being forced into the machine of war. The only option was to be labelled a coward and receive a white feather. There simply was no way out for most of them now.

As he passed Roydene Road he thought of Mrs. White, alone in her tidy little house. *Poor Mrs. White*, he thought, *and then poor Lize*.

7
Monroe, Fethard
September 1914

Ned stood fingering the envelope. ‘There’s another letter for ye,’ he said.

‘Thanks.’ Cat did not look up but carried on eating her breakfast as Ned put the envelope down next to her plate.

‘Ye know,’ he began, ‘’Tis none of me business but ’tis causin’ gossip, him keep writin’ to ye.’

‘I know.’

‘Well, ye’d better think about it, ye don’t want to get a name.’

‘Dada, ’tis only a letter.’ She pushed it across the table. ‘Read it.’ Cat studied his face as he picked it up and opened the envelope, then unfolded the paper. After he had read it he folded it in half and handed it back to her.

Without saying anything he ambled to the doorway, took a cigarette stub from behind his ear and lit it. He stood with his back to her, blowing smoke into the yard.

‘I’m not against the man, ye know that. I’m just worried for ye.’

‘I’ll not be intimidated by gossips, or the likes of Paddy Hogan.’

‘No, I’m not suggestin’ ye should be. ’Twas the best day’s work gettin’ rid of him. ’Tis just that I hear title-tattle and I don't like what I hear. I think he still hankers after ye.'

'Ha! Well he can hanker on. I'm not interested.'

Ned decided to change the subject. 'Oh by the way, I almost forgot,' he said, 'Auntie Nellie could do with a hand in the bar tonight.' He flicked the butt into the air and when it landed, stubbed it out with his boot.

'I'll go up to Auntie Nellie's after tea. But Dada, ye know I like gettin' the letters, they're interestin'.'

'I can see that, Pet, he writes nicely.'

'Anyway, what sort of tittle-tattle d'ya hear?'

'Ugly talk from people with ugly minds. Now c'mon, 'tis time for the cows and Tom's already made a start.' He picked up the milk bucket and walked across the yard. She heard the familiar sound of his boots clashing across the cobbles, the gate creaking open then closed, followed by silence as his footsteps were softened by the grassy boreen.

Cat stopped eating, pushed her dish to one side, slid the letter in front of her and read it. She thought Louis could certainly pen an eloquent letter and though a lot of it was innuendo, she sensed he was always in danger. Why shouldn't he write to her?

She read it again, savouring every word, looking for clues as to his feelings. Her lips mouthed each word as she read.

Dear Cat

The days are absolutely endless! Though full of people; there is a solitude that is unbroken amidst all the chaos. I miss your green fields and the people of your homeland who were so kind to me.

Thank you for the cigarettes they were much appreciated. Should you ever find yourself in England please feel free to contact my sister, Eliza. I have written to her about you, so this would come as no surprise. The address is on the back of this page.

Give my regards to your parents, brother and sisters. I have very fond memories of their hospitality, which I hope to be able to return one day.

Yours very sincerely, Louis

She pressed the paper over her face and breathed in, trying to capture his scent, then folded it up and put it in her pocket before following Ned to the barn.

When she opened the door to the barn, Tom and Ned were milking the cows but she heard Tom's annoyed voice above the noise.

'That Paddy Hogan should keep his feckin' mouth shut or I'll shut it for him.'

Then Ned spoke, sounding just as angry. 'If he harms a hair on her head he'll have me to answer to. So he will!'

'Keep an eye on her, Dada. I think he's turned into nasty piece of work.'

'I agree. I thought I'd settled it that day in the hotel but it seems it wasn't enough. Maybe I should have hit him harder!'

Cat stepped over the straw careful not to disturb the new litter of kittens huddled next to their mother. 'What's goin' on, Dada?'

'Nuthin', Pet. Nuthin'.'

'Aw c'mon both of ye. Somethin's goin' on, Don't take me for a fool!'

'Leave it Cat.' Tom said sharply. 'Ye don't need to know.'

'Know *what*?'

The men continued milking in silence. She heard the milk squirting into the buckets as the cows munched on hay in the darkened barn and nobody spoke.

'Is somebody goin' to tell me what's goin' on? 'Tis obviously me ye're talkin' about?' Tom stood and moved the bucket away, unfastened a rope and led a cow out without answering her. 'Dada, what's happened?'

Ned thought for a moment and stopped milking. 'Paddy Hogan's been spoutin' his mouth off and makin' threats about ye.'

'Huh, what, again? D'ye think I care?'

'Look, he's mixin' with a mean bunch now. That's what bothers me.'

'Birds of a feather! All pretendin' they're fightin' for a cause. Stupid! All of 'em.' Just a bunch of little boys with big mouths.'

Tom re-entered the barn and stood thoughtfully before tying up the next cow.

'Ye know Dada I've been approached by them to join up.'

Ned stopped milking. 'Ye *what*?'

'I've been asked to join them.'

'And ye didn't tell me?'

'No.'

'Why?'

'Because I didn't want to worry ye.'

'So, what's the verdict?' Ned looked irritated.

'Ye should know without askin'.'

'Do I have a feckin' fool in me midst or not?'

'Of course not Dada, I was careful and said I'd think about it. But I was just stalling. 'Tis not for me.'

Cat saw Ned's face relax.

'So, when're ye goin' to tell them the good news?'

'Tonight. They've told me to meet them at Crampscastle.'

'Jesus! All this goin' on and I don't know anythin' about it. I'm beginnin' to wonder if I know me own family at all these days. One of ye's liaising with a band of murderers and the other's sendin' cigarettes to a foreign soldier! Where will it all lead to?'

Cat and Tom exchanged glances as Ned turned his back and continued milking, muttering to himself.

* * *

After leaving the bar that night Cat stopped on the humpback bridge spanning the Clashawley River, and stared up at the sky. She marvelled at the number of stars and wondered whether Louis was looking up at them too. She took no notice of the motorcar stopping on the other side of the bridge and did not hear anyone approaching her from behind.

Suddenly something was pulled over her head and she was dragged backwards into the waiting car. Through the fabric a mouth pressed against her ear.

'One word. One shout and ye're feckin' dead.'

Then she heard what she thought must be the click of a gun being cocked

'Where're ye takin' me?'

'Shut yer mouth.' It was a man's voice, but because he hissed the warning she couldn't tell if she knew him.

The car drove off quickly along the bumpy road and someone tied her hands together, so she knew there were at least two of them. The twine bit into her wrists as she was thrown back and forth by the motion of the speeding vehicle.

After a while she was told to get off the seat onto the floor of the car. She slid onto her knees and a hand pushed her down forcing her to remain in position. She felt someone's boot then rested on her back, pinning her down. Her mind raced.

She tried to memorise how many bends in the road they took and guess where they were, but her thoughts were scrambled and she was unable to assemble her sense of reason. Panic set in – the hood was suffocating her. She began to scream.

'Shut yer feckin' mouth!' Someone shouted and she fell silent.

They must be somewhere with rutted mud, a farm or somewhere off the road she thought, as the bumping became more pronounced. Then the car stopped and someone got out to open a gate. She knelt shaking, but listening for clues as to her whereabouts. She thought it sounded like a farm gate with the iron clasp being lifted.

The driver got back in and drove on. The bumping had ceased so Cat gathered they were on a smooth surface. Then the vehicle stopped again and someone opened the car door and pulled her out. She was bundled into what she thought was some sort of barn as she could smell hay and hear chickens. But so many farms had chickens; she could not tell where she was.

Someone pushed her down onto a hay bale and she heard the sound of several pairs of boots approaching. The voice of the person who abducted her spoke first.

'Well Miss, ye're here to be taught a lesson.'

She didn't answer.

'I said ye're here to be taught a lesson. What have ye to say for yerself?' He paused waiting for her to reply, but she remained silent. 'Nuttin', by the sound of it.'

Cat thought she recognised his voice, but it was muffled, as though the man was speaking through a scarf on a cold day.

'Got plenty to say normally.' It was the first voice again.

The hood was hot and she felt she was going to be sick, but she plucked up the courage to sound defiant. 'What d'ye want with me?'

''Tis more like what do *ye* want with English soldiers. Filthy little whore.'

Then another voice asked, 'Is it ready?' and the sack was suddenly yanked off her head. It was dark and she couldn't see, but before there was time to adjust to the gloom, someone blindfolded her. There was no point fighting, she was out-numbered, so she decided to comply; not provoke them, then maybe they would let her go.

Suddenly one of them grabbed her by the hair from behind and started chopping at her locks with what sounded like scissors. She tried to dodge out of the way but one of the men smacked her face and told her to hold still; then little by little she felt her hair falling onto her shoulders and her lap.

Time passed until she felt there couldn't possibly be any more hair to cut, but then she felt her scalp being scored by a razor until she realised her head must now be completely bald. Soon she smelt tar and felt the tacky substance being smeared across her naked skull before she sensed something soft descending gently onto her head, then falling lightly onto her shoulders. She could smell chickens.

* * *

Tom felt unsettled after the meeting earlier that night at Crampscastle. He'd told the gang that it was not for him, and they had sworn him to secrecy before he made his way back to Monroe.

He knew one or two of them, *but where on God's earth,* he wondered, *had they conjured up the rest from*? He would not have been surprised to see Paddy Hogan, but he was not amongst them.

He had begun unlacing his boots before going to bed when he heard what sounded like one of the kittens mewing outside. He stopped what he was doing. The noise came again, so he laced up his boots and went outside to listen.

He crossed the yard and stood by the gate; and when the sound came again he walked up the boreen thinking perhaps a kitten had become separated from its mother in the barn. He opened the barn door and struck a match to light the hurricane lamp, then he saw Cat - and all he could say was, 'God in heaven!'

8
The Royal Irish Constabulary Office
Fethard,
November 1914

'So, ye're no nearer catchin' the swines then?' Ned said to Brendan and leaned on the desk holding his head in his hands. Outside the lashing November rain beat against the windows.

Brendan frowned. 'No.'

'Have ye questioned Paddy Hogan?'

'Sure, I went out to the Hogan's place ages ago to talk to him and his mother, but I'm not sure he had any direct involvement. He could account for his whereabouts that night.'

'So, where was he?'

'He says he was at home and that Father Ryan had been out to dine with them that evenin'.'

'Huh! And ye believed him?'

'His mother confirmed it.'

'Ye know as well as I do she'd lie for him. The sun comes out of his backside where that one's concerned.'

'Well every swan thinks their own signet's whiter than the rest,' Brendan said taking a bottle of whiskey from his drawer. He poured them both a shot. 'C'mon now, Neddy, drink this, ye look as though ye need it.'

Ned thumped the table. 'The feckin' names they called her an' all! English soldier's whore! Ye know yerself, Brendan, she never goes out, except to help in the shop with the girls or in the bar for Nellie. She's not even been out with anyone other than Paddy and she has certainly never gone out with a soldier! I'll kill 'em if I ever find out who 'twas did that to her.'

'Best left to me,' Brendan sighed, 'though to be honest, Neddy, 'tis goin' to be difficult to nail these bastards. I've got nowhere with the enquiries in all this time. I know this so-called company of Irish National Volunteers has sprung up - but to harm a woman is unheard of! Everyone I talk to says the same; they cannot imagine who would do such a thing.' He took a sip of whiskey and scratched the back of his head. 'I wasn't goin' to tell ye, but Paddy even put in an appearance here a while back askin' if I'd found out who did it.'

'G'w'on away wit' ye, he never did!'

'Sure he did. Now he's either innocent, or he's more canny than I'd given credit for. I'll keep me options open at present and see which way the cards fall.'

Looking thoughtful Ned rubbed his chin.

'Well, thanks for all ye're doing, Brendan. Maeve and I won't forget it.'

'Look, Neddy, even if ye weren't me cousin I'd be after this bunch of scum. We don't want this kind o' thin' creepin' in here. Ye don't know where 'twill end. But I think we're goin' to have to lie low for now, and then maybe I'll get a tip-off from someone.'

Ned took his cigarettes out, lit one and blew the smoke upwards. He sat thinking, sighed, and then leaned forward to flick ash into a saucer.

'Ye know Cat's set on goin' off to England to live. She's had an invite to go to Louis' sister and family for a while. Apparently there's plenty of work to be had in the Woolwich Arsenal packin' ammunition for the war.' His voice had a strained tone. 'Now her hair's grown back some, she says she's goin'.' He picked up the whiskey glass, but just sat staring at it.

'Jesus, Ned, ye'll miss her, and so will we. We all will. What a state of affairs that she has to run away to another country. It makes me sick to the heart.'

Ned shifted in his chair. 'God save us, I don't know what Maeve and I will do without her. Not just for the help on the land, but she's the very breath in our lungs. I feel certain Paddy Hogan had somethin' to do with this. It has to be him, or some connection don't you think?'

He sat silently swirling the honey-coloured liquid round and round in his glass until Brendan broke into his train of thought.

'Ye know, Neddy, even if I thought Paddy was at the bottom of this, how d'ye prove it? If he says he was with Father Ryan on that night, I'm not about to go and question Father Ryan about it.'

'Why not? What's to stop ye askin' him?'

'Fear, I suppose.'

'Of what?'

'I'm afraid that I may hear Father Ryan tellin' me somethin' I don't want to hear.'

'I'm not with ye, Brendan.'

'Well, 'tis true Father Ryan did go out to Hogan's that night, but I have no idea what time he left.'

'So, d'ya think Paddy was usin' the visit as a sort of cover?'

'Could be, but I have no proof, Neddy. I can't go questionin' a priest about his movements, especially if he's Paddy's alibi; there's no tellin' where that one would lead. And anyway, even if 'twas Paddy, there were others too accordin' to Cat.' Brendan lifted his glass. 'Sláinte.'

'Sláinte, Brendan.' Ned sipped the whiskey. 'I see the way the land lies with these fiends. They're too slippery for the likes of us, especially if they're hidin' behind a priest's cassock.'

'Maybe. But as a policeman I won't just look the other way, they'll thrive on that kind of inaction, to be sure. I shall have to find other means of discoverin' the truth. They'll slip up eventually.'

Ned got up and walked over to the window; his eyes welled with tears.

'Do what ye have to Brendan. I won't be expectin' miracles. Cat's leavin' and I feel we've lost the battle already.'

* * *

The railway station was full of people boarding the boat train.

'All aboard,' the guard repeatedly called as he walked along the platform slamming doors. Young folk were hanging out of the train windows saying their last tearful goodbyes to families, reminding each other to write as soon as they could.

Ned watched it all as though in a dream. He saw the family huddling around Cat, pressing rosaries and medals of Our Lady into her hands, and he couldn't speak. He thought Maeve looked pale as she tearfully kissed Cat goodbye.

'Lord above,' he heard her say, 'I never thought I'd see ye go, mo chuisle.'[12]

He wanted to say so too. Wanted to shout out, 'Don't go Cat,' but an appalling grief had gripped him and he could find no words to ease his pain.

The guard was shouting for everyone to stand back when Ned suddenly snapped out of his reverie. He pushed his way forward and elbowed the girls, Tom and Maeve aside. He went to Cat; pulled the collar of her coat straight; held her face in his hands and kissed her. Then his face wet with tears, he stepped back and watched her climb into the carriage and close the door.

A whistle blew and the train eased its way out of the station, swaying along the track until, smaller than a pinhead in the distance, it disappeared from view.

---

[12] mo chuisle – my darling (pronounced ma cooshla)

9
Plumstead
November 1914

Cat walked briskly along Benares Road until she reached No. 29. *This is it*, she thought, opening the gate and walking along the path to the front door. When she knocked, the hollow-sounding echo suggested to her that the house was empty.

Standing on the doorstep as it began to rain, panic gripped her. Everything rested on the promise of accommodation with Louis' sister, Eliza.

She drew Louis' letter out of her bag and re-read it. He had assured her she could go to his sister, but the letter had been written a couple of months ago! There was only one thing to do she decided, and looking round to make sure no one was watching her, she pushed the letter box open and peered through.

The hallway was empty; there were no signs of life and the coat hooks on the wall were bare, so she went to look through the front-room window. Cupping her hands against the glass she saw the room was completely bare.

Perhaps the people next door may know something she thought, so slipped through a gap in the hedge. As there were children in the garden playing ball, she asked them if their mother was in.

'Mum!' one of them bawled out, 'someone to see yer.'

A woman appeared wiping her hands on her pinafore, looking annoyed. She eyed Cat up and down.

'Yers, can I 'elp you?'

'Yes. I'm sorry to bother ye, but I was wonderin' if ye knew where the family next door are; only I've just arrived and was expectin' to stay with them?'

'They moved yesterday.'

A wave of panic washed over Cat and tears filled her eyes. She stood helplessly before the woman, wondering what on earth she was going to do now, but after a moment or two the woman spoke again.

'They aint gorn far, 'cross the common to Roydene Road. Number seventeen.'

'How do I get there?'

'Walk! Like I says, just 'cross the common.' She nodded her head in that direction. 'Straight over and second on the left. Easy 'nough to find.'

Cat looked in the direction of the common, and then turned to thank her only to find the woman had begun closing the door. Before she shut it though Cat heard her grumble. 'Fucking Irish!'

Shocked, Cat stumbled out of the gate with her bag and headed for the common. The grass was sodden and it wasn't long before the hem of her skirt was soaked. She hobbled across the uneven ground lugging her bag of clothes.

The enormity of leaving home and arriving at a stranger's house to beg for accommodation suddenly hit her. What if she got the cold shoulder from his sister? She had taken for granted that Louis' letter meant the invite was from both him and his sister, but was it? All manner of doubts now crowded her thoughts filling her with uncertainty about what to do. She continued staggering across the common weighed down by her bag until at last she reached the other side and was able to leave the wet grass.

When Cat found the house, knocking on the door seemed like a major step to her and she hesitated. But then thoroughly soaked, she had no alternative than to get on with it.

She knocked on the door and waited. No reply. She knocked again; then heard distant sound of children's laughter from the back of the house. She rapped a little harder, and then from around the corner of the house a boy of about ten emerged. He had a mop of straw-coloured curly hair, cheeky blue eyes and rather crooked overlapping front teeth.

'Hello,' she said, 'is your mammy in?'

'No. She's out.'

Her heart sank.

'Is yer mammy Mrs. Eliza Collis?'

'Yes, I think so. Only everyone calls her, Lize.'

'When will she be home?'

'Soon.'

'Well, can I come in and wait for her? Cat asked.

'If you want. My nan's here.'

'Well, that's good. Will ye tell her I'm here then?'

The boy nodded. 'Yes. But what's your name?'

'Miss Delaney.'

He disappeared around the side of the house and soon Cat heard footsteps approaching the front door. A small woman of about sixty opened the door with the boy close behind her.

'Yes?'

'I'm a friend of Louis',' Cat explained.

'Yes?' she repeated.

'Well, actually, Louis wrote and said his sister may put me up for a while if I were to come over.'

'Did 'e?' She sounded disinterested. 'Well you'd better come in outa the rain.' She stood back from the door to allow Cat inside. 'Shut the door after yerself,' she said and marched off down the hall.

Cat called after the woman. 'Is it alright if I leave my bag here?'

''Spect so,' came her distant reply.

Cat thought she sounded exactly like the woman she had spoken to across the common and just as indifferent, but she had no option other than to put up with the woman's attitude. She put down her bag and went along the hallway to the kitchen where she discovered the woman had seated herself at the kitchen table and was drinking tea. Cat stood in the middle of the kitchen until the woman looked at her.

'S'pose you wantacupoftea?'

Cat hesitated, trying to translate what she had said. 'Thank you. But don't go to any trouble on my account.'

'I won't. It'sallreadyinthe pot.' She sniffed and got up to get a cup and saucer from the dresser, but something attracted her attention in the garden. She opened the window and bellowed at the boy Cat had just met.

'Put that bleeding rake down, Reggie! And both of yougetinoutathe rain!'

'Ye must be Louis' mother,' Cat said as the woman poured out her tea.

'No! I'm Lize's Mother-in-law, formesins. Mrs. Collis is me name,' she replied waving cat into a chair. Mrs. Collis sat down opposite Cat and lapsed into silence reading the newspaper she had spread out on the table. Cat wondered whether she should talk or remain quiet.

In the heat of the kitchen, Cat's woollen coat began to steam, giving off a distinct and unpleasant odour of damp wool, so she undid it and slipped it over the back of the chair along with her headscarf. She picked up her cup and sipped the tea. It was very bitter and there was hardly any milk in it. The mud-coloured liquid slid down her throat scalding it, but she just didn't feel she could ask her for more milk. Cat decided Mrs. Collis didn't seem the sort of woman she could ask for more of anything.

In the silence, Cat felt she was making horrible swallowing noises, but Mrs. Collis didn't appear to notice; it was as though she had completely forgotten she was there.

It felt like an age before Cat heard a key in the lock of the front door and a voice calling out to the children.

'Reggie. Iris. I'm home.'

Thank Heavens, Cat thought, at least the voice sounded cheerful! Then simultaneously, the boy she had met before, followed by a flaxen-haired, blue-eyed girl of about seven, burst in through the back door just as the owner of the voice entered the kitchen pulling off her headscarf. Cat stood up.

'Hello, who's this?' Lize asked her mother-in-law.

'FriendaLouis,' Mrs. Collis grumbled without lifting her eyes from the newspaper. Then she folded it shut and looked up at Lize. 'Think she's Irish. Yer later than you said you'd be and now I'm late meself.' She stood up. 'I'llbeyoff.'

Cat was trying hard to understand what Mrs. Collis was saying and as she was just deciphering the last sentence, Lize spoke. To Cat's relief she understood every syllable Lize said as she had a very clear and slow way of speaking, in much the same accent as Louis.

'Yes, I'm so sorry I got held up Mother.' She turned to look at Cat. 'You must be Cat,' she said stretching out her hand. 'Pleased to meet you. You're very welcome. Very welcome indeed. Please, sit down and finish your tea.'

Cat sat with a fixed grin on her face, searching Lize's face for any resemblance to Louis. Her hair was mousy brown and she was very thin.

She had a distinctly hooked nose and blue eyes. She didn't look like him at all and Cat felt strangely disappointed.

The children stared at Cat until Lize noticed.

'Iris, Reggie, stop staring. Where are your manners? Go on now, sit up at the table, it's time for tea.'

They scrambled up to the table and Cat, feeling awkward, wondered if she would be asked to join them. She hoped so, as her growling stomach reminded her that she had not eaten all day.

'I'm so pleased to meet ye, Lize. I hope ye don't mind me arrivin' like this, but I did write. Ye may not have got the letter though.'

'Oh yes I got it,' she laughed. 'But I just did not have time to reply, what with the move and everything. You know how it is. It went clean out of my head. Sorry.'

'Well is it alright if I stay here for a bit?'

'Yes of course. It'll be company for me. My brother said you were a nice person, so you come with good recommendation.' Lize smiled and started putting fish and chips on the plates.

Mrs. Collis put her coat on and began buttoning it up. 'Well I'm off now Lize. D'ya want me to come tomorro' to help finish the unpacking?'

'No, that's alright. I can manage now thank you, Mother.'

Mrs. Collis said no more but turned on her heel, marched through to the hallway and left, slamming the door behind her. Reggie and Iris looked at each other, then at their mother.

'She didn't say goodbye,' Reggie said

'Who is *she*?' Lize asked, 'I think you are referring to your grandmother. Is that so?'

'Yes, I'm sorry, Mummy. But grandmother still didn't say goodbye.'

'Don't be cheeky and eat your food,' Lize said and clipped Reggie round the head with her hand.

Cat thought the boy was right. The woman had just gone, and not even given the children a kiss. What a strange sort of grandmother she must be or perhaps this was just the English way. Well one thing was certain, she hoped she didn't have to meet her too soon or too often.

10
Plumstead
November 1914

Lize watched Cat pegging out the washing. It was good to have another adult indoors, especially one that was proving so useful. She began buttering the children's bread, daydreaming about how she would spend her day, when someone knocked on the front door.

She called out to Reggie asking him to open the door. The next moment Lize's mother stormed into the kitchen and began shouting at her.

'You crafty little bitch! Thought you'd steal a march on me did you?'

Lize continued buttering toast, but her hands shook. She put down the knife and began pouring tea, but the pot quivered noticeably as her mother continued shouting at her.

'Not a word! Not a flaming goodbye or anything! I'm only around the corner, and you couldn't as much as tell me you were going!'

'No, that's right, Mum, I didn't.' Lize put the teapot down, and glared at her mother. 'This house was suddenly left to Louis by a Mrs. White. So I took the opportunity to get out of *your* house. You've done nothing but remind me since Charlie died, that I was getting it at a cheap rent. You certainly didn't waste any time telling me you wanted your money on time the minute he was killed, and that his death did not make any difference – you still wanted your rent!'

Lize became aware of Reggie and Iris staring wide-eyed at them both.

'Anyway, Mum, you can charge a higher rent now can't you?' Lize said pouring milk into the cups. 'You were always so fond of telling me you could charge more for the house!'

'Yes. I can and I will! Make no mistake about that my girl. And you needn't think Louis will let you stay here once he's back. If he's thinking of inviting that Irish bitch to live over here permanently, you can bet your life he's got other ideas in his mind.'

'Like what exactly?'

'You think you're sitting pretty now don't you? The older woman jabbed Lize in the shoulder with a finger. 'But mark my words, Miss High and Mighty, you'll laugh on the other side of your face one day. You'll see. And you won't be drawing his army pay for ever, you grabbing little bitch!' She poked Lize again. 'I brought him up! It's me who should be reaping the benefit, not you.' She pushed Lize. 'All those years of putting up with your drunken father; spending every penny in the pub. Years of scraping money together to get some capital behind me 'cos he'd never provided it!'

Lize watched her mother's lips opening and closing as she raged at her. She coldly met her mother's gaze then turned her back and resumed buttering bread.

After a short while Lize very calmly turned to face her mother. 'Oh and for your information Mum, the Irish bitch is already here!'

The back door opened and Cat came in. Lize stopped what she was doing and smiled at her.

'Cat, this is my mother.'

Cat held out her hand. 'Pleased to meet you, Mrs. Ross.'

Jessie Ross stared at Cat; gave Lize a withering look, turned on her heel and marched out of the house.

'Shut the door on your way out, Mum,' Lize said.

Sighing, Lize put the bread on the plates. 'Don't take any notice of her, Cat. She can be really awkward when she chooses.' She looked down at the children. 'Come on now you two, eat up.'

Reggie picked up his toast and looked up at Lize with an innocent expression on his face and asked her.

'Mum, who's the Irish bitch?'

11
Monroe, Fethard
December 1914

Ned blew on his fingertips to warm them before beginning to dig out the rotten gatepost. As he worked his mind returned, as it always did, to Cat. He wondered what she was doing right now in London. Was she happy at Louis' sister's? *Surely*, he thought, *she must miss them and would come home soon.*

The postman called to him from the main road and said he had a letter from England, so Ned leaned the spade against the gate, wiped his hands on his trousers and hurried up the boreen to collect it. He was hardly able to contain his excitement as he saw Cat's familiar handwriting and rushed back to the cottage to share the news with Maeve.

'Maeve, we've a letter at last!'

'Well read it man, g'w'on, read it!' she said, wiping her hands on a towel.

Ned screwed up his eyes and began to read.

'Seventeen Roydene Road, Plumstead, England. That's the address, then she goes on to say,

"Dear Mummy and Dada

I have not been able to write before as it took a while to settle into my new accommodation and get into the swing of things.

I am, as you know, staying at Louis' sister's house, though it is not at the address given previously because she had moved by the time I arrived. The address at the top of this letter is where you should write to me.

The weather has been fine for this time of year, though I see little of the sun because I have two jobs.

My main job is at Woolwich Arsenal, where I am in the armaments shop packing bullets. This is fairly boring work, but it allows me time to sit and think of ye all at home. I was quite slow at first, but I am becoming quicker now. The more I pack, the more I earn.

The girls I work with are a friendly bunch, though it took me some time to understand what they were saying, and they me. I work from eight in the morning to six at night with a half hour for lunch. We have a uniform for work, so it does not matter too much what I wear, though my normal clothes seem very old fashioned over here. I shall have to spend a little on some new skirts and blouses, as I do not want to look as though I have just come from a field digging up potatoes.

My other job is taking care of the house and children for Louis' sister, Lize who is a nurse in a hospital. She has been so kind to me. We have an arrangement that if I run the house and take care of the children, it allows her to work the nightshift at the hospital. In return I only have to pay her a very low rent.

It seems a good arrangement because it means I get to keep most of my earnings, so I shall be able to send you some money soon, Please God.

I have not seen Louis yet as he is still away, but I hope he will return soon.

Look after yourselves and love to all of you. Tell Ellie, if she's thinking of following me to England, there's plenty of work here for her. Just let me know.

I'll write again soon, but until then, God bless ye both.

Your loving daughter, Cat.'"

Ned frowned and put the letter back in the envelope. 'Well it looks as though she's fallen on her feet,' he said, scratching the back of his head. He was quiet for a while then said, 'I'd better get back to work.'

He dared not look at Maeve for fear she would see the tears in his eyes and discover his vulnerability. He rose and walked slowly out of the cottage and across the yard to the gatepost he was replacing.

Suddenly he did not feel like bothering to mend it, and with a sigh, he dug into the black soil reluctantly and thought about Cat sitting in a dingy factory packing bullets. Jesus, *is that what she's been brought to, working in an old factory packing bullets? And what about when the war ends, what then?* He thought she should be out in the fresh air with him now, digging up the spuds and laughing with him about some fresh joke.

Ned looked towards the Clashawly River and remembered the time before she left when they collected sallies in the sun last summer. It seemed so long ago.

Why was it he wondered, one child could twist up your heart so badly? The letter had upset him because he had hoped she would say she was homesick and was coming home.

Leaning on his spade staring into the distance, his thoughts were confused. What was the world coming to? Everything had gone topsy turvey. They'd had foreign soldiers sauntering about their streets, then his own countrymen had become savage murderers, his daughter frightened off overseas to live amongst a bunch of heathens and pack bullets for a living! It was not what he had planned.

Even Tom, he thought, was looking less enthusiastic these days, loafing about aimlessly after work. Ned decided the spark had gone out of their lives and that none of them had appreciated, until Cat had gone, that she was the axel in their machinery.

He had lost her for good and it hurt. It seemed she would probably never come home to live again unless something drastic happened or, he thought, if he demanded her return! But no. He could not do that, he needed another plan.

Tom appeared cycling along the main road, and then turned off to free wheel down the boreen towards Monroe. Ned waved and beckoned to him so Tom braked and dismounted, walking his bicycle to where Ned stood.

'What's up Dada? Are ye alright? Ye look a bit off colour.'

Ned drew himself up straight and dug in his pocket for cigarettes. Pulling out a packet he offered one to Tom and they lit up. 'Tom, I want ye to go to England and bring her home.'

Tom looked at him, surprised by the request.

'Dada, what's got into ye?'

'I just don't like the way she's livin' out there with those heathens.'

'Aw, c'mon now. How do ye know what she's livin' like, we haven't heard from her yet?'

'We had a letter today and I'm not satisfied she's happy. She says she has two jobs, but neither are what I would have mapped out for her. She's a country girl and she should be here with us courtin' a nice Irish boy, not packin' bullets from sun up to sun down in some old factory.'

'*Ah*! So that's what she's doin'?'

''Tis. As well as lookin' after a house and the children for Louis' sister. But that's not the problem. 'Tis just that, well, if she's lookin' after other peoples' children, she could be here lookin' after some of her own.'

'Ye cannot run her life for her, Dada. She's gone now and whether she packs bullets or washes floors for a livin' we have to accept it. She could *not* stay here. Not after what happened, ye *know* that.'

Ned didn't want to listen to Tom's reasoning and instead continued pouring out his thoughts to him.

'We let her down. We could not defend her and I want to have a second chance at doin' just that. So, Tom, I want ye to go over and fetch her back.'

Tom inhaled the cigarette smoke and looked at Ned. 'I'll think about it Dada, but I'm not sure 'tis the best idea ye've had.'

Ned stared into the distance at Slievenamon Mountain. 'She loves this place.' His lip quivered. 'Yer mother cannot go on without her, 'tis killin' her.'

'Mummy has not said anythin' to me.'

'No, and she won't. She's too proud. But I can tell. And don't ye go mentionin' it to her. I know her better than anyone and I can tell ye, 'tis so!'

Tom looked away, embarrassed by the emotion in Ned's voice. He started to wheel his bicycle away then stopped and turned back. 'Ye know Dada, I get the feelin' that Cat's the only one ye worry about in this family.'

Ned looked at him, surprised by the remark, then took out his handkerchief and blew his nose.

'What gives ye that idea?'

'Ye constantly bleat on about missin' all that Cat did for ye, when I do my very best after work to do all that she did, but ye never seem to notice all that I do.'

''Tis not so. And ye know it, Tom.'

'I do *not* know it, and that's the point. I just cannot seem to make up for her goin' can I?'

'Ye do fine son, ye do. I s'pose I just feel we let her down by not tryin' harder to catch those swines. 'Tis me that cannot make it up, not ye.'

Ned turned away and busied himself digging out the gatepost as bitter tears slid down his face in the cold December wind.

12
Plumstead
Christmas 1914

Alone in her bedroom, Cat sat staring out of the window well into the evening. Rain hammered relentlessly down as the wind roared along the road and across the rooftops. She watched the trees thrashing about helplessly, their black arms appearing to reach out for mercy from the burgeoning storm.

She was thinking about home and smiled to herself, remembering how on nights such as this as children they all sat around the fire thinking up scary stories about the Banshee, trying to terrorise each other!

Suddenly she felt depressed as she remembered the sound of the train door slamming, and her family weeping on the railway platform the day she left Ireland. Cat buried her face in a pillow, hoping Lize would not hear her crying.

It was Christmas Day and she had gone to her bedroom early that evening, feeling she was intruding at the family gathering. Louis and Lize's mother, and Lize's mother-in-law had arrived that morning, and were now gathered in the parlour playing games. Every so often Cat could hear them shrieking with laughter and she felt the pain of being away from home.

Cat had realised her welcome had worn thin with Lize after the first couple of weeks. She felt

Lize would prefer not to have her living there after all except, Cat reminded herself, that she was useful looking after the children and performing domestic duties.

It infuriated Cat how Lize had begun to laugh at her *funny little ways,* as she termed it. They were small things initially; such as Cat ironing the handkerchiefs in triangles rather than squares. But now it was harder to tolerate, as Lize's laughter had turned to open derision and hostility on occasions.

Lize had recently forbidden Cat to light a fire in her bedroom, because she said she could not afford to heat it as well as her own and the children's. It left Cat in no doubt that it was time to go.

So Cat had written to her sister Ellie before Christmas and asked her to join her in England, saying there was work for her and definite accommodation for them both through her job. She thought it would do Ellie good to have a change of scene since hearing her fiancé Jimmy had been killed in France.

Ellie's reply had arrived the day before Christmas Eve and Cat was delighted to read she would be arriving at the beginning of January. Thrilled with the knowledge that the end of living with Lize was in sight, Cat felt she could tolerate just one more week.

It was very cold in the bedroom, so by the light of a candle, she undressed quickly and climbed into bed, the cold air pinching her skin. The bed linen felt icy, and though she had bought herself some socks, Cat shivered violently between the cold cotton sheets. She held her rosary between her fingers and began to say a Hail Mary, but not able to concentrate, her mind drifted to her impending move.

Once I move into my own place, she thought, *I'm gonna have a fire warmin' me backside every night, if it's the last thing I do*.

She sat up and blew the candle out; but as she lay in the darkness her thoughts turned to Louis. It had been some time now since he had written and she wondered whether he had lost interest in her or perhaps found someone else to write to. She was bewildered as initially he had been very enthusiastic about receiving her letters; but he had not answered her last three. Cat saw his letters to Lize arrive, so knew he couldn't be wounded.

A few days ago Cat had asked Lize if Louis mentioned her in his letters and she had seemed surprised by the question.

'Oh no, but then he wouldn't would he? He's probably got himself a nice little French girl,' she had laughed 'you know what men are. Fickle, the lot of them!'

As she lay turning the thoughts over in her mind she could not help feeling depressed. It did seem as though Louis had forgotten her. Now she only had to pluck up the courage to tell Lize the next day that she was going and she would be able to put it all behind her.

Cat decided to write to Louis once more when she had moved, and if he didn't reply she told herself their relationship would have finished before it had even begun.

13
Plumstead
January 1915

Ellie was due to arrive the following day and Cat was moving out. The only problem was she hadn't yet told Lize! Not that it would come as that much of a surprise, she decided, because Lize had made her feel very uncomfortable for some time.

Cat was thrilled her application for a house through her job had been approved; but now it was imperative that she break the news to Lize.

She put Lize's breakfast tray on the kitchen table and arranged fingers of bread on a plate beside the eggcup. When the egg was boiled she made the tea and took it up to Lize who was having a lie in. She tapped on the bedroom door.

'Come in.' Lize called and Cat bustled in with her tray.

'Mornin' Lize I've done yer egg and will bring up some toast right away. Now is there anythin' else ye need?'

'No, thank you. This looks fine,' she said cracking open the egg. 'Has the post come yet?'

'Yes, and there's a letter for me from Louis.' Cat beamed at her and patted her apron pocket. 'Oh and one for ye too,' she added handing an envelope to Lize. Then she disappeared as fast as she could downstairs grinning to herself.

She was going to take possession of her new house today and knew she had to tell Lize today.

She resolved to do this when she took her up another cup of tea.

While the kettle was re-boiling she stood nervously in the kitchen trying to pluck up the courage to go upstairs again. She willed it not to boil too quickly as she wanted more time to plan her speech to Lize but within seconds the kettle was puffing hot steam from the spout, so she spooned more tea into the pot and topped it up with water. Before taking it upstairs she sat down at the table to read the letter.

She was surprised to find he was disappointed she had not replied to his last few letters and this puzzled her. She folded up the letter and put it in her pocket, poured Lize's second cup of tea and took it up to her. She knocked on the bedroom door.

'Come in,' Lize called, 'are the children up yet?'

'Yes, Reggie's already gone out with that boy Rodney, and Iris has gone to see yer mother.'

Lize looked relieved and settled back to drink her second cup of tea whilst reading a book.

'Lize,' Cat began, 'there's somethin' I'd like to tell ye.'

Lize looked up surprised. She waited for Cat to continue.

'Lize, I'll be movin' out now to be livin' with me sister, Ellie. Her fiancée was killed in France, so she's comin' over to join me, an' I've been offered accommodation through work. There's a development of hutments, and I'm to get one.'

There, she thought, I've said it. She waited for Lize's reaction. For a few moments there was silence until Lize put down her book and turned her face to look at Cat.

'Well that's fine actually, Cat. I had already decided to change my shift to daytime. Night duties just don't work for me. I can't sleep in daylight and I'm just worn out not getting my rest.' She sipped her tea and began to hum.

'So that's alright wit' ye then?' Cat asked, hoping for some pleading on Lize's behalf to show she cared and had appreciated having her help the past few months.

Lize smiled. 'Yes, Cat. It *is*.' She picked up a book again and began to read.

Deflated that Lize had not shown an iota of concern at her departure, Cat turned and went downstairs.

14
Paddington Station
January 1915

Waiting on the platform at Paddington Station, Cat could barely contain her excitement. As the swarm of people streamed off the boat train from Fishguard, she searched their faces for her sister's. Then she saw Ellie, with her unmistakable halo of unruly auburn hair standing on the platform looking around her. She called to her but her voice was drowned by the general babble of people; so she elbowed her way through the crowds until she was standing behind her.

She tapped Ellie on the shoulder, expecting to see the familiar dancing green eyes and sprinkling of freckles on her milk-white skin, but when Ellie turned, Cat gasped at the alteration in her face. Her skin looked grey and she had lost a lot of weight. She seemed to have shrunk, leaving her skin hanging emptily on her bony frame.

Ellie threw her arms around Cat's neck and sobbed.

'There, there, mo chuisle,' Cat said, stroking her hair. 'everythin' will be fine now. Ye'll see.' She dried Ellie's eyes with her handkerchief. 'God has a funny way of workin'. Jimmy was a good man and God's taken him. God rest his soul.'

'Amen,' Ellie whispered.

'I know he'll be sittin' up there in Heaven now on the right hand of God,' Cat said, then lifted Ellie's bag, but immediately dropped it. 'God in Heaven Ellie, what have ye altogether in here, house-bricks?'

'I've brought all I have Cat. I'm not goin' back. Not ever. I'm goin' to work, and do anythin' the Woolwich Arsenal asks of me, until those rotten Germans are sent packin'.'

'C'mon now, let's get goin',' she said hugging Ellie to her, 'at least we have each other and we've both got work. We can do our bit for the war effort together now. Oh by the Blessed Virgin Mary Ellie, ye don't know how grand it is to see ye!'

* * *

When they reached the development of hutments in Eltham, Cat stopped outside number 74 Crookston Road. She took a key from her pocket and dangled it in the air.

'This is the one,' she said going through the gateway, then opened the front door and stood aside to allow Ellie in first.

Ellie stepped into the small hallway and turned to Cat, 'Which way now?'

'Turn right'

Ellie walked into the room and gasped, 'Is *all* this *ours*?'

'Sure! *All* of it. And there's more. We've three bedrooms and a scullery and out back, our own flushin' toilet. Isn't it wonderful? Cat babbled on excitedly. 'And to think there's just the two of us here. A bedroom each and our own parlour. C'mon in here and look,' she said, rushing into a bedroom. 'Grand isn't it?'

'Yes 'tis indeed,' Ellie smiled, ''Tis nothin' short of a miracle, Cat.' She stood for a little while taking it all in. 'Now, let's set about unpacking, I've brought some things with me to make it feel like home.'

Ellie fetched her bag from the hallway, lifted it onto one of the beds and rummaged about between the clothes; then after carefully placing a statue of Our Lady on the mantelpiece, she pulled out something wrapped in muslin and handed it to Cat.

'Mummy made it specially for ye and it comes with her love.'

Cat unwrapped the bread, closed her eyes and breathed in deeply. It smelled of home and she saw in her mind's eye Maeve kneading dough, her strong arms up to the elbows in flour. Suddenly her eyes filled with tears and Ellie, seeing she was upset, put her arm around Cat's shoulders.

'C'mon now, don't let's get downhearted. We're together and 'tis all that matters now isn't it?' Ellie looked down then at the bed and changed the subject. 'One thing, Cat where did ye get the beds from?'

'Ah. Well, Lize had some spare furniture she didn't need and got someone to bring it over on a cart early today.'

'That was kind.'

'Yes. I had thought she'd be annoyed I was leavin' 'cos I only told her yesterday, but she didn't seem to care. Then she offered me some furniture she was glad to be rid of. She surely is a queer one.'

'Ye're confident that she wasn't just glad to be rid of ye? Ellie laughed. 'When I told old Mrs. Connell I was leavin' The Grange, all she gave me was the benefit of her tongue.'

Cat grinned. 'Ye were obviously goin' to be missed, whereas I clearly was not! C'mon now let's get the place sorted out.'

***

As darkness fell, Cat lit a fire and they pulled up a couple of boxes in front of it, where they sat chattering over endless cups of tea roasting the fronts of their legs, their skirts pulled up above the ankle.

'D'ya have any candles to light us to bed, Cat?'

'Oh, I can do better than that – I've bought an oil lamp. There's gas laid on, but I'm too scared to light it, so we'll make do with the oil lamp and cook on the range. 'Tis safer that way otherwise we may blow ourselves sky high.'

At last having decided they really must get some sleep, the girls undressed and climbed into bed. But they continued calling out to one another until finally they decided it was stupid sleeping in separate rooms. They tugged Ellie's bed into Cat's room and gossiped until the watery winter sunlight filtered in between the slit of the bedroom curtains at dawn.

15
Fleurbaix, France
January 1915

Louis screwed up his eyes, scouring the horizon. For hours there had been no movement from the other side; sniper fire had ceased and in its place an eerie silence hung in the space between his battalion and the enemy.

Knee-deep in a muddy trench, he eased his weight from one leg to another as he stiffened in the cold. He tried not to move too much as it encouraged little gushes of freezing water to trickle between the stitching of his boots, soaking his socks.

Soldiers to his left and right puffed hot vapour into the freezing air, giving the only visible signs of their presence above the trench line. It was quiet. Too quiet, he thought, and wondered what the enemy were doing. Somehow it was better to be on the move dodging bullets and running for your life, rather than the unnerving feeling of standing there in silence waiting to kill, or be killed. He found that too often his mind began to wander in moments like this.

He thought about a letter he had received from Lize. It gave him no pleasure to learn from his sister that he was now a house owner, not when it had been at the expense of young Private White's life. Lize's letter explained how Mrs. White had died, and had left Louis the house because of his kindness to her son. Apparently she had nobody else in the world, and having lost her only son had also lost the will to live. She had written her Will, Lize explained, and then had simply slipped away.

The only feeling Louis had about the inheritance was bewilderment. It did not seem real and he could not summon up any enthusiasm. Standing there amid filth and body parts with rats running over him when he tried to sleep - that was his reality.

Lize's letter had depressed him as she had included the fact that she had fallen out with their mother. He wished she had not written and burdened him with the news; it sounded so petty. Family disputes, lovers' quarrels, world wars, what was the difference he wondered?

He decided it all amounted to the same thing; the inability of people to listen to one another and work out their differences. It seemed to him people just ran headlong into conflict and he was sick of it all.

Then another thought crossed his mind. Now that Lize was in what was now 'his house', it may not be so easy to ask her to leave if he wished to marry. The thought had bothered him when he first read her letter but other things soon took priority and he knew he could not afford to think about anything - except staying alive for the time being.

Fighting a war was enough for him to contend with and it was made worse because his heart just wasn't in it. This was not a fair fight – they were all just cannon fodder.

As scores of men died, more arrived to take their place. It went on relentlessly. An all-too-familiar wave of depression swept over him; a feeling he knew they all felt increasingly of late.

Highlights of his life were letters or little gifts from home and he turned his mind to the letter he had received before Christmas from Cat. He pulled the letter from his pocket. It was now quite wrinkled from the many times he had read it.

The opening of her letter, My Dear Louis, had moved him. He had never received a letter before beginning My Dear. She described her days and how she looked after the children for Lize, who was working in a hospital. He thought she sounded fond of Iris and Reggie. That was nice. He thought they were nice children too.

In his mind he played games with the children and planned how he would take them to the seaside when he returned, have picnics in the park, play cricket on the common and - suddenly his mind switched back to Cat.

He recalled her walking towards him in the field that day in Fethard last summer, and felt once more the reaction of his heart quickening as it had when she stood before him laughing. He remembered the top button of her blouse had been undone, and he checked his thoughts, not wishing to sully his memory of her with lewd imaginings.

He supposed he 'had a girl' now, and it felt good. He said to himself, 'My Dear Louis,' and decided he liked the sound of it.

Later, he would write back to her. He folded the letter and slid it back in his tunic pocket and gave it a little pat for reassurance.

His thoughts were suddenly interrupted by the crack of gunfire, and immediately his horse, tethered a short way off, reared up in fright pulling wildly on the bridle. He turned to look and saw blood streaming down the horse's flank so he quickly crawled out of the trench, and crouching low, worked his way across the clearing. He tried to undo the rope tethering the animal while fighting to keep hold of the bridle but the horse repeatedly reared up onto its hind legs, kicking out in fear.

Then another round of gunfire followed as a mortar shell exploded illuminating the scene. In the instant flash of detonation, black figures silhouetted the skyline and they were cut down by gunfire.

Louis continued frantically trying to untie his horse as another shell exploded and the terrified, animal reared up, its hooves thrashing wildly. As it rose time and again into the air Louis fought to keep a grip on the reins but the ground was slimy and the animal losing its foothold, slid horizontally and pounded down on top of him.

Assailed by unimaginable pain in his leg, he only momentarily felt the impact of the horse's weight before sinking into unconsciousness.

He was unaware of being pulled away from the horse; or the medic ripping his trousers away from his smashed limb. His leg was tied to a wooden plank wrenched quickly from the trench wall, and he was taken away from the war.

16
Royal Herbert Military Hospital
Woolwich
January 1915

The sound of Cat's heels resonated on the ward's polished floorboards until she stopped at Louis' bed where he lay asleep.

She stood in awe looking at him, noticing something beneath the covers to keep the blankets away from his injured leg and a kidney bowl under his chin containing a little vomit.

She watched him for a while unwilling to disturb him, but her thoughts and emotions were in turmoil.

Until then her memory of him had been of a healthy young man with a brilliant smile and strong weather-beaten complexion, but this person looked shrunken beyond belief and his skin looked kind of green. A feeling of immense pity rose inside her and tears pricked her eyes.

The man in the next bed said, 'He was in the operating theatre four hours so he won't wake up today, Missis.'

Collecting herself, she turned to him. 'No. I don't suppose so. I just brought him in some apples, but I'll leave them on the locker. Perhaps you'll tell him I came.'

'You his missis?'

'No.'

'Sweetheart then?'

To avoid answering the man Cat leaned over and gently kissed Louis on the forehead. She was surprised to see him stirring, and his eyelids fluttered open briefly; but to her disappointment they closed again.

'Louis,' she whispered, ''tis me, Cat.' She took his hand in hers and stroked the back of it until almost imperceptibly, she felt a slight pressure from his fingers.

Alarmed that she could have done such a bold thing as to kiss him and take his hand in hers, she released his fingers quickly. His breathing slowed, and satisfied he had drifted off to sleep again, she quietly tip-toed away.

Outside the ward she saw through an open door a nurse sitting writing. Cat tapped lightly on the door to attract her attention and the nurse looked up.

'Come in,' she said, closing a book.

'Sorry to bother ye, but I wondered if ye could tell me how Captain Ross's operation went?'

'Are you his wife?

'No.'

'Oh. Well we don't normally give out information to anyone other than next of kin, but these are peculiar times.' She waved at a chair. 'Sit down' she said, and went to close the door. Cat sat down and waited.

'His leg was in a bit of a mess. The bones were badly fractured, some parts shattered beyond repair. We've had to put plates in to hold the bones together.'

Cat winced at the thought of it.

'Oh don't worry he'll be as good as new, well almost, after a while. He's lost a little length in the leg and will probably have a bit of a limp, but otherwise he'll be alright.'

Unexpectedly, Cat's eyes brimmed with tears and feeling very foolish, she opened her handbag, searching for a handkerchief.

The nurse leaned forward and patted her hand. 'Come on now don't get upset, he's not going to die. He really is one of the lucky ones. You should see some of the injuries we get in here. It's a wonder they make it home at all. The field hospital did a good job on his leg, but not good enough; that's why the plates had to be put in. At least he still has two legs.'

'Yes, of course. I'm sorry. Ye must think me an awful fool.' Cat stood up, apologised for keeping the nurse from her work, and left.

She hurried along the corridors eager to escape the atmosphere inside the hospital. Once outside she could not control her tears at the thought of Louis being injured in some foreign land, travelling home in pain, being operated on and finally ending up in hospital with a shattered leg held together with iron plates. She thought he looked awful, not the Louis she remembered at all, yet something was stirring inside her and she could not understand her feelings. She wanted to turn and run back to the hospital, fling herself on the bed and cry into his chest, Louis, ye could've been killed. But all she could do was wipe away the flow of tears as she walked toward the tram stop.

***

At home that evening with Ellie, Cat was subdued. Her thoughts persistently turned to Louis. In her mind she thought about their time in Fethard, and the night he had played the intermezzo on Breda's violin. He had looked so tall and strong, but now he lay like a broken doll in hospital with a leg that would always be held together with ironmongery. The thought appalled her.

She felt she could not share her thoughts about him with Ellie, because Ellie would love to have her fiancé Jimmy Connolly beside her, legs or no legs, but that would never happen now. She stood up and lit a couple of candles, yawned and told Ellie she was going to bed.

'Don't forget yer prayers then,' Ellie reminded her.

'I never do.'

'Well, don't forget yer extra special prayers tonight.'

Puzzled, Cat asked her what she meant and Ellie smiled mischievously. 'Ye love him don't ye?'

'No!'

'Sure ye do. Ye moon about whenever his name is mentioned and ye haven't said a word about yer visit to the hospital.' She rose and went across to Cat and hugged her. 'He's a nice fella, Cat. I like him. I'm sorry to hear of his misfortunes and with God's help, he'll be up and about soon, ye'll see.'

'Praise God, he will,' Cat murmured.

* * *

The next day Cat and Ellie went to the seven o'clock mass, then after lunch they caught a tram to the hospital. When they arrived, Lize was already there waiting for visiting time to begin.

'Oh hello, Lize.' Cat smiled. 'I didn't know ye'd be here. Where are the children?'

'My mother-in-law is looking after them for an hour, so I won't be able to stay very long.' Lize looked directly at Ellie. 'You will wait out here with your sister while I go in, won't you? It should really be relatives only, you know.'

'Sure. Ye go right ahead now; we'll just wait out here,' Ellie said, but Cat noticed there was an ironic edge to her voice.

When the Ward Sister appeared and announced that visiting time had commenced, Lize breezed through the doors, which swung shut behind her. Ellie and Cat stared at each other.

'Well! Would ye believe that one?' Ellie said. 'What a nerve! Lize clearly wants to be the only star in his heaven.' She looked at Cat. 'What d'ya want to do? Will we stay, or go?'

'For two pins I'd go, Ellie. But I'd really like to see Louis.'

'Right then, we'll stay. But don't ye let that one push ye around Cat, d'ya hear me? The nerve of her!'

'Oh well don't worry too much Ellie. After all she is his sister.'

'Sure she is. But *she's* not the Virgin Mary and *he* isn't the baby Jesus. He's a grown man and ye've every right to visit him too - she doesn't own him.' Cat saw the colour rising in Ellie's cheeks and knew she was in battle mode!

After half an hour, Lize's image appeared again inside the circular window of the ward doors. Cat could see her waving goodbye. As she came through the doors, she turned once more and waved at Louis and blew him a kiss, then approached Cat and Ellie.

'You can go in now,' she said pulling on her gloves, 'but don't stay too long, he's very tired. Got to rush now. 'Bye.' She turned away and marched off down the corridor and out of sight.

'She's jealous, that one.'

'Jealous?'

'Sure, 'tis what's up with her. Ye'll see if I'm not right.' She propelled Cat through the door then let it swing shut in front of her, but Cat pushed it open again.

'Aren't ye comin' with me Ellie?'

'Ah g'w'on. Grab yer man, Cat, and be quick about it before I do.' She laughed, 'I'll look in and say hello later on, now off with ye.' She waved her fingers at Cat to shoo her away.

Cat turned and looked along the ward. She could see Louis sitting up in the bed. He gazed at her as she walked towards him.

'Hello, Louis.'

'Hello Cat.'

He was wearing pyjamas. Cat felt a little embarrassed seeing him in his nightclothes and a slow blush spread across her face. 'How're ye feelin' today?'

'A bit weak and shaky. but not too bad.'

There was an awkward silence and Cat fiddled with her gloves.

'I came to see ye yesterday, but ye were sleepin.''

'Yes I know.'

'Oh.' She couldn't think of what to say. She looked away, then back at him, and saw that he was grinning.

'What're ye smilin' about?' she asked beginning to relax a little.

'Nothing really. Look, could you adjust my pillow, it's slipped down a bit.'

'Sure I will,' she said and approached the head of the bed. 'Can ye lean forward a little?'

She plumped up his pillows, feeling the nearness of his cheek to hers and when she told him to lie back, he was smiling. She stepped away from the bed and looked at him.

'What are ye smilin' at again, Louis?'

'Come here and I'll tell you,' he whispered, so she stepped nearer.

'Closer,' he said, 'I can't tell you at that distance.'

She shifted toward him, until she felt his hand close over hers. 'Thanks for the kiss,' he said, 'I just couldn't stay awake long enough to ask for a repeat.'

'*Louis,*' she hissed, 'everyone's listenin'!'

But they were both smiling.

17
Plumstead
February 1915

Lize was in making a fuss over Louis. Pillows under his leg; endless cups of tea; always there when needed. She could not have been happier.

She had enjoyed every minute of the week since bringing him home from hospital, trotting back and forth, from the kitchen to the front room where a temporary bed had been made up for Louis.

Lize carried his breakfast tray to him; morning paper; freshly baked cakes; lunches, afternoon teas and anything else that he desired. She had even temporarily given up her job to look after him. She thought he looked underfed and definitely needed some decent food inside him; and Lize knew *she* was the one to do it!

But something had bothered Lize about Louis since his return, though she just couldn't put her finger on it. She could wait on him hand and foot, give him everything he asked for, but still there was a strangeness about him – almost as though he had committed a terrible crime, she thought, and could not shake off the guilt or discuss it with her.

Often she found him staring blankly at the floor, hardly aware of her presence and she would slip unseen from the room, leaving him to brood about whatever it was that was tormenting him.

She had asked if there was anything the matter, but he didn't want to talk about it. She realized she would have to wait until he was ready to talk and only hoped it wasn't anything to her detriment!

Quite suddenly one day, Louis said to Lize.

'We haven't had much time to talk about your moving out of Mum's house, Lize.'

She immediately stopped what she was doing and feeling alarmed turned to face him.

'What about it, Louis. Is there something you are not saying? Did I do something wrong?'

'No. Of course not, Lize. You haven't done anything wrong. It's just that we haven't discussed how it all came about – that's all.'

She was rooted to the spot waiting for him to continue; but then she became aware that he wasn't really listening, and was staring out of the window.

'Louis?' she asked hesitantly, 'are you planning to ask us to leave when you come back?'

'No,. I was not meaning *that*, Lize, I just wondered how it all happened so suddenly. And as for the other matter of my wanting a house for myself if, say, I were to marry, well, I have not given it much serious thought really; and anyway–'

She cut him off. 'Only without Charlie now, I find it difficult to manage,' she said, 'let alone try to find rent as well now, especially as I've had to give my job up.'

He looked at her and she could tell he was now paying attention.

'Look Lize, there's no question of you finding either rent, or other accommodation. This place was a gift to me, and I now gift it to you and the children.

I promised Charlie that if anything ever happened to him, I'd look after you.' He took a deep breath, 'If it makes you feel better I'll have the house put in your name, to show I mean it.'

She beamed at him. 'Oh Louis, would you *really*? What can I say?'

'Don't say anything. But a nice cup of tea and a slice of your cake would be nice.'

She giggled and hurried to the kitchen to make the tea, singing a song as she cut Louis an extra large slice of cake.

18
Plumstead
June 1915

The war in Europe ground on. Every newspaper Louis read, his sense of relief increased, knowing that he was away from it all. He struggled with the paradox of yearning to walk unaided once more, but thankful that it had kept him from the war.

As the months advanced, he made his first uncertain steps aided by crutches; and by the time summer arrived, it was warm enough for him to sit outside in the front garden where he could chat to passers-by.

'Can you put the chair just there, where I can see everyone coming up the road?' he would ask Lize, 'so I can talk to anyone who stops.' But it was always Cat walking sprightly along the road he really sat waiting for.

Cat often travelled by tram to Plumstead to see Louis and her visits were something he looked forward to with growing eagerness.

Lize noticed that he became rather excited whenever Cat visited and that he was irritable towards her and the children if he did not see her for a few days. She complained to him about his mood, maintaining he only seemed to smile and be happy when he saw Cat. Her remarks surprised him and he realised he would have to be more careful about her feelings in future. He knew his sister was capable of saying something to Cat and offending her. The last thing he wanted was to have Lize saying anything that would stop Cat's visits.

As the season ripened into early summer, Louis struggled with whether to tell Cat how he felt about her. He practised what to say when he had the chance, but on several occasions when he had plucked up the courage, had found it impossible because Lize and the children were around.

Early in June at Louis' regular hospital appointment he was told he could dispense with crutches and use walking sticks, so he left the hospital feeling ecstatic and could not wait to see Cat and share his good news.

When Cat arrived the following Sunday Lize was out with the children visiting her mother-in-law. Louis answered the door with a big grin on his face and held his hands out wide to show her he could stand without crutches.

Cat was delighted. 'Thanks be to God, now I can stop worrying about the ironmongery inside ye goin' gangrenous and ye getting' yer leg chopped off.' She went inside the house and began taking her jacket off. 'Well aren't ye the king of the castle today, then?'

'Here, let me help you,' he said attempting to lean against the banisters for support, but he misjudged the distance and toppled. Cat grabbed him to save his fall.

'Steady on now, Louis,' she laughed.

The closeness of her body aroused him. He folded his arms round her and kissed her tenderly on the cheek. When she didn't move away, he kissed her lips. She gasped, and Louis began kissing her throat.

'Jesus, Mary and Joseph, Louis,' she said pushing him away, 'No. No. I can't. I can't.' She covered her face with her hands and in the uncomfortable silence that followed, turned away from him.

Placing his trembling hands on her shoulders he turned her round to face him.

'Oh God, I'm sorry. That should not have happened. Please believe me, Cat. It's just that I...'

He dropped his hands to his sides, unable to continue, but stood looking at her, thinking he had probably ruined their relationship now.

Cat looked up and surprised him by gently stroking his cheek. 'Louis, 'tis me who should be sorry. Sorry that I can't give meself to ye. But I just cannot.'

He fondled her hair, pushing stray curls away from her face. 'I had no right to expect it, Cat. I know you are not that sort of girl.'

'Louis, I wish I were. I wish I could change the way I am, but I just can't.'

'No.' he said stroking her hair, 'you are so right. And I would not wish you to be any different. He leaned forward and kissed the top of her head, then straightened up and cleared his throat.

Perhaps now was the time to tell her what he had practised. 'Cat, I have no idea when this war will end, but one day when it is all over, if I manage not to get myself killed, I hope to begin a new life away from the army.' He looked down at her clear grey eyes and thought how beautiful she was. He felt like a beast for spoiling things and losing control. 'But until that happens, I...' he faltered, 'I just want you to know that I - admire you, and...'

He stopped and Cat waited for him to go on. But he had lost the courage to continue, so as though he had suddenly remembered something else, he changed the subject. 'Lize has made some fruit cake, would you like some with a nice cup of tea?'

Puzzled, she nodded, and without saying another word he turned and hobbled into the kitchen. She followed him and watched as he began fumbling with the lid of the tea caddy. His face reddened with frustration as he tried to stand steadily while wrestling with the lid.

'Would ye like me to do that?' Cat asked and he passed her the tin.

He watched her deftly spoon the tea from caddy to teapot, feeling he had acted like a fool and had been unable to tell her that he loved her.

* * *

Lize battled against a gale-force wind, one hand pressed against her hat; the other clutching her shopping bag. Once home, she forced the front door closed relieved to be inside again.

'Phew, it's wild out there, Louis, 'she said entering the kitchen. Reggie was reading a comic and Iris sat patiently dressing her doll. Louis was leaning against the sink reading a letter. He wore a worried frown on his face.

'Not bad news is it?'

'I've been re-called.'

'What about your leg? You've only just come off crutches?'

'There's no arguing, Lize,' he said holding the letter out to her, 'read it.'

She turned to Iris and Reggie, 'Children, go into the parlour and play. Uncle Louis and I want to talk.'

The children left the kitchen silently as Lize began reading the letter. Angrily she looked up at him after reading. 'How can they say your injuries were not serious enough to discharge you from your duties?' She handed him back the paper, 'and it says you have to return immediately!'

'I know.'

Lize slumped into a chair.

'I don't understand it. You've barely been able to put any weight on that leg until now.'

'It doesn't matter to them, Lize. They're short of manpower and everyone is being re-called unless unfit to continue permanent service. I expect the hospital let them know I was more-or-less fit for duty.

'Fit to stand in the front line and get killed you mean.' She was clearly upset. 'When will you leave?'

'In two days.'

'*Two days*? But that's ridiculous!'

He could not answer her, and silently stared out of the window watching the clouds race across the sky.

19
Near Ypres
July 1915

When Louis rejoined his unit, he realised more than ever that he definitely did not want to remain a soldier. He was saddened to discover that only a few of the original men were left. Most of them had been killed in battle, but some, he was shocked to learn, had been shot for either desertion or disobeying orders.

Louis could tell that, though the replacement soldiers were now better trained for the job, they were less confident and many of them were dispirited.

In the dead of night, he sometimes heard the younger men cry and wished he could just let them go home.

Louis tried to boost their morale as he had done previously, but felt unable to carry it off now. How could he rally the men into thinking in terms of victory for England when inwardly it really felt futile to him? The job they were there for he thought, was simply too much for most of them and he hated what was expected of them all. He felt he was caught up in an endurance test that went beyond human capabilities.

Part of his own problem he realised was that he enjoyed the quiet life back in England and now he had no stomach for war.

Initially his unit had pushed through France relieving towns and villages from occupation on the way, with fighting becoming more intense as they drew near the German front line. As they had travelled along the route, he had witnessed slaughter everywhere and in the small villages it was commonplace to see women with their throats cut or bayoneted through the chest by the Bosch.

Now reflecting on it all brought an overwhelming sense of futility and depression which he was unable to share with anyone.

One evening they camped near a farmhouse close to a wood on the outskirts of Poperinge. All was quiet and Louis hoped they could have a few hours of peace. But just as they were bedding down for the night, they came under attack. Shells burst all around them and as well as bullets and mud flying it was raining torrents. Gas shells fell adding to the chaos.

Men, blinded by either shrapnel or effects of gas, staggered around, getting in the way of their own men firing at the enemy. Everywhere he looked there were bodies. Then, just as suddenly as it began, the gunfire and shelling ceased and all that could be heard was injured soldiers groaning.

Louis decided to push forward and take the farmhouse on the other side of the field where they were camped. He suspected the enemy were hiding there.

It was almost dark when he signalled to the men to spread out and begin moving towards the farmhouse. As they crossed the field, Louis noticed a barn ahead, to the left of the farmhouse, hidden in a copse. The men divided, some to the east and others to the west.

Within twenty feet of the barn Louis motioned for everyone to lay flat on the ground and fire at the barn. When they stopped firing, some German soldiers ran out with their hands up.

'Bitte, bitte,' they pleaded.

Poor devils, Louis thought, and turned to speak to his sergeant.

'Escort these prisoners away–' But he was unable to finish the command because gunfire from inside the hideout took him by surprise. 'Down, down,' he shouted and his men threw themselves to the ground, but the German prisoners, being in the direct line of fire, were shot by their own men.

The English gunners, some distance behind Louis' men, immediately fired their howitzer at the barn. Shells roared overhead and as Louis lay there, he became conscious of the fact that he was lying in a mire of cow dung which was emulsifying in the rain.

As soon as he felt the Germans held no more threat, Louis urged the men to move forward again.

'Keep going and stay low,' he said turning to Georgie, the youngest of their group, only to see him shot straight through the heart.

The gunfire had come from the direction of a barn on the other side of a stream.

'Carry on,' he ordered the others, 'there is no time to mourn the dead, otherwise you'll be joining them.'

So they pressed on.

On a small bridge crossing a stream between the field and the farmhouse, a sign pointing the way to Poperinge hung like a lifeless scarecrow as the soldiers, crouching low, stole across in silence.

They surrounded the barn from where Louis thought it likely the gunfire came, then without warning, two German soldiers stepped out into the farmyard waving white handkerchiefs.

They lay down their guns and with their hands above their heads surrendered to Louis. These were the men who had shot Georgie and he was face to face with them. His anger flared and his instinct was to shoot them on the spot; but his training as an officer overtook his emotions and he ordered them to be tied up.

Once the prisoners were secured, Louis pulled a packet of cigarettes from his pocket and lit one, staring away into the distance through glazed eyes.

Then he saw the door of the farmhouse open slowly and braced himself to fire again, but relaxed when an elderly man appeared waving a white cloth. The man called out, but Louis did not understand what he was saying.

Puzzled, Louis decided to try French in the hope that they could communicate.

'Parlez vous Franç ais, Monsieur?'

The old man smiled and nodded. 'Monsieur, monsieur, s'il vous plait, entré. Entré. Merci, merci.'

Louis walked up to the doorway and tipped his cap. 'Bonsoir, Monsieur.'

The old gentleman stepped aside and gestured for him to enter.

Inside was an elderly woman, whom Louis supposed was the man's wife, filling glasses of wine.

She pointed at the glasses and some bread and cheese on the table and then gestured to him to eat and drink.

'Pour les hommes, et vous, Monsieur. Et merci beaucoup.' Her voice was little more than a hoarse whisper.

'Merci, Madame. Merci,' Louis replied.

He went to the door and whistled to his men to come in, and they were given wine, bread and cheese.

The farmer and his wife were exuberant at the arrival of the British troops and explained that they had been captive for two weeks. They told how the Germans stole all their produce and shot their animals one by one for fun.

In the candlelight of the room, Louis held up his glass of wine and raised it to the old folk.

'Bon chance, Madame et Monsieur,' he said before swallowing it in one go. He thanked them for their hospitality and then they all left, calling out, au revoir, as they walked across the yard and out into the field.

Back in the camp, long after nightfall, Louis settled down to write up his field diary. The one thing that gave him a sense of reality was recording his thoughts and events on paper. It reminded him of who he was and helped him deal with the bizarre nature of events.

And as always in his mind, when the fighting lulled and the blood ceased to ooze from others' wounds, he clung to the image of Cat walking towards him, smiling, under the July sun.

20
Plumstead
Spring 1917

As daylight faded one Sunday afternoon, Cat and Ellie heard someone knocking on the door.

'Are ye expecting anyone Cat?' Ellie asked moving to the window

'No I'm not. Who is it?'

Ellie strained to see who was standing on the step. 'I can't see properly, but it looks like a woman.'

'Well open the door then and we'll know for sure.' Cat said lowering the newspaper she was reading. She listened as Ellie opened the door and heard a woman ask if Miss Delaney was in.

'Yes. I'm Miss Delaney,' Cat heard Ellie say; followed by the woman telling her she had a letter for her. Cat's curiosity was raised as Ellie appeared back into the parlour.

'What was that all about?'

'I have a letter,' she said tearing open the envelope, then as she pulled the paper from the envelope and read it was for Cat, folded it and handed it to her. 'Sorry, 'tis for ye.'

Instantly, Cat realised it was from Louis and her spirits soared. She read the letter, then flushing, looked at Ellie. 'Listen to this!' She read aloud.

'"March 3rd 1917
My Dearest Cat,
Thank you for your last letter, which as usual, I was so pleased to receive. Thank you also for asking about my leg,

which as I speak, is giving some discomfort, but I have learned to ignore this mostly. I expect it is not doing me much good constantly getting wet, and the cold has been atrocious – the past winter must be the worst in living memory. I am giving this letter to one of my chaps who is being shipped home. Poor fellow has some serious injuries, but as he lives in Eltham, he promises to get this to you, somehow.

Cat, I hesitate to write the next part, but I have wanted to ask you something for some time. Because of the war, I felt I had no right to suggest it but I feel that if I remain silent much longer, I may lose the opportunity.

What I am trying to ask is whether you would do me the honour of becoming my wife. You must know that I have been in love with you since we first met and I cannot imagine any better prospect than to return to England knowing you will be there waiting for me.

I have had a dilemma because I thought I should not ask you to become my wife as each day is filled with uncertainty. Asking you to wait for me seems such a selfish thing to do, especially since there is no guarantee that I will remain unhurt, or even return.

If you decide to say 'yes,' it must only be on the proviso that I come home in one piece. It would be totally selfish of me to expect you to wait for me just to become a nursemaid if I am injured.

If your answer is no – then I will respect this. Whatever you decide, I know that I want you in my life because life would be everything with you, and nothing without you.

I have been thinking seriously about converting to Roman Catholicism, so I would not want you to feel that religion would form a barrier between us. To this end I have been taking instruction from Father Leahy who has become a friend to me out here.

I have not taken this decision lightly Cat and would not want you to form the impression that I am only doing this to win you over. The decision to become a Catholic has been arrived at by me because I had lost my way in life. I have only found the path back to hope again through Father Leahy's serenity, sagacity, patience and friendship

If you will accept my proposal I could apply for a leave pass to enable us to marry this summer. Please take your time to consider your reply, which I hope will be yes, so that I may feel the happiest man alive - or not, as the case may be.

Yours

Louis.'"

Ellie sprang from her chair. 'Jesus, Mary and Holy Saint Joseph Cat, the man's asked ye to marry him! Sure this calls for a celebration…I'll get us a bottle,' and Cat watched as giggling like a schoolgirl, Ellie hurried to the kitchen to get a bottle of homemade wine. When she reappeared with the bottle and two cups she laid them on the table.

'C'mon let's crack it open and celebrate.'

Cat looked at her. 'Sure I haven't said, *yes to him*.'

Ellie spun round. 'What?'

'I haven't decided to say *yes*.'

'Ye've got to be joking! What d'ya mean ye haven't said yes?'

'Exactly that.'

'I don't believe I'm hearin' correctly. First ye throw over Paddy, now ye're not saying yes to Louis. Who're ye waitin' for, the King of England?'

Furious with Cat, she slumped down on the chair in front of the fire holding her head in her hands. 'Ye're twenty six years old and not gettin' any younger ye know.'

Cat could see Ellie was annoyed with her and laughed.

'What's so funny?'

'Ye are!' Cat grinned

'Oh *really*? Well I can tell ye, Cat Delaney that I am annoyed with ye. How could ye turn Louis down? He's a fine man and ye'll get none better than him. God if he asked me I'd be lickin' his boots in gratitude, I would so.'

'Who said I'm turnin' him down?'

'Well ye did didn't ye?'

'No I did not.'

'Ye did so.'

'I did not.'

'Well if ye're not turnin' him down, why did ye say ye have not said yes to him?

'Ah! I'm only griggin[13]' ye Ellie. I meant I hadn't said *yes*, because I have not done so, *yet*! But I fully intend to tomorrow, in the form of a letter of acceptance! Now, will that do ye?'

Ellie rushed over to Cat, threw her arms around her and kissed her cheek.

'Ah ye devil. Ye had me goin' there, ye did for sure. Wait now while I uncork the hooch.'

She uncorked the wine and poured two full cups out. They snatched up the cups and took enormous gulps of the wine, wiped their lips with the backs of their hands and smiled at each other.

'I'm glad ye're here with me Ellie.'

'And so am I,' she said squeezing her sister's hand. 'Tis just a pity we're not home with the family, to celebrate like.'

'Yes. Ye can imagine it. They would be puttin' on a fine craic and all of us dancing and performing. Life is funny.'

---

[13] Grigging - teasing

'How d'ya mean?'

'Well all that trouble back home. All because I wouldn't marry Paddy. I wonder what would have happened if I had never met Louis. Sure I'd probably still be home, married and all.'

'Yes, probably.'

'I would never have been happy with him, Ellie.'

'No, I know that. I felt ye did the right thing comin' over here. He can't get at ye now.'

'I miss Mummy and Dada though Ellie. Sometimes I feel I would give anythin', just to be walkin' down the boreen again.'

'Give it time. All things change and go full circle, ye'll see.'

'And what about ye? D'ya think ye've changed?'

'Probably. I've stopped bein' so angry about Jimmy now. I have become kinda resigned to it. I expect God has some other plan in mind for me. Maybe I'll become a nun or something.'

'God above, I hope not Ellie.'

'Why, what have ye against nuns?' Ellie took a sip of wine.

'Nothin' *exactly*. But most of them are like dried up old prunes. Ye're meant to become someone's wife and mother to loads of children. Don't think of wastin' yer life shut up in some old convent.'

'Ah, sure I've no intention of any such thing. C'mon, now drink up, I'm leavin' ye behind.'

Ellie poured more wine into the cups and they sat drinking by the firelight as darkness closed in and she got up to light a candle.

Then as though suddenly remembering something Ellie turned to Cat.

'I forgot to tell ye. Guess who I saw at work today?'

'No. Who?'

'Michael.'

'Michael?'

'Ye know, Michael Nagle.'

'Not Michael Nagle from home?'

'Yes.'

'Well what in the world is he doin' here?'

'He came over to enlist, but got turned down on medical grounds. He has awful eyesight.'

'Well what a surprise! Mind, he was often askin' after ye Ellie when ye were away workin' at The Grange, ye know. I always thought he would ask ye to walk out with him.'

'He did. But Jimmy beat him to it. Anyhow, he's savin' up so he can emigrate to America.'

'Is that so?'

'Yes.'

They sat for some time staring into the fire each caught up in private thoughts, until suddenly Ellie broke the silence.

'Cat, how would ye feel if I asked Michael to come to dinner tomorrow evening, so we could celebrate yer news with someone from home?'

'Yes! 'Tis a grand idea. Why don't we?'

They remained drinking wine gazing into the fire, saying silly things and becoming incoherent until only embers glowed in the grate and it was time for bed.

Slowly and unsteadily they hung onto each other as they made their way to the bedroom. Trying to enter the doorway together proved impossible and simultaneously they bumped into the doorpost. Then Ellie stubbed her toe on something and finally Cat fell onto the bed giggling.

'Get yer clothes off woman,' Ellie slurred. 'D'ya want to fall asleep in that skirt?'

But Cat was past caring and just groaned before falling instantly asleep, fully clothed.

21
Eltham
March 1917

The tram whined along the track to Eltham High Street, and Cat saw her sister on the running board as it approached. Ellie jumped off from the tram and Cat linked arms with her as they began walking quickly towards the High Street.

'I thought ye'd never get here. What kept ye?'

'Sorry, I missed the other tram. Anyway, I'm here now. Let's go for a cup of tea before we shop.'

'Did ye see Michael this morning?'

'I did.'

'Well, did ye ask him to come tonight?'

'I did.'

'And what did he say?'

'He said he was not able to come.'

Cat stopped walking and looked at Ellie.

'And what reason did he give? Did he *give* a good reason?' She felt deflated. She had been looking forward to seeing Michael again.

'I didn't ask him.'

'*Well*! I have to say, I'm disappointed in him. And I was going to buy some glasses today too. Now I won't bother!' Cat quickened her pace.

'Hey, just a minute let me finish,' Ellie said trying to keep pace with Cat. 'At first he said he could not come, but when I told him ye'd become engaged to Louis, he said he would cancel his arrangements.'

Cat stopped walking. 'So, he is comin' then?'

'Yes.'

'Well, why did ye not say so in the first place?'

'I was givin' ye the whole story. That's why.'

'Do ye have to fool around like that?'

'I thought I'd do what ye did to me yesterday, makin' out ye were not goin' to accept Louis' proposal. So there, we're on an equal footin' now.'

Ellie laughed and fell against Cat's arm. 'Ye might have known I would not let ye get away with that one. C'mon now, let's go buy those glasses so we can drink in style.'

* * *

Ellie struggled into the house with the coalscuttle, emptied some of the fuel onto the fire, and then dropped it noisily on the hearth. She looked at her dirty hands and hurried to the scullery to wash them.

Drying her hands on a towel, she returned to the parlour and glanced at the clock. She had about half an hour before Michael was due to arrive so decided she should spend it trying to tame her hair and put on her best dress.

She spread the towel out to dry on the fireguard and called out to her sister who was in the bedroom.

'Cat. Will I put that tablecloth on Mummy sent us from home?'

'Yes, and put out those knives and forks Lize gave me, and the napkins. By the way,' Cat added entering the parlour, 'I forgot to say, that Lize has a sofa she will give us, if we can find a way of collectin' it.' She looked at Ellie's unruly hair. 'C'mon now get yerself ready, he'll be knockin' on that door and we're both lookin' like a pair of wild women from Borneo.'

Ellie felt a rush of annoyance. Lize's *gifts* were usually of a sub-standard nature. Things she could not sell for love or money. She felt Cat was blind to the fact that Lize was only getting rid of things that were useless; not that she was being benevolent at all. She was a mean bitch that one.

'Father forgive me,' she murmured pulling the tablecloth from its brown paper wrappings.

Holding two corners, she threw the cloth upwards a little to allow it to spread out. It billowed as the air caught beneath the material softening the fall, then the white linen cloth landed, as gently as a bird's feather on snow, covering the rough table.

Ellie smoothed it out and ran her fingers across the embossed white embroidery of Irish harps and shamrocks that were beautifully sewn into the weave. She stopped flattening out the cloth and a sob broke from her throat as she realised that their mother must have spent all the money they sent her to buy the cloth.

'Ellie! What in the world are ye doing? C'mon in here and get yerself ready will ye?'

She could hear Cat moving about humming to herself in the bedroom, but her mind had gone home to Fethard, and that led down the painful pathway of remembering Jimmy. Suddenly, she wished Michael was not coming to call.

'*Ellie*!' Cat's voice was sounding agitated, 'Will ye get yerself in here this minute and dress up?'

'I'm about to,' Ellie said appearing in the bedroom doorway.

'There's no, *about to*, in it. He'll be here any minute and I'm not in favour of ye greetin' our first guest in yer underwear.'

'Ah! Stop yer blatherin',' she said strolling into the bedroom. She looked at Cat and was amazed at her appearance. 'Holy Mother of God Cat. What do ye think ye're doing?'

'Puttin' up me hair. Do ye like it?'

'It makes ye look, makes ye look—'

'Look what?'

'Um. Different. Yes, different.'

'Well do I look better or worse?'

'About the same. I just never saw ye without that bush all round yer face, that's all.'

Cat put down the hairpins and sat silently looking at her hands.

'Oh Cat, I'm sorry. I just forgot it happened. I'm really, really sorry.'

Cat shrugged, 'It doesn't matter. I suppose I should forget it too, but sometimes, it just comes flooding back and I can't stop it. It makes my skin crawl. I can still feel the razor goin' over my scalp. The bastards! Father, forgive me. Amen.'

Ellie sat down next to her and picked up the hairpins to finish pinning up Cat's ebony curls.

'There, ye look grand.'

A few minutes elapsed then Ellie asked Cat,

'D'ya ever wish ye could go home?'

Cat turned to face her 'Almost every day. When I wake up in the mornin's I sometimes forget where I am and wonder where my things are. And sometimes, when I'm gettin' ready to go to work, I think I'm goin' out to the field with Dada. It's peculiar. 'Tis like lookin' forward and backwards at the same time and yet not knowin' exactly where I belong, in this life, or that one.' Then after a moment she asked Ellie, 'What about ye?'

'Yes, I think the same too. The novelty of bein' somewhere different has kinda worn off for me. Has it for ye?'

''T'as. It did a long time ago. But it was better when ye came over, Ellie. I feel I can stand it if ye're here with me. Ye're not thinkin' of goin' home are ye?'

'No, of course not. Sure I don't particularly like it here but we have to be practical. The money here is far better and it gives us a chance to send some to Mummy and Dada.'

'God, I miss them Ellie. Sometimes I feel my heart is goin' to cut its way right out through me ribs, the pain it causes thinkin' of them. And I can't see a way I can go back, not now. Especially since Louis has asked me to marry him. I expect I will have to stay here, forever!'

Michael's knock on the door interrupted their conversation and the women jumped up from the bed in panic. Cat told Ellie to stay in the bedroom and get herself ready while she let Michael in.

She rushed to open the door.

'Michael! C'mon in, welcome, 'tis grand to see ye.' She laughed as he pushed a bottle of porter into one of her hands, and a bunch of daffodils in the other.

'They're lovely, Michael. Thanks, now c'mon in and sit by the fire while we finish off cooking. Ellie won't be a minute.'

She pulled a dining chair from the table to the fire. 'Sorry, we don't have any easy chairs, I've been promised a sofa from Louis' sister, but I have to arrange collection and I'm not too sure how I'll do it.'

'Maybe I can help,' Michael said rubbing his hands together before the blazing fire. As he spoke he shifted his weight from one foot to the other.

'Me landlady is goin' back to Wales and has a handcart for sale, along with some other things. She has some dining chairs, but ye already have some I see.'

'Oh no! They're not ours, they belong to Mrs. Pritchard next door, she's loaned them to us for this evening.' Cat explained. 'So how much does yer landlady want for her furniture?'

'Not too much I shouldn't think. They leave on Monday and want to be rid of it. They are goin' to live with relations and don't want the bother of cartin' the stuff back home to Wales.'

Cat poured Michael a glass of porter and one for herself then excused herself before disappearing into the bedroom.

'Guess what?' she whispered to Ellie closing the door behind her. 'Michael's landlady is sellin' up and has some furniture we could buy. Plus, Michael says she has a handcart we could use to get it here.'

Ellie finished buttoning up her dress then tried flattening her unruly hair with a brush. She turned to Cat. 'How do I look?'

'Fine. Just fine. That green really suits ye. Breda did a good job on the dress,' she said brushing a few auburn hairs off Ellie's shoulders. 'Did ye get the story? Michael can get hold of some furniture for us.'

'Well that sounds grand. When?'

'Let's discuss that later,' she whispered. 'I've had an idea.... let's do Mummy's game on Michael shall we?'

Ellie moved towards the door and just as she opened it, turned and grinned at Cat over her shoulder.

Hearing the girls enter the room, Michael stood up and greeted Ellie, offering her a glass of porter he had poured for her. She drank some and put the glass down on the table.

'Will ye sit at the table now Michael?' she asked as she went toward the range.

Michael sauntered over to the table and sat down listening to the girls clanking pots and pans.

Then Ellie placed a plate on the table where Michael sat and returned to the oven where the other two plates were warming. She quickly moved across to the table almost dropping them they were so hot. She blew on her fingertips, then quickly passed one to Cat's place and placed her own in front of her.

The girls exchanged glances then bowed their heads in prayer. Michael followed suit. Cat looked up in time to catch Ellie's eye and wink.

'Pass the salt will ye Ellie?' Cat asked and sprinkled it over her plate.

Michael watched looking puzzled.

'Can I have it back now, I can't eat these potatoes without salt, ye've forgotten to put some in the cookin',' Ellie said lavishly sprinkling salt over her empty plate. She picked up her knife and fork, but then as though remembering something, she looked up at Michael.

'C'mon Michael, dig in.' she ordered.

Michael stared at his plate, puzzled.

The girls continued cutting and forking invisible food into their mouths.

'Mm this is delicious, Ellie. 'Tis the best yet,' Cat said looking straight at Michael.

Michael sat staring, first at Cat, then his gaze turned to Ellie. They must both be crazy he decided.

'Is something wrong with the meal Michael?' Ellie asked.

'No. No. 'Tis perfectly edible, 'tis just that I like to have a bit of mint sauce on me lamb,' he said trying to humour her.

'Oh I'm sorry,' Cat butted in, 'Ellie, get the mint sauce for Michael will ye?'

Ellie obediently jumped up and went to the kitchen, then returned with a little dish. She put the dish, which Michael noticed was empty, down on the table beside his plate.

'There ye are Michael, help yerself,' she said. 'Oh but wait a minute, ye'll need a spoon too.' She jumped up and went back to fetch one and put it down next to the empty dish.

Michael picked up the spoon and scooped some imaginary mint sauce from the dish and pretended to drop it onto his plate.

'There,' he said sounding satisfied, 'that's better now isn't it?' He then set about tucking into his absent meal, wondering what the hell was taking place. He hadn't heard of any madness coming from that family back home, but maybe they had both gone that way since coming to England. He decided to go along with it and leave as soon as possible.

'This is fine meat, Ellie,' Michael said pretending to chew a mouthful.

Ellie looked at him and frowned. 'Didn't yer mother tell ye not to speak with yer mouth full?'

'Indeed she did. I apologise, Michael replied. 'Now I'll finish me meal and won't say another word.' And for several more minutes he sat cutting and forking the non-existent meal into his mouth while Cat and Ellie did the same.

Cat then asked Michael if he had to find new lodgings as his landlady was going back to Wales, but careful not to be chastised again for speaking with his mouth full, he pointed to his lips and kept chewing.

Unable to keep up the charade any longer, Cat burst out laughing, joined by Ellie who doubled up on her chair convulsed with hilarity.

Then gradually Michael began to see the joke they had played on him. He put down his knife and fork.

Cat, by now, was screaming with laughter, rocking back and forth on her chair wiping tears from her eyes as Ellie jumped up to fetch the 'real' food, which was in the oven.

Ellie lay the roasting dish with a joint of lamb on the table and asked Michael to carve. Roast potatoes snuggled round the edges of the lamb, crisp and brown, oozing juice, rubbing shoulders with parsnips laced in honey. The aroma was tantalizing, but Michael decided he was not ready to give in to normality just yet.

'Carve what?' he asked

'The meat of course,' Ellie said handing him a carving knife.

'But there's nothin' there at all.' Michael said staring at the joint, 'and anyway, I'm so full from the first meal, I couldn't eat another thing.'

Ellie grinned, 'so, ye've lost yer appetite then Michael? Well, we'll have to take this meal away then won't we?'

'Not so fast,' he said. His eyes met Ellie's. 'I think I've room for more after all,' he added and looked at her, smiling. ‘And any more tricks like that and I’ll skin ye alive young lady.’

He began carving the meat which fell from the bone tenderly, revealing pinky-brown flesh ready to be garnished well with real mint sauce.

22
Eltham
March 1917

Michael walked into the darkness whistling and Ellie closed the front door, then rested against it. She was confused; she was still mourning Jimmy's death, yet Michael had stirred something inside her. Something she thought had died. It wasn't love, she was sure of that, but in the absence of another explanation, she was at a loss. She refused to admit she was attracted to Michael, it seemed indecent, so decided she would keep her thoughts to herself until she knew him better or had let more time elapse.

Cat swept past Ellie into the bedroom. 'What in the world are ye doing, holdin' up the door?' she said interrupting her reverie.

Ellie grinned and ambled in behind Cat. 'Did ye see to the fire?'

'I did. Now get yerself into bed, we've early Mass in the mornin' and it's past midnight already.' Cat began taking out her hairpins, laying them on a box next to the bed. She undressed, put on her nightdress and began brushing her hair, mumbling the number of strokes to herself. Suddenly she stopped and turned to Ellie.

'Are ye goin' to stand all night like someone lovesick who can't spew, or are ye goin' to get undressed and into bed?'

Ellie started undressing and turned her face away so that Cat could not read her expression. She didn't feel like being interrogated, so decided to ignore the remark.

'Well?' Cat asked putting down the hairbrush, 'are ye goin' to tell me what's up or not?'

'Oh Cat, I really don't feel like talkin' right now, I'm tired and 'tis late. Let's get to bed,' Ellie said undoing the buttons to her dress which slipped down over her hips and fell to the floor.'

'Pick up the dress and hang it up Ellie, or it'll crease.' Cat slid in between the sheets and yawned, 'Oh why on earth did we agree to go to early Mass with him, we should have said we'd go to the eleven o'clock.'

'Well, it'll get it over with and leave more time to walk to Lize's for the furniture. Did Michael say whether he had to move lodgings now?'

'No, he didn't. He began to say at the table, but he got kind of sidetracked. He fell for that at first didn't he?'

'Yes. I'm surprised, I would have thought he'd have known what we were up to, 'tis an old trick.' Cat snuggled down under the bedclothes. 'Turn out the lamp when ye're done, I'm goin' to sleep.'

'D'ya think Louis will buy ye an engagement ring?'

'Goodnight Ellie!'

'Well, do ye?'

'I don't know and I don't care. Get some sleep will ye.'

'I don't think I can sleep.'

'Count sheep.'

'It doesn't work for me.'

'Then count the hours 'till ye can see Michael Nagle again!'

What d'ya mean?' Ellie's tone was cautious.

'C'mon, I've eyes in me head.'

Ellie didn't answer but put her nightdress on and crept beneath the covers where she began yawning and feigning sleep. Soon her heavy breathing indicated to Cat she had gone to sleep, but Ellie lay for hours trying to work out what she felt and the implications of getting involved with Michael. He was going to America. If he asked her to go with him, would she want to? She didn't think so but at nearly thirty, her options were narrowing.

Eventually she fell into a restless sleep, exhausted and still undecided about her course of action should Michael ask her to go out with him. Would she go? Michael had asked her out previously, but Jimmy had beaten him to it.

* * *

It was early afternoon by the time the trio had pushed the handcart, from Eltham to Plumstead. Cat opened the gate and knocked on Lize's door.

After a while the door opened a little and Iris peered through the gap

'Hello Auntie Cat,' she smiled and opened the door wider.

'Hello, Iris. Can ye tell yer mammy we're here to collect the sofa?'

Iris disappeared inside the house and returned instantly. 'Mummy said to come in. She's out in the scullery doing the dishes.'

Cat followed Iris inside and Ellie and Michael waited at the gate.

'Are ye not goin' in Ellie?' Michael asked.

'No.'

'Why not?'

'I wasn't asked.'

Michael let the conversation drop. He gathered by Ellie's tone that there was something amiss. Instead he stood whistling through his front teeth and rolling a cigarette. He pinched off spare tobacco from the end and lit it, drawing down the first rush of nicotine.

Ellie rolled a stone back and forth with her foot wishing Cat would hurry up. She wanted to get away. It was a long walk back and she was tired after a sleepless night.

'Ye look tired,' Michael said and drew on his cigarette whilst fiddling with a box of matches.

'Sure I am, t'was late before we got to bed last night.' There was a silence and Ellie continued rolling the stone around with her foot.

Then Michael turned to her. 'Would ye care to go to the music hall one evening, with Cat as well, of course?'

Ellie stopped rolling the stone around and looked up at him. 'I would. Yes, I would.'

'What about Cat?' Michael asked.

'Ask her yerself, there she is.'

Cat had appeared in the doorway and was beckoning them inside.

They went up to the door and Ellie whispered to Cat. 'Is Lize here?'

'Yes, of course, why?'

'Well, no reason, I just didn't want to go barging into her house uninvited, if ye know what I mean.' Ellie stepped into the hallway followed by Michael.

Lize approached them, drying her hands on a towel.

'Afternoon Ellie,' she said but looked at Michael, 'and you are?'

'Michael. Michael Nagle, missis.'

Lize looked at him and held out her hand.

'Eliza. But most people call me, Lize. Pleased to meet you Michael.' She pushed an errant strand of hair behind her ear and colour rushed into her cheeks.

Ellie noticed she was blushing and thought Lize had another side to her, as well as being a bitch!

23
Plumstead
April 1917

Lize strode across the playground and pushed through the swing doors of Reggie's school.

Immediately ahead she saw the door marked, *Headmaster's Office*. She didn't know why the Head had summoned her, but decided it was better to get it over with. It was an awful, rainy April day and she was cold, wet and agitated as she went into the building.

When she reached the Headmaster's office she stood still for a while composing her thoughts, trying to quell her nervousness, then tapped on the door.

Immediately the door opened and Mr. Frome waved her inside.

'Sit down, Mrs. Collis, this won't take long.'

His tone sounded unfriendly and businesslike.

Lize sat down, afraid of what he was going to say. She tucked her legs beneath the chair criss-crossed at the ankle and pushed her hands into her pockets to hide their trembling. She felt like a silly child, and wanted to cry. This man frightened her. She badly needed Charlie.

Mr. Frome sat in his chair, leaned his elbows on the desk and looked at her over the top of his glasses.

Lize's eyes settled on the blotter beneath his elbows and the inkwell neatly placed next to the inkstand and pen. It seemed an interminable wait. She wished he'd get on with whatever it was he had called her into the school about.

He let out a sigh. 'Mrs. Collis, I have a rather delicate matter to speak to you about. Normally, I would have spoken to Reginald's father, but unfortunately that cannot be.'

Whatever was he going to come out with, Lize wondered? It sounded pretty ominous and fear rose like bile in her throat. Drained of colour she looked Mr. Frome in the eye.

'Is it something bad, Mr. Frome?'

'Yes, I'm afraid it is!' He didn't continue for a while, but sat staring down at his blotter.

Lize lowered her eyes. This was awful she thought, now she was going to cry, she knew it. Lize couldn't prevent big tears spilling down her cheeks.

Mr. Frome ignored her tears and began his speech. 'You see Reginald has been involved in something rather difficult for me to speak to a lady about, but in the absence of his father I'm afraid I am forced to inform you that I am going to cane him and then expulsion will follow immediately.'

Lize straightened up. 'Why? What on earth has he done? Has he stolen something, or anything like that?' she was floundering. She felt as though she had to guess Reggie's misdemeanour.

Then, as though having given it enough time for thought, Mr. Frome told her what had happened.

'At playtime this morning your son was found outside the storeroom trying to interfere with a young girl. He had his trousers down.'

Lize gasped. Her heart pounded in her chest and her breathing became difficult; but there was more to come. Mr. Frome cleared his throat, to continue, but Lize butted in.

'My Reggie wouldn't do such a thing, there must be some mistake!'

'I'm afraid there is no mistake, Mrs. Collis, I saw him myself. I'm afraid we have to take strong disciplinary action now.'

Lize couldn't take it in. Her head spun. The room was suddenly too hot and that man was giving her an absolutely awful look. She imagined Mr. Frome thought she was horrible, just like Reggie.

'Mrs. Collis, do you fully understand the seriousness of this?'

Lize wiped the sweat from her face with her handkerchief. 'Yes. Yes of course. But surely you were mistaken. Perhaps they were just playing.'

'No. They were not playing. The little girl was extremely upset and told me that he wouldn't let her go. Her parents may make a complaint to the police.'

'Oh. No. Please, can't you do something? Not the police!'

Mr. Frome thought for a while rubbed the lobe of his ear then stood up. 'I'm going to cane Reginald. And then you may remove him from the school. Now if you can compose yourself, I shall send for him and get this over with.'

Lize sat immobilized on the chair and as Mr. Frome left the room felt she was going to vomit all over his highly polished parquet floor.

Mr. Frome re-appeared with Reggie in tow hanging his head and unable to look at his mother.

'Take your trousers down,' Mr. Frome commanded.

Reggie undid his braces and eased his trousers down a little.

'Right down boy,' Mr. Frome boomed at him whilst taking a cane from the desk drawer. He swished it a couple of times, whipping the air with vicious swipes.

Reggie trembled and his face whitened as Lize looked on helplessly. She watched as Reggie bent down and the flogging began.

Not once did he cry out, but silently took the punishment; and when it was over simply pulled up his trousers and slipped his braces back onto his shoulders.

Without looking either at his mother or Mr. Frome, Reggie asked, 'Can I go now Sir?'

'Wait outside,' Mr Frome said in a superior tone.

Reggie slunk from the room and closed the door while Mr. Frome placed the cane back in his drawer, wiped his hands on a handkerchief, and turned to Lize.

'You will now remove your son from these premises and send him to another school. I hope this has taught him a lesson. Good day, Madam.'

The ordeal was over and Mr. Frome moved to the door, opened it, and Lize slipped out without looking up.

Once outside she marched out of the playground and down the road with Reggie walking quickly behind her until they reached the house.

Lize fumbled with her keys, opened the door and motioned to Reggie to go into the kitchen.

She went upstairs and took one of Charlie's belts from the wardrobe, returned to the kitchen and went over to Reggie.

She wound the belt round her hand and lashed him across the face.

Reggie brought his hands up to defend himself but she just went on thrashing him on any part of his body she could get at - until bereft of energy, she sank to the floor and sobbed.

She wanted to scream at him, *just wait until your father comes home*!

24
The French Coast
August 1917

Louis stood on deck watching the French mainland recede, the boat pitching and rolling its way across the English Channel. He felt the tightness in his jaw relax and was relieved watching the frothy wake separate him from France.

He became mesmerised studying the white foaming sea kaleidoscope into turquoise, navy blue and green waters. They churned and tumbled in magnificent enveloping folds behind the boat heading for England. He was glad to leave it all behind and felt somehow that the sea was cleansing his soul from the blood and gore of war.

Only two days ago, he had watched a firing squad, execute Ben, an eighteen-year-old soldier, for not following orders and feigning illness.

He knew that it was really a case of Ben being unable to cope with fatigue and shell shock, but his fate was sealed by the medical officer's confirmation that the lad was fit for duty.

He could not get the incident out of his mind. No matter how much he tried, the boy's face haunted him. It had been Louis who had tied the blindfold around Ben's head and seen the terror in his eyes, and Louis' eyes were the last Ben saw before being eclipsed from the world.

How many more of his men would go down this path? He felt guilty leaving them to go off and get married, but at the same time, there was enormous relief in being able to escape for a while and turn his attention to Cat, and the wedding.

The sun's blazing rays cooled by sea breezes beat down on his face; and he relished its warmth, breathing in his fleeting freedom.

The rolling vessel made him queasy but even that was welcome. Any suffering, no matter how large or small, was easy to endure - so long as it wasn't through war.

Further along the boat a man began to play a violin and Louis' mind was drawn back to his childhood. He recalled childhood more as a series of still snapshots, like pictures he had seen in photographers' shops. Each stage of his life appeared to him as a separate event, rather than a continuous journey from childhood to adulthood, each memory superimposed with the poignancy of loss.

Louis remembered as a little boy sitting on his father's knee singing nursery rhymes as his dad played piano. His dad would count him in saying, 'One, two, three, and...' then would nod his head giving him the cue to begin singing. Over and over they would stop then re-start as often Louis giggled about something and lost his place.

Usually, he remembered, Lize was somewhere in the background practicing her dance steps coached by their mother.

Then at about eleven, or twelve he played the violin, accompanying his father on piano. He remembered the chin rest digging into his collarbone, and his dad taking out his handkerchief and tucking it beneath his shirt to soften the discomfort. Then his father's hand smoothing back his hair, kissing his forehead saying, 'My son, I'm so proud of the way you play. I hope one day you will perform in a big orchestra and make music your life, maybe travel the world. Always allow the feelings in your heart to find an exit through your playing – and play as though each day was your last day on Earth.'

Memories were also there of his mother showing Lize how to perfect her arabesque. His mother! Some time ago a much happier woman. Once a wonderful dancer - she knew how to express her emotions through movement. In those days his parents were a wonderfully matched pair.

But something had gone horribly wrong in their lives. Louis never knew exactly the reason his mother had moved into another bedroom and the door firmly locked each night. He certainly never understood why his father sat downstairs each evening drinking himself to oblivion, the piano neglected.

Things were unclear in his mind too how much time had passed listening to his mother's caustic complaints about his father; the rows, and his father's drinking becoming intolerable to the family. Eventually his mother had thrown his father out onto the street.

After that point, nothing to do with music was allowed. No more dancing or singing. The piano was sold and Louis only played the violin when his mother was out of the house.

One day a policeman had appeared at their door and told his mother that his father had been found seriously ill lying in the street in Lewisham and had been taken to hospital. But Louis and Lize were not allowed to visit him before he died, and were prohibited from attending the funeral.

The common grave in which their father was laid to rest remained unmarked and they were admonished for showing any grief. His mother, in effect, wiped him from their memories and he was never mentioned again.

He remembered with bitterness that when he was fourteen his mother had put him in the army. He could not forgive her and vowed never to return to her home on leave.

Eventually when Lize married Charlie, it became normal for Louis to stay with them when on leave.

Throughout the years, Louis had never been able to discuss or speak about his father, who remained in his heart like a lost love.

Louis had often written poetry in an attempt to make sense of his feelings. In the poems he asked his father to forgive him for all the words that had gone unsaid. It filled him with grief that his father was unable to be with him on his wedding day. He thought perhaps they would have children, but they would always be the grandchildren his father would never know, and as the salt sprayed onto his face it became merged with his tears.

Throughout his journey from Dover to Charing Cross, over London to Paddington Station, the train bound for Fishguard, the ferry to Queenstown, and finally the train to Fethard, Louis found his mind a swirling mass of thoughts.

Images of war and scenes of destruction contrasted with the pastoral scenes he saw passing by. He watched cows lazily flicking their tails in the heat, horses galloping across pastures, farmers and labourers working the fields and all the time he tried to pacify his mind and concentrate on Cat and their life that would follow once the war ended.

They would walk in the park, have some children and they would play with them and take them out to tea with relatives. Yes, life was going to be better in the future.

In his tunic pocket he carried a little jeweller's box with Cat's wedding ring, plus a little gold wishbone brooch with an amethyst cradled in the apex. He had acquired them in exchange for cigarettes from a jeweller in Ypres who couldn't sell his stock. Every now and then, as though for comfort, his hand would move to the pocket checking they were still there. Then a few minutes later, he would re-check, in case he hadn't checked it properly the previous time.

The last leg of his journey on the train to Fethard seemed the slowest and Louis occupied himself reading for a while until, too tired to concentrate, he closed his eyes. Alone in the carriage he lay flat out on the seats, his tunic unbuttoned and his hat resting in the baggage net above where he had tossed it uncaringly. He'd never known such tiredness, such complete exhaustion and wanted to sleep on the train, until the end of time.

He slept fitfully, waking every now and then when the train slowed at the country stations. Then the realisation would be there, that tomorrow was his wedding day. Cat would be waiting for him at the end of the journey and the next day he would be a married man! He was rocked to sleep repeatedly by the train's motion and only woke properly when the train approached Fethard and he saw in the distance the town cradled in the lap of Mount Slievenamon.

Quickly he inspected his appearance in the mirror above the seats, took out his comb and flicked it through his hair. As he caught sight of himself in the mirror, he was shocked. His face looked pallid and sweaty, then all-too-familiar trembling attacked him and he shook uncontrollably.

Since he'd been gassed in Ypres this had become the pattern. When he was anxious the attacks were worse, but he had learned to cope with it and wait until it passed.

Louis sat down and when the trembling had calmed, he wiped his forehead with his handkerchief. Then buttoning his tunic, he went to the door and released the leather strap to the window mechanism.

He rested his hands on the open window frame and breathed deeply, focussing his eyes on the station ahead and the small crowd he could see gathered there.

25
Fethard
August 1917

Cat heard the train before it came into view from behind the mountain, and her insides somersaulted. It hadn't occurred to her until then that perhaps when they saw each other, they may find they were not in love at all. She had screwed up her handkerchief so tightly with anxiety that it suddenly tore in two as the train, now in view, came swaying along the track towards her, bringing her man into town.

Shuddering to a halt, the train stopped and as the carriage doors opened people began spilling onto the platform. Cat tried to spot Louis. Then she saw him stepping down from the train, swinging his kit bag over his shoulder, a slow smile spreading across his pallid face. She walked towards him and he let the kit bag slide to the ground. They stood facing each other.

'Hello Cat'

'Hello yerself.'

She stood before him, pulling on the shredded handkerchief, wishing he'd say something. Louis reached down and picked up his kit bag.

'Shall we go?'

'Sure.'

Cat didn't expect to be kissed in public but somehow felt a little show of affection would have been appropriate. Still she thought, he's probably tired.

'Louis?' she began once they were outside the station and checked that nobody was within hearing range, 'Ye do still want to get married don't ye?'

He stopped walking and turned to face her.

'Yes, I do, or I would not have travelled half way across Europe to get here otherwise.'

They walked down the lane leading away from the station chatting politely about the weather. Once or twice Louis glanced across at Cat and she smiled at him, wondering what on earth to talk about. She realised she did not really know him.

They reached the end of the lane and he turned to her.

'I'll leave you here Cat, it's supposed to be bad luck to see your bride on the evening before the wedding, but I'll sleep tonight safe in the knowledge that this time tomorrow, you will be my wife. Mrs. Ross!'

Cat felt disappointed that their reunion was so brief and stilted, but managed to smile at the thought of becoming Mrs. Ross.

'Well, if ye're sure, Louis. Can you remember where the hotel is?'

'Yes, I remember.'

He stood looking at her and she wondered again whether they would get on together, as they hardly knew one another.

Louis broke the silence. 'I'll see you at the altar.' Then he stepped forward to gently kiss her lips before turning to walk away.

Cat stood puzzled, watching him as he walked up Main Street, then turned and slowly made her way home to Monroe feeling strangely let down.

26
The Holy Trinity Church, Fethard
August 17, 1917

Ned guided Cat down the aisle and could feel her trembling. He patted her hand clinging tightly onto his arm.

'Eist mo chuisle. 'Twill be fine. Just fine.'

Louis was waiting at the altar in his deep blue ceremonial dress; his spurs glinted, reflecting dozens of memorial candles flaming nearby.

Practically the whole town had shoehorned themselves into the church and there were no spaces left for any latecomers. A hush descended as Cat was led up the aisle by her father.

Ned battled with his emotions. He was completely taken by surprise at the pain he felt and wondered if he was having a heart attack. The agony gripped his throat, choking him. He tried to concentrate his mind on something else but was aware that all eyes were upon them, so he nodded at folks as he passed by, but couldn't subdue the wretched feeling of bereavement he was experiencing.

He remembered that when his other children had clung to Maeve as toddlers, Cat had been different. She had forged a love with him the others had not been able to. She'd climbed on his knee while the others were out to play, and she'd kissed his hands when they were sore with basket making.

Maeve had the other five, but he'd had Cat, and she was the star in his heaven.

When they reached Father O'Dowd at the altar, Ned nodded to Louis, and could see by the look in his eyes that he was as terrified as Cat.

Father O'Dowd asked who was giving this woman away to this man, and Ned answered that he was. He took Cat's hand and gave it one final squeeze before placing it onto Louis' outstretched palm.

Ned then stepped back leaving Cat and Louis together and the wedding ceremony continued. He sat down next to Maeve deep in thought.

Ned realised that Cat would no longer be referred to by folk as *Ned's girl*, but rather as *Louis' wife*. He sat there smiling, pretending he was happy, mumbling to himself about taking a back seat in life now until his sister Nellie poked him in the back and told him to be quiet.

'Eist now, Neddy,' she whispered.

Eist yerself, Ned thought, that's my gel goin' out o' me life for a second time. He leaned back in the pew and heard little more of the service as he slipped into a quiet reverie, only vaguely hearing Father O'Dowd bless the bride and groom before beginning to say the Mass.

The congregation chanted in unison 'Kyrie *eleison, Christie eleison*, *Kyrie eleison,'* beating their breasts in unison against the backcloth sounds of little tinkling bells and the clanking incense casket waving back and forth.

Ned's eyes wandered over the row to his other children, wondering who would be next. Tom probably he thought, as he'd been courting Norah seriously for a while and an announcement was likely soon. He thought he may temporarily give Tom the small cottage upstream from Monroe, known as *Granny's Cottage*. He only kept his basket making equipment in there, so he'd clear it out for him. It would make a nice home for him and his new wife. Tom would inherit the farm one day so he may as well start making the pathway easy for him. He felt he had to prepare to stand aside.

Also he supposed, Mary would be marrying her man Daniel, newly qualified as a doctor. His thoughts rambled on as the service unfolded over the next hour, with Ned seemingly watching everything, but in reality hearing very little.

Cat and Louis knelt at the altar and were blessed by the priest, then stood for the wedding ring to be placed on Cat's finger.

The altar boys trotted back and forth in their deep red cassocks, covered with crispy white surplices. Bright and polished, each cherubic mouth opened to chant the Latin verses parrot-fashion on cue. They did this mechanically and Ned thought they probably had their minds on football or suchlike in reality.

Remembering his own days as an altar boy, Ned smiled to himself. He'd always had his mind on football while appearing to be devoutly praying in church. Oh dear, he wondered, would he ever get to Heaven now?

The ceremony drew to an end and Ned heard Father O'Dowd saying he now declared them man and wife. Then came the point where the bride and groom went into the vestry to sign the register and they disappeared behind a door with the priest.

When they re-appeared, Ned caught Cat's eye and smiled as she walked down the aisle on Louis' arm.

He turned to Maeve. 'Right now, 'tis done and I've a helluva thirst on me so let's get over to the hotel now.'

Maeve gave him a look of disgust. 'Will ye wait now until the bride's outa the church before ye start on about wetting yer whistle?'

Nellie O'Connell hurried down the church steps ahead of the bride and groom to open up the hotel but as she crossed the road she saw Paddy Hogan lurking in a shop doorway. Furious that he had the nerve to show his face on this of all days she marched up to him.

'Now, Paddy, what is it ye're wantin'?' she demanded.

'Just watchin' the world go by, Nellie.'

'Well, Paddy, the world can be seen just as well from the other end of town, so I think 'tis best if ye do just that.' She stood her ground, hands on hips, waiting for him to move away.

Paddy stared her out for a few seconds, then decided to make himself scarce; but just at that moment the wedding guests began approaching, led by Louis and Cat.

As Cat stood at the church gates she looked across the road and saw Paddy watching her - and instantly felt fear.

Then she watched him turn and walk away.

27
O'Connell's Hotel, Fethard
August, 17th 1917

Jerry Dwyer bustled around moving chairs, sorting people by height, and when finally satisfied, shuffled over to his photographic equipment.

'Hold the pose,' he commanded as he took the photos of the wedding group. 'And now, just the bride and groom please, so the rest of ye can all g'w'on inside for a spot o' hooch now ye'll be pleased to know.'

Louis and Cat sat rigidly, afraid to move, as Jerry took more photographs until he finally announced he was finished.

'There,' Jerry said, 'captured for all time and ye can show yer grandchildren the photographs one day.' He laughed as he began to pack up his equipment and promised to send copies of the photographs to England once he had developed them.

'Well Cat, now that's over shall we join the rest?' Louis suggested.

'Sure, only I just want a few moments with Mummy and Dada.'

Louis smiled at her and made his way inside. The noise was beyond ordinary speaking level and he had to push his way through the crowd to order a glass of porter. He leaned against the bar watching the band tune up.

So, he thought, I've finally done it! I'm now a married man. He turned the names over in his mind; Mrs. Ross; Mrs. Catherine Ross; Mr. and Mrs. Louis Ross. My wife! It sounded so strange to him, yet oddly comforting. No longer alone but part of a couple.

He saw Cat come into the bar with her parents. She was looking for him among the crowd so he waved to draw her attention. She caught his gaze and in that instant he felt so elated he wanted to shout out with exhilaration, *let my wife through*, but instead decorum reigned and he merely moved towards her through the crush and said nothing.

The bandleader announced that the bride and groom would take the floor for the first dance, and gently Louis and Cat were guided to the space set aside for dancing. They stood facing one another and his arm went round her waist as she slipped her hand into his, and they began dancing, much to everyone's delight.

After a while the music grew faster and Cat broke away from Louis as she performed the dance so familiar to her, but totally unknown to him.

He stood watching; fascinated. She pulled up her dress so that her feet, freed from the material, tapped and banged the floor as she performed a traditional Irish dance.

Her footwork amazed him. The crowd clapped in time with the music and Cat swirled and danced, her cheeks glowing as Louis dropped back into the crowd, watching his woman.

He felt he was witnessing a performance that would outstrip any world-class performer. He had no idea she could dance like this.

Cat's sisters then joined her on the floor and soon the Delaney women took up the whole area. The party was in full swing!

By midnight things showed no sign of slowing down but Cat and Louis decided to slip away, knowing they had a long journey back to England in the morning.

28
O'Connell's Hotel, Fethard
August, 17th 1917

Louis closed the door behind him. 'Well you certainly can dance, Mrs. Ross,' he laughed loosening his tunic belt. 'Have you any more talents I don't know about?'

'Ah! We all dance – 'tis nothin' special.'

'*I* think it is,' he said watching her unpack her travelling bag.

She took her nightdress out and laid it on the bed, then looked up at him as he unbuttoned his tunic.

'Ye look hot, Pet. Why didn't ye take off the jacket tonight?'

'Habit really, I didn't think about it. Being in the army makes you adjust to being uncomfortable and you simply put up with it.'

'Well I'm glad I'm not in the army. I hate wearin' tight clothes, especially in this heat.'

Louis watched her fanning her face with her hand, wondering who should go to the bathroom first. He stood awkwardly, tunic undone, feeling he should make the first move but unsure what that move should be. Should he get undressed in the same room?

'Well, I'll just go along to the bathroom,' Cat finally said and gathered up her nightdress and hairbrush.

'Yes, of course. I'll go along when you come back.' He faltered over what to say now that they were finally alone.

Cat opened the door and went down the hallway to the bathroom, leaving him alone to think about what his next move should be.

Once alone Louis went to the window, slid up the sash and leaned out. The air was sultry and he thought there might be a storm later. He lit a cigarette and blew the smoke out into the night air, wishing that they did not have to return to England in a few hours.

He didn't hear Cat quietly return to the room and only became aware of her presence when he heard her slip between the bedclothes. Surprised, he turned. 'Oh I didn't hear you come back.'

'No, ye were miles away. I've finished in the bathroom. Are ye goin' along there now?'

'Yes. I'll only be a little while.' He stubbed his cigarette out and turned to close the window.

'Ah leave it open, will ye? 'tis too hot. I'll suffocate if ye close it.'

'If you're sure, only I think there might be a storm later.'

'If it rains we can close it, but there isn't a leaf stirrin' at the moment.'

He nodded agreement and went to the bathroom where he sat on a chair wondering what to do. Should he take off all his clothes and walk back in naked? No, he decided that might frighten the life out of her. Should he go back in fully dressed and take them off in front of her. Well, that could be embarrassing. Perhaps if he half undressed and just waited to see what happened? He sat trying to come to a decision until finally, after washing his face and cleaning his teeth, he was so weary he decided to just go back and see what happened.

He opened the door and noticed Cat had blown the candles out, so he tiptoed into the darkened room and made his way to the bed. He stood watching Cat in the moonlight for a while before sitting down to pull his boots off.

He took off his shirt, lowered his braces and slid his trousers down; then folded up his uniform neatly and stood in his underwear silhouetted by the moonlight. Before climbing into bed, he knelt down to say his prayers, then crossed himself and pulled back the covers gingerly to slide between the sheets.

He laid rigidly on the edge of the bed his tension rising; then the familiar nausea and shaking began and he felt he would vomit. Louis rushed quickly to the bathroom where he sat on the chair waiting for the feeling to pass.

Eventually, after splashing cold water on his face he began to recover, so returned to the bedroom. As he opened the door he saw Cat had re-lit the candle and was sitting up in bed.

'Oh! You startled me,' he said moving across the room to sit on the bed.

'Are ye sick Louis? Did ye drink too much?' She looked worried and knelt up in the bed to touch his face.

He was shivering. 'No. It's nothing, just the effects of being gassed. It happened to all of us. I just wait for it to pass. I need to rest until it goes but I don't want you to worry Cat, really!' He lay down and though the evening was hot, he felt chilled and trembled.

'Here, cuddle up, ye feel cold,' she said holding out an arm for him to curl into. He blew out the candle and shifted across the bed to her then lay cradled by her arm. He embraced her and nestling against her smelled lavender water on her skin. He thought she smelled lovely. As he relaxed against her body, he felt the attack recede.

Gently he kissed her neck, then her cheek and lifted his head a little to kiss her lips. He didn't want to rush things so softly ran his fingertip along her nose and down over her mouth, under her throat and circled the dip in her skin where her nightdress buttoned at the neck

Deftly he passed the buttons through the buttonholes and pulled back the opening until her breasts were revealed. She turned her head to him and smiled.

'I love you Louis.'

'I love you too, more than I can say.'

She kissed his forehead and he began caressing her breasts feeling her nipples harden. Then he began kissing her nipples. He sensed her excitement and was aroused.

He pulled her nightdress up and she fumbled feverishly to remove the garment, dragging it off over her head and throwing it to the floor as Louis struggled out of his underwear beneath the covers and dropped them over the side of the bed.

His hand slid between her legs, which she opened slowly, and ferocity overcame her so that she began pulling his hand into her, forcing it to go in deeper and deeper. Suddenly she cried out, and Louis stopped.

'I'm sorry, I didn't mean to hurt you,' he said, raising himself onto an elbow, 'do you want me to stop?'

In reply she merely put her arms round his neck and pulled his face closer to kiss his lips, as he eased himself onto her body.

He pressed himself against her and felt her hips lifting, inviting him into her as their bodies began writhing in unison.

Just then lightning forked the skies preceding the storm and in the neon flash Louis looked down. He imagined he saw the young German soldier beneath his grip that he had wrestled once in a desperate fight. Louis had raised his arm and his knife had stabbed wildly, slashing into the soldier's chest, which spurted warm purple-red blood. He had blood on his hands, blood on his face. He had penetrated the soldier's body with his knife.

Louis rolled away from her.

'I'm sorry. I just can't do it tonight. It's not you...'

A heavy silence fell between them. Humiliated, Cat reached down and picked her nightdress up and quickly slipped it over her head. She curled up in the bed with her back to him.

Aware of her silence, he listened to her breathing as thunder rumbled around the skies long after she had fallen asleep.

29
En route to England
August 18th 1917

On the ferry to Fishguard Cat stayed on deck with Louis, wondering how she could broach the subject of last night. She couldn't let him go back to the war with what felt like such a rift between them.

He was solicitous toward her, making sure she wasn't chilled by the sea breeze, but Cat's chill was on the inside and she couldn't find the words to cut through the tension that now existed between them.

She felt she had done something wrong, but was at a loss as to what it was. Surely she reasoned, what they were doing last night was what married people did, and as married people it was not a sin in the eyes of God. So why, she asked herself, had Louis reacted in the way he had and left her feeling she was dirty?

There was nobody she could turn to. This was not the sort of thing she could chat over with Mummy or her sisters now; it had taken on a privacy of its own. He was the only one she could talk to about their failure to consummate the marriage but Louis was not talking about it.

Ellie joined them on the deck, slipping her arm through Louis'. She smiled at him, 'Louis, ye're the nicest brother-in-law in the whole world. I'm glad ye're part of the family now.'

Louis patted her hand. 'I'm glad too Ellie. Now we just have to find you a young man and then we'll be a nice foursome.'

She laughed at this and then left the newly-weds alone as they approached the mainland where they would disembark and catch the train to London.

* * *

Louis' train was leaving from a different platform, so after seeing Ellie into her seat, Louis and Cat had a little time alone to say goodbye.

They chatted about incidental things, and though Cat longed to open up her heart to tell him how devastated she felt, she was unable to overcome the barrier between them. They strolled along exchanging niceties instead.

'Don't forget to write just as soon as you can, Cat?'

'I will. Louis–' she began, but he cut across her.

'And if you get some time I would appreciate you knitting me some more socks, the others were so useful.' He was looking away from her and she couldn't gauge what he was thinking.

She tried again. 'Louis?' But he ignored her attempt once more.

'And do write to your auntie and uncle and thank them for a splendid wedding reception. I had no idea it would be so wonderful.'

'Was it wonderful, Louis?' she asked softly.
He kept walking and looked ahead as he answered her.

'Yes, Cat it was truly wonderful. All of it. And I shall remember your dancing for the rest of my life.'

She glanced up at his face for a second and felt sure there were tears in his eyes.

Feeling alarmed, she begged, 'Louis, please look at me. I need to know how ye feel about me.'

He stopped walking and stood pondering for a moment while Cat's heart fluttered wildly in her chest. Then something caught his eye in the distance and he said to her, 'Stay here,' and strode off into the crowd.

Cat stood there being buffeted by the crowds milling around in different directions. There were thousands of soldiers marching to embark as well as civilians going about their business and it seemed to her they were all intent on pushing their way through the crowds, not caring if they shoved aside everyone in their path.

She tried to spot him amongst the rest of the soldiers teeming around the station but he was lost to her. Cat felt he had abandoned her and resolved to go back to the train where Ellie was waiting if he didn't reappear when she had counted to one hundred. She began counting.

On the count of eighty-nine and three quarters, for she had slowed the process down by adding in quarters after sixty, he reappeared holding something behind his back. He was smiling.

'Close your eyes,' he said drawing near, and though the last thing she wanted to do was play games, she did so. 'Open your hands,' he whispered.

She felt something placed across her palm and when he said, 'Open your eyes,' she saw he had given her a single red rose.

Cat looked up at him and he was smiling at her, but then she saw his face crumple and he bit his lip to stem the tears already gathering in his eyes. She was confused, didn't understand, but was speechless.

'Goodbye, Cat. Take care of yourself,' he said putting his arms round her shoulders.

Then sobbing she pleaded, 'Louis, don't go like this, can't we talk?' But he released her from his embrace, held her at arm's length, took one last look and turned away into the crowd.

She watched him go and could see his cap bobbing up and down above the rest of the crowd as he went further and further away.

Part Two

30
O'Connell's Hotel, Fethard
Christmas Eve 1920

Ned sat at the table slowly sipping his glass of porter while viewing his family. All of them were there, as was tradition, to celebrate Midnight Mass together, except Tom and his wife Norah.

Maeve nudged him with her elbow, 'Sure aren't those two late again?' She let out a sigh.

Ned took his pocket watch out and flipped the lid open.

'They've a little while left yet. They'll be here in time.' He swallowed a mouthful of porter and looked at Peggy sitting opposite.

Peggy, their eldest child, turned thirty-four last birthday. Time was running out for her to find a husband and become a mother, Ned thought.

He couldn't understand why nobody had walked out with her. She was a pretty woman with fair wavy hair and clear blue eyes. He had to admit though that she was very timid and reminded him of a little mouse scurrying away if anyone as much as looked at her.

Perhaps, Ned concluded, she had never given anyone a chance to ask her out. She would probably have darted away before they opened their mouths. Ah what a waste, she would likely remain an old maid now.

Ned's gaze drifted to Ellie, the second of their children, and as though sensing his scrutiny she looked up and winked at him. Ned thought her green eyes looked very mischievous tonight.

'Penny for yer thoughts, Dada,' Ellie laughed.

Ned raised his glass to her and smiled. 'Aye, there's more than a penn'orth in lookin' at ye,' he said, then continued to take stock of his children.

Ellie was the only one with Maeve's frizzy auburn hair and freckles and he knew how she hated them. But he'd told her often enough that a face without freckles was like a sky without stars. Anyway, he thought, they suited her, even if there wasn't much unfreckled skin left to see.

He knew she could be a fiery little minx from bitter experience, but quick to laugh and forgive. Thank goodness. Nobody could fool her. If Ellie disliked someone, there was always a good reason. Her judgement of character was sound. Ned thought Ellie was the shrewdest of the lot.

I thank the Lord that Ellie and Michael Nagle are to be married in spring. One spinster in the family is enough, he decided. Ellie is thirty-three now and 'tis about time she got a move on! I would be even more content though if Michael Nagle managed to stay in a job, Ned thought.

Each time they had a letter from Ellie, they learned Michael had lost another job. Ned hoped he would settle on one particular line of work and stay in it soon. At least there had been no mention of them going to America when they married as was Michael's original intention. If that were to happen he knew he might as well kiss goodbye to ever seeing her again.

Ned checked his pocket watch again and wondered where in God's name Tom and Norah were. Maybe they'd had trouble with the animals he thought.

He thanked the good Lord daily that he had a son to pass the farm to. Tom was his third child and he watched with pride to see Tom's confidence grow now he had handed the daily workings of the farm over to him.

Tom at over six and a half foot was tall, fair, handsome and good-humoured. Norah had a good catch there, Ned felt.

Tom was full of fun and had deep laughter lines round his eyes, which constantly gave people the impression he was inwardly amused by something.

Ned relied on Tom much more now as he had let the reins of the business fall and Tom had picked them up - but not in such a way that made Ned feel redundant. Tactfully, Tom would regularly ask Ned's opinion and this helped the older man ease the feeling in him that he was losing his place in the world.

Cat, his fourth child was chatting animatedly with Ellie. He watched her ebony curls bouncing each time she laughed. She still looked like a young girl with her pretty face and large innocent-looking slate-grey eyes. Nobody, he thought, would believe she was twenty-eight, the mother of two children and a third on the way.

Cat had stolen his heart from early on in her life, and even though it was years since she had left Monroe, not a day went by without him missing her.

'What's the joke?' he asked Cat.

'Ah, ye wouldn't want to know, Dada. 'Tis women's gossip.'

'Well, so long as the joke's not me, then go ahead.' He shifted in his seat and watched the two sisters.

Ned had not noticed until then how alike Cat and Mary, his next daughter were. Mary at twenty-six was newly married to Daniel, a doctor, and this was the first opportunity they had all had since their wedding to get together.

He studied Mary. She had the same ebony curls, milk white skin and grey eyes as Cat. Everyone used to say they both took after him for colouring, but fortunately, he thought, they had Maeve's small features and neat little nose rather than his.

Mary was like Cat, and was as petite, but she did not have Cat's vivacity. Mary would shrink away from people, much like Peggy really. It was a surprise to him that she had managed to get herself up the aisle to be married at all. Well, good luck to her and Daniel. He was a fine figure of a man and would one day take over from that old drunkard Dr. Murray.

Old Murray, Ned decided, should be put out to grass as he was always roaring around the town in his carriage blind drunk. If it wasn't for the fact his horse knew the way home, he would have probably been found long since laid out somewhere in the middle of a bog and pecked clean by birds.

Breda, his youngest offspring, now twenty-four had inherited from him, along with her large manly frame, the 'Delaney nose'.

He felt sure this was the reason for her not being able to attract a partner, coupled with the fact she was not given to smiling much. He knew she could look positively fierce at times and often thought that maybe she scared men off.

He'd heard tales of children not wanting to go into the shop if Breda was serving. She had a good head of hair though; mid-brown and so thick that when she wore it in a pleat, it took more hairpins to keep in place than any other of the women in the family.

Ned wondered about Breda's discontented nature. She always seemed cross about something; but he had long since given up trying to find out what. Perhaps, he decided, that's the way she is now and always will be. Maybe it's better if she doesn't marry; she'd lead a fella a merry dance that's for sure.

But for all their little quirks, Ned decided they were a pretty fine family and he was proud of them all. He stood up and with a fork tapped his glass.

'Eist now. I said *Eist,* I want to make a toast.' He lifted his glass, and then waited for the chatter to subside. 'As this is the first time we've all been together since Mary and Daniel's wedding, I know as a family we wish them all the luck and blessin's in the world.'

The family broke into a babble and began raising glasses and cheering. Mary looked down and blushed, twisting her shiny wedding ring round and round as Daniel raised his glass and nodded to them all in turn.

Ned went on saying how proud he was that he had such a wonderful family, which was growing by the month, and here he looked at Cat and Louis who were trying to control their fidgeting two-year-old Billy, and a fretful, teething, one year old Marie.

'It gives Maeve and me so much pleasure to know that ye're able to be with us on our Holy day.' Then there was a pause. He ran out of words at this point, so just raised his glass saying, 'Sláinte to y'all,' then sat down heavily on his chair.

Ned continued watching his daughters and saw them now as grown women for the first time, not children. It came as a shock to him. Where had all the years gone? He suddenly felt old. Here were his girls, all grown up.

His eyes misted up as he looked at his grandchildren. Billy, a rascal if ever he saw one, and little Marie, so like Cat to look at, even at a year old. He wished he saw more of them but had to resign himself to the fact that this would never happen. He'd have to make do with whatever God had planned for him. He just wished He had it in His plan to bring Cat home.

He winked at Billy who tried winking back by screwing both eyes shut together.

'Here Louis,' Ned said holding out his arms, 'pass the boy over to me and we'll teach him a trick or two.'

Ned was about to show Billy his trick about finding a penny behind his ear when Peggy stood up and said they ought to get the children to bed so that they could all be ready for Midnight Mass.

The children were then passed around to them each in turn to be kissed, cuddled and finally handed back to Cat who turned to Peggy.

'Will ye help me to get them to bed, Peggy?'

'Sure I will, just try stoppin' me.' Peggy smiled, pleased to be asked to help.

Peggy and Cat left the room like ships in full sail in a flurry of white blouses and rustling skirts as they took the children to bed.

Ned looked at Maeve. 'Well woman, are ye happy now ye've all yer chicks back home to roost?'

Maeve drank the last of her porter, put down the glass, and tying her scarf under her chin said, 'I will be as soon as Tom and Norah put in an appearance. They're very late now, as usual! That girl really doesn't know a thing about time keepin'.' She frowned looking at the clock on the wall above the bar.

'Ah c'mon give her a break, 'tis all new to her runnin' the farm. Ye weren't so hot yerself when ye came to take over from me mam.'

'I was too, Ned Delaney. Yer mother only had to show me once how to milk a cow and never twice.'

'Aye, but she had to show ye the first time did she not? And how is Norah to know all that it has taken ye a lifetime to perfect?' He laughed, then softening his tone said, 'Try not to be so hard on Norah, she tries her best.'

'Well maybe her best should be a bit better!' Maeve sounded angry and pulled her rosary beads out of her pocket to begin saying a Hail Mary and Ned took it as the signal to shut up.

He was puzzled as to why she could not take to Norah. Maybe, he considered, once a baby appeared Maeve would soften towards her as he knew that usually did the trick with women. Perhaps, he thought, Maeve had too much time on her hands now. A grandchild would be welcome as it would give Maeve something to concentrate on. He hoped Tom and Norah would get a move on in that department.

Then he remembered there were Mary and Daniel who may also produce a grandchild. Who could tell which of these couples, Mary and Daniel, or Tom and Norah would have a baby first? He thought maybe he'd put a bet on that one after Christmas.

His mind returned to Peggy. He worried about her. All the best 'pickings' in the area were now gone, so it did not seem likely that she would ever marry. At least though, she and Breda were making a success of the shop, despite losing Mary's help when she got married and left.

Ned abandoned his reverie as Tom and Norah arrived apologising for being late; so in order to offset Maeve's annoyance, he stood up and began telling everyone they should be leaving for Mass. Coats were then buttoned, scarves tied, hat donned and rosaries at the ready, the family left the hotel.

The feeling of Christmas was inside them all when they walked across Main Street just before midnight towards the church as the first snows of winter fell slantwise from the sky.

31
O'Connell's Hotel, Fethard
New Year's Eve 1921

Nellie O'Connell tiptoed into Cat's bedroom and placed a jug of water beside the bed.

'Oh, 'tis ye, Auntie. I thought maybe 'twas Louis.'

'No, Pet. He's busy tryin' to beat yer father at whist. How're ye feelin'?'

'Got an awful backache, Auntie.' Nellie frowned and felt Cat's forehead.

'Ye're not due for another couple of months yet are ye?'

'No...I'm sure it's somethin' I ate. It'll go if I just rest. G'w'on downstairs and enjoy yerself. Ye don't want to be botherin' with a big ole bloated niece on New Year's Eve.'

''Tis no bother at all,' Nellie said as she went about the room putting things in place. Cat enjoyed being fussed over by her auntie and lay watching as Nellie straightened the bedcover.

'Now, if ye're sure Pet, then I'll g'w'on downstairs an' pop back later.'

She kissed Cat's forehead and turned to leave. Just then Cat screamed. Nellie turned and saw Cat's eyes widened with pain. She immediately flew to the bedside and grabbed her hand.

'Cat, ready or not, I think this baby means to arrive today. 'Tis not somethin' ye ate. I'm goin' for yer mam and'll send for Mrs. Morrisey, and then I'll be right back.' She rushed from the room and hurried downstairs to where Maeve was sitting with Billy.

Breathlessly she addressed Maeve. 'C'mon, 'tis Cat!'

Maeve jumped up. 'Lord save us. C'mon, Billy, go sit with yer Granddaddy for a while there's a pet. I won't be long now,' she said looking worried and followed Nellie into the hallway. Nellie closed the lounge bar door and whispered to Maeve.

'I think we're about to have a new addition to the family, Maeve.'

'Jesus, Mary and Holy St. Joseph.'

'I think Ned should go for Mrs. Morrisey.'

Maeve nodded. 'Sure, will I ask him to go now?'

'I think so. Louis won't know where to find her, so 'tis best if Ned goes.'

Maeve hurried back into the lounge and whispered the news to Ned who immediately got up, dug into his pocket and pulled out a coin.

'Here, Billy boy, roll this coin along that groove in the table and see how many times ye can do it before I get back.' He patted Billy's head and the child went off to the table clutching the coin as Ned disappeared through the doorway and Maeve went upstairs.

Maeve entered the bedroom to find Cat kneeling on all fours in the middle of the bed. She tutted at her daughter.

'C'mon now, Cat, try to get out of that position and onto yer feet. The longer ye can walk about the quicker ’twill be. ’Tis a bit before time though isn’t it?’

As Cat’s next contraction swept over her she remained where she was until it passed, then assisted by Maeve began to pace the floor. Within a few minutes the next contraction came and Cat crumpled against her mother.

‘I can’t do it, Mummy, I feel too tired.’

‘C’mon, Pet. Ye’ve got to do it, for it can’t stay inside ye forever. If it has a will to arrive today, then accept it and pray to God it’s all in one piece and doesn’t have the horns of the Devil on its head!’

Cat gasped as another fierce contraction gripped her.

‘I *can’t*, Mummy, I want to push. *NOW!’* Cat grasped her tummy as Maeve, looking agitated, struggled to get her back onto the bed.

‘Let’s hope Mrs. Morrisey can be found quickly, otherwise we’ll be doin’ this on our own. Now Pet, just try to relax a little until she comes,’ Maeve whispered, placing the palm of her hand on Cat’s forehead. ‘Ye’re burnin’ up. I’ll go wet some cloth to put on yer face.’

She hurried from the room and met Nellie returning with a kettle of hot water and towels. ‘Nellie, I don’t think this baby is going to wait for Mrs. Morrisey. Daniel’s downstairs, will I call him?’

Nellie looked surprised, and then said she wasn’t sure. ‘It seems a bit indecent for a brother-in-law to see a person’s undercarriage doesn’t it, Maeve?’

Maeve bit her lip. 'Do we have any choice? Mrs. Morrisey could be away at her daughter's. Maybe we'll ask Cat what she thinks.'

When they opened the bedroom door, Cat was slumped in the bed and the sheets beneath her were steadily turning scarlet.

'Oh Jesus! Oh, Jesus!' Nellie gasped, 'Get Daniel, Maeve. *Quickly*!'

Maeve fled from the room shouting, 'Daniel, Daniel, come quick,' and he appeared at the bottom of the stairs.

Seeing the distress on Maeve's face he took the stairs two at a time and entered the bedroom where he saw blood oozing across the sheets.

'Quick,' he said, 'get the fender from the fire and place it at the foot of the bed. When I say so, slide the fender under the bed end so that we can lift it off the floor.'

Nellie and Maeve immediately heaved the fender over to the end of the bed and Daniel lifted the iron bedstead up.

'Right…now.' Daniel gasped at the weight of the bed, but held it steady as the women dragged the fender into place then slowly he lowered the bed onto it. As he let the bed go he turned to Nellie and asked her to run downstairs and fetch up his bag. ''Tis on the floor next to Mary.'

Nellie nodded and sped from the room. As she rushed down the stairs she met Louis making his way up.

'Oh Louis, Cat's in a bad way,' she gasped. 'Daniel's up there takin' matters in hand, and I'm away to get his bag.' She clattered on down the stairs without looking back at him.

Louis bounded up the stairs and rushed into the room where the sight of all the blood shocked him. He immediately sensed the old familiar trembling return. He looked across at Maeve and saw that tears were streaming down her face as she stood stroking Cat's forehead.

'What's going on?' Louis asked.

'She's havin' the baby, Louis, and she's bleedin' real bad,' Maeve cried.

He went to the bedside and lifted Cat's hand to his cheek. 'Oh my God, it's all my fault. We should never have had another child so quickly.'

Nellie returned and handed Daniel his bag

. 'Louis,' Daniel said 'would ye mind steppin' outside for a little while as I need to examine her?'

Louis just nodded and left the room to sit on a chair in the hallway.

Daniel could feel the baby's head. He slid two fingers either side of its skull so that when the next contraction arrived he could pull. To his surprise the baby slithered out with little effort, but Daniel could tell that Cat's womb had partially prolapsed, so when the afterbirth came away, he gently pushed the womb back.

'Maeve, inside my bag there's a pack of gauze, would ye give it to me?'

'Sure,' Maeve said rummaging in his bag, 'here, is this it?'

'Thanks. Now take off the wrapper and fold it in two.' Maeve did as she was asked and handed the wadding to Daniel. He packed Cat's insides tightly with gauze padding and removed the sheet from beneath her.

'Nellie,' he asked, 'can ye put a clean sheet on the bed please? and I don't suppose ye have any rubber sheeting?'

'Yes, I do, from when I had my children. I'll get it,' Nellie said and went to the chest of drawers to retrieve clean linen and rubber sheeting.

'I'll lift her if ye can slide the sheetin' beneath, it'll save the mattress. Then, Maeve, as quick as ye can, put the clean sheet on. Thanks.'

When Cat had been made more comfortable he stood and watched her for a while, taking her pulse. He didn't like the look of her as she lay there deathly pale and not responding.

He turned to Nellie and Maeve. 'The bed must be kept at this angle, until the bleedin' subsides, otherwise we'll lose her. I don't know if she'll make it through the night, but if she does, she'll stand a chance of comin' through. She's lost a lot of blood.'

Maeve was sobbing and Nellie put her arm around her shoulder. 'Eist now, she'll come through.'

Daniel met Nellie's gaze above the top of Maeve's head and he looked away and began to see to the baby. He lifted her up by the ankles and smacked her bottom until she let out a healthy cry.

Daniel smiled at Maeve and handed her the baby. 'Now, let's get this little girl washed and into somethin' warm,' he said looking at his watch.
'First baby of the New Year. She's just made it by one minute.'

32
Plumstead
January 1921

Lize answered the door, signed for the telegram and ripped the envelope apart. She read it and stood considering the contents for a while in the hallway. Slowly she climbed the stairs and made her way to the back bedroom where her mother was sleeping and tapped gently on the door.

'Mum, are you awake?' She could hear her mother's grumbling, and waited.

'I am *now!* What's the matter?'

'There's a telegram from Louis.'

'So don't just stand out there, bring it in!'

Lize went in and crossed the room to draw the curtains, but Jessie Ross complained that the light would hurt her eyes so she left them closed and went to sit on the side of the bed.

'Oh. I see you've opened it,' Jessie said.

'Yes, it *was* addressed to me. Anyway he says the baby's arrived early. It's a girl, they've called her Eileen.' Lize held the telegram out for Jessie to read, but she just waved it away.

'Another mouth to feed. God, they breed like pigs those Irish. As soon as one is out of the sty they're at it again for another one. No wonder she can't hang onto them for nine months. How is he going to put food in this one's mouth as well as the other two when *he* hasn't even got a job?'

Lize folded the telegram and placed it in her apron pocket. She stood up. 'How are you feeling, Mum?'

'I was feeling better until that piece of bad news arrived! I believed Louis had more sense; but she's really turned his head. Well they needn't think they can come to me for help. They've made their bed and they can lie on it.' She threw off the eiderdown and covers ready to get up.

'Mum, I don't think you're well enough to get up yet.' Lize put her hand on her mother's forehead. It felt hot. 'Why not have another day in bed and I'll bring your breakfast up?'

Jessie considered it for a moment, and then sank back onto the pillows coughing. 'You're probably right. I'll give it another day and maybe by tomorrow I'll feel more like my old self. I'll just have some bread and jam today, I don't feel like a cooked breakfast.' She pulled the covers up and shivered. 'It's cold up here, you can light the fire before you get my breakfast.'

Lize went to the fireplace and began raking the ashes with a poker so that they fell into the ashcan below. Then lifting the ashcan out from beneath the grate, she shook them onto a piece of newspaper. She picked up a brush and swept away the dust before screwing up some paper and setting it in the grate. Next she laid some sticks criss-cross, after which she added lumps of coal. Before lighting it, she poured on some paraffin from a can. When she had finished, she moved the paraffin can away from the fire and threw on a lighted match. The whoosh of flames was instant and Lize realized she had used just a little too much paraffin.

'Easy with that paraffin, it's got to last,' Jessie bawled from the bed and Lize, having done her first duty of the day for her mother, retreated from the room to begin the second.

As she hurried downstairs with the coalscuttle, her anger flared. She experienced a surge of self-pity knowing life would have been so different if Charlie hadn't been killed.

She felt Charlie was to blame in some way for the situation she now found herself in. She had consented to her mother selling her properties so that she could move in with her and the children on the pretext that she would buy a shop with the money. 'That way,' Jessie had said, 'you can work in the shop and won't have to worry about getting a job.' But so far, all Lize had found herself doing was waiting on her mother hand and foot and there was no sign of any shop on the horizon.

Lize gritted her teeth; marched along the hallway to the kitchen and slammed the door behind her. One day, she thought, I'll commit murder - I'm certain of it!

Iris was eating her breakfast and with a mouth full of toast asked if the letter was from Reggie who was working as an apprenticed butcher in London.

'No, it was a telegram from Ireland. You have another little cousin called Eileen.'

'Oh that's nice, isn't it?' Iris smiled, revealing her toast-filled teeth.

'Is it?' Lize snapped and proceeded to hack a slice of bread off the loaf then spread the hardened butter onto its surface. The fresh bread tore beneath her violent scraping, and maddened, Lize took the slice of bread, opened the back door and threw it into the yard. Let the birds eat it, she thought.

She came back in and said to Iris, 'Put that butter dish on the range and take it off as soon as you see the butter begin to melt.' Then she began sawing the loaf again wishing it was her mother's neck beneath the blade.

Lize went out to the coal shed, shovelled coal into the scuttle; then closed and bolted the shed door. A sharp north wind blew and glancing up she saw that the sky was heavy looking with grey clouds hanging ominously overhead. She stood for a few moments breathing in the freezing air knowing that soon it would snow.

Better get more coal ordered just in case the snow lasts she thought, and lugging the coal scuttle through the back door Lize felt her mood lift noticing that Iris had buttered the bread and laid a breakfast tray for her grandmother.

Lize went to the range, lifted the boiling kettle and poured hot water into the teapot. She put the tea cosy on and trundled upstairs with the tray, wondering how many more times she would have to make the trip that day. It would be so nice she thought, if I could lie in bed and be waited on. But she knew that it was unlikely to happen.

33
Monroe, Fethard,
February 1921

Cat watched Louis struggle with the straps of his travelling bag. ‘Ye'll squash the bread. Why not take it out and carry it?'

‘Yes, maybe that would be better. I'd be sorry to find I only have breadcrumbs to eat tomorrow.' He undid the straps and took out the loaf Maeve had given him. Lifting it to his face he breathed in the aroma through the muslin wrap. ‘There's nothing like this you know, Cat. I love it.'

She stroked the back of his neck as he refastened the straps.

He turned and saw her eyes filled with tears.

‘I hate sayin’ goodbye, Louis. I feel as though I'll never see ye again.'

‘Oh come on now you silly thing, you know you will. It's only for a little while until you are strong enough to make the trip home. You know it makes sense and your parents will love having you here. Take advantage while you can and let them help you with the children. It will be hard enough when you do come home now Ellie has to live in with her new job. You'll miss her not being around to help won’t you?'

‘Yes, I know ye're right, but I'd rather be goin' home with ye.'

'And I'd rather you got yourself fit and healthy again, otherwise I will have three children and an invalid on my hands.'

'Louis?'

'Yes?'

'I wish Ellie and Michael would change their minds about goin' to America after the wedding. I assumed the idea had died. Ye know they haven't mentioned it for a while.'

'I know it's a hell of a distance to go for work isn't it?'

''Tis. And the worst of it is Michael has no particular job to go to when they get there.'

'Well, they still have time to change their minds, the wedding isn't until April and maybe something will turn up for him before then in England. I hope so.'

'At least Ellie has a job at present, though it sounds as though that family are workin' the hide off her. The only good thing about it is she doesn't have to find cash for food, rent and clothes. D'ye suppose ye will see her on her next day off?'

'I hope so, though it depends. I expect she will want to spend her time with Michael, not me!'

He lifted his bag off the bed and heaved it outside into the main room where Maeve was busy peeling potatoes. Billy and Marie were looking on, collecting up the peelings as they curled away from her knife. He dropped the bag on the floor beside her.

'Well Maeve, I'll be off now.'

'Oh Lord ye gave me a fright. Are ye away now?'

'Yes, time to go. I'll just take my bag out and put it on the cart, and then I'll have to be going.' He lifted his bag and went outside to where Ned was waiting with the donkey cart.

Ned turned in his seat and looked at Louis. 'There ye are then. Put the bag in the back and I'll turn her round.'

Louis swung the bag onto the back of the cart and Ned made a clucking noise with his tongue and Bessie knew it was time to turn. Obediently, the animal moved forward and Ned manoeuvered the cart until they were facing the gate.

'I'll just say my last goodbyes, Ned, and then I'll be off.'

'No rush. God made time – and plenty of it.'

Louis grinned and went back inside the cottage.

'Well Cat, this is it. I'm off now.' He embraced Cat tightly then turned to Billy sitting at the table hoarding his pile of peelings away from Marie.

'Be a good boy, Billy, and look after Mummy.' Billy looked up at him, but was more interested in his pile of peelings, which he was guarding from Marie's watchful gaze.

Louis picked Marie up and kissed her. She nestled into his neck and for a moment he stood there holding the child close to him before putting her down and lifting the baby, Eileen, from her crib. He kissed her forehead and placed her back quickly so as not to disturb her sleep.

'Goodbye, Maeve,' he said hugging her, 'and thanks for everything you've done.'

'Ah g'w'on with ye, 'tis a pleasure Louis. 'Tis a real pleasure. Off ye go now or ye'll miss the train. And write as soon as ye can.'

'I will. Goodbye,' he called climbing aboard the cart.

The donkey moved off immediately, pulling the cart over the cobbles which clashed beneath her hooves until once through the gate, the grass muffled the sound.

Louis turned to look at Cat, Maeve and his children framed in the doorway of Monroe as the cart jogged its way along. Nearing the corner of the boreen where the terrain was firmer, Bessie suddenly bolted forwards just as Louis turned round, so denying him the last sight of his wife and children waving goodbye.

34
London
March 1921

Louis rested his bicycle against the wall in Villiers Street underground tunnel and placed his cap on the ground in front of him. He took out his violin, rubbed resin along bow hairs and began to play.

He didn't look at the people passing by as he played, but was aware that some walked briskly past looking away from him if they didn't make a donation. Those that did donate nodded briefly in his direction, and Louis would nod back in gratitude

Ah well, he thought, I can't blame the ones who look away as he knew that he too would have to do that if confronted with someone playing for money. He just hoped that by lunchtime he would have enough to buy a bite to eat at the tea shop in The Strand.

Louis played from memory throughout the morning, grateful for the acoustics, which amplified his music along the tunnels. Warm winds whooshed through the underground, so feeling relatively comfortable he didn't mind playing for the majority of seemingly disinterested passers-by. Occasionally someone would throw a couple of pence his way, and sometimes he got lucky and had a shilling tossed into his cap. Whatever came his way, he was grateful.

After buying some food for himself that day, he would put the rest away in a tin at home. Cat called it the *Goin' Home Tin*.

He withstood the cold in their home each night when he arrived home because without Cat and the children there, he didn't bother to light the fire. He saved the money normally spent on coal.

Nothing he felt was as bad as the cold misery he had experienced in the trenches. Often though, when he had played all day and only earned a few pence, he went to bed at night chilled, exhausted and hungry.

He had lost a lot of weight and as he rarely saw the light of day, his complexion grew more sallow and dark circles had appeared beneath his eyes. But, as he told himself each morning cycling to London from Eltham, he was working, and therefore earning money.

Unable to find work of any other kind, he had been forced to fall back on the one thing that he could do expertly and which cost him nothing to do and that was playing the violin. He didn't have to be nicely dressed to appear publicly as he would if he'd been playing in an orchestra or working in an office. In fact, if he was honest, he rather liked the freedom this life gave him.

The only thing that began to worry him as April drew nearer was the possibility of Cat finding out. He knew she would be furious at his lack of self-respect and could almost hear her scolding him for stooping so low as to beg for a living.

Consequently, his letters to her had been rather vague on the subject of work. He hadn't exactly hidden the truth from her, but after a couple of experiences of losing jobs because the next man would work for less money, he was forced to busk. His one dread was that he would come face to face with someone he knew.

Approaching midday, one particularly miserable Wednesday morning, he was playing Vivaldi's *Spring*, when he noticed a man standing a little way off, watching him. The man was neatly dressed in a dark suit and overcoat with an cream -coloured silk scarf showing between the lapels. He held a dark trilby hat in his hand.

It occurred to him that maybe the man was someone from the Underground Authorities and would report him for begging. He stopped playing immediately, put his violin away, tied the case to the carrier of his bicycle and headed for the exit. It was not too early to visit the tea shop and he could certainly do with a cup of tea and something to eat. He rode the bicycle quickly up Villiers Street, past Charing Cross Station and crossed over The Strand.

After leaning his bicycle against a building, he entered the teashop. The sound of teacups chinking in the warm steamy atmosphere cheered him as he found a table and ordered a bun and a cup of tea from the waitress.

Just as he was about to bite into his bun, the man who had been watching him in the Underground sat down at his table. Louis was instantly worried that he was in trouble as he'd seen many a tramp moved on in the tunnels and knew begging was a blight on the British public. But since the war it had increased with many thousands of men unable to find work and the most unlikely types forced to sell items such as boxes of matches to earn a living. He looked the man in the eye and put his bun down.

The man shifted in his seat and took off his hat and smiled at him. 'I hope you don't mind my following you, but I want to speak to you. I've heard you playing most days in the Underground and I've seen you come here before, so thought I may find you here.'

'Look,' Louis began, 'I don't mean any harm. I won't return if it's against the law, but I don't have a position right now and I have a wife and three children to provide for.'

The man stopped smiling and looked serious, then from his inside pocket withdrew a business card and handed it to Louis. He read the card – *Roland Andrews, Musician.*

The man continued. 'I'm not here to chastise you for producing the most wonderful sound I have heard in a long time – other than at the Royal Albert Hall my dear fellow.'

Louis' hands were trembling and his mouth had dried. The last thing he wanted to endure was the shame of telling Cat that he had been prosecuted for busking. He wasn't sure he had heard the man correctly.

'I'm sorry, what did you say?'

'I know talent when I see it my man, and I can see you are not the usual run-of-the-mill beggar.'

Louis looked down, embarrassed at hearing someone refer to him as a beggar.

'I run a small orchestra, nothing very large you'll understand, but we play every weekend in The Strand Palace Hotel.' He paused and leaned forward. 'I was wondering if you would be interested in auditioning for my orchestra?'

Louis' fear receded instantly; this was marvellous news! The very best piece of luck he'd had in years, to actually be paid for something he had considered the delight of his life! Well, what could be better?

He controlled his excitement, as this was business and felt he should react seriously to the man's proposal. They agreed that Louis would appear at The Strand Palace on the following Saturday for an audition, two hours before the orchestra struck up for the evening repertoire.

Then Roland Andrews's expression changed. 'Of course you will need an evening dress suit. I trust you have one?'

Louis thought for a moment. 'It won't be a problem. By the way, I'm Louis Ross,' he said holding out his hand for Roland Andrews to shake, in the hope it would deflect him from questioning him more about an evening suit.

'Good,' Roland Andrews was smiling, 'then we'll expect to see you this Saturday at around six o'clock.'

'I'll be there,' he sounded confident, relieved he was not in trouble, 'and thank you for this chance.'

'It's a pleasure,' Roland said standing up. 'If you play as well on Saturday as I have recently heard, I'm sure things will work out fine. We'll provide the music. Oh, incidentally, I take it you do read?'

'Yes, I do. I just play from memory normally.'

Roland Andrews left the teashop, put on his hat outside, nodded to Louis through the window and melted into the crowds. When he had disappeared from sight Louis sat thoughtfully for a while unable to take it in. Then he beckoned the waitress to his table and ordered himself a bacon sandwich, something he would never normally do, but suddenly he could see a way out of his poverty.

As he sat munching the sandwich, Louis thought about the evening suit and realised he had no idea how much such an item would cost, except he knew he would be an extravagance he could ill-afford. His next stop, he thought, had better be an outfitters shop. He just hoped they did *Easy Terms*.

35
Plumstead
April 1921

Two days after his conversation with Roland Andrews, Louis went to see Lize and his mother as he needed to ask a favour. Much as it went against his principles to borrow money from his mother, he simply had to. He knocked on the door, which was opened immediately by Iris who told him excitedly that they were packing.

'Oh. What's the big occasion; you're not moving are you?'

'Yes, we are.'

Lize called her from the kitchen, 'Who's at the door, Iris?'

'It's Uncle Louis, Mummy.'

'Oh, Louis,' Lize smiled making her way to the front door. 'This is a nice surprise. How are you? Come on in. We're just about to eat, would you like some?'

The smell of cooking was overpowering. His stomach growled, as he hadn't had a proper meal since leaving Fethard.

'I don't mind if I do, it smells lovely. What is it?'

He sat down on a chair and Iris seated herself next to him. He put his arm around her shoulder and gave her a hug. Lize smiled at him.

'It's rabbit stew. Iris, get another plate out and give Granny a shout please.'

Louis looked around the kitchen; it was in a state of disarray. It was unlike Lize to be so disorganised.

'What's going on, Lize?'

'I wrote and told you, Louis. Didn't you get my letter?'

He thought for a moment and then realised that he hadn't opened it. He had been so preoccupied with events in his own life he had put it in a pocket weeks ago and forgotten about it.

'No, sorry, I forgot to open it. What did it say?'

'That Mum and I had bought a little shop, right near where you live and that we are taking possession from the end of this week. Exciting isn't it?'

'Is this a joke?'

'No, not a joke. We really are! That's what all the tea chests are for – we're on the move!'

'Well that's a surprise, I had no idea this was happening.'

'That's why I wrote to you, to let you know. We'll be living just around the corner from you Louis, isn't that lovely.'

'Yes. Yes, I suppose it is.'

'What's up? You don't sound very pleased.'

'Of course I'm pleased for you. It's just that…'

'What?'

'Well, you know Mum is rather critical of Cat and it's easier when there's a bit of distance between them. I can pop over on my own to see you without having to tread on eggshells.'

'Oh. Louis, I'm sure it's not as bad as that, is it? And in any case, I would have thought Cat could take care of herself.'

'It's not that easy, Lize. She tries hard to keep the peace and not say anything, but Mum can be very trying…'

'You don't have to tell *me* about it, Louis! I have to live with it day and night and there's no way out for me you know.' She sounded angry.

'Lize, I'm not criticising you. It's just that Cat has been so ill since the baby was born; she's just not up to it.'

'I've had children too, Louis, and had to get on with it.'

'I know, Lize, but I'm just saying that Cat is not in the best of health and I don't want Mum upsetting her.'

'Well, I thought you would have been pleased that Mum's going to be more occupied and will definitely not have time to make social calls, so you needn't worry about *that*.'

Iris sat looking from her mother to Louis and he noticed the worried look on her face.

'Maybe we should discuss this another time,' he said and got up to leave.

'Aren't you staying after all then?'

'No, Lize, I've suddenly lost my appetite. Say hello to Mum for me, I must be off now,' and with that he strode out of the kitchen, down the hall and out through the front door.

He wished he didn't feel so angry with Lize. He'd given her the house long ago, no question about that, but in his hour of greatest need, he felt that they hadn't considered sharing even part of the profit of the sale with him.

He had intended asking his mother for a loan to buy the evening suit as the shops he had visited so far had told him they didn't do Easy Terms.

He strode down the path, mounted his bicycle and pedalled furiously away, cursing repeatedly.

'Dammit, dammit, dammit.'

36
Saturday – Woolwich
April 1921

On Saturday, Louis pawned his watch, cuff links and a gold brooch that had belonged to his grandmother in order to buy the much-needed evening suit. It would have to be second-hand he decided. He had never worn second-hand clothes in his life. But he had never been this poor. He determined to swallow his pride and take whatever he could in order to meet the deadline for his audition.

Solly Isaacs ran a little shop in Powis Street, selling all manner of uniforms, lounge suits and evening suits, mostly at affordable prices. Louis had always walked briskly past the shop, not wishing to make eye contact with anyone entering or leaving, as though the disgrace of buying second-hand clothes would embarrass them. He waited until he saw the shop was empty, took a deep breath, and went in.

Louis approached the counter where Solly was pinning up the hem on a pair of trousers. He waited patiently for Solly to serve him, though his instinct was to turn on his heels and go. But necessity drove him to wait until Solly could give him his undivided attention. Eventually, Solly put the trousers to one side and looked up at Louis.

'Now, Sir, vot is it you vont?' Solly smiled showing a row of evenly sized false teeth.

'Do you have any evening suits?'

'Vi, of course. Vee have many, but depends on how quick. You have long legs. May have to alter.'

Louis had not reckoned on this and went to check the time on his now vacant wrist.

'Do you have the time please?'

'Vell of course, but first we find the right vuns, yes?'

'No, I mean what *is* the time?'

'Oi, yoi yoi, vell,' Solly checked his fob watch, rubbed his cardigan over the watch face as it had misted up and told Louis it was just after two o'clock.

'Oh sweet Jesus, I need to get the suit now and if you would just show me a couple, I will do without the alterations, I really cannot spare the time.'

He was extremely anxious, knowing that if he waited for alterations he would never get to The Strand Palace Hotel by the appointed time. It would take him ages to cycle to London. He could, he supposed, go by train because if he got the job, he could afford that luxury. He would see how long this took before deciding.

'Here ve have vone, I sinks, dis vone, yes?'

Solly held up an evening suit that had clearly seen too many evenings, but the jacket looked about the right size and as Louis would be sitting down playing, he thought the short legs would not matter.

The price ticket on the sleeve wasn't as expensive as he had expected, which meant he could afford to go to London by train.

'Yes. Yes I'll take it.'

'Oi yoi yoi, best try goods before buy, yes?'

'I'm sorry, I don't have time. I have to be in London for an audition and I may miss it if I don't leave soon.'

'Don't vorry, time is plentiful, better to get right, uddervise you be angry vis me and say I cheat you, yes?'

Solly took the jacket off the hanger and handed it to him.

Louis could see Solly was determined he should try it on, so feeling it was better to get on with it and save time arguing, he tried the jacket on.

'It's fine. Yes I'll take it.'

'Oi yoi yoi... yes now you put trousers on vid jacket, yes?'

'Oh Good Heavens, I really don't have time for this.'

'Yes, behind curtain plis,' Solly said, pulling aside the faded velvet curtain to reveal a makeshift dressing room. He smiled at Louis, making little waving gestures with his hands to hurry him into the dressing room.

Louis sighed as he discovered the trousers were about two inches above his ankles, even if he pulled the trousers down past his waist. He knew they were really not long enough and showed too much of his socks. Frustrated, he peeked round the curtain and beckoned for Solly to take a look.

'Oi yoi yoi, this trouser has disagreement vid your shoes. Too short. Try more.'
Desperately, he pleaded with Solly, 'I *really* don't have time. Can't you just let them down for me, you needn't even sew them?'

Solly scratched the side of his nose and looked at Louis. 'Important huh?'

'Yes, *very* important. I really have to get to London.'

'Vell, take trousers off, I slit hems and you take vid you. Come back Monday and I sew. Yes?

'Yes, anything, just put the suit in a bag. Thank you.'

Outside the shop, Louis checked the time on the clock tower and realised he had no time to pedal back to Eltham and change, so decided he would go directly to Woolwich Station, change into the evening suit in the toilets and catch the train to Charing Cross. He checked the station clock and felt that with luck he could just make it to the hotel in time.

Louis left his bicycle and old clothes in the Left Luggage place at Woolwich Station before boarding the next train to London.

Sitting in the carriage he suddenly realised with horror that he'd left his violin at home! He felt the familiar shaking begin and sweat broke onto his skin as he sat wondering what to do. He decided he would get off at the next station and cycle to his house, collect the violin, then cycle back and catch an onward train to London.

As the train pulled in at the next station, he opened the carriage door, jumped down onto the platform and walked briskly out of the station. The guard blew a whistle and the train moved off.

Outside the station, Louis stopped dead as it dawned on him that he had left his bicycle in Woolwich, and the train that would have taken him to London in time for the audition had just pulled out!

Louis returned to the railway platform and slumped down on an empty bench. A feeling of hopelessness swept over him. His nerves were in shreds and the trembling had not stopped.

A porter seeing him look so unwell sauntered towards him.

'You alright mate?'

'Yes. Thank you, I'll be fine in a moment.'

'Well you don't look alright. Look as if you could do with a hot cup of tea.'

'I'll be myself again in a few minutes. It's nothing really, result of being gassed in the war.'

'Oh I see. Yers, I was out there meself. Lucky to be alive I'd say. How about that cup of tea then?'

'No. Thanks all the same. When's the next train to Charing Cross?'

'One along in about ten minutes Gov.'

'I'll just sit here and wait for it. Thanks for the offer anyway.'

'No trouble Gov'. Us vet'rans gotta stick togevver.' He cocked his head sideways, winked at Louis and wandered into the ticket office, closing the door behind him. The hands on the station clock moved towards six and Louis sat like a coiled spring waiting for the next train.

At ten minutes to seven, as Louis ran towards the doors of The Strand Palace Hotel, a doorman stepped forward and asked if he could help him.

'I've got an audition with the orchestra.'

'Have you indeed.' He looked Louis up and down. 'And whom do you wish to meet?'

'Mr. Andrews. He's expecting me.'

'Wait here,' the doorman said, and went inside the hotel.

Louis' nerves were jangling, but when the man re-appeared and told him to enter the foyer, he quickly flicked a comb through his hair, feeling hopeful.

There was no sign of Mr. Andrews inside, so he went to the receptionist and asked where he was. She said she would make enquiries if he would care to take a seat in the foyer and wait.

She left the reception desk, went across the foyer and disappeared behind a half-glazed door. After a little while she re-appeared, followed by Mr. Andrews.

Louis stood up, smiled and lifted his hand to shake Roland Andrews', but dropped it when he saw the look on his face. Roland Andrews was within six inches of Louis' face when he hissed at him.

'What time do you call this?'

'I'm sorry; I've had a few problems. I got delayed.'

Roland Andrews frowned at Louis and poked him in the chest with his index finger.

'When I say be here at six o'clock, I mean six o'clock on the dot. Not five past six, or quarter past or even half past and certainly not ten minutes to seven!' He stepped back and eyed Louis up and down.

Louis saw the look of derision on his face. He was acutely aware as he stood there in an ill-fitting evening suit, the trousers of which were flying at half-mast up his shins, that he must have looked ridiculous. Though Solly has slit the stitching on the hems, the material had crept back naturally to the original fold line leaving a distinctly large gap between his ankles and the bottom of the trousers.

'A sorry sight you look young man. And where's your instrument?'

'I forgot it.'

'You *forgot* it? You *forgot* it?' Roland Andrews shook his head. 'No. I'm sorry. We want reliable chaps in our orchestra, not people who just turn up when they think they will. The auditions finished twenty minutes ago and we've taken on a violinist who was here on time.'

Louis could not speak. His mouth opened, and then shut.

Roland Andrews turned away, but just before he disappeared through the door he turned to Louis.

'*If* you are ever fortunate enough to be given an audition by anyone again, for God sake buy yourself a pair of trousers that fit!'

37
Eltham
Saturday Evening – April 1921

The return journey to Woolwich was slow and depressing, so after collecting his bicycle from the station, Louis still had the long ride home to Eltham.

Eventually he arrived at the house, but no longer having his watch, had no idea of the time – except it must be well into the evening as it was very dark.

As he opened the gate he could see by the light of his bicycle lamp that someone was sitting on the doorstep, but he couldn't make out who it was in the gloom.

'Hello there, can I help you?'

From the doorstep, a large man uncoiled and stepped forward. 'Hello Louis, ''tis only me, Michael.'

'Oh Good Lord, Michael, what on earth are you doing here at this time of night?'

''Tis a long story Louis. Mind if I come in for a while?'

'Of course not,' Louis smiled, glad of the company. Just wait there a minute and I'll put my bike away.'

Louis wheeled the bicycle to the back of the house and returned to open the front door.

'What brings you here, Michael? Is anything wrong?'

Michael followed Louis inside and waited while he lit the oil lamp.

''Tis freezin'' in here Louis, will I light the fire?'

Louis didn't answer, so Michael asked again.

'I said, shall I light the fire Louis?'

But instead of waiting for a reply, Michael then burst out laughing. 'God above Louis, will ye look at the sight of ye. What in God's name have you got on there altogether? Is it a fancy dress costume?'

Louis sighed and sat down at the table.

'Sit down Michael, it's rather a long story. If you've got the time to listen that is.'

He proceeded to tell Michael all about it; how he had gone busking to earn some money; was spotted by Roland Andrews and offered an audition; how he had fallen out with Lize and had to pawn some things to buy an evening suit, and finally how he lost the chance of playing in the orchestra.

'So there you have it, Michael. I have an evening suit but no job and no money. I dread to think what Cat will say when she finds out.'

Michael grinned.

'Does she have to know?'

Louis shot him a glance.

'What do you mean, deceive her?'

Michael drew in his breath and sighed.

'It depends which way ye look at it Louis. On the one hand ye could say ye were foolin' her by not tellin' her, and sure enough that would be deception. But on the other hand, if by not tellin' her, ye were savin' her feelings, ye know, sparin' her the worry like – then that would be a kinder thing to do, would it not?'

'Put like that Michael, it certainly sounds kinder not to tell her. I wouldn't want her to be distressed and maybe she need not know.'

Then it occurred to him that Michael had not explained why he was there at all, so he asked him. Michael shifted on the chair a little and looked embarrassed, then began to tell *his* tale of woe to Louis.

'I was out on the town last night and unfortunately I had a little too much to drink, so to speak. Anyway the long and the short of it is, my landlady has thrown me out and I've nowhere to go.' He began picking dirt from beneath his fingernails.

'Louis, I hope you won't mind, but could I maybe bed down here for tonight and tomorrow I'll look for somewhere to stay?'

'Of course you can Michael, whatever are you thinking of looking for somewhere? You can have Ellie's room now she has to sleep in at her job. And in any case, you'll be doing me a favour, I could use the company.'

'Ah ye're a grand fella, Louis. I knew I could count on ye.'

'Stay as long as you like, Michael. The only thing is, to be honest I can't afford to feed you. The truth is I'm flat broke, apart from the money I have saved to go to your wedding and bring Cat and the children back here.'

'Don't ye worry about a thing Louis, all I ask is for a bed and I'll be no trouble. Ye'll hardly know I'm here.'

'There's no need to creep about Michael, make yourself completely at home. The problem is it isn't much like home right now. I've rather let things go.'

''Tis not a problem, Louis. Here now, I'll light us a fire and we can have a little natter about life.'

'Sorry, Michael, there's no coal. I've completely run out and don't have enough money to buy any.'

Michael looked surprised.

'Don't ye worry, I know where I can get some, *unofficial,* like.'

Louis looked concerned. 'I don't want you stealing on my account, Michael.'

'Well Louis, it depends on the way ye look at it. On the one hand ye have served this country well, away fightin' an' all that and what have ye to show for it? Not much at all. There's plenty o' rich people. Lazy rich people who have never shifted off their backsides in the whole of their lives, let alone fight for the King and country like ye've done.

'So, I put it to ye Louis. Are ye not entitled to a bit of a helpin' hand when some folks have more than their share and wouldn't even notice a tiny little bucket of coal going to an ex-soldier? Believe me Louis, ye deserve better than the cards life's dealt ye.'

Louis thought for a moment. 'But what on earth would Cat think, knowing we have stolen coal in the house?'

'It depends which way ye look at it Louis. As I said before about yer little escapade with the pawnshop and the evenin' suit. On the one hand ye could say ye were foolin' her by not tellin' her, and maybe ye would be foolin' her. But on the other hand, by not tellin' her ye could save her feelings, and that would be the kinder thing to do.

''Tis a question of perception at the end of the day. In most of life's situations I always sit down and ask meself these questions: who will get hurt by knowin' and how can I save their feelin's?'

Louis grinned. 'You certainly have a way of telling it Michael.'

'Well, that's settled then. No more qualms. Let Michael Nagle melt yer worries away. Now, is there a drink in the house?'

38
Monroe, Fethard
April 1921

'Didn't Ellie look wonderful yesterday, Louis?' Cat said, 'd'ya know, it doesn't seem five minutes since we were married ourselves, does it?'

Louis watched her as she bent over the table ironing Marie's white smock, and felt a swell of emotion seeing her small frame moving rhythmically. He walked over and stood behind her as she ironed and placed his hands on her thin shoulders. He kissed the nape of her neck then wrapped his arms around her, hugging her tight. He noticed that she had not managed to put back on any flesh since he'd left Ireland a couple of months before, despite Maeve's cooking. He thought she still looked pale and drawn.

Cat put the iron on its stand. 'That feels good Louis, I've missed ye.'

'Cat, I'm worried about you.'

'What on earth for?'

'You still don't look very well.' He studied her face. 'I think you should see a doctor when we get home.'

'Ah ye worry too much. I'm just tired all the time, that's all. Even after a good night's sleep, I feel worn out the next day; ye'd think I hadn't been to bed at all. I'll be fine. Summer's on its way. Don't fret yerself.'

'But I do worry. I don't think you've recovered from having Eileen yet, and I'm concerned that once back home, without the help of your mother and sisters, you'll find everything too much for you. Don't forget Ellie's not going to be around to help you.'

'No. I haven't forgotten. I wish she wasn't goin' to America. I think it's a foolhardy thing to do. They don't even know whether Michael will find any work, and they've nowhere to live. I know they'll go to his sister's initially, but they can't stay there forever can they?'

'No. But it's their choice Cat, and they are set on going. What I'm really worried about is *you* getting your strength back. It's a pity we can't afford to have someone to come in and help you, but without me working regularly, it's not possible at present.'

'Louis?'

'Yes?'

'There may be a temporary solution.'

'Oh and what's that?'

'Peggy and Breda have said that if we wanted to leave Marie here, they'd love to have her for a while. They said they wouldn't want a penny to keep her and we can leave her as long as we like. Marie has taken to them both a lot, in fact most days I don't see her at all.'

Louis went over to sit by the fire and began turning the bellow's wheel. The fire glowed and he threw on some peat. He took out a packet of cigarettes, lit one, and blew the smoke up the chimney.

'I should give up smoking. It's a silly expense when we can't even afford to live.'

Cat picked up the iron to finish smoothing out a smock before speaking again.

'Well, Louis what do ye think of the idea?'

'What me packing up smoking?'

'No! About Marie stayin' here for a bit?'

'I'm not sure. Let me sleep on it. It's a bit sudden isn't it?'

'Not really, they mentioned it to me weeks ago. I just haven't been able to discuss it with ye not bein' here and all.'

'I'll mull it over Cat. It would help for a while until you are strong again wouldn't it?'

'Yes. And there's no-one I'd rather leave her with than me sisters.'

'It would give your mother someone to concentrate on once Ellie leaves too, especially with us all going back to England. I suppose it would ease things for her if Marie stayed. It must be hard her daughters and grandchildren all leaving at about the same time.'

'I wasn't goin' to say anythin' but she may be havin' another grandchild this year.'

Louis drew on his cigarette, watching the smoke rise up the chimney. Then he looked across at Cat, suddenly curious.

'Promise ye won't say anythin' until it's announced?'

'Well, of course. But who are we talking about?'

'Mary! Mary and Daniel! She thinks she is expectin' a baby.'

'There you are then, more children for Maeve to dote on, and Ned too.'

'So ye'll think on it then, leavin' Marie here?'

'I will.'

May 1921, Fethard Railway Station

Cat leaned out of the railway carriage as the boat train prepared to leave. 'Don't forget now Ellie, write as soon as ye set sail next week. Let me know all about the journey, and just as soon as ye get there, send a telegram to say ye're alright, won't ye?'

'Cat?'

'Yes, darling'?'

'I love ye dearly and don't ye ever forget it.'

'Ah, mo chuisle, don't. Ye'll have me cryin' all over again. Oh dear. I wish ye weren't goin' so far. Will I ever see ye again?'

'Don't, Cat. Please don't make it any harder. We've booked the crossin' now and this time next week we'll be on our way. It breaks my heart to go. But I promise if I hate it, I'll be back knockin' on yer door.'

'Ellie, promise me. If America doesn't work out, if at any time ye're not happy, ye'll write and let me know won't ye? I mean, don't let Mummy know, she'll only worry, but I can take it. Promise?'

''Tis ye I went to when Jimmy died, and 'tis ye I'd turn to first again.'

'Any time. Any place. My door and my heart are open to ye. And I pray for the day we meet again.'

The two women hugged each other as tears poured down their cheeks. Ellie stepped back then to let Peggy, who was holding Marie, kiss Cat goodbye.

'Say goodbye to Mummy,' Peggy coaxed Marie, 'and Cat, don't ye worry at all about her. She'll be grand, ye'll see. Just get yerself fit and strong now and we'll see ye in the summer.'

Ned and Maeve bade a tearful farewell to Cat, Louis, Billy and Eileen. The whistle blew and the train slowly moved out of the station, picking up speed.

39
Eltham
May 1921

'Jesus, Louis, will ye look at the state of these sheets! Did ye never change the bed while I'm away?'

'Well of course I did! But I was out every day looking for work, you know that, and besides I couldn't get that old copper to work.'

'That's no excuse. How d'ye think I'll get them from grey to white now?'

'Oh come on Cat, it's not the end of the world. I'll change them now and tomorrow we'll sort out what to do with them. It's late, let's get the children to bed, it's been a long journey.' Louis went to put his arm around her, but she pushed him away and began to cry.

''Tis all I need, comin' home to the place lookin' like this. Look at the sink, 'tis filthy! And look at the dirt on that tablecloth! Disgusting! What's been goin' on here, Louis? Did ye ever do any cleanin' up at all?'

'Cat, I did my best, but as I said, there didn't ever seem any time left at the end of the day to turn round and start housework.'

'Well how do ye think I manage then?'

'You have all day to do it.'

As soon as he had made the remark he regretted it, because the first thing he felt after saying it, was a loaf of bread Maeve had given them, hitting the side of his head.

'Take that ye swine!'

'Cat!' Louis shouted. 'What's got into you?'

Billy began to cry and Louis sat on a chair drawing the child onto his lap.

'See what you've done now?' Louis rocked him back and forth. 'There, don't cry, Mummy didn't mean it.'

'Mummy *did* mean it,' Cat yelled, 'and what's more, Mummy *will* mean it tomorrow when ye get up off yer backside and wash those sheets.'

Louis, bristling with annoyance, put Billy down, picked up the luggage and took it into the bedroom. He sat on the bed wondering what on earth Cat's mood was all about. He and Michael had cleaned the place thoroughly before they'd left and though he hadn't changed the beds for a couple of weeks, he hadn't thought they looked *that* dirty.

The following morning Louis lay awake listening to Cat move about cooking and then she called to him.

'Breakfast is on the table, Louis.'

'Righto. Thanks,' he called and appeared in the doorway in his pyjamas. 'I was going to get you some, but you've beaten me to it.'

He smiled at her, but she looked away and went to pick up Eileen and feed her. At the sight of her breast, Louis felt the urge to rush over to her, push the baby aside and kiss her.

Cat saw the look on his face and turned her back to him.

Louis felt a dull thud in his stomach and didn't know what was going on. Cat had never behaved like this before and he wasn't sure what to say or do. He sat at the table and ate the bread Maeve had sent, albeit a little broken, and drank his tea. Not a word passed between them and all that could be heard in the room was the baby suckling at Cat's breast.

Billy appeared in the room and asked for his breakfast, so Louis passed him a plate with bread and poured him some tea.

'Where's Granny and Granddad, Daddy?' Billy asked stuffing his mouth with bread.

'In their own house in Ireland. You know that,' Louis said ruffling his hair.

'I want Granny.'

'We'll see her soon when we go for a holiday. Granny and Granddad live a long way away don't they? We'll get on the train and then the big boat in the summer.'

Billy nodded, but wasn't content.

'I want Granny and Granddad to come to my house,' he said looking at Cat. 'Mummy, can you make them come here?'

'No, Pet. They live over the water; and we are here with a man that cannot wash sheets!'

'Oh *Cat*,' Louis said throwing down his knife, 'how can you stoop so low; dragging a child into the dispute?'

He stood up and wiped his mouth with the back of his hand.

'Come on now; let's finish this here and now. What's got into you? You've done nothing but snap my head off since we came home.'

Cat began to weep and then the baby started crying too. Then Billy, sensing the atmosphere between his parents, began howling as well.

'Oh hell, what a household!' Louis shouted. 'I'm getting ready to go and look for work now, but before I go I want to see order settle back here, do you understand?' he demanded.

'Oh yes sir. No sir. Three bags full sir,' Cat spat out sarcastically, 'remember Billy, we're in the army now!'

'Cat, I'm warning you. Don't drag Billy into things. If there's something wrong, tell me. Don't use the child.'

She didn't answer him, but stood up and silently put the baby in her cot then began clearing the dishes.'

Feeling exasperated, Louis went into the bedroom, dressed and left the house, thinking that perhaps she'd get it out of her system by the time he returned.

* * *

It was dark when Louis returned home and Cat had prepared boiled bacon and potatoes they had brought back with them from Ireland. She put the meal on the table and told Louis to sit and eat.

Sitting down opposite him she began cutting up her meat, glancing from time to time at Louis.

She saw his drawn expression and dark circles under his eyes and thought he looked exhausted. Suddenly she felt ashamed of her outburst that morning.

'Is the meal alright Louis?'

'Yes, it's fine, thank you. The meat's nice isn't it?'

''Yes 'Tis.' She continued cutting her meat then looked across the table at him. 'Louis?'

'Yes?'

'I'm sorry. I don't know what came over me this morning.'

Louis put down his knife and fork and looked at her gently. He realised she was worn out and this is what he had been afraid of, but he felt helpless. They could not afford help and having three children in quick succession had been too much for Cat. He understood that but felt he couldn't do much about it unless he was to earn a fortune and employ a nanny. Both things he knew were totally out of the question.

'Cat, I know you are tired, but taking it out on me isn't going to help.'

'I know. It's not just the tiredness.'

'Then what is it?' he asked placing his hand on hers and giving it a squeeze.

'I'm lonely.'

He pushed the plate aside. 'Cat, tell me about it.'

'It's just that I want to go home, Louis.' She bent her head as tears slid down her cheeks.

Louis withdrew his hand, lowered his eyes and feared the worst.

'So that's what the outburst was really about last night?'

She didn't answer.

'Cat, I'm asking you, is that what was behind last night's row?'

'Louis, I don't know what to say. I feel isolated here. I hardly know anyone an' I've none of my family around me, and now Ellie's gone—'

She couldn't finish. The lump in her throat silenced her and Louis just stared at the floor, lost for words.

40
Eltham
June 1921

Louis left the house daily in search of work, but the queues at the Labour Exchange were depressingly long. There were always hundreds of men after so few jobs. Those prepared to take the lowest pay succeeded in being given work.

He was in the process of slipping out of the house one morning with his violin tucked under his arm when Cat questioned him about this. He brushed it off, saying he was hoping a job may come up that day playing in an orchestra.

Cat thought no more of it and began the daily task of baking bread, washing, and cleaning the house.

It was a beautiful June day and feeling full of energy she decided to tidy the outhouse at the back and re-arrange things as the mangle was in an awkward place. She began pulling out all the contents and laying them in the yard and before putting everything back, washed the floor over and then finally heaved the mangle to a new position.

Glancing up at the ceiling in the outhouse, she saw a package wedged into the eaves so poked it with a broom until it fell to the floor.

She picked it up and squeezed it. It felt soft. Cat went inside, found some scissors, cut the string and unfolded the paper. Inside was a neatly folded evening suit. She shook out the garments and inspected them, wondering who they belonged to. It could not have been any previous occupant of the house because they were the first to live there. It was a mystery how it came to be there and she decided to show Louis when he came home.

That night when Louis returned from job-hunting, Cat put their evening meal on the table and they sat down to eat. She asked him if he'd had any luck, but he said he had not.

Cat dug her fork into a potato and looked at him.

'So the musician's job didn't materialise after all?'

'No. I'll try again tomorrow.'

'What makes ye think there will be such a job tomorrow?'

'I don't mean the musician's job. I will try for another. There's talk a factory on the other side of the water are looking for men so if I leave early, I may be luckier.'

'Yes, that sounds like a good idea to me.'

When she had eaten her meal Cat put her knife and fork together on her plate to wait for Louis to finish, then she remembered the suit.

'Oh by the way, I forgot to mention, I found a parcel in the outhouse today, pushed up into the eaves.'

'Oh.' Louis said. He slid his plate aside and reached for his cigarettes.

'Well don't ye want to know what was in it?

'Not particularly.'

'Well 'twas the crown jewels and I'm goin' to pawn them tomorrow and buy meself a fur coat.'

'Oh.' His head bowed and he fiddled with his lighter unable to produce a flame.

'*Louis*! For the love of God, show a bit of interest will ye?'

'What do you want me to say?'

'I don't believe this man,' she said exasperated, 'I find a parcel in our outhouse, with a fine evening suit fit for a duke, and all ye can say is, Oh?'

'Is that what it was?'

'Yes indeed 'twas, but the mystery is how it got there.'

'I've no idea Cat. How do you think it got there?'

'Well that's what I'd like to find out.'

'Why the fuss?'

'Why the fuss? Well, if ye'd found it, not me, wouldn't ye want to know who it belonged to? After all I may be having a musician in the house while ye're out job-huntin'.'

'Now Cat you're being ridiculous. Just as if that would happen.'

'Funnier things have happened. Anyway, don't ye get off the subject!, D'ye have any idea how it got there?'

'Perhaps Michael put it there when he lived here.'

'Oh, I didn't think of that. But what would Michael be doin' with an evenin' suit?'

'I don't know, why don't you ask him?'

'How can I? He's in America.'

'Write and ask him whether he stuffed an evening suit into the roof of our out-house.

'Now ye're bein' ridiculous. Just as if I could go askin' him a thing like that. For sure if it was him and he hadn't told Ellie the reason behind stuffin' an evenin' suit out of sight, then maybe there's somethin' sinister behind it. No, I won't go writin' to him askin', it may upset them.'

She stood up, went to the bedroom, and then returned with the evening suit.

'Look at it Louis, 'tis quite a good one isn't it? Try it on, g'w'on.'

'Oh Cat, I couldn't.'

'Why ever not?'

'Because.'

'What?'

'It's not mine.'

''Tis now. C'mon, drop those pants and get these on and we'll see what a fine figure of a man ye cut in it.'

She wouldn't be deterred and began unbuttoning his jacket.

Feeling it would be better to get it over with, Louis stood and took his jacket off, then put the evening suit jacket on.

'Now the pants.'

'Oh come on Cat, this is stupid.'

''Tis not Louis. Just think of it. Say ye did manage to get a job playin' the violin, ye'd be already kitted out wouldn't ye? C'mon, get the pants on.'

Louis took off his trousers and pulled on the evening suit trousers.

'Step out here then Louis, I can't see, the table's in the way.'

He stepped away from the table and Cat let out such a roar of laughter it woke Eileen.

'Jesus, will ye take a look at the great impresario? Pants flyin' at half-mast.' Then she disappeared into the bedroom to quieten the baby. When she returned Louis had taken the evening suit off.

'Where's it gone?'

'I took it off.'

'Why?'

'You've had your bit of fun Cat, leave it at that.'

'Alright. But I'll let down the trousers for ye, so if ye get called to play in the London Philharmonic, ye'll be ready.'

Cat got up and began clearing the table laughing to herself every so often; while Louis stared out of the window feeling an absolute heel.

Next day Louis left the house by half past five and was one of the first in the queue at the Labour Exchange. Sure enough six jobs were on offer to men willing to travel to a bicycle factory in Brentford. It was assembly work, and Louis was picked for one of the jobs.

It would mean cycling to Woolwich; through the tunnel, and then all the way to Brentford in Essex, but it was *work* he thought.

Louis was out of bed like a lark the following morning; and left well before Cat and the children awoke. His one thought as he pedalled off into the dawn was that he could put some decent food on the table, and a little bit of money into the tin above the mantelpiece for *going home* to Ireland.

At this rate, if he was lucky enough to keep the job, he thought they could go home to see her folks in about two month's time. It made pedalling that distance worthwhile.

41
Eltham
July 1921

Louis was home earlier than expected one Friday afternoon and caught Cat unawares. She hurried to clear away material and the sewing machine he had bought her recently.

Cat was delighted with the machine and had begun making good use of it. It gave her a renewed sense of purpose as she had already taken in some orders for making curtains, and a couple of little girls' dresses.

She straightened up the new tablecloth she had made and asked Louis what he thought of it. But without answering her, he dropped into a chair looking depressed.

'What's up, ye look as though ye've lost a pound and found a penny.'

'I lost my job.'

'What? *Why*?'

He leaned forward, resting his elbows on the table, his head in his hands. 'They asked us to take a drop in money.'

'How much of a drop?'

'A penny an hour. But when we wouldn't agree, the boss said he had a line of men waiting outside the factory that would. So that was that. We were all out. *Sacked*!'

Cat went to him and put an arm around his shoulders. 'The bastards! God forgive me, but that's what they are, nothin' but bastards. They have ye exactly where they want ye. I hope to God they rot in hell. Ye're best out of it. The ride was too much for ye anyway.'

'Cat, what are we going to do?'

'Well one thing we're not goin' to do is sit here worryin'. It won't solve anythin'. Here now, get yer jacket off and bring in the bath, I've hot water ready for ye.'

He went to the outhouse and unhooked the tin bath then took it inside to the scullery. Cat filled it with hot water and added cold until it was ready for him.

'C'mon now off with those cacks and into the bath with ye.'

Louis took his trousers and shirt off, then slid into the water. 'I'm sorry, Cat. I *really* am.'

'Ah get away with ye. We'll survive. We have before and we will again. Ye'll see. I've some orders in to make a few things, so I'll be earning a bit too.'

'You shouldn't need to work, you've got enough to do.'

'Why don't ye ask yer mother if ye can work in her shop?'

He didn't answer immediately, but began soaping himself all over and then rinsed it off.

Cat sat on a chair watching the water glisten on his body. Something stirred inside her, a mixture of desire, pity and love. He didn't deserve this humiliation.

'I *would* ask her. But not unless I'm desperate, Cat. She has a way of making me feel I should work for her but not expect to be paid. I don't really want to be put in that position. In any case, I shouldn't think the shop could support paying Lize and me. No, I'll go back on the treadmill on Monday, looking for work. We'll see what turns up.'

He looked up at her and smiled and she dropped to her knees and kissed him as he sat in the tub, looking forlorn.

On Monday morning Louis left the house and had pedalled off on his bicycle before Cat could wave him off. She got Billy ready for a trip to the market in Woolwich where she planned to buy material for dresses she had agreed to make. Her neighbour had agreed to look after Eileen.

On the tram to Woolwich, Billy busied himself chanting nursery rhymes and Cat was free to concentrate on him alone for once. Today was going to be like a little outing, she told him, and if he was a really good boy she would buy him an ice cream from the nice Italian man in the market square.

When the tram turned into the square in Woolwich, Cat then stood up and held onto the overhead straps, craning her neck above the other passengers to see if it was raining. Satisfied that it wasn't she stepped down onto the running board. When it stopped, she caught hold of both Billy's hands and swung him off the tram, laughing as she did this.

'Again, Mummy.'

'No darlin', we can't keep at it all day, we've shoppin' to buy.'

They went along Powis Street and into a haberdashery shop where Cat bought material. Then they retraced their steps towards the market and she bought some meat in the butchers.

They were making their way towards the fruit and vegetables when Cat saw a small crowd had gathered and heard the sound of someone playing a violin. The music was wonderful and it reminded her of the time in Fethard when Louis had played Breda's violin outside Monroe one evening. In fact, she decided it sounded like the same Intermezzo he had played and her heart stirred with nostalgia.

She listened for a while, and then aware Billy was beginning to fidget, reluctantly decided to move on. Edging her way around the outside of the crowd, Cat glanced back to see who was playing so beautifully. What she saw through a gap between the people was none other than Louis!

She stood absolutely still. Her face flushed with anger. How could he? *Begging*! And right on our own doorstep too! What if people knew them?

Fury propelled Cat through the crowd, dragging Billy behind her. She positioned herself in the front row and as Louis came to the end of his piece and passed his cap round, gathering up the pennies, he saw Cat turn and disappear through the crowd.

She jumped straight on a tram to Eltham, dragging Billy behind her.

Billy's feet hardly touched the ground as she marched from the tram stop to home. All the way he had cried, as he hadn't had his ice cream.

Louis sheepishly opened the front door later and was met with chaos. Clothes were everywhere and Cat was furiously throwing items into a trunk.

'What's going on?'

'Huh! Ye may well ask. Should be me I'da thought, askin' that question. Beggin' indeed! There right in the middle of Woolwich with the entire world to see!'

Louis sat down and asked her again, 'What's going on, what are all those clothes?'

'I'm goin' home and this lot is goin' on ahead of me.'

'What do you mean, you're going home?'

'Exactly what I say!. I'm goin' home. Ye needn't think I'm goin' to sit around here and watch me husband goin' out beggin' each day. The *disgrace* of it! I'd rather go out and scrub steps meself than see ye doin' that.'

'Cat. Cat,' he moaned, 'come on now it's not begging, it's called busking.'

'Whichever way ye look at it Louis, ye were beggin', and it's the biggest disgrace ever. I don't know how ye could do it. Anyone could have seen ye. Anyone!'

'I couldn't get any work and I've made this.' He emptied his pocket onto the table and counted it. 'Ten and eleven pence,' he said, 'I couldn't have earned that in that bike factory, could I?'

Cat looked at the piles of pennies then at Louis and said nothing.

'It's not what I would choose to do but I'm not skilled in any particular trade. Playing the violin is the only talent I have.'

'Huh! So, how often have ye done this before then?'

'Well, once. I would probably have had a regular job at The Strand Palace Hotel if I hadn't missed the audition?'

'Audition? What audition?'

'I had an audition, but I missed it.'

'When was that?'

'A while back when you were in Ireland, after Eileen was born.'

'So how did this audition come about then?'

Louis licked his lips. He realised that in telling her about the audition she may now find out about him busking in London too.

Before he had a chance to answer though, Cat's puzzled frown disappeared and she began shouting.

'Oh I *see* now. Ye went buskin' or beggin' while I was away too!'

Then as if she suddenly realised something else she became quiet.

'Cat, come on now it's not worth causing a row over, is it?'

Silently, Cat folded and packed more clothes until the room was clear. She pulled out the sewing machine and finished off the dresses she was making; put them in a bag and left the house to deliver them.

Louis hoped that when she returned later she would be in a better frame of mind, but though she seemed calmer when she came back, he realised she was determined to carry out her threat.

Cat continued packing and when all the clothes were inside the trunk and she had locked it, she turned to Louis and asked if he would have her trunk picked up and sent ahead.

'So you're going after all?'

She didn't look up. 'That evenin' suit belonged to ye all along didn't it?'

42
Fethard
July 1921

Mary was sitting on a garden chair beneath the shade of a tree when Cat arrived with the children. She looked surprised and attempted to get up, but Cat told her to remain where she was.

'Cat, 'tis lovely to see ye and the children. I didn't know ye'd arrived. Mummy said ye were coming home, but wouldn't tell me when. She's kept it as a surprise.'

'Ye're supposed to be resting Mary, don't get up, stay there, I'll make us a cup of tea. Make the most of it Mary, for when the baby arrives, ye'll find ye'll never get much chance to be waited on.'

'Ye're the best Cat. C'mon now Billy, give yer auntie Mary a big kiss, and ye too Marie.' She held her arms open and the children dutifully stepped forward and kissed her. Cat turned and walked towards the house to make tea and Mary watching her retreat thought she looked pale and sad. She sat talking to the children until Cat re-appeared with a tray.

'Where's Daniel?' Cat asked as she set it down on the garden table.

'He's up at his mother's place; she's bad again with her chest, poor soul.'

'Ah, that's tough,' Cat said pouring the tea, 'She should move away from that side of the mountain, it's far too damp if ye have chest trouble.' She handed a cup to Mary.

'Thanks, Cat,' Mary said taking the tea, 'ye're right an' we keep tryin' to get her to come an' live nearer, but she won't. She wants to stay on that old mountain until she goes out in a box she says. Ah, well I guess ye can understand it.'

Cat raised her eyebrows and grimaced.

Mary continued. 'She's been there her entire life.'

Billy walked over to the table and took a biscuit.

'Billy!' Cat raised her voice. 'Ye ask Auntie Mary if ye may have one. Now put it back.'

Billy returned the biscuit to the plate and stood glaring at his mother.

'Well, are ye goin' to ask nicely?'

'Don't want one.'

'Oh ye little devil. C'mon now and we'll give ye one if ye just say, please may I have a biscuit, Auntie!'

Before Billy had time to make his request, Mary's hands began to shake and she asked Cat to take the cup from her. All colour drained from her face and her lips turned blue. She wiped her face with her handkerchief and began gasping for air.

Alarmed, Cat jumped to her feet. 'Jesus, Mary and Joseph, what's goin' on? Can I get ye something?'

'Water, just water.' Mary gasped for air.

Cat rushed into the house, poured water from a jug and hurried back to Mary who had recovered her colour a little. She took the water; swallowed some and gave the glass back to Cat.

'Thanks, Cat.'

'Lord save us us, Mary. Ye gave me a fright. What's happenin'?'

Mary shifted her weight in the chair and shivering, drew her shawl round her shoulders.

''Tis cold out here, Cat, shall we go inside now?' She held up her hand for Cat to pull her from the chair. 'I'm a fat ole lump aren't I?'

As Cat held her hand she could feel Mary's felt clammy and trembling.

'Let's get ye inside,' Cat said looking across the garden where she saw Billy was playing happily on the lawn with Marie. Eileen was sitting on a blanket watching them, so Cat helped her sister to a sofa in the lounge. After Mary was settled she asked Cat to sit with her.

'Cat, did ye ever feel as though a little bird was flutterin' in yer chest when ye were expectin' the children?'

Cat didn't want to alarm her, but she couldn't say she had. 'Well, what does the little bird feel like?'

'I feel this little flutterin' begin, and then my heart pounds like a racehorse. 'Tis as though I'm suffocatin' and I'm afraid I'll not be able to draw my next breath.'

'So, it's happened before then?'

'Oh yes, quite often actually. I expect 'tis normal though isn't it?'

Cat sat down next to her and took Mary's hand, stroking it affectionately. A little time elapsed.

'So what does Daniel say about this little bird fluttering?'

'He doesn't know. I don't want to worry him, Cat. Havin' a baby is the most normal thing in the world an' he's enough worry on his shoulders with his mother. I don't want to bother him.'

'Mary, I think ye should tell Daniel. He's a doctor and maybe he can put yer mind at rest. Ye have to see if it's normal or not. I don't think I ever experienced anythin' like this, but if ye tell him and he says 'tis normal, then normal it is. Promise me ye'll tell him when he comes home.'

Mary looked at her wide-eyed. 'Ye're frightenin' me now, Cat.'

'Ah, c'mon Mary. Ye'll do fine. But ye have to check this out. I think ye should go on up to bed and rest for the afternoon now.'

'But ye've only just arrived.'

'Don't worry. I'll be here for a bit. I'm on a little holiday.'

'Oh that's nice, Cat. Is Louis with ye?

'No.' Cat looked away.

'Is he comin' over soon?'

'I don't know exactly.' She continued to avert her face, staring out of the window, but her eyes filled with tears.

Mary reached over to her and placed her hand on Cat's and gave it a squeeze.

'Ah Cat. Ye've not fallen out have ye?'

Unable to answer, Cat continued to stare out of the window. Then she saw Billy and Marie having a tussle on the lawn so she jumped up quickly without answering and rushed outside to break up the fight. She scolded Billy but he said Marie had started it by taking a biscuit.

Cat drew Marie onto her lap and realised that in the few months since she'd left her in Ireland she had grown almost as big as Billy. Something worried Cat though - she was aware there was strangeness between her and the child. She felt that this wasn't the child she had given birth to, and that Marie ranged somewhere in her affection equivalent to a niece.

It was a strange experience and Cat couldn't work out why she should feel this way towards her daughter. Eileen now felt far more like her own child than Marie. She put her down and, satisfied the children had resolved their quarrel, returned to Mary's lounge.

'Little devils, ye can't take yer eyes off them can ye?' She stared at Mary and thought she looked a lot better; her colour was normal and her lips were no longer blue. 'Mary, are ye goin' on up to bed to rest now?'

'Yes I s'ppose so. But, Cat. I asked ye a question and ye haven't answered me yet. I'll go once ye've answered me.'

Cat looked at her, 'Ye want to know whether Louis and I have quarrelled? Well, I don't want this to be general knowledge, Mary. If I tell ye in confidence, promise ye'll not say a word to Mummy, Dada, or anyone?'

'Of course, Cat. Ye know I'll not say a word to anyone, not even Daniel. How's that?'

Cat told Mary about the job situation, how they sacked men for the sake of a penny; the constant threat of no food and no money; Louis' pride in not asking his mother for a job in her shop; and how she had found him begging in the street.

But the biggest thorn in her flesh had been the fact he had lied to her.

'Wasn't it,' she asked Mary, 'the most important thing between husband and wife that they could trust each other, and have complete honesty?'

Mary listened without comment until Cat had finished speaking.

'Cat, we're none of us perfect. If we were to go through life without doin' one single thing wrong, then we'd all be saints, not sinners.' She leaned forward and plumped up the cushion behind her. 'Soften yer heart towards him Cat, he's a good man, and he's the one ye chose to spend yer life with, isn't he?'

Cat nodded.

'It sounds to me as though he was doin' nothin' more than tryin' to put food in yer mouths, without ye knowin' where the money came from. Is that so wrong?'

'But he lied to me Mary. He told such a fantastic lie about the evenin' suit. How could he?'

Mary reached out and took Cat's hand.

'Judge not, that ye be judged, Our Lord said Cat. C'mon now, why not write to him and ask him to come on over? We'll have a grand time. The harvest is nearly ready to get in. Maybe he can help Tom and Dada and at the same time get back some of his self-respect. Ye know a man likes to feel he's providin' for his family, however he does it.' Mary watched Cat's shoulders slacken and continued. 'Cat, don't put off until tomorrow, what could be done today. None of us know what life has in store for us and it's a waste of precious time holdin' on to anger. Ask yerself what ye'd have felt if he hadn't come back from the war!'

Cat looked down and fidgeted with the lace on her blouse as tears slid unchecked down her face.

'Ye'll forgive him won't ye Cat?'

Cat sat thinking about it, wrestling with her anger and hurt.

'C'mon Cat, ye know ye're head over heels in love with the man.'

'Ye're an old sage now aren't ye?' she said smiling at Mary. 'I'll write to him. Thanks a million, Mary. I'll tell Louis the reunion is down to you.'

'Ah well, ye know the old saying, May the roof over yer house never fall in and may those beneath it never fall out. Life's too short, Cat, and we never know what's around the corner.'

Mary paused as though remembering something and then continued. 'Cat, I have somethin' for ye and Louis. It was for yer wedding anniversary, but why wait? I'd've posted it but since ye're here, well, go over to the drawer there, it's wrapped in tissue paper.'

Cat went to the drawer, opened it and lifted out the package wrapped in tissue paper. She crossed the room and handed it to Mary. 'Is this what you mean?'

'Yes thanks, 'tis.' Mary looked at her. 'Now, I've two rosaries here. One is for ye and the other for Louis, but I want ye to have the pick. Ye choose Cat, either the red one or the white, I don't mind which.'

Cat unfolded the tissue, took the rosaries out and held them up, looking from one to the other. She chose the white one then re-wrapped the red and handed it back to Mary.

'Ye give it to Louis when he comes Mary. He'd like that, he really would.' Cat drew up a chair and sat next to her sister stroking her forehead. 'Thanks a million Mary, I'll treasure it knowin' ye bought it for me.'

Mary patted her hand, 'So, off ye go now and get that letter in the post today.'

43
Eltham
July 1921

Louis was wheeling his bicycle out of the front gate as the postman arrived with Cat's letter. He leaned his bicycle against the gatepost, took the letter from the postman and lit up a cigarette before tearing the envelope open. His hand trembled slightly as he held the paper and read Cat's letter.

My Dearest Louis,

I am writing to say I have thought over what has happened and decided I was partly in the wrong - and I am sorry.

I won't lead ye to believe I came to this decision alone, because that would be a deception, which was the basis of our problem in the first place.

I went to see Mary today, and she guessed that something was the matter between us. I have not told Mummy and Dada or anyone else we have quarreled, nobody knows - only Mary.

We had a chat and she made me realise that what ye did was not just a matter of deceiving me for the sake of it, but was a way of trying to earn money to feed us and keep the roof over our heads, while retaining your sense of pride.

I don't know why I couldn't see it that way at the time, but I do now, and I want ye to forgive my hastiness in running away like that. I did not give ye the opportunity to explain, and I know I would not listen to anything ye tried to say, but I hope ye can find it in your heart to forgive a foolish woman.

Louis, I hate us being apart. It was awful when ye were away during the war and I always expected that once it was over, we would never be apart again. This is not what I want, so won't ye please come on over and join us?

Dada and Tom will be getting the harvest in soon, and could use another pair of helping hands as a lot of the local lads have either gone to England or America looking for work. I think we've enough in the tin to pay for a ticket, especially with the money ye made playing the violin - so please come.

If ye send a telegram to the Post Office here, I will collect it. Just say either, ye can come over or ye cannot. No more than that, otherwise old Niamh McNamara will spread gossip; she has a nose as long as an elephant's trunk.

One thing I have come to realise is that good marriages are not achieved by chance; they have to be worked at. So, Louis, this leaves me wishing for the entire world I was there with ye and could let ye see that I am truly sorry.

Your loving wife
Cat xx

He folded the letter, put it in his jacket pocket, mounted his bicycle and rode off towards Woolwich.

Smiling to himself as he turned the corner of the road, he freewheeled down the hill, promising himself a lovely day busking in the market place.

44
Monroe, Fethard
July 1921

Louis was no stranger to the scythe and glad of the work, threw himself into it wholeheartedly. Ned and Tom were relieved as they were up against it trying to get the hay in on their own before rain spoiled it.

The fields looked glorious to Louis' eyes after the drabness of Eltham. Though busking meant he was out in the fresh air all day, he felt so much better working on the land.

He managed to discuss things about his busking and Cat finally agreed to him continuing with it. Louis' convincing argument came in the form of an example when they sat talking following his arrival in Fethard.

'After all,' he had said, 'you would make a dress for a sister and wouldn't charge her, but you would charge someone else. I play for nothing entertaining friends and family, but charge strangers for listening – it's the same principle.'

Louis convinced her and they agreed not to quarrel over it any more. He would carry on doing it for as long as it took until he managed to gain permanent work.

Louis saw a change in Ned. He thought he looked older; his movements seemed slower and he was inclined to stop what he was doing and stand about daydreaming.

Tom didn't stop telling Louis how grateful he was for his help as he said he was finding it impossible to cope under the circumstances. Most of the local youths had drifted overseas looking for work and those that were left behind were unable to help themselves, let alone others. The price of produce had dropped and they were working harder for less.

After the long days gathering the crops, Louis, Cat and the children usually ate a meal with Maeve, Ned and Tom and his wife Norah at Monroe, then strolled slowly back to O'Connell's hotel where they were staying with her Auntie Nellie.

One evening, just before the children went to bed, Louis was relaxing in the hotel bar with Mary's husband Daniel, and Cat brought the children to him to say goodnight. As the children were kissing Louis, the lounge door burst open and Peggy rushed in.

'Daniel!' she said breathlessly, 'Mary went into labour a while back. I couldn't find ye, so I've sent for Mrs. Morrisey, she's with her now.'

'But, she's not due yet,' Daniel replied looking puzzled.

'Well any fool can tell that! G'w'on off with ye,' Peggy said flopping down onto a chair.

Louis and Cat looked at each other, and then at Daniel, who finished his drink then gathered his jacket and bag together.

Cat stood up. 'Daniel, shall I come with ye?'

He nodded, 'Maybe come along in a little while once ye've put the children to bed, Cat.' He stooped to kiss the children standing before him. 'Yes,' he added, 'that'll be a good idea, thanks.'

After Daniel left, Peggy, Louis and Cat fell silent for a while before Cat spoke.

'Are ye thinkin' what I'm thinking?'

Louis sighed. 'Yes, probably. Sounds like history repeating itself doesn't it?' He picked up his glass and finished his drink. 'Better get the children settled down before ye go, Cat. It could be a long night.'

Peggy looked worried. 'I hope she doesn't go through what ye went through Cat. Though she has Mrs. Morrisey over there with her which is more than ye had at the time. I had better get back to the shop as I have to put Marie to bed. Let me know later how things are won't ye Cat?'

'Sure I will, but it won't be for a while yet I suppose.'

'No, I suppose not. Anyway, ye know where I am; just call me if ye need me, any time.'

After Peggy left, Cat and Louis went upstairs to put the children to bed, though Cat wanted to be away as quickly as possible.

Louis felt it would be better if she did not go because he was worried about her having the memory of her last birth resurrected, but she brushed aside the suggestion. He watched her prepare to leave.

'Cat?'

'Yes?'

'Last night was pretty special to me. I just hope you do not become pregnant again as a result.'

'Ah, Louis, 'tis not a worry of mine ye know.' She was pinning her hair up and turned to face him.

'But it would not be wise to have another baby, now or later.'

'Perhaps we should have thought of that before last night, my love.' She smiled at him, put the hairbrush down and crossed the room to fold her arms around his neck. 'Louis, c'mon now quit worrying. We can't stay celibate forever, 'tis just not possible. Ye only have to look at me and, well, ye know!'

'Cat. Cat. I don't want anything to happen to you, I was so frightened that night.'

'Nothin's goin' to happen to me. Nothin' at all.'

Louis looked down at her thinking how mischievous she seemed. He gave her a squeeze, and then playfully slapped her on the backside as she turned to finish her hair.

As she stood before the dressing table mirror, she watched him. He looked worried.

'I'll be here long after ye're pushin' up the daisies,' she laughed.

'Oh don't say that. I hate thinking about that sort of thing Cat. Maybe I saw too much of it in the war, but I can't bear to imagine us being parted by death, it's horrible.'

'C'mon then let's not think about it. 'Twon't happen.' She straightened her blouse and tucked it into the waistband of her skirt.

After checking the children were asleep, Cat told Louis she was ready to leave for Mary's house.

He was sitting by the window in the bedroom reading a book and she went over to him and from behind, put her arms around his neck, kissing the crown of his head.

'Don't wait up, I may be some time.'

He caught hold of her wrist and kissed the palm of her hand before she slipped quietly from the room and ran downstairs, emerging on to Main Street just as Breda arrived.

'Hello there Breda, where are ye off to?'

'I'm walkin' out to tell Mummy Mary's in labour. Ye're goin' over to Mary's, aren't ye?

'Yes.'

'Good. I hoped I'd catch ye before ye left. I'll walk part of the way with ye.' They fell into step walking a little quicker than normal, each anxious to get to their destinations.

Dusk diminished into nightfall, the country sounds subdued, so that church bell striking every half hour was all that could be heard. Midnight came and went followed by the early hours preceding dawn. Mary made little progress and was showing signs of exhaustion, so Daniel had to send for Dr. Murray as he was unable to tend to her himself.

Daniel and Cat slipped outside the house and strolled in the garden at around three in the morning leaving 'Old Murray' to minister to Mary.

They both felt the atmosphere in the bedroom was oppressive. Daniel had become irritated with Doctor Murray who had exchanged several cross words with both Mrs. Morrisey and himself.

'Why on Earth won't he just retire and let me take over the practice?' Daniel complained to Cat. 'His methods are antiquated and I feel my more up-to-date training would be far more effective. He's out of touch and would be better as a horse doctor.'

Cat smiled, though she was beginning to feel very anxious. 'I'm worried she's gettin' awful tired, Daniel.'

'Yes, that's what I mean. He won't listen and let me give her somethin' to help the birth along. I have some medicine in my bag which would mean it could be all over and done within an hour.'

'What is it ye have?'

'Somethin' most girls that get into trouble would pay a lot of money for.'

'Oh. Not somethin' dangerous is it?'

'Can be in the wrong hands. It's a derivative of Ergot, not commonly used by all, as it can be disastrous, but I have a little and wouldn't hesitate to use it now if necessary.'

'What's that when it's at home?'

'I'll explain some other time, Cat. But if only he'd let me give it to her.'

'Why don't ye insist?'

'I can't administer to anyone in my own family. It's against medical ethics.'

'That seems a bit harsh.'

'Not really. After all, say I wanted to commit a murder and it was a member of my own family, then it would be easy if I were allowed to treat them. It's there to protect the doctor as well as the members of a family. It stops mal-practice. So ye see I have to let Doctor Murray have his own way, regardless!'

They strolled around the garden several more times, sometimes falling silent, then striking up conversation simultaneously and laughing.

Eventually they decided to go back inside and as they climbed the stairs they could hear a slapping noise coming from the bedroom. They looked at each other and grinned.

'The baby's been born, Cat, I can hear him slapping its bottom,' Daniel said, and charged up the stairs followed by Cat.

They burst into the bedroom only to find that Mary was lying motionless in the bed and Mrs. Morrisey, kneeling beside her, was sobbing.

Dr. Murray, in a futile attempt at revival was slapping the back of Mary's hand. The doctor turned and bowed his head.

'I'm sorry,' he said.

45
Eltham
September 1921

Louis opened the front door and could sense bedtime had arrived for the children. Silently he tiptoed to Billy's bedroom and saw Cat was folding up clothes as the little boy knelt before his bed saying his prayers.

She looked up and saw him, so put a finger to her lips as he crept nearer the bedroom door. They listened to Billy.

'Holy Mary, mother of dog pray for us shinners now and at the hour of our deaf. Army.'

Cat smiled at his mistakes, but he was too young she felt to drum into him the prayers she had to learn by heart at such a young age. And anyway, she was beginning to feel that maybe there was more to life than always praying.

She was angry with God right now because He'd let her down. He'd taken the perfectly good life of her sister, as well as that of her unborn baby, for no reason at all.

Heart failure, the coroner had put on the death certificate, but Daniel's words resounded in her head and she felt if Doctor Murray had let him administer to Mary, she would be alive today.

Cat wore her grief daily; but it had also had the effect of awakening in her a feeling of living for the moment, for she knew that she had to grab happiness by the throat otherwise it could evade her.

'He sounds so sweet, doesn't he?' Louis said as Cat closed the bedroom door.

'Yes, he does. C'mon and sit down now while I get yer meal.'

'Don't rush, sit down first. I've something to tell you,' he said pulling a chair out for her, and she sat down curious as to what his news would be.

'What would you wish for most if you could have it?'

Cat thought for a little while.

'Nothin' material would bring me much comfort, Louis. But if Mary could walk through that door, I would never wish for another thing.'

Louis' shoulders slumped.

'Ye look disappointed, Pet. Have I said anythin' wrong? I'm only bein' honest ye know.'

'No. It's not you, my darling. It's my ability to say the wrong thing at the wrong time. I'm sorry I should have just come straight out with it instead of asking you to wish. Of course, you would wish to have Mary here more than anything in the world. I should have thought.'

'C'mon now. Don't let's get downhearted. What was yer secret anyway?'

'I've got a job!'

'*NO*!'

'Yes! A real job.'

'Where?'

'At the Post Office. I just got to the Labour Exchange at the right time today and up it came, like magic. I prayed as I walked through the doors, *"Please God let me get a job today,"* and as if my prayer was answered, I was just the person they were looking for!'

'That's absolutely grand. I can't tell ye how pleased I am. Let's tell Billy.'

'No don't Cat. Not right now. Let's eat, then sit and work out some plans about what we'll do with the money.' He rubbed his hands together and she went to the range and lifted out his plate.

'Don't touch the plate, 'tis hot.'

'That looks good. I'm starving. I just don't know how you manage to produce such wonderful food on our budget Cat. You're a miracle worker.'

For the second time in less than half-an-hour, Louis felt he had said the wrong thing.

'Sorry, Cat. I seem to keep saying the wrong thing.'

''Tis alright. 'Tis bound to come up. Like anythin' that goes wrong in life, if ye lost yer leg for example, ye'd keep seein' people with one leg missing. 'Tis so raw, that every little thing relatin' to death reminds me of Mary. I want to speak about her, but there's nobody here who knew her, so I find myself talkin' to her in my head. If only I had done this, or that, maybe she wouldn't have died.'

'I don't think there's anything *you* could have done to save her, Cat.'

'There *was*, Louis.'

'What?' Louis poked his fork into a potato.

'I could have made sure Daniel knew about her heart.'

'What do you mean?'

'I knew there was somethin' wrong.'

Louis put down his fork. 'How?'

'When I first went home, the day Mary convinced me to write and forgive ye, she had a funny turn.'

'What happened?'

'She kind of went all shaky, her lips were blue and she was perspiring.'

'Well, you're not a doctor, Cat, so why are you feeling guilty about it?'

'Because she explained how her heart was flutterin' in her chest, like a little bird she said, and then it went like a race horse.'

'I still can't see that it's your fault.'

'She hadn't told Daniel because he had his mother to worry about. I knew, and she promised to tell Daniel, but I got too involved worryin' about whether ye were comin' over to join us and I forgot to check.'

Louis sat looking at her, then stood and went over to her. He drew her to him and wrapped his arms around her little frame. She was still so thin, he thought.

'Cat, you know if everything in this world could be done twice, it would be done perfectly wouldn't it? Life isn't like that. I have things I wish I had not done because of the outcome afterwards, but we're human, and humans make mistakes.'

'Yes. And that mistake haunts me Louis.'

'Well it mustn't. I don't suppose Daniel missed it anyway; he's pretty good at his job. Maybe nothing could have been done anyway.'

'Maybe.'

'Try to put it behind you now. You did nothing wrong, Cat. Mary loved you and you must remember that. She was a lovely lady, but it was her time to go.'

Cat pulled out a chair and sat down at the table and began playing with the saltcellar. Louis returned to his seat to continue eating.

'By the way I've got some news for ye too,' Cat said smiling at Louis.

Louis looked up and smiled, glad to see she was looking less unhappy.

'Do ye want to guess or shall I come right out with it?'

'Come right out with it, we don't seem to get it right with our guessing do we?'

'I'm not quite sure how to tell ye.'

He grinned and asked her if she had robbed the Bank of England.

'No nothin' like robbin' and stealin'.'

'Then tell me, I can't bear the suspense.'

She drew in her breath and looked at him.

'I'm pregnant!'

46
Eltham
Christmas Day 1921

Louis was asleep in an armchair by the fire when Cat put the children to bed. After she returned to the room, she picked up the paper he had dropped and began to read. The fire crackled noisily as it ravaged the coal and Cat basked in its warmth as she tried to concentrate

But her mind was elsewhere, and after a while she let the paper fall, deciding to just sit and think. She looked across at Louis, his mouth slightly open, arms dangling over the sides of his chair. Not a sound came from outside as all families had closed their doors to the outside world, spending Christmas Day at home.

Cat thought about their last Christmas. They had all been together in Fethard, had gone to Midnight Mass as a whole family and everything had seemed perfect. Then there was that dreadful night of New Year's Eve and her desperate fight with death when Eileen had been born.

She couldn't remember much about the immediate events after the birth, but it had been a long slow road back to health. Just as she could have recovered fully, she discovered Louis had lied to her about busking in the street and she had run away. It was Mary who had encouraged her to forgive Louis, and now she was dead.

As a family they would not be celebrating Christmas together this year, so Cat, Louis and the children had stayed in England. It was all too painful. Maeve and Ned would have gone to Midnight Mass last night Cat knew, probably with Tom and Norah.

She ran her hand across her swollen tummy. Less than four months to go now, she thought. If it was a girl they couldn't call her Mary because they had already had Marie. She would like to call the baby Ellie, but felt it would upset her remaining sisters, so she would have to decide on something different. If it was a boy they could call him Edward after her father. The baby moved inside her and she stroked her tummy, trying to soothe the child's movements. Eileen will be one next week, she reflected.

Her eyes wandered across to Louis again and she sat studying him. His hair had fallen across his forehead untidily and his shirt was undone. It was good to see him relax.

Today, she thought, though it had been quiet, had really been rather nice, just the four of them. Next year there would be five.

Louis stirred in the chair, mumbled something and continued to sleep as Cat sat contentedly staring into the flames.

47
London
April 1st 1922

Louis waited on the platform for the boat train from Fishguard. He had been standing around for half an hour as the train was late, but when it did arrive he spotted Peggy leaning out of the carriage window as soon as it approached the station. He stepped towards the edge of the platform and trotted alongside her carriage as the train shunted to the end of the line.

'It's very good of you to come over, Peggy.' He opened the carriage door and helped her down.

'Ah I wouldn't miss it for the world, Louis. How is Cat?'

'Not so bad. It's just me worrying she will have a bad time again that's all. Just a moment, I'll get your bag.' He stepped up into the compartment and lifted her bag down onto the platform, then turned and closed the carriage door.

'Yes. Let's hope we're not in for another episode like the last time. D'ya have a midwife arranged?' Peggy asked picking up her bag.

'I'll take that, Peggy,' Louis said trying to take the bag from her.

'There's no need, Louis. I'm used to liftin' things ye know.'

'Yes, I know, Peggy. But please, allow me,' he said offering her his arm. 'Now what was it you were asking?'

'D'ya have a midwife arranged?' She took his arm.

'Yes, we do. We have a very nice woman who only lives a few doors along, and we have also seen a doctor to check that Cat is fit.' They stopped to hand in Peggy's ticket at the barrier.

'And what did the doctor have to say?' she asked as they walked across the station towards the underground.

'He says everything looks in order and she should be fine.'

'Praise be to God then.'

'Yes, let's all pray this birth will be different.'

* * *

Louis paced up and down in the grounds of Lewisham Hospital and though he had been told to go home, he would not.

Cat was in the operating theatre undergoing a caesarian and he had no intention of leaving. He alternated between being outside and worrying he should be inside and being inside and wanting to be out in the air. And why, he thought, was it taking so long?

Eventually on one of his visits inside the hospital a consultant approached him and after checking he had the right person, invited Louis into the Sister's office on the ward where Cat had been before the operation. The surgeon sat down and motioned for Louis to take a seat.

'We've delivered the baby safely, but there were complications Mr. Ross.'

Louis waited for the explanation, not daring to ask what the complications were.

The surgeon continued. 'The uterus completely prolapsed and after considerable effort on my part, I have managed to put everything back in place. This has necessitated a lot of internal stitching. She should have no more children after this.' He studied Louis' face.

'I understand.'

'I hope you do, because if she does, she could well lose her life next time. I believe she prolapsed after the last birth with considerable haemorrhaging!'

'Yes, that's right. Luckily my brother-in-law was there. He's a doctor. He managed to stem the bleeding. But she was quite ill for a while afterwards.'

'Then why is God's name have another baby?'

'It wasn't planned. It just happened.'

'Well make sure it does not *just happen* again. If it does, you could find yourself a widower. And maybe worse, you'll be responsible for her death. Don't say you weren't warned.'

Humiliated, Louis hung his head, then looked him in the eye, thanked him and asked if he could see her.

'Yes, but only a short visit.' He began to walk off, but then as if remembering something he spun round. 'By the way, you have a lovely daughter. What will you call her?'

Louis gave a grim smile. 'We'd thought of Anna, but as it's Easter Sunday, she'll be Anna Esther.'

'Jolly good. Well, I have to go; you can see your wife now.

They shook hands, but Louis waited a while before going to see Cat, shocked at what he had been told.

48
Eltham
June 1922

'Goodbye, Peggy darlin' and thanks a million again for comin' over. I don't know what I'd have done without ye.' Cat cradled the new baby Anna in her arms and called Billy and Eileen to come and kiss Auntie Peggy goodbye.

'Don't forget now, Cat. I'll come over any time ye need me, Breda can manage Marie and the shop, 'tis no trouble. I just want ye to keep well.'

'I know, Peggy,' Cat assured her lifting first Eileen then Billy up to kiss Peggy. 'Kiss your auntie goodbye now, Billy.'

He put his little arms around her neck and kissed her cheek. 'Bye, Auntie,' then wriggled to be set free.

Louis took Peggy's bag outside and waited for her at the gate before setting off together towards the station.

As Cat stood waving she felt a wave of depression wash over her, and tears which were always near the surface these days, streamed from her eyes. How she longed to be going with Peggy.

She closed the door, went into Peggy's empty room and sat on the edge of the bed. Remembering the nights she and Ellie had spent giggling in this same room she felt desolate.

The feeling wrapped itself around her like a black cloak as she thought of her family back home.

Mary, now dead; Ellie in America and Peggy returning home and she wished she was going too. She lay on the bed, curled herself into a ball and cried huge body-wracking sobs for her life that had gone.

After a while she became aware that Billy and Eileen were watching her from the doorway, so she swiftly wiped her eyes and told them to go and play while she changed the beds.

Louis' bed, now in Billy's room, was the last one she changed. She smoothed the pillow with the flat of her hand as though caressing Louis face and felt the familiar constriction in her chest.

She mourned the loss of nights lying together in bed, sharing their thoughts and love. Louis would not sleep with her. He had absolutely refused after Anna was born.

Peggy's stay made it impossible to discuss the issue but now Cat decided she was determined to address it. She longed for his touch and craved the affection he denied her, but Louis had avoided contact with her since the birth and the subject had become one that neither of them could address. When he came back from seeing Peggy onto the train in London she would speak to him about it. They couldn't go on like this.

* * *

It was teatime when Reggie suddenly appeared. Cat was setting out Eileen's nightclothes before bathing her ready for bed.

'Hello Auntie,' he said opening the back door.

'Oh dear God, Reggie, ye gave me such a fright. C'mon in and close the door, I'm just gettin' Eileen's bath ready.' He closed the door and went to stand beside the table where Cat was arranging the soap and towel.

Reggie poked his head round the door to the parlour. 'Where's Billy?'

'He's out playin' in the back. G'w'on and call him in will ye, Reggie?'

'Is Uncle Louis out there too?'

'No, he's away seein' me sister Peggy off back to Ireland.'

'Oh,' Reggie said unenthusiastically.

'Is anythin' wrong with ye?'

'No, Auntie. I just wanted to speak to him, that's all.'

'What about?'

Reggie blushed, and Cat, thinking he wanted a man-to-man talk with Louis as his own father was dead, decided to drop the subject.

'So, will ye call Billy in Reggie, there's a good lad.'

Reggie went out to the back garden where he found Billy digging a hole in the soil so asked him what he was doing.

'Planting flowers.'

'Oh. Where are the flowers then?'

'Here, silly.'

Reggie looked to where Billy was pointing and saw a few sticks poking out of the earth.

'They're not flowers, Billy, they are just an old pile of sticks.'

Billy looked up at Reggie and then down at his collection of little sticks. 'I put them in the ground. Then I put water on and they grow to flowers, Granddad said!'

'Well they won't Billy, because they are not flowers, they are just sticks.'

'Granddad said they are.'

'He probably only meant that if you were planting flowers. You can't grow flowers from old sticks. Anyway your mum wants you to come in now.'

Billy continued to twiddle the sticks in the earth.

'Come on, Billy, you've got to come in now and get ready for bed.'

'No.'

'Come on now, Billy, your Mum said so.'

Billy continued to push the sticks further into the soil, patting the base of each one so that it would stand upright.

'I'll tell your mum you won't come if you don't do it this instant!'

Billy stood up and rubbed his hands together freeing them of mud. He looked at Reggie sternly, then stomped past him, saying, 'Them is flowers!'

Reggie followed Billy indoors where Cat was undressing Eileen on the table. He sat next to Cat as she deftly removed Eileen's clothes.

'Can I do that Auntie Cat?'

She was surprised. 'Well, Reggie I think maybe she would be a little difficult to hold right now, she can be an awful wriggler you know.'

Reggie looked downcast and Cat felt awkward. It was a surprise that a young lad of nearly seventeen should show an interest in helping with a small child. This was strictly a woman's domain and she felt there was something a little odd in his request. Then as though relenting because she had hurt his feelings, she asked if he would like to dry Eileen once she had bathed her, and Reggie seemed cheered by the suggestion.

After bathing her, Cat wrapped her in a towel and showed Reggie what to do, ensuring that every part of the child was dry.

Cat was surprised at how gentle he was with Eileen and impressed at how deftly he towelled her dry before asking if he could put her nightdress on.

Once more Cat felt uncomfortable, but again not wishing to thwart Reggie, she allowed him to do this task. He then brushed her hair and sat her on his lap tickling her chin making her laugh while Cat prepared Billy's tea.

'Can I put Eileen to bed, Auntie?'

Cat was about to cut into a fresh loaf and stopped. She looked across at Reggie who was bouncing Eileen on his lap. Eileen was laughing and Reggie looked perfectly natural, almost like a man twice his age and certainly at ease with the child.

'Well, yes. I suppose so. G'w'on then. Pull the curtains and once ye've laid her down, leave the room quickly, or she'll think she's in for more fun and games with ye.'

'Come on Eileen,' he said standing up with the child in his arms. 'Bed time.'

Reggie walked into the bedroom and Cat heard him pull the curtains, speaking to Eileen as he did, then he re-appeared in the kitchen. Cat looked across at him.

'Reggie, would ye like some bread and jam with Billy?'

'Yes please, Auntie.'

'Sit yerself down then and I'll get ye some,' she said. 'I hear ye lost the job in London?'

'Yes.'

'So what'll ye do now?'

'Work in the shop with Mum until I can find another job. It's not that easy.'

Cat looked at him. 'Yes, I know all about that, Reggie. What was the reason they let ye go?'

Reggie blushed and looked away from her.

'Something about not being able to afford to keep me on.'

'Oh. Well, I expect somethin' will turn up. In the meantime, if ye can help your mam, it'll be good for her.'

Reggie didn't answer.

After Cat had put their food on the table she sat down to feed Anna while they ate. She unbuttoned her dress and put the baby to her breast.

Every once in a while Reggie cast his glance in her direction, but Cat was unaware of the interest she had stirred in him. When the boys had finished eating, Cat asked Reggie if he would like to get Billy ready for bed.

'I should be going home actually, Auntie.'

'Oh. I thought ye were goin' to wait for Uncle Louis, he won't be much longer now.'

'No. It is getting on a bit and I have to be up early tomorrow, so I'll get off home now.'

'Will I tell him what it was ye wanted to talk to him about then?'

'Oh, no. I'll come and see him another time.'

''Tis alright to tell me, Reggie. I can keep a secret. Is it about a girl or something?'

Reggie blushed, quickly stood and pushed his chair into the table. 'No. It's nothing, Auntie. I must go now. Goodbye.'

He walked across and kissed her cheek. Then bending over Eileen he kissed the baby's forehead.

Cat felt his breath on her breast and moved back a fraction, feeling that perhaps Reggie was becoming a little too interested in her breast. Still, she supposed it was bound to happen sooner or later; after all he was of an age where he was probably becoming curious about women.

'Well, goodbye then Reggie. I'll tell Uncle Louis ye came round. Will I ask him to call at the shop to speak to ye?'

Reggie was walking towards the door and without turning said, 'No please don't...er, I'll come and see him another day. It's nothing, really!'

He disappeared through the doorway and left Cat wondering what it was that had bothered her so much.

* * *

Cat encouraged Louis to pop round and see what Reggie wanted, and when Lize opened the door to him she said she'd been expecting him.

'Oh, really? Did Reggie say what he wanted me for?'

'It's a long story, Louis, you'd better come in.'

Lize related how the situation was becoming unbearable between their mother and Reggie since he'd lost his job and moved back home.

'Mum actually accused Reggie of stealing from her purse, and no amount of intervention by me seems to make any difference. I'm at the end of my tether, Louis. Can you go up and speak to Reggie?'

Louis climbed the stairs, knocked on Reggie's door and went in.

'Auntie Cat said you wanted to speak to me, Reggie.'

'Um, yes.'

'Well, what was it about?'

Reggie looked down and began fiddling with a thread on his pullover.

Louis felt tired having just got back from London and sat down on the bed next to Reggie.

'Come on Reggie, spit it out, I haven't got all night.'

'Uncle?' he began.

'Yes?'

'I was wondering if I could come and live with you, that's all.'

Louis was taken by surprise; he had not expected anything of this nature.

'And what's brought this idea about?'

Reggie outlined how difficult his life was living with his grandmother and how she constantly picked on him and tried turning Iris and his mother against him. He finished by telling Louis how he'd been accused of stealing from his grandmother's purse. An accusation he flatly denied.

'So you see Uncle, it's really quite difficult here.' His words trailed off and he sat looking at Louis dejectedly.

Louis thought for a while.

'Look Reggie, I know things are difficult, but you can't come and live with us, not just like that. You'll have to try harder to not get under Granny's skin. Keep out of her way. Go out in the evenings and you'll find it works.'

Reggie looked down and Louis got up to leave.

'You can't run away from life, you must learn to work things out, Reggie. You know… find a way of resolving issues yourself.'

Reggie didn't answer so Louis left him to think it over and went downstairs.

As Louis entered the kitchen Lize was making a pot of tea, but Louis said he wouldn't stay for one as he'd only just returned from London and was tired.

'So did Reggie tell you what he wanted you for?'

'Yes, he wanted to come and live with us.'

Lize poured out her tea. 'And what did you say?'

'I told him, he'd have to work harder at making the situation work here.'

Lize turned on him, her brow furrowed and lips quivering.

'It's not that easy Louis. Mum made Dad's life a misery, then yours and now it's Reggie. I think she hates men and she's ruining all our lives. You don't have to put up with her day in and day out picking on everything he says and does.' She took out a handkerchief and blew her nose. 'And this latest thing, this idea he's stolen from her, well it just about finishes it all off!'

Louis let out a sigh. 'Lize, we've got five mouths to feed already. I can't take on another one.' He looked at her and thought she did look worn out.

'I don't suppose you pay him enough for him to live independently do you?'

She gave a little laugh.

'Of course I don't. But if he could live with you, I could manage by myself, with perhaps a little help from Iris.' She began to bite her fingernail.

'I'm sorry Lize, I can't ask Cat to do this. She really has enough to do.'

'Well you can choose, Louis. Either you take Reggie, or you'll have to take on a larger share of the load with Mum. She'll have to go and live with you. I can't take much more and I can't have them both under the same roof!'

'You know that wouldn't work, Lize. Mum doesn't exactly warm to Cat does she? I mean look at that notice she's had put up on the gate, No Hawkers, No Trespassers and No Irish. How do you think that makes us feel?'

'I know she's got some prejudices against the Irish, Louis, and I don't know why. But I can't be the go-between.'

Louis looked at her and noticed for the first time her hair had begun to grey at the temples and she had a deep furrow between her eyebrows. Tears welled up in her eyes and he could see that she was at breaking point. He sat down and thought. After a little while he said he would go home and talk it over with Cat.

'Perhaps if Reggie were to get another job it would help.'

'He is looking for one, Louis.'

Louis remained silent for a while, and then looked at Lize.

'This is only an idea, but one of the chaps I work with has a brother with a butcher's shop in the High Street. I happen to know they are looking for an apprentice. Would you like me to ask him if he'd give Reggie a chance?'

'Oh, Louis – would you?'

'I will, but don't say anything to Reggie at present, not until I've had time to ask whether it is viable. Or perhaps we should ask Reggie first whether he would like to do that.'

'Lize looked horrified. 'He'll do as he's told, Louis. He's not in a position to pick and choose.'

'That's settled then. I'll let you know.' He got up to leave. 'I'll speak to Cat about him too; she seems quite fond of the boy.'

Lize just nodded in agreement and Louis left before she could ask him to do anything else.

When Louis reached home he braced himself; worried about breaking the news to Cat about Reggie. But he was surprised at her reaction. She had simply smiled at him.

'Of course he can move in, Louis.' Then she had mumbled something else which sounded to Louis like, *God moves in mysterious ways*.

Too tired to question her about what she had said, Louis slumped down at the table and poured himself some tea while Cat put his evening meal in front of him.

'There ye are now, Louis. Eat this up and ye'll feel better, Pet.'

'You seem in a good mood, Cat. Are you sure about this business with Reggie?'

She turned away so that Louis could not see the smile on her face.

'Of course I don't mind, he can share the bedroom with Billy!'

49
Eltham
August 1922

'Things seem to be working out well with Reggie here don't they Cat?'

'Sure.'

'Oh, by the way this letter just came,' Louis said dropping an envelope onto the table. 'It's from Ellie, judging by the American stamp.'

Cat read the letter, then re-folded the thin blue sheets and put them back in the envelope without saying anything. Expecting to hear her news Louis looked across at her. 'How are things in New York then?'

Cat's voice sounded flat. 'She lost the baby.'

'Oh dear, not again! Poor Ellie.' Louis remained silent for a while, and then began buttering a piece of bread. 'Does she say whether Michael is working?'

'He's got a job as a docker. At least that's one good thing. I wish she were nearer. Why in God's name did they have to go so far?'

Louis sighed. 'Well by the look of things here, they'll be glad they did if it continues this way. The dockers here are devils; they have the whole of our economy dependent on their actions. I've never known a more powerful force than them, even the Germans weren't able to overrun us in the way they have.'

'Oh, I can't be bothered with politics, Louis. Give me a simple old film any day and I'm satisfied.'

'Talking of pictures darling, as it's our wedding anniversary on Friday I wondered if you would like to go and see the latest Charlie Chaplin?'

'Yes that'll be good. D'ya think Reggie will mind the children?'

'I should think so. He never seems to want to go out; so I don't suppose he'll mind. Will you ask him, or shall I?'

'Would you ask him, Louis?'

'Right, but let's make it Saturday night. I'll ask him when he gets in from work tonight.'

'Has he said anythin' to you about how his job is going? He hasn't said much about it to me.'

'He seems to have settled in well. Ernie's brother has taken a liking to him. At least it's helped the atmosphere at Lize's, especially now Iris is helping to run the shop with her. Seems things have worked out well all round doesn't it?'

* * *

'We're off now Reggie – and thanks again. 'Tis not often your uncle and I get out.'

'Goodbye, have a nice time both of you, and enjoy the film.'

'Don't forget now, Reggie. Help yerself to anythin' you want, there's some apple pie in the pantry and plenty of bread and jam.'

'I will Auntie. Goodbye now.'

Reggie closed the door and strolled into the lounge to sit in Louis' chair. After a while, feeling restless, he ambled out to the back garden and stood listening to the birds quarrelling in the hedgerow.

He liked living with Louis and Cat. He was treated more as an equal and felt more grown up than at home. He also knew he was getting on better with his Grandmother, now there was some distance between them.

The evening sun washed over him and he felt at peace. Then as though remembering something he suddenly went inside and closed the door. He sat back down again in Louis' chair for ages, thinking.

It was growing dark and Reggie heard Eileen call out in her sleep, so he tiptoed into the bedroom and stood watching over her for a while. She settled in her sleep and became peaceful again, so he crept out of the room and went to see if Billy was asleep. Satisfied that he was, Reggie returned to watch Eileen and Anna.

Eileen had kicked the covers off in her sleep and lay sprawled out on the bed, her nightdress riding up over her buttocks which were peach-coloured in the diffused evening light.

Slowly, and carefully, Reggie lifted Eileen from the bed and cradled her in his arms then slid silently from the bedroom into Cat and Louis' room.

He laid the sleeping child on the bed and, satisfied she had settled back into sleep, carefully lifted her nightdress and stood gazing at her tiny body.

Part Three

50
Eltham
July 1925

'Uncle Louis, a chap I work with has a dog that's had pups. He's looking for homes for them and, well, I wondered if I could bring one home for the children?'

'Oh I don't know, Reggie. Dogs cost money and I'm not sure we could afford to waste food on a dog.'

'Well I've thought of that, and it shouldn't be a problem. I would be able get all the meat scraps from the shop. What do you say? Only Billy's been going on about having a dog for ages.'

Louis looked across at Reggie and seeing the enthusiasm on his face found it hard to refuse him. He shook out the paper he was reading and folded it up.

'You'd have to ask Auntie Cat. She's in charge of that sort of thing. If she says yes, then you may. What sort of dogs are they?'

'Something like a Border Collie. I've already seen them. They are mostly black and white with little brown patches over their eyes.'

Louis smiled at him. 'So you've already been and picked one out have you?'

Reggie looked embarrassed. 'Not exactly. But I, well I was invited to tea last Friday and—'

Louis put down his paper. 'Do you mean the Friday just gone?'

'Yes, that's right.'

'But you said you were going to the church dance.'

'Yes, I did. But this was before the dance. I went to tea with Maureen first and then on to the dance after.'

'Oh Yes? And *who* is Maureen?'

Reggie blushed. 'A girl I know.'

'Clearly, it's a girl you know. You would hardly go to tea with a stranger. Tell me about her. Where did you meet her, and everything else about this Maureen?'

'Well, she comes into the shop pretty regularly.'

'Go on.'

'And, well... we struck up conversation.'

'What about, liver and kidneys or was it the hearts?'

Reggie looked distinctly uncomfortable, so Louis decided to stop poking fun at him.

'Go on Reggie, I'm only joking.'

'And, so I asked her out. She wanted me to meet her aunt and uncle, so I went to tea last Friday.'

'And are we to be presented to this Maureen? Or are you keeping her away from us for some reason?'

'Oh no, Uncle. It's not like that. I didn't know whether you'd mind me bringing a young lady home, that's all.'

'Well, I'd rather you did, so that we can see the kind of company you are keeping.'

'Alright. I could bring her to meet you and Auntie Cat on Sunday if it's convenient.'

Louis picked up his newspaper again, shook it straight and began reading. From behind the paper Reggie heard him mutter.

'Bring her to tea. Four o'clock on the dot and don't be late. Now go and tell your aunt all about it and don't forget to ask her about the dog.'

Reggie hurried out to the garden where Cat was deciding which lettuce to pick. He silently walked between the rows of lettuce until he was about three feet from her.

Hearing someone behind her, she turned quickly and gave a gasp. 'Reggie, you gave me a fright. You shouldn't creep up on me like that!'

'Sorry Auntie, but Uncle Louis said I should discuss something with you.'

'G'w'on then. I'm all ears,' she said turning her back to him and continuing to look for a good lettuce.

Reggie related the conversation he had just had with Louis, and Cat listened, amused at Reggie's enthusiasm.

'Well aren't ye the dark horse? I was wonderin' when ye'd start takin' an interest in girls. Yes of course ye can bring her home on Sunday.'

'What about the dog then?'

'Yes, the children would love it. When will it be ready to leave its mother?'

'Soon. Maybe by Sunday even.'

'Fine. We'll have to think of some names then.'

Billy had been listening intently to this conversation and, delighted at the prospect of the puppy, ran off to tell Eileen and Anna.

* * *

On Sunday Billy stationed himself at the garden gate waiting to catch the first glimpse of the puppy. As soon as he saw Reggie and Maureen appear in the distance he darted inside the house, slammed the door shut, and announced that he'd seen them coming. Then he went to sit next to Louis and waited for them to knock on the door.

'Oh well, I'll say one thing for them,' Louis said looking up at the clock, 'at least they're on time.'

A little while later, he heard Reggie open the front door and some muffled voices in the hallway. The children rose from their chairs expectantly and Louis looked at them with a grave expression so they lowered themselves back down, to wait.

Reggie poked his head round the door.

'Is it alright to bring Maureen in now?' he asked.

Louis stood up, 'Yes of course it is, bring her in.'

Reggie reappeared, his hand cupping the elbow of a petite redhead.

'This is Maureen, Uncle Louis and Auntie Cat.'

Louis stretched out his hand to shake Maureen's, saying he was pleased to meet her. The girl smiled revealing a row of slightly uneven teeth, the front ones crossing over at the tips. Strangely enough, Louis thought this looked rather endearing.

'Ach, 'tis good to meet yerselves too.'

'Ye're Irish?' Cat laughed.

'Sure I am. And 'tis lovely to make yer acquaintance, Mrs. Ross.'

'I didn't realise ye're from home. Welcome, Maureen, c'mon and sit yerself down and have a nice cup of tea and somethin' to eat. Where is it ye're from now?'

Louis was astonished and looked from Maureen to Cat, then to Reggie wondering what on earth his mother would have to say about this. Not one, but two Irish women in their midst.

'I'm from Fermoy.'

'Well, that's not a million miles away from Fethard. I can see we'll have plenty to talk about, Maureen.'

Reggie cleared his throat as if to remind Maureen of something.

'Oh yes, I nearly forgot, so if ye're not getting' too much in one go, I've brought the puppy along with me for the children.' She turned to Reggie. 'Would ye go out now to me basket and bring in the puppy for them?' Maureen then turned to the children who were lined up waiting to see Reggie's young lady.

'Well these must be the darlin' children Reggie keeps goin' on about.' She stooped down and kissed them all on the cheek one by one as

Reggie brought Maureen's basket in and placed it on the floor.

The children gasped. Sitting in the basket was a small black puppy with a snow white breast and two little brown patches over his eyes that looked like eyebrows. They swooped over the basket, each wanting to pick the puppy up first.

Billy grabbed at it. 'My go first 'cos I'm the eldest.'

'Let me have it first.' Eileen argued and tried to pull the puppy from his grasp.

'Oh dear, we seem to have caused a problem,' Maureen laughed and the children completely forgot about their esteemed guest as they jostled for supremacy over the little dog who licked their faces furiously.

Cat stepped forward and rescued the puppy from Billy's grasp.

'We'll call him Tipper,' Cat said, 'because I'm from Tipperary. What do ye think Louis?'

Louis stroked the puppy's ears and took him from Cat.

'Right then. Tipper it is. Funny, I've never thought of getting a dog. But it's rather nice isn't it?'

Louis headed for the garden with Tipper under his arm and fondled his ears while the children scrambled behind him, arguing for the next hold.

51
Eltham
December 1925

Cat read the letter from America while eating her breakfast, then looked up at Louis with tears in her eyes.

'Praise be to God, Louis. Ellie's given birth to a little girl and both are fine. At last, she's done it!'

'That's wonderful, Cat. Does she say what they've called her?'

'Catherine, after me! Oh Louis, I wish I could see her. It's been so long.'

'Yes, but there's a big stretch of water between them and us, it's not going to be possible. Not unless they come to us.'

She put the letter from Ellie down and picked up the dress she was hemming. 'I bet Michael's over the moon, don't you?'

'Sure to be.' Louis lit up a cigarette, then bent down and stroked Tipper's head. The dog licked his hand, turning faithful brown eyes upwards to his master.

As much as Billy had tried to take control of the dog's loyalty, Tipper had chosen Louis. Wherever Louis went, Tipper wasn't far behind. At night he would lay before Louis' chair by the fire at the feet of his master, sighing as if in ecstasy and making little yelping noises in his sleep.

'What else did Ellie have to say?'

'Only that she'd heard Paddy Hogan has married.'

'Only! Well, I should think you'd be mightily relieved to hear that piece of news.'

'I'm not bothered either way. Why should it matter to me? Good luck to the fool who's taken him on.'

'Does she say who the blushing bride is?'

'Yes, it's someone from Thurles. Nobody I know. I wonder if he's still up to his old tricks with that band of murderin' thugs.'

'Probably. They've certainly not curbed their ways since the signing of the treaty. It seems to go from bad to worse.'

They sat quietly for a while, listening to the crackle of the fire as the embers shifted and blazed in the grate. Soot, clinging to the fire back, glowed and faded simultaneously - like an advancing army climbing the chimney in the darkness. Louis sat mesmerised watching the coals, deep in thought.

Suddenly he stood up and took the savings tin down from the mantelpiece. He counted out their savings and Cat watched his lips moving as he added up the money.

'What are ye up to?'

'Adding up what we have?'

'Yes, but why?'

He smiled and put the money back in the tin.

'What would you say to us buying a motor cycle and side car?'

Cat drew in her breath, puzzled by his suggestion, not knowing how to react.

'Well, what do you say, woman?'

'I'm not sure what ye're on about, Louis.'

'Someone at work has a motor cycle and side car for sale.'

'What on earth would we do with such a machine?'

'Go out for a spin. Go to Ireland! We could drive all the way to the ferry in Fishguard, get off on the other side and drive to Fethard. Go for little breaks to the seaside, and.'

'Whoa. Slow down! Are ye suggestin' we actually go ahead and buy this machine?'

'Cat, it's going for a song. We can afford it and I think it would be ideal for us. So what do you say? No don't say anything. Just think about it. Imagine yourself speeding along in the sidecar with the wind in your hair as we make our way to the coast. The sun on your face and the children with their buckets and spades - even Tipper could come.'

'Louis, how could we all get into a sidecar?'

'You, Eileen and Anna in the sidecar with Tipper, and Billy can ride behind me on the pillion. So what do you say?' He rubbed his hands together in excitement.

Cat thought for a while. There were other things they needed like some decent furniture to sit on, clothes for the children, for her and Louis. But then she decided there was little fun if they couldn't enjoy life while the children were still young. And then there was the prospect of going to the seaside!

Her face suddenly lost its serious expression and animatedly she threw her arms round Louis neck, reflecting his enthusiasm and laughing.

'Yes, Louis, let's do it!'

52
Eltham
June 1927

The church bells peeled as Reggie and Maureen emerged from the church smiling. She wore an oyster coloured silk wedding dress and Reggie looked handsome in a charcoal grey suit with matching silk tie. Iris, Eileen and Anna wore pink bridesmaid's dresses and Billy, much to his annoyance, was dressed as a pageboy.

'Can we have the bride, bridegroom and bridesmaids please?' the photographer said, then as Cat whispered something to him he added, 'Oh, and the page boy.'

Cat slipped a silver horseshoe on a satin ribbon over Maureen's wrist and kissed her cheek.

'I hope ye'll both be very happy.'

'Thanks Cat. Ye've been wonderful and the dress is gorgeous, ye've made a perfect job of it, I feel like a queen.'

'Yes and ye look like one.'

Louis shook hands with Reggie wishing him good luck, and agreed to help him move his belongings from their house once the couple returned from honeymoon. They were off to Ireland to spend a week with Maureen's parents.

As Louis stood talking to the couple, confetti rained down on them from the crowd and the children scampered about trying to pick it up from the ground.

'Don't do that girls, ye'll get dirty and you've to get the photographs done yet,' Cat scolded.

'Yes, put that down and line up, the photographer's already called for you,' Louis said. He shook Anna's hands to free the coloured pieces of paper. 'Eileen,' he commanded, 'throw that confetti down and come here. That's right, stand next to Maureen and smile.'

Slowly the entourage made their way back to Cat and Louis' house for the wedding celebrations. As they approached the road leading to their home, Louis said he'd go on ahead and shut Tipper outside as he didn't want him jumping up on the guests, spoiling their wedding clothes.

Louis quickened his pace and was soon quite a distance ahead of the crowd. When he reached the house he entered through the back door calling Tipper to him. Initially the dog seemed reluctant to come to him but with a little coaxing Louis soon managed to get him into the out-house.

On entering the parlour, disaster met his eyes. Tipper had been helping himself while they were at the church, and sandwiches were scattered across the floor; the pile of sausage rolls was considerably depleted and the plate of cold meat had clearly provided the animal with more than he could devour, as he'd left a few slices uneaten.

Louis rushed to the front door, glanced up the road and saw the wedding party was nearing the house.

'Oh Lord, what a mess,' he said rushing around to re-arrange the sausage rolls, and picking sandwiches off the floor. He inspected the ones that were not broken and put them back on the plate. Then he removed the plate of cold meat and put it in the kitchen. He was just about to cut some more to replace it when the guests poured through the front door and into the parlour. Quickly Louis took off the pieces nearest the outside edge of the plate. It wouldn't kill them, he decided, and it was certainly a lot better than what they'd eaten in the trenches!

Cat filled small glasses of sherry for the women and Louis ladled out some of his homemade beer to the men. The children were in high spirits and more than once Cat had to reprimand them for trying to grab at the food before the guests were served.

In pride of place amid all the food on the table stood the wedding cake that Cat had made them, and on top of it stood the tiny forms of a bride and groom. Maureen was delighted and thanked her.

'That's my pleasure, Maureen. Ye'll be makin' Reggie's cakes from now on though - so 'twill be me last task. I'm glad ye've found somewhere to live, 'tis a better start to be on yer own, ye know, not livin' in with family.'

'Yes. It was so lucky to get the flat over the butcher's shop. And Reggie shouldn't be late for work living above now should he?'

'No indeed he should not. Now, I had better circulate with the sandwiches, we'll speak later.'

Cat mingled among the guests with the plate of sandwiches and Reggie, seeing Lize pulling on her gloves, went up to her.

'What, going so soon Mum?'

'Yes, your gran's at home alone, so I'd better be off now.'

'But we haven't even cut the cake yet.'

'Oh. Well I'll stay until you've done that, then I'll have to go. You know how she is.'

Reggie pulled a face thinking that even on his wedding day his grandmother was controlling him from afar. 'But why not stay on for a little longer Mum? The children were dying to see you!' He turned and beckoned to Billy who immediately came to his side.

'Billy, say hello to Auntie Lize.'

'Hello, Auntie Lize.'

Lize bent down and kissed Billy. 'Here you are, sonny,' she said, fishing out a penny from her purse, 'come round to my shop in the morning and you can spend it.'

'Oh thanks Auntie. Shall I get Eileen and Anna to come and get a penny too?'

'Billy, don't be saucy.' Reggie laughed and Lize re-opened her purse.

'Here, Billy, give this to your sisters, and mind you do!' she said placing two more pennies in his hand.

'Look Reggie, I really must go now. Have a good time and come and see me more often.'

'I'll try Mum, but now the boss is retiring I'll be working much longer hours and may find it difficult for a while.'

'Well I'm sure if you wanted to do it you would.' She pecked him on the cheek and went in search of Louis and Cat to say goodbye.

Louis and Cat walked to the front gate with Lize and they stood chatting for a while. Then Lize, feeling agitated, said she must get back as she didn't like to leave the old lady on her own for too long as she was prone to dizzy spells.

Lize walked off into the late afternoon and Louis couldn't help feeling sorry about the way her life had turned out. He thought she looked so pitiful walking away from her son's wedding party alone.

At that moment he felt he could forgive her anything, even the way she had insisted they take Reggie in. And they had the better end of the bargain. Having Reggie was infinitely easier than taking his mother in.

He wished he could turn the clock back and return to the old days when Lize's husband Charlie was alive – they had been so happy then. Fate had turned his sister into an old woman long before her time.

His conscience pricked him. 'You go in, Cat. I'll follow you in a minute.'

'Are you upset about somethin' Louis?'

'Look, I just want to walk Lize home, she looks a bit forlorn going off alone. I won't be long.'

'Sure ye go on; I'd better go back in now.'

It didn't take Louis long to catch his sister up. She wasn't used to walking in high-heeled shoes along the unmade road, and she was clearly pleased.

'Louis, what are you doing here?'

'I thought I'd walk you home. You know, just like the old days. Remember how we used to walk out in the evenings when I was on leave?'

Lize slipped her arm through his and they walked along arm in arm.

'You know Louis, I don't like weddings much.'

'Why not, for heaven's sake?'

'Don't sound so surprised.'

'Well, I am.'

'Because it reminds me of all I've lost. Of what will never be now.'

'I'm sorry Lize, I should have realized you would be affected by today.'

'I didn't think I would. But as I stood there looking at Reggie in the church, I couldn't help thinking how much like Charlie he looked and how it had all been snatched away in the blink of an eye.' She rummaged in her handbag for a handkerchief and blew her nose.

'Sorry, I should have known you would find it difficult. I suppose I'm not much good at anticipating things, I'm more of an 'afterthought' sort of person.'

'It just made me feel like screaming standing there listening to the marriage vows. I can't explain why, but hearing the words 'till death do us part' brought it all home to me. I didn't expect to be a widow – it never occurred to me. Do I sound too sorry for myself?'

He squeezed her arm, 'No, Lize. I don't think so. I used to think I was the only soldier who had suffered in the war, but I know now I was just one of millions. It touched all our lives and we all remain scarred in some way or other. Some scars don't show, but they don't heal either.'

'Louis, do you ever think about death?' They had reached the corner of Lize's road.

Why?'

'I'm not sure why but lately I've been borne down with a dreadful feeling that I'm going to die before my time and I can't bear it. I still have Iris to look after; though she seems to do more of the looking after me these days. It's just a feeling of foreboding I have and I'm not sure whether it's a dread of life or of death. I can't work out why I feel the way I do.'

They reached the shop; Lize took the keys from her bag and opened the door. 'Do you want to come in for a moment, say hello to Mum?'

Louis hesitated and he saw Lize's expression change to one of annoyance.

'Yes, I suppose I'd better. Why wouldn't she come to the wedding?'

'She said it was too far to walk. But that's not the whole truth. There's nothing wrong with her legs. I think it's because Maureen is Irish.'

'I wondered. She's never really taken to Cat has she?'

Lize paused before answering, sighed and agreed that she hadn't.

'It's made it quite difficult for me at times, Lize. The children would love to come to see her but I have to make excuses most of the time because I'm not subjecting Cat to Mum's indifference. What's she got against the Irish anyway?'

'Probably the same as most other people have,' she said, beginning to climb the stairs. 'They think they are all stupid drunks and you have to admit it, Michael Nagle didn't do much for their reputation did he?'

'Oh he's a nice enough fellow really, Lize. He's just a heavy drinker, that's all. And he's not so stupid either. He's had a good education; he just can't leave the liquor alone.'

They had reached the top of the stairs and Lize called out.

'Mum, I'm back.' There was no reply. 'She's probably fallen asleep; I'll go and see. Make yourself at home.'

Louis sat in an armchair listening for any sign from the room above that his mother would be joining them and when Lize called out for him to put the kettle on to make tea, he realised that for her, even though it was her son's wedding, it was just another day.

53
Eltham
March 1929

'It's a boy!' Reggie beamed at Cat as she opened the front door.

'Oh, congratulations Reggie. How's Maureen?' She stepped aside to let him in.

'Fine. Just fine. Bit tired, but that's to be expected.'

'Yes. I know all about that, Reggie,' she said closing the door. 'C'mon inside now, Louis should be home any minute. Here, take off yer coat and g'w'on over to the fire.'

Reggie shed his coat and as Cat hung it on the coat pegs he rubbed his hands together, moving towards the fire where he squatted before it warming himself.

'What'll ye call him?'

'Charles, after my dad.'

'That's nice. Yes, I like the name.'

Cat looked across the room as Billy came in from his bedroom. 'Billy, ye've a new baby boy cousin.'

'Oh,' he said unenthusiastically, and pulled a chair in front of the fire before burying his head in a book. Undeterred by Billie's lack of enthusiasm, Cat called to the girls who were in the scullery.

'Eileen, Anna, the baby's arrived. A little boy. His name's Charles.'

The girls rushed into the room jostling each other and it was Anna who managed to fire the question at Reggie.

'When can we see him, Reggie?'

Reggie said they could go as soon as they liked, but Cat shook her head saying the children should wait until Maureen felt like having them there. Cat and Louis would visit the next day, but the children must wait.

'Now, Anna,' Cat hugged her, 'g'w'on and get that bottle of homemade wine down from the dresser, 'tis time to open it.' She looked at Billy who was still reading.

'Billy, did ye finish yer mathematics yet?

'Ages ago.'

'Good, well then clear all these tridlums[14] off the table and the girls can set it up ready for tea. C'mon now girls, set the table for me, there's good children, while I talk to Reggie.'

Billy scowled and lowered his book. He glanced at the table, saw that the girls were already clearing his books and pencils away, and continued to read.

Cat poured two glasses of homemade wine and they welcomed Charles into the world. She and Reggie each took a long gulp and Cat gasped.

'That's powerful stuff.'

'Phew! It really has a kick in it,' he agreed.

'Well, how does it feel to be a father?'

'A little strange really. It hasn't sunk in yet.'

---

[14] tridlums – term used to describe lots of bits and pieces

Cat laughed, 'Huh! It will when he keeps ye up all night cryin'.'

Reggie nodded, took a sip of the wine, then put the glass on the table.

'Where's Louis? Is he working late?'

'No, he's at the doctor's.'

'Oh! Nothing serious I hope?'

'Just an irritatin' cough. It won't shift, so I made him see the doctor finally. Honestly Reggie it's been like tryin' to move a mountain to get him to go.'

'How's his work?'

'Steady at the moment. But things are lookin' bad. Unrest an' all that. I don't suppose ye've got that in yer job. After all, the dead animals aren't goin' to talk back at all are they?' She filled their glasses again.

'No. One thing's certain,' Reggie said, 'whatever happens, people have to eat.'

'Yes, or die! That's another good line to get into, Reggie, funerals! People always need burying, so ye'd never be out of work would ye? Sláinte,' she said, lifting up her glass.'

'Here's mud in your eye,' he laughed.

* * *

Louis arrived back long after Reggie had left and when he entered the parlour Cat thought he looked pale. After stoking up the fire she asked him what the doctor had said.

'Not much really. Just the usual thing – rub camphor into my chest at night and have onion soup regularly. Don't get wet; or stay in damp clothing, and keep away from draughts.' He took his coat off, went into the hallway to hang it up, and then ambled back into the parlour.

'Oh well, at least ye went. C'mon now sit down and have a glass of this.' She poured him a glass of wine and he asked what the occasion was.

'Maureen's had a little boy. They've called him Charles. I said we'd go round tomorrow and see the baby.'

'That's nice. Does Lize know?'

She probably does by now. Reggie was goin' round there when he left here. I wonder how she'll feel bein' a grandmother. It doesn't seem possible does it?'

'No. I suppose one day we'll be grandparents too. That seems unbelievable, doesn't it?' Louis flopped into his armchair and looked around for Tipper.

'Come here Tipper, come on boy.'

Tipper left the bone he was gnawing and slumped down at Louis' feet.

'That's right, there's a good boy.'

He fondled Tipper's ears and rested his head back against the chair, closing his eyes. He looked deathly pale and Cat stood looking at him.

'Are ye feelin' alright, Louis?'

'Just tired.'

''Tis this weather. Rain, rain and yet more rain. I'm sure I don't know where it all comes from.

Here, take off yer boots and I'll get yer slippers.' She fetched his slippers, worried about his pallor.

'D'ya want yer meal now?'

'In a minute. I'll just have a little doze. It's been a long day.'

54
Fethard
August 1929

'Louis doesn't look so well, Cat,' Maeve said as they walked into town together.

'No, he's had such a cough Mummy, all last winter, and it took everythin' out of him. I hoped comin' home would help; the fresh air and all.'

'He's got awful thin, Cat.'

'Not really, he's still wearin' the same size shirts Mummy.'

They arrived at Peggy and Breda's shop and Cat felt a wave of nostalgia. She could smell toffee apples. Peggy must have been busy. Then she remembered Mary filling up the sweet jars - so long ago now.

'Well here we are then,' Maeve said, opening the shop door, 'and where's my little darlin'?'

'I'm here Granny,' Marie called from the back of the shop.

'C'mon out then, here's yer mammy to see ye.'

Marie came running out and threw her arms around Maeve who kissed the top of her head repeatedly.

'C'mon now pet, give yer mammy a kiss.'

Marie stepped forward and raised her lips up for Cat to kiss.

'Hello darlin',' Cat said putting her arms around Marie, 'my ye've grown into a big girl, ye have.'

Marie extricated herself from her mother's embrace and Cat noticed that her child didn't seem to want her to hold her. She felt a stab of jealousy, quickly replaced with the sobering thought that she couldn't expect anything else. They had decided to leave her to be brought up in Fethard so it was no wonder Marie felt distant from them.

'Where's Billy, Eileen and Anna, Ma?' Marie asked Cat.

'At Monroe with Granddad. Ye can walk back with me when I go.'

It amused Cat that she called her *Ma*. None of the others did and it set Marie apart, as well as her strong Tipperary brogue.

Peggy finished serving a customer and rushed to greet Cat.

'Ah Cat, 'tas been too long. And will ye look at this one,' she said pointing at Marie, 'nearly as tall as her mother.'

'Well that's not very hard, there's nothin' of her at all,' Maeve laughed.

Cat walked into the side of the shop where Breda usually worked, but she wasn't there.

'Where's Breda, Peggy?'

'She's away up at Paddy Hogan's doin' a fittin' for his wife's new outfit.'

When Cat came back into the sweet shop Peggy could see by the look on her face that she'd made a mistake telling her.

Cat felt as though she had been kicked in the diaphragm. She couldn't say anything, but her thoughts were running riot. What on earth was Breda doing cavorting with Paddy Hogan's wife?

Suddenly Cat wanted to get away. She burned inside with anger at what she felt was their betrayal but was also confused because she felt deep sorrow. She made an excuse about having to get back to Monroe as Louis wasn't feeling too well.

'Shall I come with ye, Ma?' Marie asked uncertainly.

'Oh yes, if ye want to.'

Marie turned to Peggy. 'I'll be back later, Auntie.'

'That's fine,' Peggy said turning to Maeve. 'Mummy, ye're stayin' for a while, aren't ye?'

'Sure I am. Is the kettle boilin'?'

''Tis. I'll just make the tea. Cat, stay for tea won't ye?'

'No. No thanks Peggy. I'm away now.' And she left the shop quickly with Marie running to catch her up.

Peggy nervously bit her lip and stared at the empty doorway after Cat had left.

'Oh Lord, I've said the wrong thing haven't I, Mummy?'

Maeve nodded and raised her eyebrows.

'She's been gone from home a long time, Peggy. She probably has no idea that things have settled down here and that Paddy has changed now he's married.'

'I didn't think. I could bite my tongue off for lettin' it come out like that. We should have warned her before. I wouldn't hurt her for the world.'

'I know, Peggy. But what else could we have done? It's not easy to put in a letter that Breda is makin' Paddy's wife's clothes now, is it?'

Peggy continued biting her lip and Maeve could see she was worried.

'All the same Mummy, it must have been a shock for her to find out in that way that we've forgiven him. She doesn't know he's changed because we've not spoken of him in years. I think I wrote and told her he was getting married, that's all.

I'm worried what she'll say if she finds out Marie has been to his place ridin' around on his horses too. I hope Marie doesn't tell her before I get a chance to.'

Maeve crossed herself. 'Jesus, Mary and Holy St. Joseph let's hope the saints keep all our mouths shut.'

55
Eltham
Christmas 1929

'Holy Mary, Mother of God, Louis, that cough's gettin' worse, I swear it.' Cat lifted the kettle from the range and walked across to the table where she poured some hot water into a bowl.

Louis used his shirt cuff to wipe sweat from his brow and lit a cigarette. She saw his hand trembling as he put it to his lips.

'And smokin' won't help either. Now, look here, I've Friars Balsam for ye to inhale. C'mon here and put yer head over the bowl.'

Louis stood and slowly ambled over to the table where he sat heavily on the chair and leaned over the bowl of steaming liquid. Cat placed a towel over his head and told him not to lift it until he had inhaled at least twelve times. He sat breathing in the vapour, occasionally coughing.

The children were playing dominos as snow fell softly outside, covering the houses and roads in a soft blanket of white. Cat stood looking out of the window thinking that if they had much more snow it would completely block the front gate and she would have to dig it away. Louis was in no fit state to go out in the cold clearing snow.

She looked across the room at his hunched form leaning over the bowl and fear gripped her. What if he was sicker than they thought? The doctor had only told Louis to do simple things earlier on in the year, but none of it had worked and now he couldn't look at onion soup without feeling physically sick. She resolved she would go to the doctor after Christmas and demand that Louis was sent to the hospital for a diagnosis. He wasn't getting any better and she knew he had been coughing up blood lately.

Tears filled her eyes and she turned her back on the room so that the children and Louis would not see how upset she was.

'Cat?' Louis called, breaking into her thoughts.

'Yes, Pet I'm here,' she said in a bright tone, quickly blinking away her tears.

'Could you let Tipper out? He's at the door.'

'Of course.'

She went to the scullery and opened the garden door. 'C'mon Tipper. There's a good boy.'

Tipper gingerly stepped out of doors, his nose held high as he sniffed the air.

'G'w'on ye coward, get yerself outside,' she said pushing him with her foot. She closed the door and returned to the parlour. 'He should have been born a lamb, not a dog. He's too scared altogether to go out in the snow.'

Louis emerged from beneath the towel and wiped the vapour off his face. He remained where he was, staring into the distance.

'I said he's too scared to go out, Louis.'

'Oh what was that you said?'

'Nothin'. 'Tis not important. Look why don't ye go to bed, ye look banjaxed.'

'Yes. Maybe I will.' He stood and looked down at the children playing and then without warning he began coughing. He rushed from the room into the scullery where Cat found him spitting blood into the sink.

'Louis, this can't go on. Ye've to go to the doctor straight after Christmas and get an appointment for the hospital. I *insist*!'

'Yes. I will. I promise. Now I simply must go and lie down. I'm sorry Cat. I didn't want to spoil Christmas.'

'Just go to bed Louis. I'll come and wake ye later, Pet.'

* * *

It was dark when Cat slid into bed next to Louis. The whole afternoon and evening had passed as he slept. He woke as she cuddled into his back.

'Oh Cat, I feel so much better. It's dark. Is it late?'

'Yes. Ye've been asleep all afternoon and evenin'. 'Tis ten thirty now. The rest will have done ye good. I'm glad ye gave in and went to bed. Is there anythin' I can get ye before we go to sleep?'

'I wouldn't mind a drink of some sort.'

'What sort of drink. Would ye like tea or hot milk or somethin' a little stronger?'

'I'd actually like a small drop of your homemade wine if there's any left.'

'There is,' she said slipping out of bed and wrapping a shawl around her shoulders. 'I won't be a minute.' She disappeared from the bedroom to return immediately with two glasses and the bottle of wine. The bedroom was cold and she shivered. 'Sit up now and hold the glasses while I pour.'

Louis sat up and held the glasses as Cat filled them with wine. She put the bottle on the floor and climbed back into bed where Louis sat scrutinising the glass of wine against the light of the candle.

'It's a good colour. Probably very potent, Cat.'

'Sure it should be. 'Tis a couple of years old.' She raised the glass to her lips. 'Sláinte.'

'Cheers. And here's to us.'

'Yes, Louis. To us!'

They poured another glass each and were soon chattering and laughing. Louis had colour in his face.

Relieved that he looked so much better, Cat relaxed. Maybe it wasn't so bad after all. But he must still go to the doctor she thought, pouring their third glass of wine.

'I'm getting a bit tiddly, Cat.'

'I'm more than a bit tiddly, Louis. C'mon now, give us a kiss.' She closed her eyes and puckered her lips, but Louis just kissed her briefly on the cheek and took another sip of wine.

Disappointed, Cat opened her eyes. 'Not that sort of peck on the cheek, Louis… I want a *proper* kiss.'

'That *was* a *prope*r kiss woman. You're just wanton you know,' he laughed putting his glass down on the floor. He lay back on the pillow and looked at her.

'Wanton or not. I demand to be kissed properly, just like a film star.'

'You know where that will lead, Cat.'

'I don't care. I've waited long enough to be kissed properly and I'm not waitin' any longer. Kiss me. Now!'

They reached down and put their glasses on the floor, before Louis turned to Cat smiling.

'Right, you asked for it! Don't say I didn't warn you!'

56
Eltham
March 1930

'How much longer will Mummy be, Reggie?'

'Oh quite some time yet, Anna. London's a long way. Try to get some sleep now both of you. You need to be good girls for Mummy.'

'Reggie?'

'Yes, Eileen?'

The child's lip trembled. 'Is Daddy going to die?'

'No, of course not. They just want to do an operation to make him better.'

'That's good. I don't want him to die.'

'Settle down now then...I'll be back later after I've talked to Billy.'

Reggie left the room and went to talk to Billy in his bedroom.

Tipper lay in front of the fire but pricked his ears up as Reggie moved about the house. The dog had guarded Louis' slippers all day, waiting for his master to return.

Reggie appeared at Billy's doorway. 'Right, Billy have you finished reading your book?'

'Yes, sort of. But I can't concentrate. I'm too nervous about my exam on Monday.'

Reggie nodded. 'Ah yes. I forgot about that. It'll be good if you win the scholarship. Not many boys have that chance. I certainly didn't.'

Billy slid beneath the covers. 'Daddy says I can go to a Grammar School if I pass.'

'Good. That will be very nice. So you don't want to be a butcher then?'

Billy thought for a moment. 'No. Actually I would rather like to become a doctor.'

'A doctor eh?' Reggie smiled, 'Well you'll certainly have to work hard to do that.'

'I intend to, Reggie. It's what I'd really like to do one day.'

'I should think your parents would be very proud of you if you manage it.'

Billy remained silent for a while and Reggie turned to go, but then Billy called him.

'Reggie. It's pretty serious with Daddy isn't it?'

Reggie hesitated. 'We don't know at the moment, Billy. Let's wait and see what they say after the operation tomorrow. We'll keep our fingers crossed. Now come on settle down and try to get some sleep.'

Billy blew out his nightlight. 'Alright. Goodnight, Reggie.'

'Goodnight, Billy.'

Reggie closed the bedroom door and went over to sit in Louis' chair beside the fire. Tipper whined and Reggie got up to let him out, but the dog wouldn't leave Louis' slippers.

'Come on Tipper, out you go.' Reggie tried to coax him, but it was no use. He made one last effort. 'You silly old dog. Why don't you go out for a little while?' He gave up trying to coax the dog and instead sat down, opened the evening paper and began reading. After he had spent an hour catching up on the news he heard a door open and Anna came into the parlour rubbing her eyes.

'I can't sleep, Reggie. Eileen's making snoring noises.'

'Come over here then…sit on my lap and I'll tell you a story.' Anna tiptoed across the floor and hopped up onto Reggie's lap. 'What sort of story do you want?'

Anna thought for a moment, and then smiled at Reggie. 'A fairy story.'

'I'll make one up out of my head and you can put little bits in as we go.'

'That's a good idea.' Anna shivered. 'I'm cold, Reggie.'

'I'll get my coat and we can snuggle up together,' Reggie said, easing Anna off his lap. He went to the hallway for his coat, returned to the fire and drew Anna back onto his lap, laying the coat over them.

'There, that's better isn't it?'

Anna lay against Reggie's chest. 'Yes, much better. Start the story then, Reggie.'

Reggie began his tale, using his finger to show how tiny the little fairy was compared to Anna.

'You see she's a really little person and she likes to hop on and off peoples' shoulders without them knowing…just like this.' He tickled Anna's neck and she giggled.

'What else does the fairy do, Reggie?'

'She goes tippy toeing along your leg and lifts your nightie up and has a look to see if you've eaten all your dinner up.'

Anna giggled and Reggie lifted the hem of her nightie, and then tickled her knees.

'That tickles Reggie,' she laughed. What does the fairy do then?'

'She tickles my tummy too to see if I've eaten all my dinner.'

'Go on then, let her tickle your tummy.'

'Just a minute, I have to undo my trousers so she can tickle my tummy.' He undid his trousers and pulled his shirt out exposing some flesh.

'Now the little fairy can see whether I've eaten my dinner too. Do you want to feel my tummy like the little fairy does, to see if I've eaten my dinner?'

'Yes, and then I can see what the fairy sees, can't I?'

'Give me your hand then and I will let you feel my tummy.'

Reggie took her hand and guided it through between his unbuttoned flies.

'Can you feel my big tummy?'

'Yes. I think you've eaten all your dinner it's very big.'

Reggie pressed her hand against his penis.

'There, can you feel that?'

'Yes. You must have eaten a lot of dinner, Reggie.'

Reggie moaned and began forcing her hand faster and faster against his penis until with a gasp he released her.

Anna looked at him in surprise. 'My hand's got all wet Reggie.'

Reggie sat breathing deeply before he answered her.

'You mustn't tell anyone about our little fairy story – it's a secret.'

'Why?'

'Because if you do, the little fairy will be very cross with you and put a spell on your daddy and something bad will happen, so do you promise?' He wiped her hand on his shirt.

'Yes. I promise. Can I tell Eileen though?'

'*No*! Not Eileen or *anybody* else. If you do, a spell will be cast on whoever you tell and they will die as well as your daddy, so it's very important that it's just our secret. It's our story. So do you promise?'

Anna stared wide-eyed at him and nodded. She didn't want anyone to die because of her; so she knew she would never tell anyone about the little fairy story.

Suddenly Reggie kissed her cheek. 'Come on now, it's time you went back to bed.'

Anna slid off his lap and walked away towards the bedroom.

'Remember now, it's our secret, Anna,' Reggie called.

'Yes Reggie. Goodnight.'

She crept beneath the covers and cuddled up to Eileen, thinking how careful she would have to be not to tell. She had been a little afraid of the fairy and how she had to feel Reggie's tummy. She felt it was wrong, but she couldn't ask anybody about it in case they died - because of the spell.

57
Eltham
1930

'Good luck, Billy. And remember, Daddy will be so proud of ye if ye do well.'

'I'm very nervous, Mummy.'

'Ye can only do yer best darlin', that's all any of us can do. Now off with ye to school and don't be late or they won't let ye in to do the exam.'

Billy kissed Cat's cheek and she hugged him, squeezing her eyes shut tight against the tears that were welling up in her eyes.

He pulled away and ran down the steps, along the path and out of the gate without a backward glance. Turning round as he got to the house next-door-but-one, Billy grinned at Cat who waved again, before returning inside.

The girls had a day off school because of the examinations and were helping to clear the breakfast table. Eileen was dashing back and forth while Anna was dragging her heels not doing much.

'Anna, c'mon now, look lively Love, ye're half asleep.'

The child looked mournfully at Cat and tears formed in her eyes.

'What's the matter my darlin'?' Cat said, sitting at the table. She pulled Anna onto her lap. 'Is it Daddy ye're worried about?'

She nodded and began sobbing uncontrollably. Cat rocked her in her arms as Eileen stood watching, then she picked up the remaining cup and saucer from the table and disappeared into the scullery to wash up.

Cat kissed the top of Anna's head and her sobbing subsided. After a little while Cat suddenly squeezed Anna.

'C'mon' she said, 'let's get ready and go up to London to see Daddy shall we?'

Anna smiled and slid off Cat's lap looking happier. Cat looked at the child's solemn little face and stroked her cheek softly.

'That's better now isn't it? G'w'on now and get dressed. I'll help Eileen to finish off in the scullery, and then we'll go.'

* * *

They approached the ward through a small dimly lit corridor, but all visitors had to report to the Ward Sister for permission to visit, so Cat and the girls stopped outside her office.

'Stay here, and sit quietly on those chairs while I just speak to the Sister to see if it's alright for us to see Daddy,' she whispered.

Cat knocked on the Sister's door and when she heard someone call out for her to enter, she opened the door and disappeared inside.

The girls grew restless as Cat didn't reappear for ages.

Eileen whispered in Anna's ear. 'Shall we creep in and find Daddy, Anna?'

'No! I'm scared.'

'What are you scared of?'

'All those people in there.' She nodded toward the ward doors.

'They're only people who've had operations, silly.'

'Yes, but I don't like them. They're scary.'

'Oh you're just a cry-baby.'

'I'm not!'

'You are.'

'No I'm not.'

Cat came out of the office. Her face was ashen and she signalled for one of the girls to get up and let her sit down.

Eileen stood up. 'What's the matter Mummy?'

Cat couldn't answer, but sat gasping and wiping her brow with her hankie. The girls fell silent watching their mother, trying to read her expression and assess the situation. They waited for Cat to speak.

Then the door to the Sister's office opened and a doctor in a white coat came out, followed by a couple of nurses. The doctor pushed through the swing doors to the ward and led his entourage of uniformed staff inside.

Eileen caught a glimpse of the patients inside and something made her shudder.

Suddenly Cat got up and told the girls to wait on the chairs outside the ward.

Eileen immediately anxious said, 'But I thought we were going to see Daddy.'

Cat sounded agitated when she answered.

'I'll have to see how he is first. Now just ye wait here and I'll g'w'on in. Be good girls now. I need ye to be good.'

Something in Cat's manner alarmed the girls, so they just nodded and sat down again to begin their vigil. As Cat disappeared through the swing doors Eileen took hold of Anna's hand and held it tight.

Cat tiptoed towards the bed.

'Louis? Louis?' she whispered stroking the back of his hand. She thought he looked shrunken; he seemed half his normal size.

Louis opened his eyes and she saw his pupils were very large and he had difficulty focussing on her face.

'Cat? Is that you?'

'Yes, my darlin' I'm here.'

Louis sighed and licked his dry lips. 'Water, please.'

She poured water from the jug and held a glass to his lips while he sipped some, then sank back on the pillows, exhausted.

Cat sat watching Louis as he drifted off to sleep again and realised it wasn't such a good idea bringing the girls to see him. She thought she should go, but didn't want to leave him. When she stood up Louis opened his eyes as if sensing her impending departure.

'Going so soon?'

'I've got Anna and Eileen outside. I think it may be best if we come back another day when ye're feelin' better.'

'Don't go Cat,' his voice was so quiet, she could barely hear him. 'I want to tell you—'

Cat sat down again and waited for Louis to gather his strength and speak.

'What is it ye want to tell me, Pet?'

'Insurance. Lize has it. Since before the war.'

There was a long pause while Cat waited for him to explain about some insurance, but he had stopped speaking. Then he opened his eyes and began again.

'Ask Lize.'

There was another long pause, and then he sighed, 'Oh God Cat, what will you do?'

Maybe he's rambling, Cat thought. Probably the anaesthetic was mixing up his mind. She felt it was best to let him sleep. She kissed his lips.

'Now ye just settle down and stop worryin'. I'll go now and come back again soon. Billy has his exam today and I'd better be gettin' back now.'

Louis frowned. 'Exam?'

'Ye know, the one for him to get a scholarship to the Grammar School.'

'Oh. Grammar school.'

Cat realised he was confused, so just told him he'd forgotten. She stood up ready to leave.

'Louis, I'll be gettin' off home now.'

'Children at school?'

'No, Louis. I already told ye, Anna and Eileen are here with me.'

'Can't hear them.'

'They're outside the ward, waitin' for me.'

'I want.' he coughed, and Cat saw pain register on his face. She sensed he needed to see the children, but was afraid it would tax him.

'Oh Louis, I don't think ye're well enough to be bothered with them. They may tire ye out.'

He shook his head.

'Cat, please.'

She tiptoed down the ward and pushed the swing doors open and motioned to where the girls sat waiting for the signal to enter the ward. Just then the Ward Sister appeared from behind some screens. 'I'm sorry, no children allowed in the ward.'

'Oh, but we've come such a long way and they'll be so disappointed not to see their daddy.' Cat said, her eyes filling with tears.

'I'm sorry, it's hospital rules. No children.' She turned on her heel and walked out of the swing doors into her office.

Cat looked down at Anna and Eileen's faces and could see their disappointment. She held a finger up to her lips and beckoned them to follow her into the ward. Softly the threesome approached Louis' bed. His eyes were closed and Cat stroked the back of his hand again to let him know they were there.

'Cat?'

'Yes, my darlin', I'm here. Anna and Eileen are here too.'

Louis opened his eyes and smiled, but Cat could see his unfocussed eyes were looking past them. She looked at his waxen complexion and saw him struggling to see them, but she could tell he didn't have the energy to hold a conversation.

'Kiss Daddy, girls,' Cat said. 'I think we'll go now because he's very tired. We'll come back again when he's a bit better.' Her voice was high pitched and the lump in her throat constricted further conversation.

Eileen leaned forward and kissed Louis' forehead but Anna stepped back hesitating.

'C'mon now Anna, kiss Daddy goodbye,' Cat encourged.

Anna stood rooted to the spot. So Cat kissed Louis lips; took hold of Anna's hand and led her from the ward.

Irritated with Anna, Cat turned to her.

'What's got into ye? Why wouldn't ye kiss Daddy goodbye? It would have made him feel better.'

But Cat didn't notice that Anna had failed to answer, or see the look of terror on the child's face, because her mind was focussed on her conversation earlier with the doctor, and all she could think of doing now was praying. 'God in your mercy, help us.'

58
Eltham
April 16th 1930

'Happy Birthday to you, Happy Birthday to you, Happy Birthday dear Anna, Happy Birthday to you,' Cat, Billy, Eileen, Lize and Iris sang.

'Come on blow the candles out, Anna,' Lize said pushing the cake towards her.

'Don't forget to make a wish,' Eileen reminded her as Anna began to blow. But then, as though remembering something, Anna stopped blowing, closed her eyes and thought hard about her wish, then opened her eyes and blew the candles out in one go.

'Hooray,' Iris said and lifted the knife to cut the cake. 'The next cake I cut will be my wedding cake, won't it, Mum?' she said looking round at Lize.

'You getting married, Iris?' Billy asked.

'Yes.'

'Who to?'

'My fiancé of course.'

'It's not that one that I saw you with is it?'

'Yes, that's him. His name's Fred.'

Cat smiled at Iris. 'It doesn't seem five minutes since ye were a child, Iris.'

'Maybe not to you, Auntie, but I am twenty two now.'

'Yes, time flies doesn't it?' Cat turned to Lize.

'Piece of cake, Lize?'

'Thanks. Cat, can we talk for a minute?'

'Sure. Let's go out there,' Cat said nodding towards the scullery and the two women disappeared through the doorway. Cat anticipated what Lize was going to ask before she said it.

'Cat. How serious is it with Louis?'

'More than I knew, Lize. They removed one lung and the other's no better. 'Tis cancer.'

Lize drew in a breath, visibly moved.

'How long?'

'Not long, Lize. They couldn't be specific.' She began to cry.

Lize's eyes filled with tears and she rummaged up the sleeve of her cardigan for a handkerchief.

'Sorry. Look don't cry Cat,' Lize said offering her the handkerchief. 'Oh God. How will you manage, Cat, with another baby on the way?'

'I'm not thinkin' about it, Lize. I haven't been able to make any plans, I'm kinda numb. I can't seem to take it in.'

Billy opened the door. 'Shut the door, Billy,' Cat snapped at him. 'Auntie Lize and I are talkin'.' He scowled and closed the door.

'Cat, I don't know what to say.'

'There's nothin' *to* say. I'm goin' to lose him and there's *nothin'* anyone can say, or do. I sent a telegram to my parents today, just to let them know; only there's Marie to think of as well. He's her father too, she has a right to know and I thought they could break it to her.'

'I see,' Lize answered, 'well let me know if there's anything I can do, Cat, won't you?'

'Thanks, Lize. Just knowin' ye're around is a help. I'm takin' the children up to see him tomorrow. Maybe he'll be a little better. I hope so. They need to see him, they miss him so much.'

Lize patted her arm and tears slid down her cheeks.

'We all do.'

* * *

'Louis, we're here, all of us. Billy, Anna, Eileen and me. Are ye awake?' Cat stood nervously by his bed.

Louis opened his eyes and smiled. He seemed coherent when he answered.

'There you all are my darlings. I've been wanting to see you. Louis looked at Anna. 'Anna, Happy Birthday for yesterday. So, you're eight years old now.'

Cat noticed how difficult it was for him to speak, as in order to finish a sentence he had stopped several times to take a breath before continuing. Anna pushed something wrapped in greaseproof paper into his hand.

'What's this?' he smiled unwrapping the little parcel. 'Oh birthday cake, how lovely. Thank you Anna. Sorry. I don't have a present for you. Mummy will get you something, won't you, Mummy?'

Cat put on a bright smile. 'Yes, there's a little doll she's seen. I'll get it for her shall I?'

'Take the money from the savings tin,' he said to Cat, and then looked back at Anna. 'What are you going to call your doll, Anna?'

'I don't know, Daddy. If you and Mummy have another little girl, what would you like to be her name?'

'Oh, hard question, Anna.'

Louis' rasping breath was worrying Cat.

'C'mon now Anna, that's enough questions for today.'

'No, it's alright, Cat. I just thought of a name. The Duke and Duchess of York's little daughter, is Elizabeth. I like that name.' He smiled at Cat directing the suggestion to her. 'So shall we call the new baby Elizabeth if she's a girl?'

Anna smiled. 'I like that name.'

'I think we all do,' Cat nodded. 'Elizabeth it is then.'

59
Eltham
18th April 1930

'Someone at the door, Mummy,' Billy called from his bedroom, so Cat, drying her hands, hurried from the scullery to open it.

'*Dada*! Oh *Dada*!'

Ned dropped his bag and opened his arms to hug Cat.

'I came as soon as I got yer telegram. Jesus, I'm that sorry Cat. How bad is it?'

She pulled away a little, caught him by the hand and drew him inside the house.

'C'mon in,' she whispered, 'we don't want to talk out here.'

Ned picked up his bag and swung it into the hallway.

''Tis bad, Dada. I've to tell the children; but can't pluck up the courage.' She wrung her hands together. 'I'm so thankful ye've come. Dear God, this is the answer to a prayer.'

They went into the parlour and he pulled Cat into his arms. She sobbed against his chest, thinking to herself that she would never be held in Louis' arms again.

Ned sighed. 'C'mon now, ye go right ahead and have a good cry. What a hand ye've been dealt. What a hand!'

Billy appeared in the doorway.

'*Granddad!*' he said dropping the book he was holding. He rushed to embrace him. 'I didn't know you were coming.'

'No, I didn't know meself either until I was on the train and on me way, then me head caught up with me body.'

Ned did some mock boxing with Billy then pulled the boy toward him again and hugged him.

'Tis good to see ye, Billy.' He held the boy at arm's length looking at him from top to toe, 'Ye're lookin' grand, and so grown up!'

Hearing a commotion, the girls then came into the room and Eileen joined in the excitement with Billy.

Anna slipped her hand into Cat's, burying her face against her mother's body as Eileen glanced across at Cat.

'Have you been crying, Mummy?'

Cat looked across at Ned, shrugged her shoulders and sat down.

'C'mere. All of ye. I've somethin' to tell ye.'

Silenced, the children gathered around Cat; and Ned stood watching his daughter tell his grandchildren their daddy was going to die.

* * *

Cat ripped the telegram open and read the four words printed on the inside:

COME QUICK, SINKING FAST.

Her mouth dried and her legs began to shake. Gripping the edge of the table she fell into a chair, calling to Ned who was in the scullery shaving. He appeared immediately in the doorway, wiping his chin with a towel. Barely able to speak, her breath coming in short bursts, she held out the telegram for him to read.

'Dada. I have to go to the hospital immediately.'

Ned went to her instantly and took her hands in his.

Cat, mo chuisle. If 'tis God's will to take him, then go he must. Ye have Louis' children and he's left ye with the finest gift a man can give. A family. Let's pray together, Pet.'

They knelt on the parlour floor and Ned prayed that Louis' passing be as quick and painless as possible; and asked God to open the doors of Heaven and admit him.

When they had finished praying Cat rose and went to the bedroom to collect her outdoor clothes. She opened the wardrobe door and took out her coat and boots. When she saw Louis' old army greatcoat hanging on the rail she wanted to wrap herself in the material; bury her face in the fabric; anything to be near him to experience him once more.

Sitting on the bed her thoughts of Louis avalanched into her mind. Like an album of snapshots her memories flicked over each picture of him: all those years ago as a dashing young soldier inviting her to tea in the barracks, their developing love when Louis had serenaded her playing the violin after haymaking; being away in the war, their wedding, their ups and downs, the children. And soon he would be gone.

Inside her, deep within the very cortex of her mind, Louis had taken up residence and she didn't know how she could go on living without him.

They had made such plans. When they were such and such an age they would do this, and then when they were old they would go home to Ireland and live there because the children would all have flown the nest. This *wasn't* the way things should be. She felt it defied the natural order of things.

And then the child in her womb stirred as though reminding Cat that it would never even know its father. She slumped forward, her hand reaching out to touch the arm of his greatcoat but the sleeve was empty of the man.

Automatically she put on her boots, laced them up, and then donned her coat. She fumbled with buttons that wouldn't go through the buttonholes, and then placed her hat on her head. She dropped the hatpin on the floor but when she bent to pick it up between her numbed fingertips, she couldn't feel it.

She felt as though someone had hit her head with an iron bar and that she was in some sort of bewildered trance. It wasn't really her going through the motions of preparing to see Louis for the last time. Totally adrift, it was as if she was in a boat without oars. Even Ned's voice seemed distant and muffled as he called her from outside the door.

When Cat didn't answer he opened her bedroom door.

'Are ye ready, Pet?'

She was standing before the window staring out onto the garden, where the promise of summer swayed tantalizingly before her eyes in every blossom.

'Cat, I think I'll come with ye. Is there someone who will watch over the children?'

She seemed to emerge from her reverie.

'Oh, yes. Mrs. Pierce next door.'

'Right then. I'll go ask her now.'

He disappeared and Cat continued to stare out of the window, immobilised.

When Ned reappeared he gently guided her from the bedroom into the parlour.

Mrs. Pierce was in the room. How did Mrs. Pierce get there, she wondered?

More muffled conversation between Mrs. Pierce and Ned took place and then Cat was aware of her father holding her arm as they went down the steps into the garden out onto the road ahead.

60
Royal Free Cancer Hospital, London
April 23 1930

Louis' bed was empty when they arrived. Shocked, Cat turned to Ned.

'We're too late.'

Then the Ward Sister appeared and beckoned her into a side room where Louis lay struggling to breathe. The Sister whispered to Cat.

'He's holding on. I think he knew you were coming, Mrs. Ross.'

The nurse and Ned then left the room, closing the door to leave Cat and Louis alone.

Cat leaned over and kissed him.

'Louis, I'm here.'

'Cat? Oh Lord Cat, how will you manage?'

'Don't worry Louis; ye've enough to think about. Don't worry about me and the children.'

'But the baby. I should have–'

'Louis. 'Tis a gift from God. Somethin' between us, like the others. Don't fret.'

Her words seemed to pacify him and he looked at rest. Then he became agitated again.

'I haven't–'

'What, my darlin'? Haven't what?' She waited as his laboured breathing filled the air with rasping sounds. 'What haven't you done, Pet?'

'Said, how much you filled my life, my soul. Wanted it to be forever.'

Her tears fell unchecked, dropping onto his pillow as Cat struggled to remain controlled. She couldn't run away and couldn't escape from the room because it was all too painful. She knew she had to sit there and see it out as this would be their last conversation.

Louis slept for a while and Cat sat waiting and wondering how much longer he had.

A priest had been summoned and he quietly slipped into the room, opened his bag discreetly and put on his garments for reading Louis the last rites.

After a while, Louis seemed to rouse again.

'Cat, my love.' The rasping breaths continued, interspersed with his words of love.

'First time I saw you. I knew you were the one.' He stopped talking and became restful.

She sat rigidly in the chair afraid to move, watching his chest rise and fall, listening to the rasp of breath.

The priest came round to her side of the bed and took hold of Cat's hand.

'Cat?'

'Yes, Louis I'm here, Pet,' she said and took hold of his hand.

Suddenly he opened his eyes, looked at her and said in a very clear voice. 'Cat. Don't let go.'

'I won't, Louis. I won't.'

61
Eltham
May 2nd 1930

The sun was high overhead as six jet-black horses with black feathered plumes across their bridles stopped outside the gate. Cat saw their shining flanks quivering occasionally as they waited, but only their perfectly groomed tails showed any sign of movement in the May morning sun.

Her heart palpitated in her chest but she was determined to see things through with dignity. She would be brave, for Louis' sake.

Seeing the funeral director and coffin bearers approach the house, she slipped her arm though Ned's and he squeezed it tight. Then she released his grip and went along the hallway to open the door.

As the door opened the funeral director bowed his head.

'We are ready to receive your husband now, Madam.'

Speechless, Cat merely stepped aside and the black-coated men went quietly into the parlour.

'Wait,' she called. 'Wait just a moment please,' and she pushed through the men who had gathered around the coffin, about the screw down the lid.

'Let me say one more goodbye, please.'

For the last time, Cat leaned over and kissed Louis' lips, his closed eyes and his forehead, and murmured. 'Goodbye, my darlin'.'

Then, unable to watch the men closing the lid on Louis, she turned away and went into the scullery to wait with the rest of the family.

They all stood listening until finally they heard the last sounds of the men's feet scuffing through the parlour, along the hallway and out of the front door.

Soon after, the funeral director returned and said they were ready to go; so, composed, Cat left the house supported by Ned.

Following Cat and Ned was Billy holding hands with Marie. Maeve came next holding hands with Eileen and Anna. Peggy and Breda followed with Lize, Iris and Fred, Maureen and Reggie. Louis' mother, unable to walk the two miles to the cemetery, was absent.

Led by Cat and Ned they all went quietly to stand in place behind the glass-sided hearse. The only sound breaking the silence was the gentle clinking of the bridles as the horses moved their heads, as their black plumed feathers lifted and fell in the slight breeze.

In the stillness Cat became vaguely aware of neighbours lining the roadside to pay their last respects; of curtains drawn on every home; the men lifting their hats, and the sound of horses' hooves clashing against cobbles as they became impatient to proceed.

The funeral director stepped up to her and asked if she was ready to go and when she nodded, the hearse drew gently away.

As they left, Cat's mind raced through past events. She thought about the home they had lived in which had known both harsh times and laughter. Visions of their life together flashed through her mind. All the joint memories kaleidoscoped, and she found it hard to grasp that they were now taking this last journey together, moving towards Louis' final resting place, where he would lie alone in perpetuity.

Throughout the walk Cat was transfixed with the sound of the coffin bearers' boots crunching along in unison with the wheels of the hearse and the clip clop of horses' hooves. The rhythm somehow soothed her. It felt like the ticking of a clock.

On and on she walked, thinking that life was just like a treadmill, and that they were all on it together. Sometimes, she thought, someone just steps off the wheel a bit earlier than the rest. Ultimately she knew that her parents, her sisters, her children and herself would all step off somewhere, at some time, further along in time from life's eternal wheel.

Walking in the early summer sun, up slight inclines and down gently sloping roadways, became therapeutic to her. If only she could just go on walking like this, with Louis in front of them and the children behind. She could walk forever and not let this day end. Just to walk on endlessly, following her man.

After a mile the procession stopped and the funeral director approached Cat and said they would rest for five minutes.

Ned thanked him and took a hip flask out of his pocket. He offered the canteen to Cat.

'Here, I've brought some water for ye.'

She took it without a word, drank some, and handed it back.

'When you are quite ready, Madam,' the funeral director said, 'we will go on, but please take your time, there is no hurry.'

Cat looked at him quizzically. No hurry? No, she thought, there's no hurry. Time means nothing at all now. There's no today, no tomorrow, and no next week or anything anymore. It didn't matter how much time it took to get there, the longer the better, because it meant Louis was still with them.'

She nodded to Ned. 'I'm ready now. We'll make a start again.'

So he indicated to the funeral director that they should go and once more they began following the hearse along the cobbled road.

* * *

The priest blessed Louis' coffin with holy water and the coffin bearers lowered him slowly into the grave.

Cat watched as the oak casket bumped the sides of the hole on its way downward and felt angry, wishing they would be more careful.

Ned, sensing her anguish, squeezed her arm and stepped forward to take up a handful of earth. He handed it to her and one by one the children stepped forward and did the same.

The priest was chanting.

'Ashes to ashes, dust-to-dust, earth-to-earth.'

She took one final look at the coffin and with her eyes shut threw in her handful of earth. The children watched her and did the same, then wiped their hands on their clothes.

Cat left the cemetery with the children and stood for a while looking over the stone wall as the gravediggers filled in the grave. Then sadly she turned and began walking home to life without Louis.

Part Four

62
Hogan Stables, Fethard
May 1933

'Paddy! Will ye look at me?' Marie called as he leaned on the paddock gate.

'Sure, I am after lookin' at ye, Madam!'

'Well, here I go now,' she laughed as she spurred the pony into a canter to jump the pole propped up on two straw bales. As she landed Marie looked back to see if Paddy was still watching, and in that moment became unseated and fell off.

Quickly Paddy unlatched the gate and ran to where she lay motionless.

'Are ye hurt, Marie?' he asked lifting her from the ground, but she was limp and fear gripped him.

'Oh God, don't let her be hurt,' he murmured.

Suddenly she giggled.

'Huh! That fooled ye!'

'Oh ye little devil,' he said dropping her, 'I thought ye were dead.'

Marie pointed a finger at him.

'Ha ha, that caught ye out.'

She scrambled to her feet and continued to laugh as he chased her around the paddock. When he caught hold of her, he tickled her until she yelled for him to stop. But he wasn't prepared to give in that easily,

'Say ye're sorry then,' he demanded.

'Oh *sure* I am.'

He let go of her.

'Don't ye be cheekin' me now, Marie, or I'll have to set about ticklin' ye again,' he said breathing heavily, 'Now, get back in the saddle and finish off yer exercises before I put her away for the night.'

Paddy lit a cigarette and stood watching Marie remount the pony, then sit perfectly straight in the saddle and trot around the paddock practicing her show jumping.

He checked the time on his watch.

'Now then. Same time tomorrow and we're ready for the show on Saturday, where we intend to win – is that right?'

Marie jerked her head to flick the hair off her face and smiled at him

In her face Paddy suddenly saw a vision of Cat. His chest constricted and he felt his jaws tighten in the familiar way he once experienced whenever he heard Cat's name, or saw someone that reminded him of her.

All these years later, and he still could not rid himself of anger at being jilted. She haunted his dreams; burned a huge jealous streak into the calm of his life. Damn her, he thought!

Marie called to him and reluctantly he dragged his thoughts into the present. He opened the gate to allow her to trot through with the pony then closed it behind her.

Smirking, she looked down at him.

'Thank ye yer Lordship.'

'Don't ye get too cheeky young lady,' he laughed as she steered the pony towards the stable.

Marie turned in the saddle at the stable door. 'Are ye goin' to rub her down or will I?'
He thought for a moment. 'Why don't we do it together, 'twill be quicker.'

'Right, together it is then,' she said slipping down from the saddle and began unbuckling the girth strap.

Paddy pulled the saddle off and heaved it up onto the side of the horse stall

'Now, Miss,' he said looking serious, 'ye'll need to be here nice and early on Saturday, we've to plait the tail and give her a good brush before the competition.'

'Have I ever been late? Ye know ye don't have to worry about me bein' here I'll arrive before ye've had yer breakfast.'

'Good. Now be off home or yer aunties will be eatin' supper alone again.'

'Aw they don't mind, Paddy.'

'Nevertheless, off ye go now.'

'I'm goin',' she said moving toward him and raised her chin. 'Kiss before I leave?'

'C'mon now,' he said giving her a peck on the cheek, 'away with ye.'

She turned and walked toward the stable door.

'See ye tomorrow then, Paddy. Bye.'

After she left he stopped what he was doing and stood thinking for a while. What in the name of

God was he doing? He had begun to feel something different for this young girl who reminded him so much of her mother.

He reflected that there was no hope of any children of his own as years of marriage had failed to produce one single baby. Now, with his wife so poorly, it was final – there would be no heir.

Strange thoughts had begun to creep into his head of late. He'd begun thinking that if his wife died then he could wait a few years and maybe, just maybe - Marie and him? No, don't be so stupid, he chided himself. She was just a child. And yet - what was wrong with having a little daydream to help him through?

He finished putting the pony to bed, left the stable, bolted the door and strolled across to the house.

The silence enveloped him like a heavy black blanket. He liked peace and quiet, but he had begun to feel he was dying a slow suffocating death along with his wife; just going through the paces of living out the months until he was a single man again.

The atmosphere oppressed him but there was no way out. Oh well, he thought, better get inside and cook the supper and then sit alone reading some old book until bedtime.

He sat brooding long into the evening and as often occurred, his mind turned to the events of years gone by, of his involvement with the Irish National Volunteers and their attempts to disrupt the political endeavours of the British Government.

All a long time ago now, he thought, and for what purpose? Nothing had come of it all and they were no better off. True, he was comfortable himself as he had inherited everything from his parents, but many of the local population were in dire straits and most young people left to work in England or America once they finished school.

There was no work around in Fethard other than on the land, the railway or the dairy. The place was dying along with his wife.

Paddy did not have to worry about money as the thoroughbred racehorses he bred were much sought after. He had the finest bloodline in winners throughout Tipperary, if not the whole of Ireland.

But there was a void in his life. A big hole that was never filled. He knew that it was because he had no family other than his wife, and she too would soon be gone.

63
St. Mary's Convent School,
Eltham
June 1933

Anna knocked on Mother Superior's door. She heard her call *come in*, and slipped inside.

'Sister Monica said you wanted to see me, Mother,' Anna said, looking worried.

'Yes, Anna I do,' the nun answered pulling an envelope out of her desk drawer. 'Just wait one minute and I'll be finished. I want you to take this letter home to your mother.'

She wrote something on the envelope and looked up, smiling at Anna. 'It's alright Anna, you are not in any trouble; it's just a letter for your mother. Nothing to worry about.'

Mother Superior saw Anna's visible relief so opened her drawer again and pulled out a bag of sweets.

'Come here and choose yourself a sweet,' she said.

'Oh thank you, Mother. I thought I was in trouble.'

Anna went to the desk and took a sweet from the bag Mother Superior held open, and popped it in her mouth.

'Should you be in trouble over anything then, Anna? '

'Well, Mother, I thought maybe it was because of my socks.'

Mother Superior stood up and peered over the edge of her desk to view Anna's socks. She noticed they were not the uniform grey woollen ones, but were white and crocheted. She sat down and smiled.

'They are rather smart socks, Anna. Were they a present?'

'No not really, Mother. The lady Mummy cleans for gave them to us as her daughter had outgrown them.'

'Well that was very kind of her. But why would you think you were in trouble over the socks?'

'Because Sister Monica told me I was bold wearing them to school, Mother, and she said that I was never to wear them again. She made me stand in front of the class and said I was showing off by wearing them to school.'

Anna's face burned with embarrassment and she stared at the floor.

'Come here my dear,' Mother Superior said pushing her chair away from the desk. 'Our Lord entered this world without clothes, without a house and with nowhere to sleep. Since that time, throughout history, we have remembered the Inn Keeper, as he was kind enough to show some pity towards the family and allow them to stay in their cattle shed. It may not have seemed much, but for those days I suppose you could say it was a big act of kindness, wouldn't you agree?'

'Yes Mother I would.'

'So, Anna, just remember that if people are kind enough to give something to less fortunate children we should remember that they are only following the example of the Inn Keeper and that accepting that kindness is nothing to be ashamed of.' She ran her hand over Anna's curls. 'Wear the socks as often as you like, it's far too hot to wear wool.'

'But I'll get into trouble from Sister Monica, Mother.'

'I'll have a word with her, Anna. We are about to change the uniform rules for summertime anyway, so this will remind me to see to it. Run along now,' she said.

As Anna reached the door Mother Superior called to her.

'Anna, finish the sweet before you go back into class, we don't want you to be in trouble for eating in Sister Monica's lessons do we?'

Anna grinned at her before closing the door behind her.

* * *

Cat bustled into the parlour with Elizabeth and dumped a huge pile of washing on the floor. She saw the table had been set, the kettle was boiling on the range and Eileen and Anna were busy buttering bread.

'Ah 'tis good gels ye are,' she smiled at them. 'I can always rely on ye and I don't know what I'd do without ye.'

She went over and kissed them both and gave them a hug. 'Now Billy, will ye get off yer backside and take that pile o' clothes outside for me?'

Billy dropped the book he was reading, scowled, and reluctantly picked up the washing.

'Where do you want it?' he asked, clearly annoyed he had been requested to do something.

'Where d'ya think? Where it always goes. And ye shouldn't need to question that.'

Billy dragged the pile into the scullery muttering, and Eileen and Anna glanced at each other with raised eyebrows.

'How come Billy never has to do the housework, Mummy?' Eileen asked.

'Well ye know he has a lot of reading to do for school. It's hard work in a Grammar School and if he's to get into the medical profession, he has to do it.'

'Huh. Lucky old him,' Eileen said. 'Well, he'll have to get off his backside a lot more if he does ever get into the medical profession – then he'll get a shock. Lazy devil!'

Cat turned on her.

'Eileen, that's enough of that. Ye know we all have our tasks to do and Billy is the man of the house since Daddy died, ye know that. And I don't want to hear any more arguments about who does what – we all do our fair share.'

Elizabeth went to the corner of the room and took her bricks out.

'Billy,' Cat said, 'play with Elizabeth while we finish gettin' the tea will ye?'

The one thing Billy never minded doing was playing with Elizabeth and he gladly pulled the toy brick box over to the hearth and tipped them out so that they could build something.

'Did ye feed Tipper, Billy?' Cat asked him as he started placing the bricks in a row.

'Yes, Mum. And I took him for a walk, but that horrible Chow down the road went for him again so I we didn't get any further, I just brought him home.'

'They want to get that animal put down, vicious thing. Was he hurt?'

'No, we got away in time,' he said sitting down next to Elizabeth where he began telling her a story about the train he was making her.

'Mummy, Mother Superior gave me a letter for you,' Anna said pulling the envelope out of her pocket. 'Here, I'm sorry it's a bit crumpled.'

'Oh what's it about?'

'I don't know, but I thought it was about my socks.'

'What about yer socks?'

'Sister Monica scorned them. She made me stand out the front of the class so everyone could take a look at them, and told me I was bold for wearing them to school.'

'She did *what*?'

'She said I wasn't to wear such things to school, but it's alright because Mother Superior said I could, and she's going to have a word with Sister Monica.'

Everyone had stopped what they were doing and watched for Cat's reaction to this piece of news, but Cat then sat down to open the letter, thinking it was on the same theme as the socks.

The children watched for her reaction and when Cat began to smile and then jumped up from the chair and began hugging them all, they wondered what the letter had contained. Puzzled, it was Anna who asked what the letter was about.

'This letter,' Cat said waving the piece of paper about, 'is the answer to a prayer.'

The children all looked at one another and Anna thought it must surely be about the socks as Mother Superior had talked about Our Lord and the way we have prayed to him in thanks for his kindness.

'I can't believe it, I just can't believe it,' Cat repeated as she re-read the letter, and having satisfied herself she had the facts right, told the children the contents.

'The letter from Mother Superior is offerin' me a job in the convent, doin' the cleanin' and I can take Elizabeth with me and she can go into the class with Anna while I'm workin.' Cat went on explaining excitedly, 'and because I am goin' to be on the staff, we will all get a free dinner. Oh Lord above, I cannot believe this. 'Tis too good to be true. Now Anna, get me some paper and a pen and I'll write to accept it immediately.'

'So it's not about the socks then?' Anna asked.

'No, Pet. But don't ye worry, I'll still be seein' that Sister Monica and remind her just what she's supposed to be doin' in her job, not criticising people who have nothin'. Now, let's sit down to eat – I'm starvin'. And just think, we'll have more food on the table from now on, thanks be to God.'

64
Eltham
May 1934

'C'mon now Anna, hurry up and put Tipper out for a quick run before we go.'

'Do I have to go, Mummy?' Anna groaned.

'Of course ye do, Auntie Maureen and Uncle Reggie will be so upset if ye don't, not to mention the boys.'

'But I don't want to go there. I'd rather stay here and look after Tipper,' Anna moaned, opening the scullery door for the dog to exit. She waited on the step while he sniffed around the back garden then stood smelling the air, nose pointed upward. 'Come on Tipper, hurry up, I can't wait here all day,' she said impatiently.

Cat called to her from the parlour. 'Anna, c'mon now we're late.'

'Oh alright I'm coming,' she replied and ambled indoors with Tipper close at her heels.

'Lay down now, boy, we won't be long,' Anna said stroking the dog's head. His sorrowful eyes told her he did not want to be left. 'Look, Mummy, Tipper's really sad we're leaving him. Can't we take him with us?'

'No, of course not. The flat is small enough without a dog, five children and three adults to squeeze in.'

Anna counted up the people on her fingers and turned to Cat.,

'It's six children not five.'

'No, Billy won't be comin' today, he's got to read up for his examination.'

'Oh I see! *He's* allowed to stay behind but not *me*. I *hate* going there!'

'Anna, what's got into ye? Auntie Maureen's always so kind to ye, and she makes those special little butterfly cakes for ye.'

'Oh alright then. But do we have to stay for long?'

'Aw c'mon now and stop fussin', we've a long walk so let's get goin'.'

All the way to the High Street Anna felt a sick feeling in the pit of her stomach. She couldn't remember why she didn't like going to Uncle Reggie and Auntie Maureen's as she always liked it when she got there. She enjoyed playing with her cousins Charlie and little Louis, the youngest addition to their family, but it was invariably nicer when Uncle Reggie wasn't there. She hoped it was one of the days when he was out.

Cat knocked on the door to the flat over the butcher's shop that Reggie now owned. Apart from bones and scraps for Tipper, Reggie regularly gave them meat they couldn't afford.

Often Reggie called after the girls as they passed his shop on the way home from school. He would usually have a bundle of meat wrapped in paper for them to give Cat.

Anna couldn't work out why she resented him pushing the food on her, as her mother often reminded them, it was their salvation. But somehow she felt she would prefer to give up eating meat entirely rather than have to say thank you to him so often.

Maureen answered the door.

'C'mon in, lovely to see ye again. Hello, Cat. Hello gels. What big gels ye're growin' into,' she laughed as the family trailed up the stairs to the flat.

'Reggie,' she called, 'put on the kettle will ye, we've a thirsty bunch of people here.'

Anna's heart sank – so Reggie was in!

Once upstairs Maureen rushed around tidying newspapers off chairs and plumping up cushions for Cat and the children.

'Aw, don't be botherin' now about that Maureen, 'tis good of ye to ask us, and I don't see the point in worryin' about tidyin' up, t'will soon be messed up again.'

Cat sat down and picked up Reggie's youngest child, Louis.

'Hello there, little Louis,' she crooned, rocking the child in her arms. 'Shall I do Round and Round the Garden?'

Louis nodded so Cat began doing the game that he so loved her to do when they visited.

Reggie brought a tray of tea into the lounge and they sat chatting for a while.

Then Maureen told Cat that she was going home to Ireland in the summer with the boys to see her parents, but Reggie was staying behind as he had the shop to run.

'Well that'll be grand for ye all; I know my parents love it when we go home. When are ye thinkin' of goin'?'

'August, probably. I haven't actually let them know as they'll get too excited and Dada's heart isn't so good these days, so I don't want to tell them too soon.'

'Well, Reggie, ye'll have to come and eat at our house when ye can while Maureen's away.'

'Thanks, Cat, that would be nice – I'll keep you to that.' He didn't see the look of horror cross Anna's face, but Eileen did and resolved to ask her about it.

* * *

It was dark by the time they left Maureen and Reggie's, but the night was warm and it felt good to be out in the open. Cat suddenly stopped walking.

'I've an idea,' she said. 'Why don't we do a bit of a detour and visit Daddy's grave?'

Delighted with their change of route they set off to the churchyard at the crossroads of Eltham High Street and Well Hall Road.

As they opened the gate it creaked, and in the gloom the girls became agitated.

'Suppose there's a ghost in there?' Eileen whispered.

'Don't ye be so silly, there's no-one there at all, only yer sleepin' daddy,' Cat laughed.

'I've got the heebie-jeebies,' Anna said and clung onto Cat's dress.

They ambled through the churchyard and by the light of the moon came upon Louis' grave.

They stood praying in the darkness for his soul and reminiscing about whatever they could about him, but the girls found it difficult. His memory was beginning to fade and neither of them could clearly remember his face.

Cat sniffed and wiped her nose on a handkerchief, knelt down and patted the soil as though Louis was just in bed and she was tucking in the covers.

'Sleep well my love,' she whispered then stood, and clasping Elizabeth and Anna's hands she slowly strolled out of the churchyard as she had done so many times now since Louis had gone.

The following day, Cat received a registered letter from her sister Peggy and inside was the fare for the children to go on a visit to Fethard.

Billy and Eileen were very excited by the idea, but Anna became withdrawn and said she didn't want to go anywhere without her mother. So it was agreed that just the two of them would go once the school holidays arrived, and Cat would take Anna and Elizabeth to visit some other time.

65
Granny's Old Cottage, Monroe, Fethard June 1934

Summer was approaching and Ned sat in the doorway of the old cottage, once the home of his parents, weaving the supple willow leaves in and out of the basket frames.

He had handed over total control of the farm to Tom who had taken to managing stock, buying, selling and making day-to-day decisions, like a duck takes to water. Ned helped his son when asked, but otherwise kept out of the way.

In the mornings he often busied himself making baskets from sallies growing along the riverbank, and he had begun sending some to England for sale.

From lunch time onwards he could usually be seen in O'Connell's Hotel passing the time of day, reading the newspaper or chatting to other old locals who, like himself, had retired.

Maeve and Ned had left their farmhouse just after Christmas in 1933 to make way for Tom and Norah's growing family; but settling in had not been easy for Maeve as she found the cottage too small, too damp, and far too near the Clashawley River for her liking.

Hardly a day went by without Ned hearing her muttering to herself about being put out to grass like some old donkey. When it rained she would snatch up her rosary and feverishly begin praying whilst keeping an eye on the swelling river lapping towards the back door of the cottage. She hated the water with a vengeance and feared more than anything that one night while they were in bed it would crash through the door and take them in their sleep to a watery grave.

Ned looked across the field and could just see the rooftop of their old home, Monroe, where he saw smoke twisting out of the chimney rising into the fresh spring air. A current of wind blew smoke in his direction, and he smelled the familiar aroma of burning peat; the scent of home.

He did not dwell on the fact that he missed his home because he liked the thought that Tom, Norah and their children now occupied the cottage he had been brought up in, and where he and Maeve raised their family. Ned accepted the fact that he and Maeve would live out their days in the smaller home, known as Granny's Cottage, until God called them to Him

Ned was, by and large, content with his lot. He had Tom and Norah nearby; and their two children Edward and Theresa were always running in and out as though it was their home too. The door was never locked and the children would crash through it each morning, filling their grandparent's days with delight. Even Maeve seemed content with the pattern of her days, so long as the children came to be with them each day.

Maeve put the kettle on to boil and went across the room to Ned.

'I'll shut this door now, the weather is turnin' and I feel cold.'

'Please yerself woman,' Ned said and pulled his stool further outside to continue basket making in the open. He stood for a while watching the river and lit up a cigarette, just as Edward turned onto the pathway leading to the cottage.

'Well hello there, I expect ye've come to eat up Granny's special cake,' Ned said, ruffling the boy's hair. Edward smiled at his granddad.

'Me ma said she'd be glad if she could borrow some sugar, sure she forgot to buy it when she was in town.'

'C'mon inside and we'll see what Granny can find then,' Ned said, opening the door, but when he went into the room, Maeve was not there. She must be in the bedroom, he thought so went to open the door.

At first he thought the door must be locked, but how could it be when there was no lock on it? He pushed against it calling out.

'Maeve. Maeve! Will ye open the door, Edward is here after some sugar.'

Maeve did not reply, so he pushed against the door until it gave a little, but it felt as though there was something inside preventing him from opening it.

'Maeve, are ye in there?' Ned called, becoming irritated. 'Will ye open this door?' He shoved the door with his shoulder and it gradually gave enough to enable him to slip inside.

Edward stood watching and waiting for Granny to come out, but when he heard Ned shout, '*JESUS*!' he became alarmed and knew there was something wrong.

'Granddad is Granny in there?' he called.

'Edward, run and get yer Dada as quickly as ye can,' Ned commanded.

The boy ran off to find Tom who was in the yard feeding the pigs. When Edward told Tom what Ned had said he dropped the bucket of food, told Edward to fetch Norah, and ran towards the little cottage.

Once inside, Tom saw the bedroom door was open slightly.

'Dada are ye in there?' he called.

Ned appeared in the doorway, but told Tom he was unable to open the door wide as Maeve was lying behind it.

'She seems to have had a fall and I can't move her, Tom,' Ned said.

Tom wedged himself through the gap in the door and saw his mother's ashen face twisted sideways against the floor. She wasn't breathing. He gasped and looked at Ned.

'Is she...? Has she...? Oh *Dada*...I think she's gone.'

Ned stared at Tom, and then slumped onto the side of the bed.

'No. No.' He struggled for breath. ''Tis just a fall she's had. Go get Daniel, as quick as ye can.'

Tom stood up.

'Put a blanket on her Dada and I'll get Daniel,' he said moving around Maeve's body. He looked at Ned. 'Norah will sit with ye, Dada. C'mon in near the fire and warm yerself, and I'll be back soon.'

'No, I'll stay here and watch her; she may wonder what has happened when she wakes up. Ye get on now and fetch the doctor.'

Tom squeezed out of the doorway and met Norah just outside the cottage.

'Be prepared,' he told her. 'I think Mummy has passed away.'

Norah blanched. 'Oh *no*!' She drew her shawl tightly round her shoulders. 'What'll I do, Tom? Will I go in, or not?'

'Sure, ye should go in, Norah. Dada's in there but I do not think he is in full command of his thoughts. He says she has just had a fall, but I think Mummy has died. I'm away to fetch Daniel now, so are ye up to goin' in?'

Norah nodded, but inwardly she dreaded walking into the room and having to deal with the situation. She looked Tom in the eye. 'Off ye go then, Tom. Edward is lookin' after Theresa so don't worry, but maybe ye should ask yer sisters to come.'

Tom agreed. He hurried away and disappeared around the corner, leaving Norah alone on the pathway to Granny's Cottage.

66
Mother Superior's office – St. Mary's Convent Eltham 1934

'So ye see, Mother,' Cat explained, 'I have to go right away, but I'll leave Anna and Eileen here, I'll just take Billy and Elizabeth.'

Cat wiped away the tears that were running unchecked down her cheeks and meeting beneath her chin.

Mother Superior shifted in her chair, and then leaned on her forearms across the desk, reaching out a hand to touch Cat's.

'There's no problem as far as your job is concerned Cat, so don't worry about that, you won't lose it, especially not over this.' Her voice was calm and comforting and Cat looked up and tried a fragile smile.

'Thanks so much, Mother, ye've no idea how much it means to me workin' here, but ye do see I have to go. Poor Mummy and I didn't get to say goodbye.'

'Try to draw solace from the knowledge that she is in good hands now Cat, and that her soul is at rest. I wish we could all say the same.'

'Yes, Mother. But I've an idea, if it would please ye. Would ye allow Anna and Eileen to do the work while I'm away, then I'll not be lettin' ye down?'

'That sounds like an excellent idea to me Cat, and you can rest assured that they will be well looked after in your absence.'

'Ah Mother, ye're far too good to me.'

'You're worth it, Cat. I know what a struggle life is for you and if we can help in any way it would be an honour. You're a good, fine Catholic woman and have suffered enough. If I had my way, I'd just give you your wages without expecting you to work for it but I know you wouldn't accept that sort of arrangement.'

A huge lump constricted Cat's throat preventing her from replying, so she just nodded her thanks and stood up to leave.

Mother Superior stood too, moved around her desk and went across her office to open the door for Cat.

'When are you leaving, Cat?'

'First thing in the mornin', Mother,' and as she uttered the nun's title another wave of grief overtook her as she realised she would never speak to Maeve her mother, ever again. She hurried from the office, down the corridor and out into the fresh air where she leaned against the wall and wept.

* * *

Tom was waiting on the platform as the train drew into the station and Cat, leaning out of the window, waved to him.

He raised what looked like a weary hand in reply and walked towards the carriage as the train drew to a halt.

'Oh, Tom I can't believe it.' Cat sobbed against his neck as his arms folded around her. They clung together for what seemed ages, and bewildered, Billy and Elizabeth exchanged glances waiting for instructions on what to do next.

Eventually the pair parted and Tom turned and picked up the luggage.

'I've got the cart waitin' so ye've not far to walk,' he said winking at the children.

'Can I ride up next to you, please?' Billy asked.

'Sure ye can.' Tom stood aside to let Cat out of the platform gate first. 'And ye can drive too.'

Excited at the prospect of driving, Billy ran ahead and scrambled up onto the cart.

Cat shouted at him. '*Billy*!'

He turned, wondering what the problem was as Cat sounded angry.

'Will ye get down from there and think of others first for once!' she snapped.

Confused, Billy slowly climbed out of the cart.

'Have ye no manners, child?' she chided him. 'Help yer uncle with the bags and make yerself useful, ye can seek yer own pleasures after ye've helped others.'

Billy scowled and picked up a bag which he threw onto the cart with a vengeance. 'Is that enough?' he asked sulkily.

Tom, sensing a battle of wills between Cat and Billy, was careful not to take Billy's part against his sister. She was right that the boy had acted selfishly and Tom didn't like his tone of voice. He lifted Elizabeth onto the cart and then as Cat jumped up to follow, he turned to Billy.

'Righto, Billy ye can step up here now and take the reins.'

Billy sullenly climbed up to the seat next to Tom, took the reins, and made a clicking noise to urge the donkey forward.

As they bumped along the Cashel Road toward Monroe, Cat's thoughts darted from one image to another as she saw Maeve in every step of the way. Maeve waving from a field, Maeve guiding the cows in, Maeve lifting the heavy milk churns, Maeve brushing her hair when she was a child, and now no Maeve.

When they arrived at Monroe, Billy remained motionless in the driver's seat until Cat and Elizabeth were helped down by Tom. He then turned the donkey round in the yard so that she was facing up the boreen, ready for their next journey to O'Connell's where they would be staying.

'Thanks, Billy,' Tom said and looked up at the boy sitting stubbornly in the driver's seat. 'Ye know Billy, this is hard for all of us and I'm relyin' on ye to help me out here.'

The boy looked down and began picking at a piece of skin on his finger.

'How d'ya mean, Uncle?'

'Well, ye're goin' to learn now how to handle losin' someone–'

But Billy didn't let him finish.'I've *already* lost someone and I *know* what to do.' His voice was tight.

Tom was surprised by Billy's response, but quickly recognised that the boy wasn't just being stubborn, he was fighting to keep his emotions under control.

'Ah sure, I know ye have, and a fine boy ye've been since, so ye'll know what yer mam's havin' to go through right now. So if she seems a little snappy, ye'll know it's because she's tryin' not to cry in public kinda thing.'

Billy continued to pick at his finger while Tom talked to him. Then, feeling he should be with the women and Ned, Tom sighed.

'C'mon inside when ye're ready.' He left Billy sitting on the cart and walked into the cottage.

Billy sat outside on the cart until spots of rain began to fall, first intermittently then more regularly, and though he tried to ignore, it he knew that eventually he would have to go in and face everyone.

The last funeral he had attended was his father's and he dreaded going to Maeve's. Billy tried to push down the horrible feeling he was going to cry. He'd been very brave since Louis' death, had not cried once. He was proud of having kept this record for four years.

But as Billy sat out on the cart in the rain, something inside him burst like a dam and all the misery of becoming the man of the house since his dad died frothed up inside him, threatening to choke him.

Unable to prevent the tears of loss, he succumbed to his grief and sobbed.

67
O'Connell's Hotel
Fethard
1934

Ned's sister Nellie put a glass of porter on the table and sat down opposite him. Her husband Mick, Cat, Mary, Breda and Tom were subdued, making arrangements for a funeral they never dreamed would have come so soon. They all agreed Maeve had always been so healthy, never a day's illness in the whole of the time they had known her.

Silently Ned picked up the porter and sipped it. He hadn't said a word, couldn't bring himself to make a decision about which sort of casket, the lining, or what sort of gown Maeve would wear. It just wasn't true.

Numbed, he let the whole thing whirl about his head and somewhere he found a comfortable lodging place for his thoughts. Going back to when Maeve and he were newly wed and had moved into their first home - Granny's old cottage where they had finally ended up. Curious, he thought, how things go full circle.

Nellie looked across at him, saw the dreamy look in his eyes and knew he wasn't hearing a word that was said. She nudged Cat who looked up, and following the direction of Nellie's glance, looked at her father.

Cat got up and moved around the table to sit next to him.

'Dada, are ye feelin' alright?' she asked gently, rubbing the back of his hand.

Ned looked at her. 'No, I'll never be alright again.'

'Oh don't say that Dada, Mummy wouldn't want ye to!'

'I don't know. I don't know anythin' anymore.' He sipped his drink and Cat sat watching him, feeling utterly helpless.

Oh why is death so painful she wondered, why don't we rejoice that someone is out of all this suffering? She looked at Nellie and raised her eyebrows. Nellie decided to take the lead and involve Ned rather than let him just drift off into his private reverie.

'Ned, we need ye to make a decision on this now Pet.'

He looked up. 'On what?'

Nellie continued. 'On the sort of casket ye want Maeve to have and the other bits and pieces.'

'Oh ye go ahead and choose, I have no opinion on the matter,' he answered quietly. 'Don't mind me, Nellie; I'm no good at this sort o' thing. Just choose amongst yerselves. I'll go along with it.'

Nellie shot a glance at the three sisters who all nodded, so they went ahead and chose the casket, handles, lining and Maeve's gown, while Ned sat appearing to listen to them, but not hearing a word.

* * *

On the day of the funeral the sun shone brilliantly and the whole of Fethard gathered in their age-old custom to bid Maeve farewell.

As funerals go, Ned thought, it was a very good one. So many people gathered to greet him and the children and he drew comfort in knowing that all these familiar faces were there for Maeve and to help them get through the awful ordeal.

After the funeral, O'Connell's was opened to the mourners, the priests and anyone who wanted to join the family for a drink. They would reminisce, laugh at funny things they remembered about Maeve and many offers were made to help Ned.

Of course they all meant well he realised, but what help could anyone be now? All the years Maeve had scolded him for not doing this, that or the other, and now there would be nobody to do that, and he'd grown used to it. It was her way.

But that didn't mean that there was no love between them because there was. They just didn't have to go around shouting it out. Now what was he going to do? How would he cope without her rough matter-of-fact personality and the fact she would stop at nothing until he did as he was told? Had he been the man of the house, or had she? It had all happened so subtly. They had slipped into that way of co-existing.

Ned was afraid. He didn't think he could bear to be alone in that cottage without her. But what choice did he have? It was out of the question for him to burden any of his children, and kind as Nellie and Mick were, he didn't want to live at the hotel, he would rather keep his routine of going there for a drink with his pals. Each suggestion made to him was dismissed for one reason or another.

Despite all the offers, Ned came to the conclusion that he had, in fact, very little choice. He would just have to endure living in the old cottage with Maeve's ghost and try to make the best of it.

The awful part of it all though Ned recognised, was that this was the first time in his life he had ever lived alone, and it scared him.

68
Peggy and Breda's Shop
Main Street, Fethard
1934

'So,' Cat said, 'If ye could keep me posted about Dada I'd be much obliged, only I think he's lookin' so lost and I'm worried about him.'

Peggy poured the tea out, put the tea-cosy back on the pot and handed the cup to Cat.

'Sure we will, Cat. And don't ye go worryin' about him, he'll be grand, ye'll see once he gets over the shock.' She took a handkerchief from her pocket and wiped away her tears. 'Though who'd have ever thought Mummy would go, just like that?'

Cat went to Peggy and put an arm around her shoulders.

'There, pet. None of us know when the Good Lord will call us, and we have to comfort ourselves that she didn't suffer. A lingerin' death is painful for all to endure.'

Peggy hugged Cat.

'Sorry Cat, I know ye've had yer own troubles, sure ye have, 'tis just that we'd no warning. She never complained of feelin' ill or anythin'.'

'Well, thanks be to God for that then, it means she's left this world as she came into it, free from worry and pain.'

''Tis a good way of lookin' at it, that's for sure,' Breda said, poking Marie in the arm.

'Go give yer mother a kiss now Marie, as she's away back to England.'

Marie went to Cat and raised lips for Cat to kiss.

'And ye'll write to me more Marie, won't ye?' Cat asked before kissing her.

'I will Ma. Though I've a lot of work to be doin' at present as I'm studyin' for my music exams and then there's the dancin' and horse ridin' competitions too–' She broke off, aware that Cat had stiffened at the mention of her horse riding.

'And where are ye gettin' the horse ridin' lessons from, Marie?' Cat questioned

Breda came to Marie's rescue.

'She's still goin' up to Hogan's, Cat. Paddy's been awful kind to her and doesn't charge for the lessons and all, not to mention takin' her to all the competitions in his new motor car.'

Cat turned to Marie.

'Marie, will ye go downstairs and look out in the street to see if Billy is comin' up the hill from Auntie Nellie's please? He's late.'

Marie obediently left the room and Cat immediately took up the topic of Paddy's involvement with her daughter.

'Look, I know he's been doin' a lot for Marie and maybe he has changed but I can't help feelin' uneasy about him.'

Cat looked from Peggy to Breda, trying to gauge whether she had an ally.

Peggy kept her head bent studying her tea cup as though she'd only just noticed the pattern on it for the first time. It was Breda who took up the challenge.

'Listen, Cat, ye've nothin' to be worryin' about. Paddy's a different person now to the wild young thing he used to be, and Marie is really havin' such a good time competin' on the horses. I think it would break her heart if ye forbade her to continue.'

Forbidding her to continue was exactly what Cat had in mind, but she felt she was treading on shaky ground with her two sisters.

In her heart Cat knew that they had given Marie everything she and Louis were unable to, and that their intentions were for Marie's benefit. Cat knew that she would be forever in their debt.

But she was now aware that in accepting their generosity throughout the years, she had relinquished her right to direct Marie's life.

69
Granny's Cottage
Monroe - Fethard
1934

Cat entered the cottage and found Ned sitting before the empty fire.

'Dada, have ye no fire? 'Tis a cold day, will I light it for ye?'

Ned looked up, perplexed at her presence.

'Well hello there, Cat. I didn't expect to see ye. Sit ye down and I'll get ye a cup of tea.'

He rose slowly and plodded over to the dresser, lifting down one of the best cups, a residue of his and Maeve's wedding present. Never used, the tea set had adorned the dresser for more than half a century, but Ned was going to use it now. He realised there was no point hanging on to the china, not without Maeve, though in his head he heard her moan at him for using it.

'Dada, ye know 'tis time for us to go today don't ye?'

Ned spun round, puzzled. 'Is it? Ye didn't say ye were leavin'.'

Tears filled Cat's eyes, and she battled to overcome the intense emotion that was rising inside her, making it difficult to answer Ned. She too was in such pain. The pain of losing her mother and now of leaving her father to return to London.

'I expect ye've forgotten, Dada, but I have to get back now, I've left the children alone in England.'

'But ye've got Billy and Elizabeth with ye.'

'I know Dada, but there's also Eileen and Anna at home on their own. I've been gone longer than I expected already.'

'Oh,' he said, and then became silent. After a while Ned put the cup and saucer on the table and gazed at the kettle. 'I've forgotten to light the fire, so I can't boil the water for tea. I'm sorry.'

Cat went to him and put her arms around him, nuzzling into his chest, smelling his familiar scent.

'Oh Dada, I wish I could stay here. I want to look after ye. Nothin' would give me more pleasure, especially with Mummy gone, but I have to go.'

'Can't ye come back home now, Cat?' he murmured into her hair. C'mon home now.'

'I *can't* Dada. *Please* don't ask me to. I've the children in school over there and Billy is hopin' to go on with his studies, he'd never be able to do that here; I wouldn't have the work to pay for him.'

Ned didn't answer but she could see his shoulders shaking as he cried silently following her reply.

'Dada. If I could stay I would, believe me. I'd love to come home and look after ye, but I can't.

The girls are gettin' big and take every penny I can earn to feed them. I can't be dependent on the family, there are too many of us.'

As though realising it was useless to continue the request, Ned sighed and held Cat out at arm's length, studying her face.

'Ah mo chuisla, I know ye've a big burden yerself, and I don't mean to add to it, I shouldn't have asked. Forget it.'

'I feel awful, Dada, but ye do see don't ye, that I can never come home, not permanently, not ever again.'

'I know, Pet, I just thought there's no harm in askin'.' He lifted the empty kettle. 'I'm just a silly old fool, can't even remember to light the fire and we've no hot water.' He set the kettle back over the empty fire.

'Never mind the tea Dada, why don't we go into Norah's? She'll have hot water boilin' and she's lookin' after the children for me.'

'Sounds like a good idea to me. But before we go Cat, I want to give ye somethin'. Just wait there will ye?'

He went into the bedroom and she could hear him rummaging in a drawer and muttering to himself. After a while he returned with something wrapped in tissue paper.

'Here,' he said pressing the little package into her hand. 'I bought this for yer mummy when I first decided to marry her.'

'Oh, no Dada, I can't take it.'

'Course ye can, 'tis for ye. And when I'm gone, I intend to leave ye this little cottage, so's ye'll always have somewhere to come back to.'

'Oh Dada, I can't take this, or the cottage. What about the others?'

'They're all set up, don't ye worry. Peggy and Breda have that little business which gives them a good life, and Tom and Norah have the farm now, so ye see 'tis only right ye have a little slice o' the cake. Open that now before we go into Norah's, I want ye to see it while we're alone.'

Cat unfolded the tissue paper and revealed a silver brooch designed in a circle with a bar across the centre on which were three little green shamrocks. She'd never seen it before and was deeply moved by the gift.

'Mummy always said that I was to give it to ye, I just never believed 'twould be so soon.' His eyes filled with tears and his bottom lip quivered.

'Oh Dada, 'tis lovely and I'll treasure it, thank ye. Ye know Dada, I've never thanked ye and Mummy for the wonderful life I had with ye as a child. 'T'as been the one thing that's kept me goin' ye know, the thoughts of home.'

Ned looked at her as though seeing her for the first time. He nodded and then surprised Cat.

'Ye know, in all the years I was married to yer mummy, I don't think I ever told her I loved her. I wish I had.'

70
Hogan Stables, Fethard
1935

Paddy rode ahead of Marie, opened the gate to the stable yard, and she followed on her pony. It had started to rain; slowly drizzling initially which was refreshing after a strenuous cross-country ride. Then the downpour increased and with their slower pace nearing the stables, Paddy and Marie found they were becoming chilled.

'C'mon, let's get these animals in for a quick rub-down then we can dry ourselves,' Paddy said looking back at Marie. 'Ye're lookin' cold and we don't want ye catching pneumonia.'

'Ah I'm alright, Paddy, but glad to be back now. The rain looks to be really settin' in.'

They stabled the horses and then set about rubbing them down.

'I don't think we'll make too much of a job of it today, Marie 'twill be gettin' dark soon and ye need to be goin' home,' he said briskly brushing his horse. When she did not answer he turned and saw she was drinking from a bottle. Astonished, he asked her. 'What's that ye have there?'

She giggled and wiped her mouth with the back of her hand. ''Tis wine from home.'

'And what in the world are ye doin' with it here?'

'Ah gettaway Paddy, 'twill not do any harm. C'mon, have a sip. 'Tis real nice.'

'I will not, young lady! And you put that bottle down at once!'

'Or what?' she leered at him.

'Listen Marie, 'tis not nice for a young gel to go about drinkin' especially not in broad daylight.'

'Well then, I'll wait 'till dark.'

'Ye know what I mean.'

She tipped the bottle up again and took long gulps before offering him the bottle.

'Try some, Paddy, 'tis real good.'

He looked at her, seeing her for the first time as a woman, not a child. Her hair was wild and bushy and it had turned frizzy in the rain. There was a blush on her cheeks that lit up her eyes making them appear full of lust. He had never seen her looking lovelier and his heart gained pace in his chest. An old memory of Cat stole into his mind, igniting an angry lust he thought was quenched long ago.

Marie continued to taunt him.

'C'mon Paddy, take a swig o' this, 'tis lovely.' She moved around the horses and stood before him waving the bottle back and forth. 'G'w'on, I dare ye. Are ye a man or a mouse?'

'Ye're a wicked gel, Marie, I'll say that.'

'Sure, we all know that, Paddy. But c'mon now, take a swig. 'Twon't hurt ye, 'twill warm ye up.'

He looked at her. He'd never had the heart to say no to her for just about anything, but this was looking a mite dangerous. Drinking in the stable with a girl, and him a widower! What would folks say?

'C'mon, nobody will know.'

Tantalised beyond caution he put aside the brush and went towards her.

'Ah give us the bottle ye little temptress,' he said and took a long drink from the bottle. 'Ye're right, 'tis pretty good stuff this. Where did ye say ye got it?'

'Auntie Peggy makes it.'

'Well then surely, she's goin' to miss it if ye've stolen it.'

'Oh no. She gave it me for ye.'

'Seriously?'

'Sure. She said to me, to give it to ye for all the trouble ye take with me and anyway she has too many to store.' Marie smiled at him and took the bottle, then swallowed another long gulp. 'So ye see, I'm not so wicked am I?' She handed him the bottle again and he sat down on the straw before taking another long drink.

'Sure is warmin' after that rain.'

She slumped down beside him, took the bottle back and continued drinking.

'Slow down, Marie, 'twill make ye dizzy,' he said leaning back on his elbows.

'Ah, ha,' she said 'I think it already has.'

'Stop right there then, Marie. Ye don't want to get sick on it.'

'Give us a kiss then and I will,' she teased.

'I'll give ye a smack on the backside.'

'C'mon then, I dare ye.'

But Paddy just laughed and wrenched the bottle away from her.

'Give it back now, Paddy, I need some more,' she demanded.

'I will not, ye little madam, that's enough now,' he said and looked around for the cork. 'D'ye have the cork?'

'I do.'

'Then give it here.'

'No.'

'C'mon now Marie, I won't ask again, give me the cork.'

Marie picked up some straw and began tickling Paddy's nose with it and he laughed.

'Stop that will ye, it tickles.'

But she was feeling very giggly and ran the stalks down his arm and over his hand.

He shuddered; it was rather nice having the light sensation caressing his skin.

She ran it up his arm and over his neck to his face again. Then she positioned herself in front of him, sitting cross-legged on the straw and raising her hand, traced around his lips with her finger.

He pulled back for an instant but she just smiled and shuffled nearer him.

'Hold still will ye?' she said and kneeled up so that their faces were level. 'Kiss me, Paddy.'

He hesitated, drawing back from her, but Marie merely leaned toward him. He studied her face. She had her mother's eyes and he could feel her breath on his face. Then her lips were on his and they tasted so sweet, so irresistible his resolve melted away and all thoughts of whether it was right or wrong dissipated.

She lay on the hay next to him and he folded her into his arms, kissing her forehead, nose, lips, and throat.

Marie, thrilled by the experience of her first kiss from a man, was giving him as much encouragement as she could. Sure the boys at the convent school had planted one or two slobbery kisses on her during play time but this was something different and she was hungry for more.

The rain outside intensified, hammering down on the stable roof, as Paddy, drawn irrevocably to the edge of desire, ignored Marie's belated cries of '*No.*'

71
St. Mary's Convent, Eltham
1936

Anna poked her head round the scullery door. 'Mummy, are you in there?' she called.

Cat was scrubbing the floor and stopped when she heard her. 'Sure I'm in here. Wait now and I'll be with ye.' She dropped the scrubbing brush into the bucket, scrambled to her feet, and wiping her hands on her apron went to the doorway. 'What is it, Pet?'

'Is it alright if I go home with my friend Laura Kennedy, and have tea there, Mummy?'

'What about Elizabeth? 'Tis yer turn to take her home isn't it?'

'Yes, but I've agreed to swap with Eileen and do Monday and Tuesday of next week instead.'

''Tis fine by me, so long as there's no arguing next week when ye have to do two nights on the trot.'

Elizabeth was sitting at the table drawing, waiting for Cat's reply.

'Thanks, Mummy. I won't be late home. Oh, and Eileen said to remind you to get some sausages for tea.'

'Sure I won't forget. And see that ye're not home late, I don't want to be marchin' out to Mrs. Kennedy's to get ye.'

Anna was then aware of someone behind her and turned to find Eileen standing there. She hadn't heard her approach. ‘Oh, it’s you,’ she said, ‘you made me jump.’

‘Well you asked me to pick up Elizabeth, so that’s what I’m doing, if it’s alright with *you.*’

Cat sensed an argument developing between the girls and looked at them wearily.

‘Can’t ye two get along better instead of this constant griggin’?’

Eileen pushed past Anna and marched into the room and glared at Elizabeth.

‘Elizabeth, put your coat on, we’re going now,’ she demanded, ignoring Cat’s plea. She turned to Anna. ‘And don’t forget, you’ll be picking Elizabeth up Monday and Tuesday of next week, not me!’

‘I won’t,’ Anna said and turned to leave.

‘’Bye Mummy. ’Bye Elizabeth, see you at home.’

Anna hurried down the school corridor and Cat ambled over to the doorway, watching her receding form. She wondered where all the years had gone as Anna was looking so grown up now.

Eileen took Elizabeth by the hand and marched her out of the room, but as she left, she turned to her mother.

‘I have to call in on a friend so I may not be home until after you, Mummy. But don’t worry.’

‘Fine. Do as ye please,’ Cat said, but Eileen was already stomping down the corridor and Cat’s heart sank as she watched her dragging Elizabeth by the arm. ’Tis at times like these she thought, I miss their father most. What would he have been like now? How different would life be if he were around? Would Eileen and Anna always be arguing or would his presence have calmed them down?

But she had to admit to herself that Anna was a good girl and of all her children, though she was the cheekiest, she was undoubtedly the most helpful and the least quarrelsome. She was well aware that Eileen was often at the root of most friction at home.

Cat grinned to herself as she thought of Anna swaggering down the corridor practicing her latest walk, one that she knew she had copied from a film star she had seen at the cinema. Maybe she would take her to see the film with her favourite actor, Ronald Coleman, which was showing next week. She took the brush out of the bucket and continued the relentless task of scrubbing the scullery floor.

The nuns liked the way she brought the woodwork up so brightly, plus the wonderful smell of polish on the boards. Once it was dry it looked good enough to eat their meals from.

Everything that Cat cleaned was left gleaming, to the delight of the sisterhood. She prided herself in her ability to turn the dirtiest of jobs into a work of art, and Mother Superior was always very complimentary and so kind to her, there was nothing Cat would not do in return.

Tired at the end of a long day, Cat swilled the water down the sink, washed the bucket out and stored it away in the cupboard.

After cleaning the sink and making sure everything was neat and tidy, she folded her apron and put it in her shopping bag. Then wearily she took her coat off the peg behind the door, pinned her hat on and left the scullery after taking one final satisfied look at the floor.

Well now, she thought, let's see how dirty they can get the place before Monday. It never ceased to amaze her how a bunch of women could make so much mess, and nuns too! But it keeps me in work and that's all I care about. God forbid the day if it ever dawned when they would not need her any more.

She made her way across Eltham High Street and called in at Reggie's shop. The assistant who served her explained that Reggie was cutting up a pig in the back of the shop, so she bought some sausages and after paying for them, poked her head around the doorway.

'Hello there,' she called.

Reggie looked up and smiled at her.

'Hello, Cat. All finished for the day then are you?'

'Sure, and I'm just off home now,' she said putting the sausages in her shopping bag.

'I shall not be sorry to sit down and put me feet up now.'

'Long day, Cat?' Reggie asked, wiping his hands on his apron.

'Yes, and I feel quite tired tonight. Still, 'tis Saturday tomorrow and God willin' I can take a break.'

Reggie fished about beneath his bench and brought out a package wrapped in brown paper tied with string. 'Glad you called, Cat. This is for you.'

Cat knew it would be a parcel of meat, plus bones for Tipper. 'Oh, Reggie, ye shouldn't.'

'Come on now, Cat,' he laughed, 'we can't have these bits going to waste now, can we?' He winked at her and she went to him and kissed his cheek.

'Thanks, Reggie. How're Maureen and the children?'

'Fine, thanks. Really fine.'

'Why not come to tea on Sunday? 'Twould be lovely to see ye all.'

'Done!' Reggie said without hesitation. 'I'll bring some nice ham with me, so don't go out buying any.'

'Aw, there's no stoppin' ye Reggie, is there?'

Cat left the shop stuffing the parcel into her shopping bag. She would write a letter to Lize and get one of the girls to pop it round to her shop; maybe she would join them too.

She knew it was pointless inviting her mother-in-law as she never left the flat above the shop now. She had not visited once since Louis had died. The children would often call to see her on a Sunday after mass, but Cat did not go as she knew she would not be welcome. Over the years Cat had given up trying to be accepted.

She stood at the end of Westmount Road and looked at the long route ahead. For the first time Cat felt it was too far and she was tired. *If*

Louis had lived, she thought, as she began the long trek, *he would probably be meeting her on his motor bike.*

Ah, the motor bike, she thought. *What fun they'd had on it, short-lived though it was.* She had sold it to the man next door after Louis died; but each day she saw him arrive home on it, she experienced a bitter-sweet reminder of not just the motor bike, but of longing for the man who once rode it.

Tipper greeted Cat when she arrived home though his movements were now very much slower. His tail still wagged, but Cat noticed he was lethargic these days. He slept almost constantly and she was worried there was something wrong with him. She undid the parcel Reggie had given her and found a nice marrow bone in it, about a pound of bacon and some lamb chops. Reggie had done her proud again.

'Here ye are, my lovely old friend,' she said, placing the bone on the hearth for him. Wagging his tail, Tipper walked over and slumped down in front of it. He licked it all over and then began gnawing at it with relish. 'That's more like it isn't it?' Cat said to him. Happy that he seemed to be enjoying the bone, she went into the kitchen and put the kettle on.

Eileen was still out with Elizabeth and there was no sign of Billy, so Cat made herself a cup of tea and decided to take a nap before starting to cook the sausages.

She was awoken by Eileen shouting, ‘Oh you *naughty* dog.’

‘What in the world’s goin’ on?’ Cat said struggling to clear her head.

‘It’s Tipper, Mummy. I came in to find him eating the sausages you bought for our tea.’

‘Oh no! He must have pulled them off the drainin’ board, I didn’t think he’d do a thin’ like that anymore. Tipper!’ Cat shouted at him, ‘Ye *naughty* dog.’

Tipper slunk out to the kitchen, tail between his legs and cowered by the back door.

‘Aw, look at him. How can I tell him off?’ Cat asked. She patted her thigh calling to him, ‘C’mere boy.’ Tipper looked uncertain at first, then ventured slowly over to Cat and sat before her, ears back and not looking up.

‘Well I don’t know how you can forgive him so quickly, Mummy,’ Eileen snapped.

Elizabeth, copying Eileen’s tone of voice joined in.

‘You are a very *naughty* dog, Tipper!’

‘He doesn’t know any different, do ye, Tipper?’ Cat chuckled. ‘Anyway, as it happens, I have some eggs in the pantry and Reggie gave me some bacon, which I don’t think Tipper has touched, so we’ll just have egg and bacon.’

Cat looked at Eileen and Elizabeth. ‘C’mon now, look lively and set the table, ’tis not the end of the world.’

* * *

The next day Cat lay awake wondering if perhaps one of the girls would bring her breakfast in bed. She felt worn out and just for once wanted to lie there and be waited on.

As though she had read Cat's mind, Anna popped her head around the door at that moment and saw Cat was awake.

'Mummy, how would you like me to bring you breakfast before I go to work?'

'Lord save us, I was just prayin' someone would come and offer me breakfast in bed today, I'm so tired. Thanks, Pet. That would be grand. I'll have a piece of bacon and some tomatoes with a fried egg. Oh and some toast to dip in the egg too.'

Anna nodded, smiled, and closed the door as Cat snuggled down beneath the blankets, relishing her first lie-in for ages. Oh it was so nice now the children were getting bigger, she thought. Maybe I can stop worrying so much and depend on them more.

Eileen was not working that day, so perhaps she could help with the cooking and cleaning. She needed to do some baking if the family were coming to tea the next day.

By the time Anna shuffled in with the breakfast tray, Cat had dozed off again. She was woken by Anna calling her.

'Come on Mummy, sit up. Did you go back to sleep?'

'Yes, I did and I can't remember when I had that privilege, Anna. Thanks, Pet,' she said as Anna put the tray on her lap. 'Sit here and talk to me. Have ye had yer breakfast yet?'

'No, it's on the table waiting.'

'Well why don't ye bring it in here and we'll have a picnic together.'

Anna grinned and went out to the kitchen to get her breakfast just as the post arrived, so she picked up the letters and took them with her breakfast tray into Cat.

'Post's arrived, Mummy,' she said and dropped the letters onto the bed.

'Ah let's eat first, whatever it is can wait.'

They sat on the bed and between mouthfuls Anna told Cat about her visit to Laura's the evening before. She told Cat in detail about Laura's older brother who was all dressed up in black shirt and trousers, going out to a meeting. There were lots of other men there all in black too.

'Black eh?' Cat questioned. 'And who in God's name goes out all in black unless 'tis to a funeral?'

'Well he belongs to a special group and they all wear black to their meetings. Laura says she's going to the next one and asked me along too.'

'We'll see, but I'm tellin' ye Anna, we won't go wastin' money on black anythin''.

Anna looked downcast, and then remembered the other letter which she handed to Cat.

Cat finished her breakfast then opened the letter. Slowly a smile spread across her face. Suddenly she let out a loud '*YES*!'

Alarmed, Anna asked her what it was and Cat passed the letter to her which she read. Awestruck, Anna looked at her mother after reading it.

'Does this mean what I think it means?'

'It surely does, Anna. We are being re-located to a proper house at last.'

'But Mummy, this is a proper house and I want to stay here.'

'Ye'll think differently when ye get into the new house, Anna. Just think of it now, no more damp and no more mould growin' up the walls; a proper brick house. By God, won't we be laughin'? C'mon now we'll go and tell the others, then I'll go shoppin' 'cos we've Reggie, Maureen and the children comin' tomorrow and I want ye to slip round on yer way to work to take a note to ask yer Auntie Lize too.'

'Oh,' Anna said in a flat tone.

'Anna, why is it whenever I say they're comin' here, ye start with that tone of voice?'

'I don't know, Mummy. I just feel creepy when I know they are coming.'

'Well, maybe ye've a touch of the green-eyed monster about ye. So snap out of it - and the quicker the better!'

72
Eltham
1936

Cat looked around the room that had been her home for so many years: remembering how she had first acquired the wooden home which was no more than a log hut, and the time she had spent there first with her sister Ellie, then Louis and the children.

Then Ellie had gone to America with Michael Nagle and she had not seen her for years. Sure, they kept in touch by letter and she was thrilled when she heard they had called their little girl Catherine after her, but the years had passed so quickly and though Ellie was still important to her, Cat had to admit that her own family had now taken centre stage in her day-to-day focus.

She smiled as she remembered the tricks they had played on Michael, pretending there was a dinner on his plate when it was totally empty. How they had laughed, feeling they had nearly convinced the poor man they were mad.

Michael had been a good match for Ellie, but her letters of late had worried Cat. She told of Michael's drinking and constantly losing his job because he was too drunk to go to work. Reading through the lines, Cat wondered if they would ever return from America; Ellie had certainly hinted that she would if she had the money for the passage. She could not help her, though she would dearly love to, because every penny she earned was spoken for.

Cat sighed as she put the last of the crockery and cooking pans into a tea chest. Billy was away in London at the hospital training school so would not be there to help. How glad she was that at least one of them would be 'making it' in the world. He was advancing quickly to fulfil his dream of becoming a doctor and Cat was so proud of this she could burst.

She had a job not to keep slipping it into her conversation at the slightest opportunity, because Eileen had made it clear to her that she was sounding very boastful, and this was frowned upon by the church.

Eileen worked in a shoe shop in the High Street near Reggie's butcher's shop, and Anna had a job in an office above an electrical engineering works. She helped to make up the men's wages and was learning how to enter the accounts as well as general filing. On Tuesday evenings she went to night school to learn typing and was picking it up well, though it was not her first choice. But as Cat often told her, she was lucky to have a job at all so she had better be satisfied with not liking it.

Mr. Pierce next door had offered to help Cat with the move and she had accepted because she would not let the girls stay off work and lose money. Mr. Pierce was retired and glad to have something useful to do.

Cat would miss Mr. and Mrs. Pierce; they had been good neighbours and had helped her through her loss of Louis years ago. She would of course no longer hear Mr. Pierce riding around on Louis' motorbike, but maybe that was a good thing because it never ceased to stir memories that evoked sadness.

'When ye leave work tonight,' she had told Eileen and Anna, 'make yer way to Alwold Crescent. Number fifty one. I'll be there. Now off ye go so's ye're not late into work and get yer money stopped.'

The girls had said goodbye and waved as they trotted down the road. Both of them turned and looked back at their home, sighed, and continued on their way.

'Well, that's that then,' Anna said resignedly, 'we won't be going home to that house ever again.'

'No,' Eileen said.

'Are you sorry or glad?'

'A bit of both I suppose. It won't make much difference; we'll still have a jolly long walk to work every day.'

'Yes, but I'm excited about having a new place to live, aren't you?'

'Suppose so.' Eileen sounded uninterested. 'So which of us is Elizabeth sharing with?'

'I don't mind. If she wants to share with you it's fine by me but if she wants to share with me, then that's fine too.' Anna was not going to get into an argument about this. 'When Billy comes home, we'll all have to share I suppose.'

Eileen shrugged. 'He won't be back for a while, so we can count him out.'

'Maybe,' she said, and then added, 'I miss him. Do you?'

'No, not really. I don't miss his bossiness and lazy attitude, just because he's a boy and doesn't do the housework. I'm telling you that if ever I have a boy he'll do the whole lot.'

Anna laughed. She could not imagine Eileen having a baby, or herself for that matter. She decided to change the subject as they continued walking. 'I'm going to Laura Kennedy's on Friday night.'

'What, more black shirt meetings?' Eileen sounded annoyed.

'You could come too if you wanted,' Anna offered.

'No thank you, I have better things to do.'

'Oh. What's that?'

'Never you mind.'

'Come on tell me.'

'No.'

'Please yourself.'

'Anyway Mummy doesn't like you getting involved with Laura's crowd, she thinks it has sinister overtones, and I agree with her.'

'What sinister overtones?' Anna sounded surprised.

'Ask her yourself.'

'I will.'

They walked in silence the rest of the way to the High Street where they normally parted company. Anna paused before continuing in the direction of her work.

'Eileen, you *can* come Friday night if you want.'

'I'll see if I'm busy or not.'

Anna knew then that she did not have anything better to do and was merely covering up the fact that nobody ever asked her to join them. She wondered why.

Anna accepted that Eileen could be rather sharp-tongued, but she knew of other girls with equally scathing ways who didn't seem to go short of invites. Perhaps, she thought, it was because Eileen was inclined to be quarrelsome and wasn't much fun to be with. She is rather dull and boring Anna decided, crossing the High Street.

She then made her way jauntily down the other side of the road as Eileen entered the shoe shop where she worked. Maybe handling feet all day is what made her so sour, thought Anna.

As soon as she arrived in the office, Anna asked her boss Mr. Catherall if he would like a cup of tea. They had fallen into this ritual right from the beginning of her employment and it seemed to cement their relationship. Anna thought he was a nice old gentleman and often day-dreamed that he was her father and she was doing things for him because of that.

Mr. Catherall never stood too close, or breathed on her neck or touched her when he should not, and slowly she came to trust his company.

Before that, she cringed when a man came within her arm's length of her and froze if one as much as brushed against her accidentally.

Mr. Catherall was safe Anna had decided. Other men were not.

73
St. Mary's Convent, Eltham
April, 1937

Cat tidied the kitchen in the convent and was about to put a newspaper into the corner to be used for lighting the boiler when a headline caught her eye. She picked up the newspaper but it was in French and she had no idea what it said, other than the fact the Pope's name was mentioned.

She scrutinised the article trying to make sense of the words:

L'Oest-Éclair	**22 Mars 1937**

Le Nouveau Kulturkampf

Energique prostestation du Pape contre la persecution des catholiques en Allemagne…

It was hopeless! She couldn't read it; but it alarmed her. Were Catholics being persecuted somewhere in the world and the Pope had heard about it? Or was the Pope in danger of persecution?

And what in the name of God's was Allemagne? She folded the paper and thought for a moment. Mother Superior may be able to read it she decided, so took off her apron, smoothed down her skirt and headed for her office.

Cat tapped gently on the door and when she heard Mother Superior call for her to enter she opened the door and went inside.

'Good mornin' Mother, I'm sorry to disturb ye, but I happened to see this newspaper in the kitchen and wonder if ye can make sense of it for me?'

'Ah, I see you've picked up Sister Cecile's paper from France. Bring it here and we'll see.'

Mother Superior took the paper from Cat and stared at the headline, then folded the paper and laid it on the desk.

'I can't tell you word for word what it says Cat, but I do know what it's about as I was discussing this today with Sister Cecile. As you know she's French and her relations send the paper over here regularly.'

'Well, is the Pope in trouble, Mother?'

Mother Superior smiled, 'No. No, Cat. It's about an important message he sent out in his summer encyclical to all churches of the Reich encouraging the faithful to resist violating the 1933 concordat in the Catholic churches of Germany.'

'So what does it mean exactly?'

'It's a reminder to have faith in God, in Jesus Christ and the Church, and to remember Christian morals. He implores divine forgiveness for all those that are persecuting and said that it went against the preachings of Christ.'

'Is this about what's happenin' to Jews and the like over there?'

'Yes, it is Cat.'

'So that's all 'tis about then?'

'More or less, but he did end by saying, if I can remember Sister Cecile's translation, that St. Peter prays for them and all who suffer for their faith, in prisons and concentration camps, and asks Catholics everywhere to resist physical force.'

Mother Superior looked at Cat. 'Does that help to explain the article, Cat?'

'Sure, in a way it does, Mother.'

'You sound doubtful, Cat. What's going through that mind of yours?'

Cat laughed, 'Ye know me too well.'

'So, Cat. Come on tell me what's worrying you.'

'Well, Mother. I'm hearin' certain talk that's makin' me uneasy. I hear folk sayin' the likes of people in Germany, and over there generally, are bein' tipped out of their houses and businesses and that in some towns, Jews are bein' made to scrub the streets. Now why in God's name would anyone want to make them do that?'

'I think you are right to be concerned, Cat. I don't like what I'm hearing either and I deplore people who get so swept up in, well whatever you like to call it, politics, power, greed, or wanting something someone else has, that they have to torment the life out of others. I fear for us all, there are movements going on even in this country that I just don't agree with. It causes disharmony, brain-washes people into thinking they are part of some super-race that sets them apart from the ordinary folk.'

'Mother, I think I know what ye mean and that's somethin' else I've been meanin' to discuss with ye.'

Mother Superior took off her glasses and rubbed the bridge of her nose where they had left indentations and little red marks.

'You can talk to me about anything you wish, Cat. You know whatever you say to me will be treated in complete confidence.'

'Anna has been goin' to meetin's with Laura Kennedy, and I'm worried about it.'

'Oh. What kind of meetings are these, Cat?'

'Well, they all wear black shirts and 'tis some kind of political party, one I'm not acquainted with, but I don't like the sound of it.'

'You don't have to say any more, Cat. I know exactly the party you are talking about, Mosley's fascists - and you are right to be worried.'

'I'm glad ye agree, Mother.'

'What I suggest you do Cat, is persuade Anna to stay away from such company and if she needs any guidance about it, she can either come and speak to me or Father Fitzgerald after work one evening.' She replaced her glasses. 'I must say though I'm surprised at Laura Kennedy, I would have thought she would have more sense than to get mixed up with that sort of thing.'

'Right then Mother, I'll do that. I'm mighty relieved ye understand the problem. I had experience myself of so-called political parties back home when I was a girl, and I don't want anythin' like that creepin' into our lives now. We're away from it here and I fear for my girls gettin' mixed up with any trouble.'

'You're a good mother, Cat. You're on the right side of things, and if I can help you in any way, just ask. I'll be glad to help.'

Cat looked at the clock. 'I must let ye get on now Mother. I'm away home as I've finished work.'

'Good night then, Cat. And we'll see you tomorrow.'

'Good night Mother, and thanks for the advice.'

All the way home, the talk she had with Mother Superior went round and round in her mind. She would have to tell Anna not to go about any more with Laura Kennedy and just hope she had the sense to see that getting mixed up with that lot would only lead to trouble.

74
Alwold Crescent, Eltham
May 12th 1937

Anna laid the table for the evening meal and asked Elizabeth to fill the kettle and put it on the range to boil. She began slicing a loaf of bread as Eileen was plucking her eyebrows in front of the mirror above the fireplace.

'Mummy's home late,' Anna said to Eileen

'She's probably gossiping to someone about the King and his coronation. I expect she'll be back soon but I think we should start on the meal, I'm going out and don't want to be late.'

'Where are you going?' Elizabeth asked her.

'None of your business,' Eileen snapped.

Anna looked across at Eileen. 'You don't have to speak to her like that.'

'Who are you telling Miss High and Mighty?'

'I'm telling something that the label has fallen off, so I don't exactly know.'

Elizabeth sniggered, and pretended to read her book.

Eileen stepped away from the mirror and moved her head first one way and then the other to see if she had removed all unnecessary hairs, and satisfied she had, turned and looked in her make-up bag for an eyebrow pencil.

As Eileen carefully drew lines on her brows, Elizabeth watched her.

'Where are you going tonight, Eileen?

'Dancing.'

'Oh. Who with?'

'None of your business.'

'That's all you ever say,' Elizabeth said, and feeling thwarted fell silent, deciding to drop the conversation and get on with her story. When Eileen was in one of her moods, Elizabeth knew better than to try holding a conversation with her.

The front door opened and Elizabeth looked up.

'That's Mummy now,' she said slamming her book shut. 'Now we can get on with the cooking.'

Cat came into the room, her face chalk white. Anna looked up and stopped slicing the loaf of bread.

'What's the matter Mummy, you look dreadful!' She went to her and helped her to a chair. 'Elizabeth, get Mummy a drink of water will you?

Cat held up a telegram and put it on the table.

'I just got this from the telegram boy. 'Tis from my sister, Ellie in America. Her little girl's been killed.'

Eileen and Anna both said, 'No!'

'How? What happened?' Anna asked.

'I don't know for sure, it just says 'Catherine was killed yesterday by a truck, letter follows.'

Anna put her arms around Cat's shoulders.

'Mummy, how terrible. Poor Auntie and Uncle.' She looked at Eileen who stood still, clearly shocked by the news.

'I'll make you a cup of tea Mummy,' Eileen said. 'I won't go out tonight.'

'Thanks, Pet,' Cat said, 'but ye've no need to stay in, the poor little soul has gone and there's nothin' we can do here for her. God in heaven, my poor sister, this'll kill her. Her only child.'

When the letter explaining what happened arrived a week later, Ellie described how Catherine had run out into the road to buy ice-cream and was hit by a truck. She died in Michael's arms soon after. Ellie left Cat in no doubt now that she was saving every penny to travel back to England, she hated America. She said she didn't care how long it took but they were determined to return.

Stunned by the horror of how Catherine had died, Cat found it hard to write to Ellie. When she did, she felt she had made a poor job of it.

Whilst walking to work that day, Cat questioned herself. What can I say to my poor sister after losin' her child? I can't make the words understandin' enough to help her pain and every word I have written is inadequate.

She just hoped Michael stayed away from the drink long enough to keep a job and save money for their fare back.

75
Main Street, Fethard
January 1938

Breda sewed the last button on a jacket she had made for a customer, snipped off the thread and stood to hang it on a hook behind the door. She went across to the window and looked out at the layer of snow settling on Main Street. It looks so serene like this, she thought. Pity it doesn't last.

Nobody was out and all curtains were drawn against the cold, except hers. She stood breathing against the window, her breath misting the glass, then condensing in little droplets which ran downwards onto the woodwork.

She sighed. Another year! Another round of making suits, coats, skirts, trousers and anything else she was asked to do. Another year older with no hope of breaking the trend.

She picked up the poker and prodded the peat burning in the grate. As it burst into flame, she was aware of feeling heavy-hearted. If the truth were known, she thought, I am worried that in another ten years if I don't do something about it, I could be here still staring out of this window on a cold January night, not having done anything different in all that time.

In the reflection of the window Breda studied her silhouette and saw nothing but a huge heap of a woman and she felt she could scream. Wake everyone up. Shock them out of their slow little lives.

'Oh God,' she murmured, 'please make some change in life for me. I don't want to die before I have lived.'

She drew the curtains over, blocking out her image and the whiteness outside, and sat thinking about her life, aimlessly prodding the fire. She heard Peggy upstairs moving about, then her footsteps on the stairs, so got up and opened the door to the hallway.

'Are ye alright, Peggy?'

'Sure. I just need to get some more water.' Peggy sniffled into her handkerchief.

'G'w'on back to bed now. I'll get ye some. Shall I boil it up and put some lemon in it for ye?'

'No, don't go to any bother now. I'll just get some water and try to get off to sleep.' She continued into the scullery, poured some water from a jug and then turned to go back to bed. When she reached the bottom of the stairs she called to Breda who had gone back into her sewing room.

'Goodnight Breda, are ye comin' to bed soon?'

'Yes, I s'pose so, though I'm not tired. I'll maybe have a read for a while, and then I'll be up.'

Just then they both heard Marie groaning in the room above. Peggy looked at Breda saying, 'Is that Marie I hear callin' out?'

''Tis.' Breda said. 'I'll go up and see what she wants.'

'No, ye sit and read yer book Breda, I'm goin' up anyway, so I'll look in on her. Goodnight.'

'Right then, up ye go or ye'll be getting' cold and ye don't need to feel any worse than ye already do.'

Peggy climbed the stairs and turned to go into Marie's room when she heard her cry out. She opened the door and found Marie curled up on her bed clutching her stomach.

'What's the matter, Pet?' Peggy asked.

'Oh Auntie, I've got a terrible pain in me tummy.'

''Tis probably all those dried figs ye ate. I said they'd upset ye didn't I?' she smiled, 'c'mon now, settle down and if ye need to go to the toilet, put yer coat on, 'tis like the Arctic out there, snow everywhere. 'Twill freeze the hide off ye.'

Marie nodded and slid under the covers. Peggy kissed her on the forehead and went to her own bedroom where she got into bed and drank her water, coughing and sneezing. Feeling quite cold and dreadful she decided to put a cardigan on. She climbed out of bed, opened a drawer, and put her thickest one on. Warmer now, she got back into bed, blew out her candle and was soon asleep.

Peggy didn't know what had woken her but she sat bolt upright in the middle of the night. Something had disturbed her sleep, but when she couldn't hear anything, decided she must have been dreaming. In the gloom she could see Breda in the next bed.

Then she heard it again. Something *had* woken her! It sounded like a muffled scream. She thought maybe it was the Banshee and sat shivering in the bed. Then there was a louder scream and she realised it could only be Marie. She leapt out of bed and rushed into Marie's room. By the light of the moon she saw her niece gasping for breath, holding her stomach, unable to speak for the pain she was in.

'Dear God, whatever's the matter?' Peggy asked, lighting a candle. Alarmed at Marie's obvious pain and not knowing what to do, she hurried to rouse Breda.

'Breda, wake up, Marie's ill.'

'What's up with her?'

'I don't know. She has an awful pain. Will ye go and fetch Daniel?'

'Is it really that bad?'

'Sure it is, she's in agony.'

'I'll see for meself before I go getting' Daniel out of bed!'

Breda went into Marie's room and it didn't take her more than a heartbeat to decide she should go for the doctor. She pulled on her clothes and hurried downstairs.

'I'll take Marie's bicycle, t'will be quicker,' she said to Peggy. 'Maybe 'tis her appendix. Oh Lord, I hope it isn't. The hospital is miles away.'

She opened the door to the back yard, brushed the snow off the saddle and dragged the bike through the gate to the side alley where she mounted it and drove off into the dark.

As Breda entered the driveway of Daniel's house the snow made an eerie scene, with the trees pointing their empty branches skyward.

Dismounting, she tried to catch her breath as she surveyed the windows, looking for signs of life, but the house was in darkness. She banged on the door relentlessly until she saw a light appear upstairs.

He must have that new fangled electricity, Breda thought, because she saw one light after another spring to life until Daniel opened the door.

'Hello Breda,' he said. 'C'mon in. What's the matter?' he asked, though with the sight of Breda covered in snowflakes and looking rather dishevelled in the middle of the night he knew it must be serious.

'Daniel. 'Tis Marie. She ate a load of figs yesterday and now she's writhin' about in pain.'

'Silly girl,' he smiled, 'they can have that effect if ye eat them in abundance.'

'Well I wouldn't bother ye if 'twas just figs, but she's in awful pain and we're worried it may be her appendix.'

'G'w'on into the lounge Breda while I get dressed.'

'No, 'tis fine if ye just come on after me, I have the bicycle.'

'Not at all,' he laughed, 'leave the bicycle here and I'll give ye a ride in my new motor car. It will be faster.'

'Oh. I don't know, Daniel, I've never been in a motor car.'

'Then tonight will change your life. Your first drive,' he said closing the door. 'Sit yerself in there,' he yawned pointing to the lounge, "tis warmer, and I'll be down straight away.'

Breda walked toward the lounge and stood inside the doorway. She looked at the light switch placed in the wall and feeling a little afraid of the gadget, pushed it downwards with her finger.

Suddenly the room came alive. Shocked, she flicked the switch back up and the light faded. She chuckled to herself. Electric light. It wasn't so bad and very effective compared to candlelight.

She flicked it on again and walked into the room. It was all as it had been when her sister Mary was alive. So sad, she thought. Daniel had never stepped out with anyone else and was living the life of a bachelor, except that he had a housekeeper who went in daily. He was clean of any gossip and she was glad of that. Fethard was such a small place; folk couldn't afford to be the object of speculation.

Daniel broke her train of thought as he appeared downstairs.

'I'm ready, Breda. Turn off the light and we'll go. Ye can pick up the bicycle any time, t'will be fine in the porch.'

He opened the front door and raised the collar of his overcoat. 'Phew, 'tis awful cold. Hope the car starts well,' he said, gingerly stepping towards it. He fished the starting handle out from the back seat and fitted it into place at the front of the car. After a couple of turns it burst into life and

Breda climbed in just before Daniel deftly turned the car around and drove out of the gates.

He parked the car outside the shop and Peggy was waiting with the door ajar.

'She's upstairs, Daniel,' Peggy whispered closing the door behind them. 'She's been kickin' up an awful din. I think it may be appendicitis, but then ye're the doctor, so I'll leave it up to ye now. I'll put the kettle on, and maybe ye'd like a hot toddy before ye leave.'

Daniel smiled and made his way upstairs. Peggy and Breda stood at the bottom of the staircase and heard him knock on Marie's door, open it and disappear inside. After the door shut they hurried into the scullery to make hot toddies.

'Peggy,' Breda whispered, 'Daniel has electric lights installed.'

'Never!'

'Sure he has. And I tried it!'

'Ye did not. Did ye?'

'Yes, he has a little switch thing on the wall and ye just flick it up and whoosh! 'Tis like magic. The whole room lights up in one go.'

'Jesus, Mary and Holy St. Joseph, I'd be too scared to try it.'

'Ah 'tis easy when ye know how,' Breda smiled, 'and I didn't feel any tinglin' or anythin'. Maybe we should think about gettin' some electric lights too.'

'Oh I don't know 'tis a bit worryin', the thought of it.'

'Ah Peggy, ye need to move with the times. Electric light is here to stay.'

Breda couldn't help smiling. She had asked God to change her life and already tonight she had taken her first ride in a motorcar and used an electric light. She thought her prayers had been answered pretty quickly for once.

The kettle had been boiled, cooled off and re-boiled many times and still Daniel had not come downstairs. Peggy and Breda had re-kindled the fire in Breda's room and sat before it trying to keep warm. Peggy's cold was making her feel dreadful so Breda suggested she went back to bed.

'I will not. How could ye suggest it? I'm not leavin' ye to cope on yer own.'

'Think of yerself, Peggy, I will cope if I know ye're feelin' better tomorrow.'

'No. I'm kinda worried to be honest Breda. Daniel's been up there so long. D'ya think he's fallen asleep?'

Breda laughed. 'The very idea!'

Then they heard Marie's door open and close and Daniel softly descend the staircase. He was greeted by the two sisters looking up towards him, with faith in their hearts that he was the best person to rely on in a crisis.

But there was something amiss. Daniel wasn't smiling. His face was ashen and he wasn't delivering the verdict that it was the figs causing the problem.

'C'mon in and sit down both of ye,' he said softly, not waiting to be invited. He went into Breda's room and waved the sisters into chairs to join him.

'What I have to tell ye is one of the hardest things I've ever had to say.'

Breda and Peggy looked at him bewildered, but remained silent. Daniel looked down. Then he spoke in a quiet voice.

'I think maybe we'll need that whiskey now if ye don't mind.'

'Why of course,' Peggy said standing up, thinking that he was just tired and needed a drink to pick him up. 'I'll just be a moment,' she said and disappeared into the scullery to collect the bottle and three glasses.

''Tis bad news isn't it?' Breda probed.

'We'll wait for Peggy if ye don't mind, Breda,' he said and wiped his forehead with his sleeve, just as the door opened and Peggy came in with a tray holding whiskey and glasses.

She poured the drinks, offering Daniel one first. He drank it in one go and held his glass up for a re-fill before Peggy and Breda had even taken hold of theirs. Surprised, Peggy replenished his glass and then sat down ready to toast him, but Daniel didn't look in the mood for frivolities.

He took a deep breath and faced the two sisters who had no idea what he was about to tell them.

'What I have to tell ye both is not somethin' ye're ready for.' He heard their intake of breath; saw their apprehension and their trusting eyes focussed on his.

'Marie did not survive the delivery, and neither did her baby.'

Speechless, Peggy and Breda stared at Daniel and did not react. Eventually Breda spoke.

'What in the world are ye talkin' about? Wasn't it figs?'

'No, Breda. 'Twas not the figs. Marie was in labour.'

'Labour? But…' Peggy could not grasp it and the sentence died on her tongue.

Minutes passed. Nobody spoke. After some time, Daniel stood and re-filled his glass, then sat down again. Peggy and Breda had not touched their drinks.

'Ye need to drink the whiskey, 'twill help,' he said glancing at Peggy who looked in a worse state than Breda. 'Peggy, ye need somethin' for the shock. Drink yer drink while we decide what to do.'

76
Eltham
January 1938

Cat saw the telegram boy pedalling toward her as she left for work; her mouth dried as she felt instinctively it was for her, and knew it would be bad news. The only telegrams she ever received brought bad news. Sure enough, as she approached he stopped his bicycle and handed her the telegram.

'Thank ye,' she said stuffing it into her pocket. She couldn't open it in the road and would be too late for work if she returned to the house to read it, so decided to open it later when she was more composed.

As she plodded along the road towards the High Street, she conjured up every imaginable disaster that the telegram would bring her. It was, she feared about her father. It had to be. Peggy had written telling her several times he wasn't looking so good and had lost a lot of weight. She would prepare herself for the shock and would be surrounded by the nuns who would support her when she found out the nature of her bad news.

Wiping away tears that kept misting her eyes, Cat made her way to Eltham High Street and entered the school through the back door. She hung up her coat, took the telegram from her pocket and laid it on the table in the kitchen.

After fishing her apron out of her bag she tied it around her waist and sat down to open the telegram. But she couldn't do it. She just could not bring herself to open the envelope, dreading what she would read. Glancing up at the clock, Cat speculated that Mother Superior would be available if she hurried along to her office, so she snatched up the envelope and made her way there.

'Come in,' Cat heard Mother Superior call. Cat opened the door and slid inside.

'Good morning, Cat,' the kindly old nun smiled at her, 'what can I do for you?'

'Mother, I've received a telegram and I'm that terrified to open it, for I'm sure 'twill be bad news.' She held the envelope out to the nun. 'Would ye open it for me please, and break it to me gently. I think 'twill be about me father.'

'Of course, Cat. Here, take a seat and we'll do this together. First let us say a Hail Mary for strength to help us out. She bowed her head. 'Hail Mary, full of grace, the Lord is with thee. Blessed art thou among women and blessed is the fruit of thy womb Jesus. Holy Mary, Mother of God, pray for us sinners now and at the hour of our death. Amen.'

'Amen,' Cat echoed.

Mother Superior opened her eyes a fraction of a second before Cat, and looking at her bowed head, noticed for the first time that her hair was turning grey at the crown. Poor Cat, she thought, what has this woman ever done to attract such misery? The Lord must have a plan though she thought, so we must just accept whatever is sent to try us. She looked at Cat who nodded for her to begin opening the envelope.

Agonising about the contents Cat twisted the material of her apron round and round, anxiously awaiting the terrible news.

Mother Superior looked puzzled as she read, then folded the telegram and put it back in the envelope. She looked at Cat's white and anxious face and rose from her chair and went to a heavily carved oak cupboard in the corner of the room. She opened the cupboard door and took out a bottle of brandy and a glass, then returned to her desk where she poured out a large measure and handed it to Cat.

'What is it, Mother? 'Tis me father isn't it?'

'Drink this, Cat, it will help.'

'Oh Lord, I *knew* it. I *knew* it!'

She took the glass which shook in her hand, then drank a little of the brandy before she realised that Mother Superior had not said a word.

Cat looked at Mother Superior. 'Tis me father, isn't it, Mother?'

'No, my dear it is not your father.' Mother Superior moved around the desk and pulled a chair up to sit beside Cat. 'Brace yourself my dear; it was not about your father. It is about your daughter.'

'My daughter? Which daughter? Anna? No, not Anna! Eileen? Elizabeth?' Cat gasped for breath.

'I'm sorry my dear, but it's about Marie.'

'Marie! What about Marie?'

'The telegram says, "Marie died yesterday with a burst appendix. Please come. Peggy."'

Cat couldn't speak. She couldn't cry. All she was aware of was the sound of her heart pounding in her ears.

77
Fethard
January 1938

Tom was waiting at the station when Cat's train arrived. He dreaded meeting her, what could he possibly say? It was bad enough when their mother had died, but to lose a child! It was not in the natural order of things for a child to go before the parents. He wondered what on earth he would do if it was any of his children he was coming home to bury.

The train drew to a halt and he moved along the platform searching for his sister's face, but when he spotted Cat he hardly recognised her.

The person who waved wanly from the carriage window bore the face of an old woman. The young, raven-haired capricious Cat had been replaced by a sad looking, shrunken, middle-aged woman. A sob rose in his throat, but he steeled himself not to weaken as she would need him to be strong.

But the truth was, Tom had never felt he was as strong as Cat. He regretted any feelings he had in the past of envy over her relationship with their father; he could see clearly why her spirit was nearer to him than his was. She should have been born a boy he thought.

Oh Hell, his mind was whirling off in all sorts of stupid directions, like an escape route, away from facing the inevitable.

She stepped down from the train and her face crumpled as their eyes met. Then his arms were around her tiny frame as she wept uncontrollably.

'C'mon now. There, there,' Tom soothed. 'I'm here for ye, mo chuisle. Let's get ye outta here and home to Monroe.'

With one arm around Cat he lifted up her bag and ushered her out of the station to the waiting donkey cart. He helped her up and they began heading towards Monroe.

***

It was a grey, drizzling, miserable morning as Marie's coffin was lowered into the family grave at The Abbey graveyard in Fethard. The whole town had come to pay their respects and each person crossed themselves as the cortège passed by before they followed behind the family.

Cat was supported by Tom, and his wife Norah held onto to Ned, who was shaking uncontrollably, tears raining down his craggy features.

As the last link with her daughter was broken Cat cried silently, thinking to herself that she had let this child down. She had left her in a land backward in medicine, whereas if she had lived with them in England she would have been in a hospital and mended in no time. She would never forgive herself. They would have survived the financial hardship of another mouth to feed all those years ago. After all, hadn't they gone on to have two more children anyway? Her guilt lay on her like a black stain and she imagined everyone in Fethard was thinking what a bad mother she was.

The wake in O'Connell's Hotel was a very quiet affair. Normally, when burials were over, folk gathered together and celebrated the person's life. Musical instruments would appear and drink flow as everyone remembered the person and would find something to rejoice and laugh about.

But for Marie there was no such celebration. She had not dipped her toe into the waters of life, let alone gone for a swim.

Nellie and Mick provided food and people sat around the tables murmuring and drinking quietly, taking the odd bite to eat. Not one person raised their voice or their glasses for a toast. All were subdued by Marie's death. Nobody suggested clearing the tables and chairs to one side so they could dance, and eventually the mourners drifted away with nothing more to say to Cat than that they were sorry for her troubles. When they had all gone the hub of the family was left alone; sorrowful and silent.

Daniel finished his drink and stood up saying he must go, but before he left he turned to Cat.

'Will ye come to the house later? I know ye've to get back to England tomorrow, but I want to talk to ye before ye go.'

Peggy and Breda glanced at each other, but this went unseen by Cat as she looked at Daniel with her earnest expression; dry-eyed for the first time since she had arrived.

'Sure I will.'

She expected he wanted to console her and it would be nice to speak to him alone again after all the years since Mary's death.

They had not shared a moment together since that terrible night when they entered her sister's bedroom and witnessed her death, and that stupid old doctor slapping her hands, trying to revive her.

Later that day Cat rang Daniel's doorbell and he opened it within a second.

He must have been looking out for me, she thought, as she entered the hallway.

'C'mon in, Cat. Ye're most welcome.'

'Thanks, Daniel,' Cat murmured taking her hat off, 'ye know 'tis the first time I've been here since poor Mary went, God rest her soul,' she said crossing herself.

Daniel bit his lip and guided her into the lounge where he asked her to sit while he made them a pot of tea.

'I'll be back with ye in a trice,' he said, 'make yerself comfortable and get warm by the fire.'

Cat sat rubbing her palms together trying to get some life back into her numbed fingers. *Jesus it was a cold day*, she thought. Her eyes scanned the room and settled upon the place where her sister Mary had rested the day she died. That was the last day she had seen her and Mary had given them rosaries as a wedding anniversary present.

In her mind she counted her losses. There had been Mary and her baby; Louis; Mummy; Ellie's daughter Catherine, and now Marie. Six deaths she thought, as she sat gazing at the fire which roared up the chimney, yet gave her no warmth.

Daniel returned shortly with a tray of tea, poured them both a cup and sat in a chair opposite Cat. H e shifted about restlessly.

Cat could tell he felt uneasy. Maybe 'tis because he doesn't entertain many people these days he feels shy, she thought. Then he put his cup and saucer down and cleared his throat.

'Cat, I asked ye to come here for a specific purpose.'

'Oh?'

'There's somethin' ye should know. Somethin' that's not easy to tell ye, but neither Peggy nor Breda could bring themselves to discuss with ye.'

She put her cup and saucer down on a small table and looked him straight in the eye.

'What is it, Daniel?'

'Before I tell ye, I want ye to promise ye'll hear me out and not go rushin' off before I finish.' His voice was tight in his throat. He leaned forward, hands joined together across his knees.

'G'w'on, I'm listenin'.'

'Marie did not die from a burst appendix, 'twas a little more complicated than that.'

'How d'ya mean? Wasn't it peritonitis?'

'No, Cat. 'Twas nothin' to do with her appendix at all. But if I tell ye, and I mean to, I must have yer promise ye'll not breathe a word of this to anyone. Do I have that promise?'

Mystified, she nodded, unsure what it was she was agreeing to. 'Well if 'twas not her appendix, then what was it that took her?'

'Yer sisters believed Marie had eaten a load of figs prior to her fallin' ill. They were tendin' to her, but she seemed to be gettin' worse so Breda, in the dead of night, got onto a bicycle and rode here to ask me to go to her.'

'Right, I'm with ye so far,' Cat nodded.

'When we got to the shop, Peggy was waitin' and I went upstairs to see to Marie. Neither Breda nor Peggy knows the next bit because I did not tell them. So painful though it is, Cat, I feel morally bound to explain. But I have to tell ye that my destiny is in yer hands. If ye ever let out as much as a hint about it, I'll be struck off the medical register.'

Cat's eyes widened and her heart began to thump in her chest, but she could not stop him now, she had to know what it was about her daughter that only he knew.

'I'm listenin'.'

'I have to trust ye, Cat. So can I have yer assurance that ye'll not report me over tryin' to help yer daughter?'

'Daniel, I've known ye a long time and ye've known me too, long enough to realise I am able to keep me mouth shut. Tight! So long as 'tis for a good reason.'

'Right then.' He ran his fingers through his hair. 'When I got into the room Marie was in a lot of pain.'

'Lord save us,' Cat whispered, her eyes filling with tears.

'I soon saw the cause of the pain, Cat.'

'Yes,' she nodded wiping her eyes, 'g'w'on, Daniel,'

'Well, she was in the late stages of labour, the baby's head was crowned, but she could not push him out.'

'What in the world are ye sayin'?' Cat gasped.

'I had to act quickly. Marie was slippin' away. She had bound herself up tightly to conceal her pregnancy. Which as I've told ye, yer sisters knew nothin' about and she began to haemorrhage.'

'Dear, God. I can't believe what I'm hearin'.'

'I had to perform a procedure to release the baby, but he was stillborn. I was too late for either Marie, or her son. Cat, I'm very sorry.'

Cat sat very still and neither of them spoke for a while. Daniel saw the colour had drained from her face leaving a ghostlike image behind, but it was Cat who broke the silence.

'So which part of this is it ye would get struck off for? I don't understand.'

Daniel drew in his breath and began to explain.

'Well, not for performin' the procedure to release the child, but for the disposal of the child's body.'

'Oh, don't, Daniel! Don't say ye did anythin' horrible. *Please*, I couldn't take it.'

'No, Cat. I did what I could to preserve his soul, but as ye know, any talk of a baby out of wedlock in a place like Fethard would mean yer family would be shunned and the little fella was already dead.'

'So what about Marie? What happened to her then?' Cat sobbed.

'She just slipped away, Cat. I could not stop the bleeding. I tried. I tried so hard, but she had lost too much blood.'

'And the baby? What did ye do with the baby?'

'That's the bit I would be struck off for Cat. I concealed both the cause of death and reporting a stillbirth. There will be no record of this. I drove out to Mount Carmel and buried him beneath the statue of Our Lady.'

Cat broke down upon hearing all the facts while Daniel sat helplessly witnessing her heart-wrenching wails of grief, crying her daughter out of her life.

Daniel knew he had committed a crime, not for his own advancement, but to preserve the Delaney's good name in Fethard. He couldn't help drawing a parallel in his mind about the time he had helped Cat in a similar predicament during childbirth all those years ago, except that he had been on the scene quicker then and had managed to save her and the child. Hopefully, he thought, when Cat recovered from the shock, she would realise he had done it for the best.

If she did not come to this conclusion, Daniel knew he could wave goodbye to his practice. It was not just his job though, it was his very existence. If this got out, he could not stay in Fethard and he would most certainly never work as a doctor again, even if he managed to escape prison.

His destiny was in Cat's hands; as hers had once been in his.

The minutes ticked by until Cat's crying diminished and she was able to speak.

'Well Daniel, ye have no fear that I'll ever say a word about this. Apart from anythin', ye've been a wonderful husband to me poor sister Mary, God rest her soul, and friend to us all. T'would kill Daddy if he knew the truth and ye're right, most people in Fethard would cut us dead.'

Cat sat silently for a while, and then looked at Daniel. 'But thinkin' about it, who *was* the father of the child?'

'I don't know, Cat.'

'Did Peggy and Breda know?'

'No, they did not. They were as shocked as ye about the whole thing. I had a job convincing them not to go to confession about it. None of us can, so we've to live with this on our conscience. 'Twill never be cleansed from our souls, all three of us.'

'And mine too now,' she added dully. 'That makes four.'

They were quiet for a while then Cat looked directly at him.

'But I've never heard that Marie had a boyfriend even. Not that she wrote much, but neither Peggy nor Breda ever mentioned one.'

Silence ensued as Cat gazed unseeing into the fire. Then, as though something had fallen into place in her mind, she suddenly looked up at Daniel.

'I *hope* this has nothin' to do with Paddy Hogan!'

78
Daniel's House
January 1938

Cat was about to leave when someone rapped on the front door, shouting for Daniel.
'It sounds like Tom,' Cat said and Daniel rushed to open the door.
'Daniel,' Tom struggled for breath as he had run across the fields for speed, 'can ye come to Monroe quickly, 'tis me father, he's collapsed.'

'I'll come straight away.'

He turned to Cat. 'I'll drive ye both down in my motor car. I didn't think he was lookin' good. C'mon now, I'll just get me bag and we're away,' he said to them.

Daniel drove quickly out of the town, raced along Cashel Road and straight down the boreen to Monroe.

Tom and Daniel ran into the cottage, followed by Cat where Norah was sponging Ned's face as he lay on their couch.

It was so dark inside it took a few moments for Daniel's eyes to adjust to the gloom, but soon he could see that Ned was in a bad way and had probably had a heart attack.

Daniel turned to Tom.

'Can ye send the children into the bedroom with Norah?'

'Sure,' Tom said looking at his wife. 'Norah take the children into the bedroom.'

Norah instantly ushered the children away from the room.

'Just call if ye need me,' she whispered and closed the door.

Daniel listened to Ned's heart and held his wrist feeling the pulse. It was too irregular and weak for his liking, but Ned was conscious, looking alarmed and struggling to speak. But then without warning Ned became very calm and closed his eyes.

Stricken speechless by yet another dilemma for this family, Daniel hesitated to turn and tell Tom and Cat that Ned needed a priest, but he knew what he must do this time, everything must be correct.

'Tom, I think we should go for the priest, yer father's heart is not in good shape.'

'Right, I'll send Edward on his bike, 'twill be quicker than me runnin'.'

Tom opened the bedroom door, beckoned to the child and whispered the errand to him.

Edward shot out of the cottage and began pedalling for all he was worth in the direction of the priest's house.

Cat sank to her knees holding Ned's hand, buried her face in his rough old jacket and cried.

'Daddy, don't leave us. Please, don't go. We've not had long enough. Please open yer eyes.'

She felt Tom's hand on her shoulder.

'Don't, Cat. Let him go. He's not been the same since Mummy died. He's tired and he's ready to join her. Let him rest in peace.'

'Why does all this keep happening to our family?' she cried.

It was Daniel who answered. 'It happens to all families, Cat. It's just tough it's all happened in a short space of time for all of ye.'

The men stood watching Ned labour for breath, his face pallid and swathed in perspiration. He was slipping away and Cat could not bear it.

'Give him some brandy, or somethin' to bring him round, can't ye?' she cried to Daniel.

'Twould be dangerous to introduce any drink at present, it could choke him as he isn't awake, Cat.'

'Well ye can't just stand there both of ye's. Do somethin' for God's sake,' she yelled.

Daniel bent down and lifted Cat up, putting his arm around her shoulders. He spoke to her soothingly.

'Cat, yer father has a weak heart; all the emotion of recent months has taken its toll. When he's called to the Lord, 'tis his time, and as mere mortals we cannot override God's will.'

They heard Edward skid into the yard, throw down his bike and burst through the cottage door.

'Father O'Dowd's on his way,' he said 'he's drivin' in his motor car.'

Norah brought Teresa in from the bedroom and they all drew up chairs around Ned's prone form, now covered with a blanket. Minutes later they heard the unmistakable sound of the priest's car chugging down the boreen.

The car door slammed and Father O'Dowd appeared, framed by the doorway, his figure silhouetted against the light outside. He strode into the room and donned his robes.

They were aware of the clock on the wall marking off the minutes of Ned's life, and when he began to make a strange noise in his throat Daniel shot a glance at Father O'Dowd.

The priest immediately made the sign of the cross above Ned's body and began to recite words that were the most unwelcome sounds to all of them.

'Ego te absolvo. Omnibus peccatis tuis. In nomine Patris et Fillii et Spiritu Sancto…'

79
O'Connell's Hotel
January 1938

Cat sat with her arm around Ned's sister, Nellie. She had been deeply shocked, unable to work since hearing about Ned's death, and as a result her husband Mick had to take over all her duties in the hotel.

'We've to go to the solicitor's in the mornin' Auntie,' Cat said softly, 'to hear Daddy's Will read. Will ye come?'

'No. No. I don't think so Pet. 'Tis for all his children to go, not me.'

'As you please, Auntie. But I don't want ye to feel we're leavin' ye out of things.'

'Ah, Cat. This is somethin' I wish I'd been left out of entirely. Ye've hardly buried yer own little darlin' and now this! 'Tis a cruel world at times ye know,' she said patting Cat's hand, 'God forgive me, but I wonder who in the world's lookin' out fer us up there.' She pointed skywards.

'I know what ye mean,' Cat murmured, 'what a time of it we've had. It cannot get any worse now, can it?'

Inwardly Cat was hoping Auntie Nellie didn't go the same way soon. She felt all the people that she held onto in the back of her mind, her securities in life, were falling away. Disappearing, leaving her to face things alone.

* * *

Tom knocked on the solicitor's door and turned the brass knob when he heard him call for them to come in. Cat, Peggy and Breda followed him.

Sean Burke rose from his leather chair and took off his glasses which he placed on the desk in front of him.

'I'm sorry to meet ye all on this sad occasion,' he began, 'please accept my condolences. He was a fine man, yer father. Yes, a fine man.' Then he seemed to be counting up something in his head, nodding. 'Two, three, four, me five and Miss O'Carroll, that'll be six,' he said.

He called for Miss O'Carroll to join them from the outer office and soon a mousey little woman poked her head around the door. Sean Burke raised his eyebrows.

'Please Miss O'Carroll,' he said to her, 'would ye bring in another chair?'

He then turned his attention back to the family. 'Sit yerselves down. Yes indeed, sit yerselves down.'

Sean Burke went through the preliminary details of the paperwork and said that he had been empowered to deal with Ned's estate.

Tom shifted in his chair, clearly ill at ease. If Ned had written anything into his Will that altered his position he could find himself in a difficult situation.

The solicitor put on his glasses and began reading out Ned's Will, outlining the features that incorporated his estate.

Some of it seemed a little odd to Cat as the Will referred to the farm at Monroe eventually being taken over by Tom, his eldest son, when he became of age, and of an amount compensating his daughters, Peggy, Mary, Ellen, Catherine and Breda to the sum of £50 each.

Sean Burke read on.

'The estate comprisin' of the cottage known as Monroe and the smaller cottage known as Granny's cottage beside the bank of the Clashawley River to be passed to his only son, Thomas Delaney.'

Cat took a sharp intake of breath. Daddy had expressly told her he was leaving the cottage to *her*, so that she would always have somewhere to come home to.

Sean Burke finished reading the rest of the Will and drew a piece of paper from his folder.

'If ye take a look at this account I have of yer father's estate, ye'll see that there is now no money left to pay any compensation to ye ladies as the taxes on the land have been increased since this was written and eaten away any surplus put aside for that purpose. So if ye'll all sign to that effect, then our business is done.'

He looked up, took off his glasses, smiled and pushed the piece of paper towards Cat.

'Ye'd better read what ye're signin' for,' he said grinning, 'or ye may find ye owe someone a fortune.'

He clearly thought the whole thing was some sort of joke, Cat thought, and tried to quickly take in the words on the paper. But the writing swam before her eyes and she felt hot and faint. It had all been too much for her and she wanted nothing now but to get out of the solicitor's office, pack her bag and travel back to England.

Without another word, and not having read what the solicitor had pushed over the table for her signature, she signed.

The other sisters signed too, obviously in a state of shock themselves, and Tom, looking distinctly uncomfortable, signed last of all.

Then Cat decided to ask the question that had formed in her mind.

'Excuse me Mr. Burke, but can ye tell me when this Will was written, only it mentions me sister, Mary and she's been dead some years now.'

'Ah. Yes. Good point,' he said twisting the Will round so that he could re-read it. 'Yes, 'twas written in 1915.'

Twenty three years ago, Cat thought. Long before all this happened! Before any of us married, and had families, or when Mummy had died. She realised that Ned had obviously forgotten to update it. His wish that she should have Granny's cottage to always give her a home in Ireland, had disappeared as quickly as rain drops evaporate when kissed by the sun.

80
Hogan's Stables,
January, 1938

Paddy lay slumped on his couch, where he had passed out drunk the night before. He had not washed or changed his clothes for days and had drunk himself into oblivion.

In his madness, the images, first of Marie and then Cat, danced before his eyes; tormenting, laughing at him, drowning him in kisses, then scratching his face with a thousand razors, tearing his hair out...they kept interchanging until he was driven crazy and had drunk enough to poison himself.

Cat pulled the donkey cart to a halt, dismounted and marched up to the house with a riding whip in her hand. She was hot with anger as she banged on the front door.

'C'mon out Paddy Hogan!' she shouted.

But deeply asleep, Paddy didn't hear.

Undeterred, she hammered on the door again and when there was no reply she tried the latch. It opened. So she marched in unafraid to face the man who had, in her estimation, been responsible for initiating all her problems for so long.

She stood inside the doorway and listened. The sound of loud snores came from the room to the left of the hall so she pushed the door open and saw him asleep, mouth wide open, shirt unbuttoned and trousers undone. The sight of him repelled her.

She stormed out and made her way down to the kitchen at the end of the hall, filled a jug with water, returned to the sleeping Paddy, and threw the contents over him.

He stirred and then sluggishly tried to sit up.

'C'mon, get up ye filthy swine,' Cat shouted. 'Did ye think yer little game would go undetected eh? Did ye think ye could just take advantage of Marie and that nobody would find out? Ye stinkin' worm of a creature.'

'Wha' ye talkin' about?' Paddy slurred without moving. He frowned as he focussed on Cat's angry face.

'Ye know what I'm talkin' about, and if ye think for one minute I'm sucked in by yer feigned ignorance, it won't wash.' Cat took a step backwards. 'This is what I should have done years ago.'

She lifted the whip and slashed it across his face. The first slash drew blood, and egged on by her success, she whipped him again and again.

He raised his arms and tried to shield his face but when he did she just slashed across them too, pleased when red wheals stood proudly out on his flesh. His shirt split under the assault by the leather thong, blood oozing from the slits.

Satisfied he would bear the marks for all to see, she lowered her arm. Then she stepped towards him and spat in his face.

'There, that's for me daughter.'

Then she spat on him again.

'And that's for me Dada, 'cos yer actions robbed him of both his daughter and granddaughter.'

Finally she spat at him once more.

'And that's for *me*. If ye thought ye were bein' clever coverin' me head with a sack all those years ago, ye *weren't*! I knew all along it was *ye*. Ye great spineless heap. Look at ye! Never able to stand up and own up to what ye've done. Yer nothin' but a murderin' bastard and I hope ye rot in hell.'

Cat turned and strode from the room, along the hall and out of the front door, which she left swinging open.

Satisfied, she climbed aboard the cart and rode away.

81
St. Mary's Convent, Eltham September 1939

Mother Superior had asked Cat to pop in to see her after she finished work, so having put her apron in her bag, she combed her hair and went along to the nun's office.

'Come in Cat.'

Mother Superior's door was open and Cat saw she was stacking books on her desk from the shelves.

'Ye wanted to see me, Mother.'

'Yes, Cat. Sit down my dear; it's a sad day for us all.'

'What is it, Mother? Is anythin' wrong?'

'Yes my dear. Now that war has been declared, the convent is being requisitioned by the army and we have to leave. So I'm so sorry, Cat, but this means we have to let you go I'm afraid.'

The news hit Cat like a body blow.

Mother Superior could see that this poor woman, who had stood by them for a number of years, was to lose not just her job but a way of life. They had existed together in such harmony and she knew that in the absence of any family in England, she had been a substitute, a confidant, and a friend.

'Cat, I can't tell you how sorry I am. You've meant far more to us all than just our cleaner. There will never be another one to take your place and I mean that from the bottom of my heart.'

She opened a drawer and took out an envelope. 'Don't be offended, I know you are a very proud woman, but we've had a little collection for you as a sign of our appreciation and our love.' She pushed the envelope toward Cat.

Overwhelmed, Cat could not speak. Tears brimmed from her eyes and pushed their way down her cheeks. She wiped them away with her hand, and then pulled a handkerchief from the sleeve of her cardigan.

'Ye know, Mother, I never dreamed the day would dawn when I didn't work here. It's become a kinda home to me.'

'I know my dear, and you have been our sister all the way along the years.'

She then took another envelope from her drawer. 'In here, Cat, is a reference for the future should you ever need it, with our address in Surrey where we are to be sent for the duration of the war. But in the meantime, I hope you don't mind but I've spoken to the Father Fitzgerald and he has agreed to employ you for as long as possible. That way, you will not suffer financially.'

'I don't know what to say, Mother. I'm desolate at the thought of not seein' ye again, ye've been everythin' to me over the years, and to my children. God bless ye for all the kindness ye've shown me.'

'Well, Cat. I'm afraid we will have to say goodbye. Hopefully we may re-convene after the war, and I'm sure that you will be the first one I shall contact upon our return. Unfortunately the Ministry of Defence has not given me any time to tie up the ends, we have to go immediately.'

'Goodbye then, Mother. And until we meet again, may God keep ye in the palm of his hand.'

82
Eltham,
July 1940

Cat had been in her new job for nine months. It wasn't the same as working for the nuns and her heart wasn't in it.

Father Fitzgerald was kind enough, but she couldn't talk to him in the same way. Often when things were going wrong in her life she yearned to turn to Mother Superior and pour out her heart.

But now, at last, things were about to change for her. Ellie and Michael were on their way home from America.

Their inability to raise the money for the passage home from America had been overcome. The Woolwich Arsenal required an increase in their workforce and so paid the fares of any worker who was employed during World War I. Ellie had the experience to re-convene without too much time wasted.

So when Ellie and Michael arrived they had accommodation waiting for them, and even some furnishings.

Cat's spirits soared. At last, another family member to be with her. She had arranged to be at their new flat when they arrived, having acquired the key in advance for them.

Out of her meagre wages, Cat had bought them the basic foodstuffs and hoped it was enough to get them started until they could provide their own.

On the appointed day, Cat waited at the flat. Around three in the afternoon she heard them arrive in a taxi and flew down the steps to throw her arms around Ellie. Both broke down crying as they hugged each other and Michael stood watching them until Cat finally let go of Ellie and embraced him too.

'By God, ye don't know how good it is to see ye,' Cat said, helping to lift some of the luggage, but she was breathless and seeing this, Michael took it from her.

'Thanks, Michael,' Cat said, 'I'm a little out of practice for weight liftin'.'

Ellie clutched her beneath the elbow and they ran up the stairs like two children.

Michael was glad. It was the first time he had seen Ellie spring to life since Catherine had been killed. Perhaps now, he hoped, she would be more herself.

'C'mon in and sit yerself down while I make us a nice cup of tea,' Cat said, then turned to look at her sister.

'My Ellie, ye're awful thin.'

'New York didn't agree with me at all,' Ellie said.

When she took off her hat, Cat gasped. Ellie's hair was as white as snow. All her lovely auburn locks had disappeared.

Ellie saw Cat's surprised expression.

'Sure, I look awful don't I?'

'I don't care if ye had two heads. I sure am pleased to see ye. Both of ye,' she added for diplomacy.

But it was Ellie she wanted to see most. Ellie she wanted to hold; gossip to, and cry with. She wanted to do just about everything with her, but had to hold back. Ellie had a husband and she would have to share her sister with him.

Michael was stacking the trunks and suitcases in the room and straightened up moaning about his back strain.

'Jesus this woman has more clothes than the Queen of Sheeba, he laughed.

'Michael,' Cat said, 'D'ya remember when ye first came to dinner at our house in Crookston Road?'

'Would I ever forget it, ye little minxes? I've played that trick on several people since. Always works a treat.' He laughed, and Cat knew then that the same old fun-loving Michael was back. He hadn't changed and they would get along just fine.

Every so often, Cat stole at glance at Ellie. She looked so old. Her hair was not the only change in her. Something had died in her sister. She seemed subdued and resigned. Maybe she would feel better once they saw more of each other. She hoped so.

After a while Cat decided it would be diplomatic to leave the couple to themselves.

'Well, I'll be gettin' off home now. Why not come up to my house and have dinner tomorrow after Mass, I assume ye'll be goin'?'

'Probably give Mass a miss tomorrow, Cat. We'll take some time sortin' everythin' out and we're pretty tired. Too tired for either seven o'clock or eleven o'clock Mass, but we'll come to dinner – if that's okay with ye?'

'Okay? What kind of a word is that?'

'Oh 'tis an American word – it means alright, or somethin' near to that.'

'Well, then it is okay. I'll see ye about one o'clock. Now I'll explain how to get there.'

Next day, Ellie and Michael arrived for lunch and Cat was deliriously happy. She opened a couple of bottles of her homemade wine and it wasn't long before they all were quite merry.

Anna, Eileen and Elizabeth had stayed in specially to greet their aunt and uncle, although Elizabeth went out to play in the afternoon with her friend next door.

Ellie seemed more relaxed than she had the day before and Cat put her sister's mood down to travel weariness. She couldn't wait to take up the threads of their former relationship. So much had happened to them both. Scarred by tragedy, they had come through and out the other side, only to be left denuded of something neither could define.

Ellie wanted to know all about their life so Cat spent quite a while talking about Reggie and Maureen and their children, and Lize and Louis' mother, who even now still wouldn't receive her.

She explained about the shop and how her mother-in-law lived above it in a flat with Lize, Louis' sister. She told about Iris and Fred's family, Brian and George their children, but said they lived in Essex so hardly ever saw them.

Cat noticed as she mentioned Reggie that Anna sneered, and she meant to have it out with her later but not until after Ellie and Michael had gone.

Photographs came out and they poured over them laughing at the old fashioned clothes, but beneath the mirth was an undercurrent of unspoken melancholy.

By the time Ellie and Michael decided they should go they had covered quite a distance in remembrance, but some of the things that had caused most pain were avoided. They did not mention Catherine or Marie. It was as though both sisters knew the safety boundaries – and to go no further. It would wait.

* * *

Later that night, Billy arrived home unexpectedly.

'Good Heavens, Billy,' Cat laughed, 'this is a lovely surprise. Why didn't ye let me know ye were comin' home? We'll have to have a bit of a re-shuffle with the beds,' she added. 'Wait now, I'll put the kettle on before I do that.'

She called to Anna and Eileen to come downstairs and greet their brother and within seconds both girls flew downstairs and threw their arms around his neck.

Cat watched them with a tinge of sadness. How like Louis he had grown. About the same height, that same chestnut brown hair and Louis' eyes.

'Anyway Billy,' Cat said as she disappeared into the kitchen to fill the kettle, 'ye haven't told us what brings ye home on a Sunday night.'

Billy hesitated and both girls looked at him as though anticipating what he was about to say.

'I've got my call-up papers,' he said.

Cat spun round from the kitchen doorway.

'Oh no! Oh my God. I thought ye were safe workin' in the medical profession. I didn't think they'd call ye up from the hospital.'

Billy sighed and sat down.

'I have to report for duty in two days for training and then I'm to go into the R.A.M.C.'

'What's that, a department at the hospital?'

'No, it's the Royal Army Medical Corps, Mum. I won't be fighting, but I will be out there amongst it all, bringing home the wounded and tending to them once we get them here. That's if I don't get shot on the way.' He gave a funny little laugh.

'Billy! I don't want to hear ye joke about it – ye'll put the mockers on yerself. Oh God I never thought I'd see the day. First yer father, now ye. God help us.' She went back into the kitchen and turned on the tap, hoping the noise of running water would drown the sound of her crying.

83
Eltham
June 1941

'C'mon in, Reggie. Hi there Maureen, and here's the little darlins' come to see their auntie too. 'Tis good to see ye.'

The family went into the front room and Ellie and Michael stood to welcome them.

Cat smiled at them.

'Reggie, ye remember me sister Ellie, don't ye?'

'Yes, I think so. How are you Ellie?'

'Oh I'm grand thanks. This is Michael, me husband, Reggie.'

Reggie shook hands with him and Charlie, the elder of his two boys, shook hands with Michael too. *Little Louis*, as Reggie's youngest boy had become known, held back and hid behind his mother.

'Louis,' Maureen coaxed, 'c'mon and say hello now.'

'Ah, don't worry him. He he'll be grand once he gets to know us,' Ellie laughed.

'So, Ellie,' Reggie said, 'Cat tells us you are back working at Woolwich Arsenal.'

'I am indeed and it doesn't seem as though I ever left England. We're both workin' there at present, Michael and I, that is.'

'Bet the noise gets you down, doesn't it?'

'Ah, ye get used to it,' Ellie said sitting down again, 'and anyway it's work, that's the main thing.'

'Sure is,' Michael added.

'Is my mum joining us this afternoon, Cat?'

'Sure, she'll be along soon. Anna popped round there earlier to give her a hand in the shop now she opens Sundays, and she said she'd be here about four o'clock.'

'I ought to go and see Granny some time,' Reggie said, 'but to be quite honest, by the time I get finished up in my shop at night, I just don't get time to do much else except sit in the armchair and fall asleep.'

Cat uncovered the pile of sandwiches and salad she had prepared, along with butterfly cakes and some scones baked that morning.

'C'mon now and dig in folks,' she said, then squatting before little Louis added, 'will I get ye a sandwich?' Louis nodded and she planted a kiss on his forehead. 'Good boy,' she said smiling at him, 'I'll get ye an egg one, ye like them don't ye?' The boy nodded and she went to the table to put some food on a plate for him.

Maureen sat chatting to Eileen and Cat asked Reggie if he'd open a couple of bottles of beer for himself and Michael.

'Eileen, will ye go next door and fetch Elizabeth now please?' Cat asked 'and Anna, will ye put Tipper outside for a run please, there's a love?'

Eileen went next door to bring Elizabeth home and Anna shut Tipper out in the back garden, then closed the door with a bang.

'Jesus, Anna I asked ye to put the dog out, not shake the whole house down.' Cat laughed.

Anna just scowled.

Oh don't say she's going to get into a mood just because Reggie and the family are here again, Cat thought, I don't know what gets into her when they are here, and it makes me feel as though I'm walkin' on eggshells.

She felt a knot of anguish in her stomach.

'Yoo, hoo. Came Lize's voice as she let herself in through the back door. 'Cat I've brought you some bits and pieces from the shop and, I'd better spell it out Maureen, but I've got some s.w.e.e.t.s for the boys.'

'Ah ye spoil them, thanks though 'tis very good of ye,' Maureen said.

Lize turned to Billy. 'When are you off?'

'First thing tomorrow, I can't wait.'

'Oh don't be in too much of a rush, Billy. If it's anything like the last war, everyone thought it was something magnificent to join up to, a touch of glory for all the boys, except it wasn't so glorious for all of us left as widows.'

'No, I don't suppose so Auntie, but I'll be fine. Just look after Mum for me will you?'

'Of course. Don't worry.'

'Well we're all here then, except Eileen and Elizabeth,' Cat said, taking some sandwiches for herself just as Eileen came in, minus Elizabeth.

'Where's Elizabeth?' Cat queried

'She doesn't want to come. She said she's playing with Carol next door.'

Furious, Cat told Eileen to go right back and fetch her and there was not to be any nonsense from her.

Eileen shrugged and left once more to get Elizabeth. When they returned Elizabeth crept in and sat on the arm of the chair next to Ellie.

'Well, Pet,' Ellie said stroking her arm, 'were ye havin' a nice game with Carol?'

Elizabeth nodded.

'Well get yerself some tea now, and maybe yer mummy will let ye out again after,' Ellie said, and Elizabeth slid off the arm and approached the table.

Reggie happened to go to the table for some food at the same time and Elizabeth immediately took a sideways step away from him.

'Elizabeth,' Cat said, 'say hello to yer cousins.'

'Hello,' she said without turning round.

'Here, young lady, where's yer manners? Turn round and say it properly,' Cat said, furious that Elizabeth was displaying what she thought to be downright rudeness.

Elizabeth turned and said hello to Charlie and Louis in an unenthusiastic tone and then continued putting food on her plate.

Maureen accidentally dropped a sausage roll onto the floor and Cat then asked Elizabeth to go and fetch a dustpan and brush from the kitchen.

'No, don't pick it up to eat it Maureen, take another one. Tipper can have that,' Cat said.

Elizabeth took the dustpan out to the kitchen and opened the back door. She stepped outside and called Tipper and was then aware that Reggie was behind her.

She ran into the middle of the garden and Tipper frolicked around her thinking it was a game. She gave him the sausage roll and then ran around the circumference of the garden, out of the side gate and through to the front garden.

Reggie stood still for a moment and then strolled back indoors.

'Where's that child?' Cat asked him.

'Gone off out to play again I think,' Reggie said, stuffing a sausage roll into his mouth.

'Eileen, will ye go and get her in here this minute, I won't have her runnin' off in the middle of eatin'. We're all here to send Billy off and she's not goin' out to play with Carol while all the family are here.'

'I'll get her, Eileen. You stay there and finish your food,' Anna offered, and Eileen, looking surprised at the offer, sat down to continue eating.

Anna went to the side of the house and through the gate to the front garden where she found Elizabeth sitting on the front step.

'Shove over,' she said to her and Elizabeth moved over to make room for her. Anna put her arm around Elizabeth and cuddled her.

'What's up?' she asked.

'Nothing.'

'Come on, Elizabeth, you seem very jumpy.'

'No I'm *not*! I just don't want to be inside, I want to go out and play and Mum won't let me 'cos *they're* here.'

'Well it's a send-off for Billy; can't you just stay in a bit for that?'

'Yes.'

'Then why don't you come in now, stay for some food and then maybe Mum will let you go out again later.'

'Anna, I don't want to come in.'

'Why not?'

'I don't know. I feel as if I'm going to choke on the food.'

'What on earth for? Have you got a sore throat or something?'

'No.'

'Then what is it?'

Elizabeth began screwing the hem of her dress round and round her finger. 'Don't tell Mum will you?'

'Not if you don't want me to.'

'Cross your heart and hope to die?'

'Of course.'

'Say it then.'

'Look, what's this all about?' Anna sounded impatient

'Say it or I won't tell you.'

'Cross my heart and hope to die.'

'I don't like Reggie.'

Anna felt a wave of fear wash over her. How could she deal with this?

Anna sat silently for a while, but eventually she thought of something to make her laugh.

'Is it because he's got a big nose?'

Elizabeth laughed.

'No, silly.'

'Is it because his front teeth stick out like a pantomime horse?'

Elizabeth began to laugh and just then the front door opened and Cat scolded Elizabeth for running off.

'Now get back in here this instant young lady,' she said, 'and ye won't be goin' out later on now.'

Elizabeth cast a sideways glance at Anna, looked down, and then stood up to follow Cat inside.

Anna remained on the step for a while and then was aware of Reggie behind her. Goose pimples stole across her flesh as he spoke to her.

'Penny for your thoughts, Anna.'

She stood immediately feeling agitated and tried to push past him, but he just barred the way.

'Excuse me, Reggie,' she said in a loud voice hoping everyone in the front room could hear her.

He quickly stepped aside. 'Oh sorry, Anna,' he said in a voice that made her skin crawl.

She pushed past him and disappeared into the front room, leaving him by the open front door. She would try to speak to Elizabeth again to find out what was behind her fears, although she already had a good idea.

When Anna went inside, Cat said she wanted to say something now they were all together.

Reggie ambled in as she said she wanted them all to wish Billy God's protection as he went off to war.

'Come home safely, Son, that's all I want,' she said, and embraced him.

'Don't worry. I'm not going for any bravery award; I just want to stay in one piece.'

Anna glanced at Reggie and wished it was him going off to war and not Billy. She doubted she would shed any tears.

84
Eltham
July 1941

'Quick, we've to get down the shelter,' Cat shouted to Anna, Eileen and Elizabeth.

All four of them had a rigid routine and dropped everything they were doing to scramble into the dug-out. They paddled into the water that had surfaced; the earth having reached field capacity after days of rain. It was cold, dank and petrifying. But Cat knew it was better than taking the risk of staying indoors.

The bombardment was ferocious; shaking the ground beneath them as they sat huddled together.

'This is the worst we've had,' Cat said, shielding her ears with her hands. 'Lord save us,' she murmured as bombs fell from the sky. 'Billy, Billy,' she sobbed into her handkerchief, 'Oh Lord don't let my boy be killed - or any of us.'

Elizabeth began to scream when the next explosion splintered the door to the shelter and she scrambled onto Cat's lap. Eileen and Anna drew closer, putting their arms around their mother and little sister. The four hung onto each other as the pounding continued, breaking up the world they knew forever.

All night they sat petrified awaiting the most brutal predator of all, their fellow human beings. They feared this was their last night alive.

* * *

Fatigued, yet thankful for survival, they emerged next morning from the air-raid shelter.

Anna came out first.

'Oh my God,' she gasped. 'There's nothing left.'

Cat, Eileen and Elizabeth followed her to find the whole landscape had gone from the end of Alwold Crescent.

Speechless, the four walked to the end of what had been their road and viewed the devastation. Cat's eye traversed the horizon and she took a sharp intake of breath.

'What's the matter, Mummy?' Anna asked.

'Jesus, I hope I'm wrong.'

'Wrong about what?' Eileen queried.

'I don't want to say it, I just need for us to go and find out.'

Puzzled, Eileen looked at Anna, raised her eyebrows and shrugged indicating that she didn't know what their mother was on about.

'Quick girls, we have to go to the High Street,' Cat said and started to hurry off in that direction.

Along the way they crossed rubble that was once the main road and then took the direction of Crookston Road.

Once they arrived at what Cat thought must be roughly where they used to live, she had difficulty in orienting herself. The whole area had suffered a direct hit and had been flattened by the worst bombardment they had experienced. But Cat was driven towards finding exactly where they had once lived.

She scrambled relentlessly over rubble, craters and debris; the girls following in her wake, until they reached the corner of the road that Lize's shop was in.

Nothing was left to identify the shop and Cat couldn't even begin to imagine where it had been as the whole area was flattened into a mass of smoking rubble.

Firemen were working relentlessly to quench fires and free trapped people. Cat saw that the WRVS was there handing out cups of tea.

Frantically she clawed her way over bricks and piles of concrete attempting to locate the shop; desperate to find Lize and her mother-in-law.

She asked various people if there were any survivors from where she estimated the shop would have been. But all she could discern from the ARPs was that nobody had survived between this point and that. The points described included Lize's shop.

Cat stood, running her fingers through her hair and turned to look at the girls who were desperately trying to keep up with her.

'Wait a minute Mummy,' Anna pleaded, 'we can't get over this stuff, it's too hard.'

Then Cat arrived at the point she knew, absolutely, must have been where the gate to the shop had been. There was just a massive hole in the earth with tons of concrete, splintered and charred wood sticking up at all angles. She then knew in her heart it was pointless looking for them. They must have all died.

She turned to the girls.

'I'm sure the shop was here.'

Cat looked at their faces, pinched and white from lack of sleep. 'Oh Lord...Auntie Lize and Granny,' was all she could whisper.

They stood among the rubble staring in disbelief at the devastation, embracing each other, unable to fathom the enormity of events.

'We should go and see if Reggie, Maureen and the boys are alright,' Cat said wearily.

Gingerly they picked their way across lumps of concrete that once marked the roads they knew to make their way towards the High Street.

As they turned the corner into the High Street, they all realized that Reggie's shop had gone too.

'Maureen!' Cat cried out running towards the place where the shop and flat had once been. But all that remained was a yawning cavity in the ground.

'Oh my God. *Oh my God.*'

Cat ran back and forth, trying in her mind to shift the location of the shop to further along the road where some buildings had remained intact.

'No. No, it couldn't be here. It *couldn't* be.'

She fell onto her knees trying to throw aside pieces of broken concrete, gashing the skin on her arms and legs.

Anna reached out to her mother. 'Mummy, *stop* now,' she pleaded.

'But I have to find them,' Cat cried clawing at the rubble.

'Mummy, *stop*!' Anna yelled.

'Ye don't understand. I have to find them. I have to tell Reggie and Maureen about Lize and Granny–'

'Mummy, it's all over. They're gone,' Anna said. She tried pulling on Cat's arm, forcing her to leave her desperate rummaging.

Elizabeth drew closer to Anna and clutched her hand. 'Are Charlie and Louis dead, Anna?'

'Yes, I think so. Nobody could have survived this,' she said looking desolately across the devastation.

Cat stood up amongst the ruins, dazed.

'Dear God,' she murmured, 'they're all gone.'

They stood in bewildered silence staring at the heaps of wood and bricks that were once the butcher's shop and flat knowing that under it, somewhere, were Reggie, Maureen and the boys.

ARP wardens were rushing around trying to dig out people calling for help. Some, able to walk, emerged from the rubble covered in dust with trails of blood trickling down their whitened bodies, were wrapped in blankets and led away. The men continued working frantically pulling aside planks of wood and bricks searching for survivors.

Cat began to shake and Anna took off her cardigan to wrap around her shoulders.

'We should leave them to it and go home now Mummy,' she said, holding her mother tight. 'It's all over. We can't do anything to help.'

Cat nodded her agreement and reluctantly they began retracing their steps - picking a way out of the chaos.

Walking arm-in-arm they made their way home in silence, but as they entered Alwold Crescent the sun drifted out from behind the clouds.

Anna turned to Cat. 'That's good the sun's coming out.'

Looking at Anna's face Cat was suddenly reminded of Louis.

'You look so much like yer father ye know.'

'What's made you suddenly say that?'

'I was just remembering yer dad, and that July day – so many years ago.'